THE OTHER DAUGHTER

Twenty-five years ago such crimes had been committed, both big and small. Twenty-five years ago such sins had been tolerated, both big and small. He had always thought human nature would take care of everything in the end. Someone would break, someone would talk, maybe even Larry Digger would finally put the pieces together.

But year had passed into year, and everyone did absolutely nothing. Told nothing, asked nothing, remembered nothing. Everyone got away with it.

He had had enough. Now he was taking matters into his own hands.

His preparations were complete.

Time for the opening gift. He studied his list. He studied his pile. He made his decision: Melanie. Melanie, who had actually found happiness as the Stokeses' other daughter. Melanie, who in all these years had never done him the favor of remembering.

He got out his butcher's knife. He sharpened the blade.

He was ready.

Do you know the perfect crime?

I do.

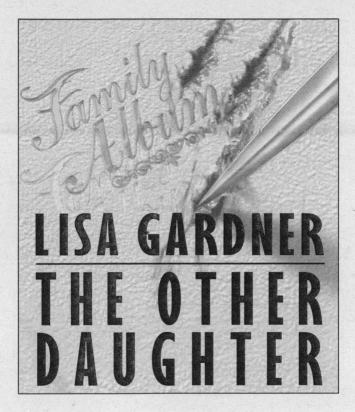

LISA GARDNER
THE OTHER DAUGHTER

BANTAM BOOKS

NEW YORK TORONTO LONDON
SYDNEY AUCKLAND

THE OTHER DAUGHTER
A Bantam Book / July 1999

ISBN 0-553-57679-8

Published simultaneously in the United States and Canada

Bantam Books are published by Bantam Books, a division of Random House, Inc. Its trademark, consisting of the words "Bantam
Books" and the portrayal of a rooster, is Registered in U.S. Patent
and Trademark Office and in other countries. Marca Registrada.
Bantam Books, New York, New York.

PRINTED IN THE UNITED STATES OF AMERICA
OPM   20   19   18

ACKNOWLEDGMENTS

AS ALWAYS, I'M indebted to quite a few people for their expertise and patience in helping make this book a reality. Being myself, I took artistic license with a great deal of the information but tried to keep things as rooted in the real world as possible. All mistakes are mine, of course. Special thanks to:

Special Agent Nidia C. Gamba and Supervisory Special Agent John C. Ekenrode of the Boston Federal Bureau of Investigation healthcare fraud squad. I know I didn't have the space to do your job justice, but I hope you'll appreciate the fact that I tried.

Bob and Kim Diehl, former corrections officers for the Texas Department of Corrections. Not just anyone will answer e-mails from a total stranger, particularly a stranger inquiring about proper protocol for the electric chair.

Larry Jachrimo, custom pistolsmith and true artist. I've never liked guns, but you helped me appreciate them.

The Arthritis Organization for the general information on AS and to my brother, who is living with it. The older we get, Rob, the more you are my hero.

Jennifer Carson, R.N., my dear roommate from college and one of the few healthcare professionals who doesn't mind answering all my inquiries about poisons. You've got a devious mind, Jenn, and I love you for it.

Finally, to my agent, Damaris Rowland, for riding this roller-coaster with me, and to my new husband, the love of my life. I couldn't do this without you.

AUTHOR'S NOTE

FANS OF THE death penalty in Texas will notice an immediate discrepancy in my novel—that a man is sent to the electric chair in 1977. In fact, Old Sparky was retired in 1964 after the execution of 361 men, and the death penalty was not carried out again until 1982, when Texas got lethal injection. Never let it be said that historical accuracy got in the way of a writer.

For the record, the Huntsville Prison Museum does exist and is an excellent source of information on the colorful world of the Texas Department of Corrections. Bonnie and Clyde are among the most famous prisoners documented there, though I like to think that Russell Lee Holmes would be worthy of similar notoriety. The Captain Joe Byrd Cemetery also exists in real life, and, yes, the day I visited it, there was a freshly dug grave just waiting for the next recipient—I was told there was another execution planned that night.

And the owl did hoot while I was there, and there was one helluva thunderstorm, and I do so solemnly swear I will never commit a crime in the state of Texas.

THE OTHER DAUGHTER

PROLOGUE

September 1977
Huntsville, Texas

AT SIX A.M. the Huntsville "Walls" Unit went to full lockdown.

Outside the redbrick walls, protesters were already gathering for Texas's first execution in thirteen years. Inhumane, picket signs read. Cruel and unusual. The "Texas thunderbolt" should never have been brought out of retirement. The death penalty was capricious and irresponsible.

An equal-sized crowd begged to differ. Cruel and unusual was still too good for Russell Lee Holmes. Send him to the chair. Let him fry. Execution candidate number 362 was worth bringing back the electric chair—in fact, they should bring back hanging.

Inside the Death House, where he'd been brought just the night before, Russell Lee Holmes settled his sparse frame more comfortably on the lone bunk in his cell and ignored them all. He had watery blue eyes, a thin face, and a hunched, lean frame. After thirty years of chewing tobacco and drinking soda, his teeth were crooked, stained, and half-rotted. He liked to pick them with his thumbnail. He definitely wasn't a pleasant man or a brilliant man. What he was was quiet and, for the most part, indifferent. Sometimes it was difficult to remember just what his small, finely boned hands had done.

In January, when Utah had ended the Supreme Court's moratorium on executions by throwing Gilmore in front of the firing squad, there hadn't been any doubt that Texas would reenter the death business. And there hadn't been any doubt that Russell Lee Holmes would be the first man up to bat.

Maybe that's because when the sentencing judge had asked him what he had to say about kidnapping, torturing, and murdering six small children, Russell Lee had said, "Well, sir, basically, I can't wait to get me another."

The warden arrived at Russell Lee's cell. He was a fat, barrel-chested man, nicknamed Warden Cluck due to jowls that reddened and shook like a rooster's when he was angry or upset. Russell Lee knew from experience that it didn't take much to get Cluck upset. Now, however, the warden seemed kind, even benevolent, as he unrolled the warrant and cleared his throat so the other four men in the Death House could hear.

"Here's your sentence, Russell Lee. I'm gonna read to you your sentence. You listenin'?"

"They're gonna fry my ass," he said casually.

"Now, Russell Lee, we're all here to help you today. To get you through this with less fuss."

"Go to hell."

Warden Cluck shook his head and got to reading. "It is the mandate of this court, that you, Russell Lee Holmes, shall be executed for the following crimes."

He ran down the list. Six counts of murder in the first degree. Kidnapping. Rape. Molestation. All-round sadistic bad ass deserving to die. Russell Lee nodded to each charge. Not a bad list for the kid his mama had simply called Trash, as in "filthy white trash," as in, "no betta than yer father, that piece of no good, filthy white trash."

"You understand the sentence, Russell Lee?"

"It's a little late if I don't."

"Fine, then. The Father's here to meet with you."

"I only want to speak with you, my son," Father Sanders said soothingly. "To be with you in this time of crisis. To allow you to unburden your soul and understand this journey you are about to take."

Russell Lee, always cordial, said, "Fuck you. I don't want to meet no pussy God. I'm looking forward to meetin' Mr. Satan. I figure I can teach him a thing or two about how to make babies scream. Don't you got a kid, Warden? A little girl . . ."

The warden's pudgy face had suddenly turned beet red. He stabbed a thick finger in the air while his jowls started shaking. "Don't start. We're trying to help you—"

"Help fry my ass. I'm no fool. You want me dead so you can sleep at night. But I think I'm gonna like being dead. Then I can go anywhere I want, be like Casper. Maybe tonight I'll find your little girl—"

"We ain't gonna bury your body," the warden yelled. "We're gonna put it through the chip machine, you son of a bitch. We're gonna dice you into dust, then dump the dust into acid. Won't be no trace of your sorry ass left on the face of this earth by the time we're done with you. No fucking molecule!"

"Can't help myself," Russell Lee drawled. "I was born to be bad."

Warden Cluck hiked up his gray pants, jerked his head at the priest to join him, and stomped out of the cell.

Russell Lee lay back down on his cot and grinned. Time for a good nap. Nothing more to look forward to today. Nothing more to look forward to period, Trash.

His grin faltered when in the corridor, the four dead men took up the chant.

"How do you like Russell Lee? Baked, crisped, or fried? How do you like Russell Lee? Baked, crisped, or fried?"

• • •

THREE-THIRTY P.M. Russell Lee got up, his last meal of fried chicken, fried okra, fried sweet potatoes finally arriving. With it came an uninvited guest, reporter Larry Digger—the warden's way of punishing him for his morning display.

For a moment the two men just stared at each other. Larry Digger was thirty years old, his body trim, his face unlined, his dark hair thick. He carried the wind of the outside world with him like a special scent, and all the men stared at him with sullen, resentful eyes. He breezed into Russell Lee's cell and plopped down on the cot.

"You gonna eat all that? You'll burst your intestines before you ever get to the chair."

Russell Lee scowled. Larry Digger had been latched on to him like a leech for seven years now, first following his crimes, then his arrest, his trial, and now his death. In the beginning Russell Lee hadn't minded so much. These days, however, the reporter's questions made him nervous, maybe a little scared, and Russell Lee *hated* being scared. He fastened his gaze upon the meal cart and inhaled the oily scent of burnt food.

"Whaddya want?" Russell Lee demanded, digging into the pile of fried chicken with his hands.

Digger tipped back his fedora and adjusted his trench coat. "You seem calm enough. No hysterics, no pledges of innocence."

"Nope." Russell Lee ripped off a bite of chicken, chewed noisily, swallowed.

"I was told you'd sworn off the priest. I didn't think you'd take the Jesus route."

"Nope."

"No purging of sins for Russell Lee Holmes?"

"Nope."

"Come on, Russell Lee." Digger leaned forward and planted his elbows on his knees. "You know what I want to hear. It's your last day now. You know there won't be a pardon. This is it. Final chance to set the record straight. From your lips to the front page."

Russell Lee finished the chicken, smacked his greasy lips, and moved on to the charcoaled okra.

"You're gonna die alone, Russell Lee. Maybe that seems okay to you now, but the minute they strap you into Old Sparky, it won't be the same. Give me their names. I can have your wife flown in here for you. And your baby. Give you some support, give you *family* for your last day here on earth."

Russell Lee finished the okra and plunged three fingers into the middle of the chocolate cake. He collapsed a whole side, excavated it like a tunnel digger, and started sucking the frosting from his palm.

"I'll even pay for it," Digger said, a last-ditch effort from a man who was paid jack shit, and they both knew it. "Come on. We know you're married. I've seen the tattoo and I've heard the rumors. Tell me who she is. Tell me about your kid."

"Why does it matter to you?"

"I'm just trying to help you—"

"You gonna bring 'em here and call 'em freaks, that's what you're gonna do."

"So they exist, you admit it—"

"Maybe they do. Maybe they don't." Russell Lee flashed a mouthful of chocolate-coated teeth. "I ain't telling."

"You're a stubborn fool, Russell Lee. They are going to fry you, and your wife will never have benefits and your kid will get raised by some other junkyard dog who'll claim it as his own. Probably become a loser just like you."

"Oh, it's all taken care of, Digger. It is, it is. Matter of fact, I got me more of a future than you do. That's what they call irony, ain't it. Irony. Good word, goddammit. Good word." Russell Lee turned back to his cake and shut up.

Larry Digger finally left in a rage. Russell Lee tossed his leftover food, including most of the cake, onto the concrete floor. He was supposed to share his dessert with his fellow death row inmates; that was protocol. Russell Lee ground the cake into the cement floor with the heel of his right foot.

"Let them all share that. Let the motherfuckers share that."

Abruptly a loud *crunch* rang down the corridor, the noise growing, swelling, into a fierce, angry crescendo. It paused, dipped low, then soared high, going from a whine to a snarl.

The executioner was warming up the chair, testing his equipment at 1800 volts to 500 to 1300 to 300.

Suddenly the moment was very real.

"How do you like Russell Lee?" the corridor pulsed. "Baked, crisped, or fried? How do you like Russell Lee? Baked, crisped, or fried?"

Russell Lee Holmes sat down quietly on the edge of the cot. He drew in his shoulders, thought of the nastiest things he could think of. Small, soft throats, big blue eyes, shrill little-girl screams.

I won't say a word, baby. I'll keep it to my grave. 'Cause once there was someone who at least pretended to love Trash.

Boston, Massachusetts

JOSH SANDERS TRUDGED down the brightly lit halls. A first-year resident, he was going on hour thirty-seven of a supposed twenty-four-hour ER shift and he functioned purely on autopilot. He wanted sleep. He must find an empty room. He must sleep.

He came to the door of room five. No lights were on. Dimly he recalled that the boards listed five as unoccupied. Slow night in the ER.

Josh entered the room and yanked back the curtain surrounding the bed, ready to collapse.

A whimper. A hoarse, strangled wheeze. A moan.

The freshman doctor caught himself and snapped

on the overhead light. A fully clothed little girl lay magically sprawled on top of the bed.

And she was clutching her throat as her eyes rolled back into her head and her whole body went limp.

THE DEATH TEAM was well trained. Three guards snapped Russell Lee Holmes into leg irons and a belly chain. He informed the warden he could walk out on his own, and everyone fell into position.

The guards flanked Russell Lee. Warden Cluck led. They marched down the forty-five-foot corridor, where the green door that had greeted 361 men now held Russell Lee's number.

At five the barber had shaved his head, sculpting a perfectly bald crown for the electrode plate. Then there'd been one last shower before he'd donned the execution whites. White pants, white shirt, white belt, all made from cotton grown on the prison farms and cut, spun, and sewed by prison inmates. He was going to his death looking like a fucking painter and without a trace of the outside world upon him.

The door swung open. Old Sparky beckoned. Rich burnished wood, over fifty years old and gleaming. High back, solid arms and legs, wide leather straps. Looked almost like Grandma's favorite rocker except for the face mask and electrodes.

The executioner took over and everything happened in a blur. The guards were strapping Russell Lee to the golden oak frame. One thrust a bite stick between his teeth, the other swabbed his left leg, head, and chest with saline solution to help conduct the electricity. The executioner followed up with metal straps around his calves, metal straps around his wrists, two diodes on each side of his heart, and finally a silver bowl on top of his shaved head. In less than sixty seconds Russell Lee Holmes had been crowned king.

The executioner taped up his eye sockets so there

would be less mess when his eyeballs melted, and
stuck cotton balls up his nose to limit the bleeding.

Eleven-thirty P.M. The death squad left the room,
and Russell Lee's "torture time" began. He sat,
strapped to his death chair, surrounded by blackness
and waited for the phone on the wall to ring, the
phone connected directly with the governor's office.

In the three viewing rooms across from him, others
also waited. In room one were the witnesses—Larry
Digger and four relatives of Russell Lee's victims who
could afford to attend. Patricia Stokes had lost her
four-year-old daughter Meagan to this monster's
handiwork. Her husband was on duty at his new job,
so she'd brought along her fourteen-year-old son instead. Brian's young face was immobile, but Patricia
was sobbing quietly, her thin arms wrapped tightly
around her tall, gaunt frame.

In room two, the executioner stood ready. This
room contained the second phone connected directly
with the governor's office. It also boasted three large
buttons, an inch and a half in diameter, which jutted
out of the wall. One main inducer and two backups.
The state of Texas always got the job done.

Room three was for family and friends of the inmate. Tonight its only occupant was Kelsey Jones,
Russell Lee's beleaguered defense attorney, who was
wearing his best suit—a mint-colored seersucker—for
the occasion. Kelsey Jones had a special assignment.
He was to watch. He was to report back, Russell Lee's
last consideration to the woman who had loved him.

Then Kelsey Jones was to forget all about Russell
Lee—a task he would gladly accept.

Eleven thirty-one P.M. The countdown began, and
the many subterfuges and manipulations that had
started more than five years before finally came to a
head. All rooms were quiet. All occupants were tense.

The man who was responsible sat in the chair with
tape over his eyeballs and ground his teeth into the
bite stick.

I AM POWERFUL. I AM HUGE!

His bowels let loose. And he gripped the end of the armrests so hard his knuckles turned white.

Love you, baby. Love . . . you.

"CODE BLUE! CODE BLUE!" Josh simultaneously shouted orders and checked the little girl's pulse. "I need a cart, stat! We got a young female, looks to be eight or nine, barely breathing. Somebody call peds!"

Dr. Chen rushed into the room. "Where did she come from?"

"Don't know."

Staff and crash cart arrived at the same time, and everyone fell into a fast, furious rhythm.

"She's not on the boards," Nancy, the head nurse reported, grabbing a needle. The IV slipped in, followed by the catheter. Immediately they were drawing blood and urine.

"She's running a fever! Oh, we got hives!" Sherry, another nurse, had finished snipping away the cotton sweatshirt to attach the five-lead heart monitor and revealed the little girl's inflamed torso.

"STAND BACK!"

The chest X ray flashed, and they fell back on the patient, working furiously. The girl's body was covered with a sheen of sweat and she was completely nonresponsive. Then her breathing stopped altogether.

"Tube!" Josh shouted, and immediately went to work to intubate.

Shit, she was small. He was afraid he was hurting something as he bumbled his way around her tiny throat like a water buffalo. Then the tube found the opening and slithered down her windpipe. "I'm in!" he exclaimed at the same time Sherry whirled out of the room with vials of fluid for the CBC, chem 20, and urine drug screen.

"Pulse is thready," Nancy said.

"Assessment, Josh?" Dr. Chen demanded.

"Anaphylaxis reaction," Josh said immediately. "We need one amp of epi."

"Point-oh-one milli," Dr. Chen corrected him. "Peds dosage."

"I don't see any sign of a bee sting," Nancy reported, handing over the epinephrine and watching the doctor administer it through the breathing tube.

"It could be a reaction to anything," Dr. Chen murmured, and waited to see what the epi would do.

For a moment they were all still.

The little girl looked so unprotected sprawled on the white hospital bed with five wires, an IV, and a bulky breathing tube sprouting from her small figure. Long blond hair spilled onto the bed and smelled faintly of No More Tears baby shampoo. Her eyelashes were thick and her face splotchy—smudges under the eyes, bright red spots staining her plump cheeks. No matter how many years he worked, Josh would never get used to the sight of a child in a hospital.

"Muscles are relaxing," Josh reported. "Breathing's easier." Epinephrine acted fast. The little girl's eyes fluttered open but didn't focus.

"Hello?" Dr. Chen tried. "Can you hear me?"

No response. He moved from verbal to tactile, shaking her lightly. She still did not respond. Nancy tried the sternal rub, pressing her knuckles against the tiny sternum hard enough to induce pain. The little girl's body arched helplessly, but her eyes remained glazed.

"Hard to arouse," Nancy reported. "The patient remains nonresponsive." Now they were all frowning.

The door burst open.

"What's all the ruckus about?" Dr. Harper Stokes strode into the room, wearing green scrubs as if they were tennis whites and looking almost unreal with his deep tan, vivid blue eyes, and movie-poster face. He had just joined City General Hospital as a hotshot

cardiothoracic surgeon and had already taken to
striding the halls like Jesus in search of lepers. Josh
had heard he was very good but also seemed to know
it. You know what the difference between a cardiac
surgeon and God is? God doesn't think he's a cardiac
surgeon.

"We got it," Dr. Chen said a bit testily.

"Uh-huh." Dr. Harper sauntered over to the bed.
Then he spotted the little girl sprouting tubes and
drew up cold, looking honestly shocked. "My God,
what *happened?*"

"Anaphylaxis reaction to unknown agent."

"Epi?"

"Of course."

"Give me the chest X ray." Dr. Stokes held out a
hand, peering at the girl intently and checking her
heartbeat.

"We got it under control!"

Dr. Stokes raised his head just long enough to look
the younger M.D. in the eye. "Then, why, Dr. Chen,"
he said somberly, "is she lying there like a rag doll?"

Dr. Chen gritted his teeth. "I don't know."

MIDNIGHT. THE DOCTOR entered the executioner's
room and took up position against the back wall, his
hands clasped behind him. The executioner picked up
the phone connected to the governor's office.

He heard dial tone.

He recradled the receiver. He counted off sixty seconds.

He stared at Russell Lee Holmes, who sat in the
middle of the death chamber with his lips peeled back
from his scarecrow teeth in an idiot's grin.

"He's too dumb to know what's going on," the
doctor said.

"Don't matter now," the executioner said.

His watch hit 12:01. He picked up the phone. He
still heard the dial tone.

He hit the main inducer button and 440 volts/10 ohms of electricity surged through Russell Lee Holmes's body.

The lights dimmed in the Death House. Three inmates roared and clapped while one curled beneath his cot and rocked back and forth like a frightened child. The relatives of the victims watched stoically at first, but when Russell Lee's skin turned bright red and began to smoke, they turned away. Except for Brian Stokes. He remained watching, as if transfixed, while Russell Lee Holmes's body convulsed. Abruptly his feet blew off. Then his hands. Behind Brian, his mother screamed. He still didn't look away.

And then it was simply over.

The doctor entered the death chamber. He'd wiped Vicks VapoRub beneath his nose to block out the smell. It wasn't enough, and his nose crinkled as he inspected the body.

He looked at the middle window, into the executioner's room. "Time of death is twelve-oh-five."

"I GOT DRUG screen results!" Sherry plowed through the door, and Josh grabbed the reports, just beating out Dr. Harper Stokes.

"She's positive for opiates," Josh called.

"Morphine," Dr. Stokes said.

"Narcan," Dr. Chen ordered. "Point-oh-oh-five milli per kilo. Bring extra!"

Sherry rushed away for the reversing agent.

"Could she be allergic to morphine?" Josh quizzed Dr. Chen. "Could that be what caused the anaphylaxis reaction?"

"It happens."

Sherry returned with the narcan and Dr. Chen quickly injected it. They removed the breathing tube and waited, a second dose already in hand. Narcan could be repeated every two to three minutes if necessary. Dr. Stokes checked the young girl's pulse again, then her heart.

"Better," he announced. "Steadying. Oh, hang on. Here we go . . ."

The little girl was moving her head from side to side. Nancy drew a sheet over her and they all held their breath. The little girl blinked and her large eyes, a striking mix of blue and gray, focused.

"Can you hear me, honey?" Dr. Stokes whispered, his voice curiously thick as he smoothed back her limp hair from her sweaty forehead. "Can you tell us your name?"

She didn't answer. She took in the strangers hovering above her, the white, white room, the lines and wires sticking out of her body. Plump and awkward-looking, she was not a pretty child, Josh thought, but at that moment she was completely endearing. He took her hand and her gaze rested on him immediately, tearing him up a little. Who in hell drugged and abandoned a little girl? The world was sick.

After a moment her fingers gripped his. A nice, strong grip considering her condition.

"It's okay," he whispered. "You're safe. Tell us your name, honey. We need to know your name."

Her mouth opened, her parched throat working, but no sound emerged. She looked a little more panicked.

"Relax," he soothed. "Take a deep breath. Everything is okay. Everything is fine. Now try it again."

She looked at him trustingly.

This time she whispered, "Daddy's Girl."

ONE

S HE WAS LATE, she was late, oh, God, she was *so* late!

Melanie Stokes came bounding up the stairs, then made the hard left turn down the hall, her long blond hair whipping around her face. Twenty minutes and counting. She hadn't even thought about what she was going to wear. Damn.

She tore into her room with her sweatshirt half pulled over her head. A strategic kick sent the heavy mahogany door slamming shut behind her as she shed the first layer of clothes. She toed off her tennis shoes and sent them sailing beneath the pine bureau that swallowed nearly a quarter of her bedroom. A lot of things came to rest beneath the battered dresser. One of these days she meant to clean it out. But not tonight.

Melanie hastily shimmied out of her ripped-up jeans, tossed her T-shirt onto the sleigh bed, and hurried to the closet. The wide plank floorboards felt cool against her toes, making her do a little *cha-cha-cha* along the way.

"Come on," she muttered, ripping back the silk curtain. "Ten years of compulsive shopping crammed into one five-by-five space. How hard can it be to locate a cocktail dress?"

To judge by the mess, pretty hard. Melanie grimaced, then waded in fatalistically. Somewhere in there were a few decent dresses.

At the age of twenty-nine, Melanie Stokes was petite, capable, and a born diplomat. She'd been abandoned as a child at City General Hospital with no memory of where she came from, but that had been a long time ago and she didn't think of those days much. She had an adoptive father whom she respected, an adoptive mother whom she loved, an older brother whom she worshiped, and an indulgent godfather whom she adored. Until recently she had considered her family to be very close. They were not just another rich family, they were a tight-knit family. She kept telling herself they would be like that again soon.

Melanie had graduated from Wellesley six years earlier with her family serving as an enthusiastic cheering section. She'd returned home right afterward to help her mother through one of her "spells," and somehow it had seemed easiest for everyone if she stayed. Now she was a professional event organizer. Mostly she did charity functions. Huge black-tie affairs that made the social elite feel social and elite while simultaneously milking them for significant sums of money. Lots of details, lots of planning, lots of work. Melanie always pulled them off. Seamless, social columnists liked to rave about the events, relaxed yet elegant. Not to mention profitable.

Then there were the nights like tonight. Tonight was the seventh annual Donate-A-Classic for Literacy reception, held right there in her parents' house, and, apparently, cursed.

The caterer hadn't been able to get enough ice. The parking valets had called in sick, the *Boston Globe* had printed the wrong time, and Senator Kennedy was home with a stomach virus, taking with him half the press corps. Thirty minutes ago Melanie had gotten so frustrated, tears had stung her eyes. Completely unlike her.

But then, she was agitated tonight for reasons that had nothing to do with the reception. She was agitated, and being Melanie, she was dealing with it by keeping busy.

Melanie was very good at keeping busy. Almost as good as her father.

Fifteen minutes and counting. Damn. Melanie found her favorite gold-fringed flapper's dress. Encouraged, she began digging for gold pumps.

During the first few months of Melanie's adoption, the Stokeses had been so excited about their new daughter, they'd lavished her with every gift they could imagine. The second floor master bedroom suite, complete with rose silk wall hangings and a gold-trimmed bathroom, where she needed a stool just to catch her reflection in the genuine Louis IV mirror, was hers. The closet was the size of a small apartment, and it had been filled with every dress, hat, and, yes, gloves ever made by Laura Ashley. All that in addition to two parents, one brother, and one godfather who were shadowing every move she made, handing her food before she could think to hunger, bringing her games before she could think to be bored, and offering her blankets before she could think to shiver.

It had been a little weird.

Melanie had gone along at first. She'd been eager to please, wanting to be happy as badly as they wanted to make her happy. It seemed to her that if people as golden and beautiful and rich as the Stokeses were willing to give her a home and have her as a daughter, she could darn well learn to be their daughter. So she'd dressed each morning in flounces of lace and patiently let her new mom cajole her straight hair into sausage curls. She'd listened gravely to her new father's dramatic stories of snatching cardiac patients from the clutches of death and her godfather's tales of faraway places where men wore skirts and women grew hair in their armpits. She spent long afternoons sitting quietly with her new brother, memorizing his tight features and troubled eyes while he swore to her again and again that he would be the perfect older brother for her, he would.

Everything was perfect. Too perfect. Melanie stopped being able to sleep at night. Instead, she would find herself tiptoeing downstairs at two A.M. to stand in front of a painting of another golden little girl. Four-year-old Meagan Stokes, who wore flounces of lace and sausage-curled hair. Four-year-old Meagan Stokes, who'd been the Stokeses' first daughter before some monster had kidnapped her and cut off her head. Four-year-old Meagan Stokes, the real daughter the Stokeses had loved and adored long before Melanie arrived.

Harper would come home from emergency surgeries and carry her back to bed. Brian grew adept at hearing the sound of her footsteps and would patiently lead her back to her bedroom. But still she'd come back down, obsessed by the painting of that gorgeous little girl whom even a nine-year-old girl could realize she was meant to replace.

Jamie O'Donnell finally intervened. Oh, for God's sake, he declared. Melanie was Melanie. A flesh-and-blood girl, not a porcelain doll to be used for dress-up games. Let her pick her own clothes and her own room and her own style before the therapy bills grew out of control.

That piece of advice probably saved them all. Melanie left the master bedroom suite for a sunny third-story bedroom across from Brian's room. Melanie liked the bay windows and low, slanted ceilings, and the fact that the room could never be mistaken for, say, a hospital room.

And she discovered, during a clothing drive at school, that she liked hand-me-downs best. They were so soft and comfortable, and if you did spill or rip something, no one would notice. She became Goodwill's best customer for years. Then came the trips to garage sales for furniture. She liked things banged up, scarred. Things that came with a past, she realized when she was older. Things that came with the history she didn't have.

Her godfather was amused by her taste, her father aghast, but her new family remained supportive. They kept loving her. They grew whole.

In the years since, Melanie liked to think they all learned from one another. Her well-bred southern mother taught her which fork to use for which courses. In turn Melanie introduced her depression-prone mother to the reggae song "Don't Worry, Be Happy." Harper instilled in his daughter the need to work hard, to consciously and proactively build a life. Melanie taught him to stop and smell the roses every now and then, even if just for a change of pace. Her brother showed her how to survive in high society. And Melanie showed him unconditional love, that even on his bad days—and Brian, like Patricia, had many of those—he would always be a hero to her.

The doorbell rang just as she unearthed her shoes. Jesus, she was cutting it close tonight.

Hair and makeup, quick. At least her pale features and baby-fine blond hair didn't require more than the lightest touch of color and a simple stroke of the hairbrush. A little blush, a little gold eye shadow, and she was done.

Melanie took a deep breath and permitted herself one last assessment in the mirror. The event was coming together in that crazy way each one did. Her father had volunteered to greet the guests, a definite overture of peace, and her mother was appearing more composed than Melanie had expected. Things were working out.

"It's going to be a great evening," Melanie assured her reflection. "We got rich patrons, we got a blood donor room. We got the best food money can buy and a stack of rare books to collect. Your family is doing better, and to hell with Senator Kennedy—it's gonna be a great night."

She gave herself a smile. She pushed herself away from her bureau. Took a big step toward her door. And suddenly the world tilted and blurred in front of her eyes.

Black void, twisted shapes. Weird sense of déjà vu. A little girl's voice, pleading in the dark.

"*I want to go home now. Please, let me go home. . . .*"

Melanie blinked. Her cluttered room snapped back into view, the fading spring sun streamed through the bay windows, the hundred-and-ten-year-old floor felt solid beneath her feet. She discovered her hands pressed against her stomach, sweat on her brow. She glanced around immediately, almost guiltily, hoping no one had noticed.

No one was upstairs. No one knew. No one had seen or suspected a thing.

Melanie quickly descended the stairs where the sounds of gathering people and clinking champagne glasses beckoned gaily.

Four spells in three weeks. Always the black void. Always the same little girl's voice.

Stress, she thought, and walked more briskly. Delusions. Neuroses.

Anything but memory. After all this time, what would be the point?

THE BOEING 747 TOUCHED down badly, bumping and skipping on the runway. Larry Digger was in a foul mood to begin with, and the botched landing did nothing to improve it.

Digger hated flying. He didn't trust planes, or pilots, or the computers that were installed to imitate pilots. Trust nothing, that was Larry Digger's favorite motto. People are stupid was his second favorite.

Gimme a drink was probably his third. But he wasn't about to say it then.

Time hadn't been kind to Larry Digger. His trim frame had turned soft at pretty much the same rate his promising investigative reporter's career had turned sour. Somewhere along the way his mouth adopted the perpetually dour look of a hound dog, while his cheeks developed jowls and his chin got too fleshy. He looked ten years older than his real age. He felt about another ten years older than that.

At least he had until the phone had rung three weeks earlier. Within days he'd hocked his stereo equipment for a first-rate tape recorder, then sold his car for a plane ticket and traveling cash.

This was it for Larry Digger. Twenty-five years after he'd started the search for the Holy Grail, he was in Boston, and it was boom or bust.

He hailed a cab. It had taken him a week to track down the address in his fist. Now he handed the piece of paper to the tired-looking driver who was paying more attention to the Red Sox game on the radio than to the other cars on the road.

Digger was traveling light, just clean underwear, a couple of white shirts, the tape recorder, and a copy of his own book, published fifteen years before. He'd started writing it soon after Russell Lee Holmes's execution when most nights he woke up with the scent of burning flesh polluting his nostrils. The other guys had gotten a break that night. Blowing an inmate apart had given the anti–death penalty liberals all the ammunition they'd needed. Texas had gotten to hastily re-retire Old Sparky, not entering the execution business again until 1982, when the state got lethal injection.

It hadn't helped Digger though. He'd thought Russell Lee would be the big story for him, finally break him out of Pisswater, USA, and move him to national news. They'd kept him in Huntsville, covering the retirement of Old Sparky, covering the debate. Then he got to cover the setup of the lethal injection, and way before he was ready, he was back to watching men die.

He had started needing a drink before going to bed. Then he started needing two or three. Most likely he was on his own slow road to dying, when lo and behold, the phone had rung.

Two A.M., May 3. Exactly three weeks ago. Larry Digger remembered it clearly. Fumbling for the ringing phone on the bedside table. Swearing at the thundering sound. Pressing the cold receiver against his ear. Hearing the disembodied voice in the dark.

"You shouldn't have given up. You were right about Russell Lee Holmes. He did have a wife and child. Do you want to know more?"

Of course he did. Even when he knew he should've given up, when he knew that his obsession with Russell Lee Holmes had cost him more than it had ever given him, he hadn't been able to say no. The caller had known that too. The caller had actually laughed, a weird, knowing sound that was distorted by some machine. Then he'd hung up.

Two days later the caller was more specific. This time he gave Digger a name. Idaho Johnson.

"It's an alias. Russell Lee Holmes's favorite alias. Track it down, you'll see."

Digger had tracked the name to a marriage certificate. He'd then traced both husband's and wife's names to a birth certificate for a child listed as Baby Doe Johnson. No sex or hospital was listed, but there was a midwife's name. Digger found her through the Midwives Association, and there he'd struck gold.

Yes, she remembered Idaho Johnson. Yes, that picture looked like him. A slight hesitation. We-ell, yes, she understood that his real name was actually Russell Lee Holmes. Not that she'd known it then, she informed Digger crisply. But when the cops had arrested Russell Lee and the papers had carried his picture, she'd sure figured it out. Then the midwife thinned her lips. She wasn't willing to say another word. Baby Doe Johnson was Baby Doe Johnson and she didn't see any reason to infringe upon the privacy and rights of a child simply because of what the father had done.

Digger had tried tracking down the child and mother on his own, only to hit a wall. The woman's name on the marriage certificate also appeared to be an alias, having no social security number, driver's license, or tax history to back it up. Digger had combed through old records, old files. He'd hunted for photos, property deeds, any damn kind of paper trail. No sign of Angela Johnson or Baby Doe.

Digger had gone back to the midwife.

He'd begged. He'd pleaded and argued and browbeat. Offered money he didn't have and glory he'd never known. The best he could get out of the woman was one last grudging story, a small incident that had happened to her after Russell Lee's arrest. Really, it had probably been nothing.

But to Larry Digger it had been everything. Within seconds of hearing the midwife's little tale, he thought he knew exactly what had happened to Baby Doe Johnson. And it was a bigger story than any dried-up, washed-up, half-drunk reporter had ever dared to dream.

But why dredge it up twenty years later?

He'd asked his three A.M. caller that question, actually. And he still recalled the weird, high-pitched answer.

"Because you get what you deserve, Larry. You always get what you deserve."

The cab was slowing down and pulling over. Digger glanced around.

He was in downtown Boston. One block from the Ritz, one block from the landmark Cheers, limos everywhere. This was where the Stokeses now lived? The rich did get richer.

God, that pissed him off.

Digger slapped ten bucks in the cabbie's hand and crawled out of the taxi.

The sky was clear. He sniffed a couple of times, wiped his hand on his rumpled trousers. Air definitely smelled like flowers. No exhaust fumes here. Rich folks probably didn't stand for such things. Some big park loomed behind him, filled with cherry trees and tulips and, of all things, swan boats. He shook his head.

He turned away from the park and inspected the row of buildings. They were all stone town houses, three stories high and rail thin. Old and grand. Nestled shoulder to shoulder but still managing to appear aloof. Built by blue bloods, he figured, one hundred years ago, when everyone was still tracing their lineage to the *Mayflower*. Hell, maybe they still were.

He checked the addresses. The Stokes home was the fourth in. It was currently lit up like the Fourth of July, with two red-coated valets guarding the doorway like matchsticks. As he watched, a Mercedes-Benz pulled up and a woman stepped out. She'd draped purple sequins and white diamonds all over her plump body and looked like a moldy raisin. Her husband, who was equally portly, waddled like a penguin in his tux. The couple surrendered their keys to a valet and sauntered through heavy walnut doors.

Digger looked down at his old trench coat and rumpled pants.

Oh, yeah, he could just stroll right in.

He walked into the park, took a seat on an old wrought iron bench beneath a vast red maple tree, and contemplated the Stokes house once more.

As the reporter who'd tagged Russell Lee Holmes to the grave, Larry Digger had gotten to know all the families of the murdered children. He'd met them when their grief was still a raw, ragged wound, and he'd interviewed them later, when the horror had leached away and left only despair. By then the fathers had a vengeful gleam in their sunken eyes. They fisted their hands and pounded already beat-up furniture when speaking about Russell Lee Holmes. The mothers, on the other hand, clung to their surviving children obsessively, and stared at all men, even their husbands, mistrustfully. By the time the state got around to killing Russell Lee, most of the families had imploded.

Except the Stokeses. From the very beginning they had been different, and from the very beginning the other families had resented them for that. Except for Meagan, Russell Lee's victims lived in poor neighborhoods. The Stokeses had lived in a mansion in one of the newly rich neighborhoods of Houston. The other families had had that worn, mongrel look of two working parents. Their kids had had torn clothes and uneven teeth and dusty cheeks.

The Stokeses belonged on the cover of *Better Homes and Gardens*—the strong, noble doctor-husband, the slender, classy, former-beauty-queen wife, and their two golden children. Gleaming blond hair; perfect white teeth; pink, rosy cheeks.

They were the kind of people you half *wanted* something bad to happen to, and then, when it did . . .

Digger had to look down at the grass. Images from that time still shamed and confused him.

The way Patricia Stokes's clear blue gaze had softened when she spoke of her daughter, trying to describe to reporters the perfect little girl who'd been kidnapped from her family, begging them to help her find her daughter. Then, the way her face had broken completely the day Meagan's body had been ID'ed. Her blue eyes grew so bleak that for the first time in his life, Larry Digger would've given up a story, hell, Larry Digger would've given up his *soul* to give this perfect woman back her daughter.

Right after the execution, when Patricia had been overcome by grief and horror, Digger followed her to the hotel bar. Her husband hadn't come. Work, Digger had heard. According to the rumor mill, since the death of Meagan Stokes, all Dr. Harper Stokes did was work. The man seemed to have some misguided notion that saving other lives would make God give him his daughter back. Rich men were stupid.

So, the fourteen-year-old Brian had gone to Texas as his mother's escort. He'd even followed his mother into the bar as if he owned the place. When the bartender tried to protest, the kid gave him a look. A don't-you-mess-with-me-after-the-things-I've-seen look. The bartender shut right up.

Christ, what kind of kid attended an execution?

Right about then Digger figured that the Stokeses weren't so perfect or golden after all. There was something there, something beneath the carefully manicured surface. Something dark. Something sinister. In all the years since, he'd never shaken that impression.

Now here he was, twenty years later. The Stokeses had a new daughter, and this one had gotten the chance to grow up. But somehow the demons couldn't all be settled, because someone had called up Larry Digger and invited him over to play.

Someone still thought the Stokeses hadn't gotten what they deserved.

Digger felt a chill.

He finally shrugged. He spared one last thought for the other daughter, wondering what she was like, if she'd found any happiness there on Beacon Street. He decided he didn't care.

This was his shot and he was going to take it. He'd done his research. He had his information. And he knew by then how to make his opportunity.

Ready or not, Melanie Stokes, he thought indifferently, *here I come.*

TWO

B Y NINE-THIRTY, guests were filling up the
Stokes home like glittering jewels. White-
tuxedoed waiters cut clean lines through the
expensively dressed crowd, offering silver trays
heavy with champagne flutes or sizzling garlic shrimp
or wild boar with blueberry demiglaze. Baccarat
chandeliers threw sparkling lights over carefully
coiled hairdos and captured handsome men whispering to beautiful young ladies.

Rushing down the stairs, Melanie waved merrily at
the Webers and the Braskamps and the Ruddys, then
exchanged nods with the Chadwicks and Baum-
gartners. Lawyers, deans, chiefs of surgery, and management consulting VPs. Investment bankers and a
few politicians. Boston was full of new money and old
money, and Melanie had shamelessly invited it all. Everyone brought a rare book to donate for literacy, and
if they were all jockeying to give the best book, the
most priceless donation, even better. When it came to
fund-raisers, Melanie was a true hussy.

She exchanged smiles with her father, who stood by
the door, looking elegant in his favorite satin-trimmed
tux. At nearly sixty years of age, blue-eyed, golden-
haired Harper was in his prime. He worked like a
dog, jogged religiously each morning, and was an avid

golfer who'd finally gotten down to a nine-handicap. More important, *Boston* magazine had just named him the best cardiac surgeon in Boston, a long over-due triumph. Tonight Melanie thought her father appeared happier than she'd seen him in months.

Satisfied, she went in search of her mother. Parties had always relaxed Melanie, hence her job. She felt comforted by the throng of milling people, the flutter of multiple conversations. In her mind, hell was soli-tary confinement in a room that was cold and stark and unending white. Fortunately with her job, her volunteer work at the Dedham Red Cross Donor Center, and her family, she didn't have much time to waste on worrying about being alone.

Melanie finally spotted her mother across the room and altered course straight for her.

Patricia Stokes was tucked in a corner, standing next to one of the sterling silver juice carts, and chat-ting with the young male server. This was a sure sign that she was nervous. A tall, striking blonde who had conquered the hearts of most of the men in Texas by the time she was eighteen, Melanie's mother had grown more beautiful with age. And when scared or unsure, she had a tendency to migrate toward men, as they inevitably gushed over her every word.

"Melanie!" Patricia had spotted her daughter. Her face immediately lit up, and she waved enthusiasti-cally. "Darling, over here. I've spoken with catering and the juice stations are all set."

"Wow," the waiter exclaimed. "Your daughter looks just like you!"

"Of course," Patricia declared breezily. Melanie rolled her eyes. She didn't look like her mother any more than a yellow buttercup resembled a yellow rose.

"Are you harassing the help?" she asked her mom.

"Absolutely. Charlie here was just pouring me a drink. Orange juice. Straight up. I figured that would keep the room buzzing. 'Does she have vodka in that or doesn't she?' 'Does she/doesn't she?' You know I love to be the life of the party."

Melanie squeezed her mother's hand. "You're doing fine."

Patricia merely smiled. She knew people still whispered such things as *They found her first daughter murdered. Just four years old and her head was cut off. Isn't that horrible? Can you imagine?*

And these days they were adding *Her son just announced he was gay. You know he's always been, well, troubled. And get this—she's started drinking again. That's right. Fresh out of rehab . . .*

"Everything looks great," Patricia said too cheerfully. Two women walked by, then whispered to each other furiously. Patricia's grip on her crystal glass grew tight.

"They'll get over it," Melanie said gently. "Remember, the first public outing is the worst."

"It was my own fault." More hesitation now, genuine remorse.

"It's okay, Mom. It's okay."

"I shouldn't have been so weak. Fifteen years of being sober. Sometimes I don't know myself. . . ."

"Mom—"

"I miss Brian."

"I know," Melanie murmured. "I know."

Patricia pinched the bridge of her nose. She had worked herself up to the point of tears, and Patricia Stokes did not cry in public. She turned, giving the room her back until the worst passed.

The waiter looked reproachfully at Melanie, as if she should be doing something. Melanie would love to do something. Unfortunately the rift between her father and brother was old, and there was little she or her mother could do. Harper looked in good spirits tonight, so maybe the end would soon be near.

"I'm . . . I'm better now," Patricia was saying. She had pulled herself together, adopting that firm

smile she'd learned in some finishing school umpteen
years earlier.

"You can go up anytime you want," Melanie said.

"Nonsense. I just need to get through the first hour.
You're right—the first public outing is always the
hardest. Well, let the windbags talk. I've certainly
heard worse."

"It's going to be okay, Mom."

"Of course, it is." Patricia was back to her overbright smiles, but then she leaned over and gave her
daughter a genuine hug. Her arms were strong around
Melanie, the scent of Chanel No. 5 and Lancôme face
cream comforting. Melanie looped her arms around
her mother's too-thin waist the way she had been doing since she was nine and let the embrace last for as
long as her mom needed it to.

When they drew back, they were both smiling.

"I have to get to the kitchen," Melanie said.

"Do you need help? I'm really not doing much."

"Nope. This show is on the road." She was already
stepping away, but then her mom caught her hand.
She looked intent.

"William coming?"

Melanie shrugged. "He *is* dad's favorite anesthesiologist."

"Nervous?"

"Never. What's one ex-fiancé among three hundred
people?"

"William's a jerk," her mom said loyally.

"And you are the best." Melanie gave her mother's
hand a squeeze, then plunged into the crowd.

A sudden movement caught her eye. She turned just
in time to see the flapping tail of a brown overcoat
disappear into the kitchen. That was odd. Who would
be running around in a soiled overcoat?

She was about to follow up, when she heard a com-
motion from outside. The valets were fighting over
whose turn it was to park a Porsche. By the time Mel-

anie sorted it all out, the matter of the out-of-place overcoat had completely slipped her mind.

AN HOUR LATER Melanie realized she still hadn't checked in on the blood donor room that her friend Ann Margaret had set up in the front parlor.

"I'm so sorry!" she apologized immediately, bursting into the wood-paneled room that now boasted four blood donor stretchers instead of the usual leather sofas. "I wanted to see if you needed anything, but it's been so crazy!"

"Completely understandable," Ann Margaret drawled as she finished rubbing iodine on the exposed skin of a man's arm and in the next heartbeat slid in the needle. "As you can see, life here is just fine."

"Hey, gorgeous," the man said. "I've been wondering where you've been hiding."

Melanie burst into a smile. "Uncle Jamie! Here you are. I should've known my godfather would fly all the way from Europe just to hole up with a beautiful woman."

"Can't help myself," Jamie informed her. "It's the gift of being Irish."

Melanie shook her head. She'd heard it all before but didn't mind hearing it again. A longtime friend of her parents from their days in Texas, Jamie O'Donnell was one of her most favorite people in the world. He jetted all over the globe tracking down rare items for his import/export company, then blazed into town twice a year to spoil her rotten with imported chocolates, exotic toys, and larger-than-life stories.

Now he was sprawled on the raised donor bed, looking just off the docks even in a three-thousand-dollar tuxedo. It was probably the single diamond winking in his left ear, or the mischievous look on his face.

"They take your blood, Uncle Jamie? Somehow I figured with the life you've led . . ."

"Ah, I'm a saint, lass. A pure, angelic sort, I swear it."

"Hardly," Ann Margaret murmured, and snapped a rubber band around an empty donor bag.

Melanie looked back and forth between her godfather and best friend. Maybe it was just her, but she would swear there was a light blush on Ann Margaret's face, a reluctance to meet Jamie's direct gaze. Very interesting.

Melanie climbed onto the stretcher next to Jamie's and offered up her arm to donate while she and her godfather caught up.

Jamie didn't waste any time. "Brian really thinks he's gay?"

"I don't think he merely 'thinks' it."

Jamie sighed. "And your dad, being the open-minded fellow that he is, tossed him out on his arse."

Melanie grimaced. "Brian didn't exactly help matters with his method of announcement. I mean, one minute Harper is serving duck à l'orange to the hospital's head of surgery, the next his own son is bolting up, yelling he's tired of the goddamn lies and he's a goddamn homosexual and Harper had better goddamn deal with it. I don't think I've ever seen Dad hold a duck leg in midair for so long. If the whole thing hadn't been really happening, I think it might have been funny."

"Brian always lets things build too much," Ann Margaret stated knowingly, having followed the family saga for the past ten years. "Wasn't he seeing a therapist?"

"He stopped. I believe his lover is the therapist's brother, or something like that."

"You're kidding!" Both Ann Margaret and Jamie managed to be aghast.

"Well, at least tell me your brother is doing okay," Jamie said to Melanie.

But Melanie couldn't. "I don't know. Brian . . . Brian isn't speaking to me."

"No." Jamie shook his head. "Stupid young fool. He and Harper have always gone head to head—they're both too damn thick, that's the problem—but the boy's crazy about you. I used to tease your parents that he mistook you for a puppy, the way he'd run around feeding you toys and feeding you chocolate. He's got no good reason to be taking out this newest tiff on you." Jamie paused, then asked carefully, "He *doesn't* have any reason to be mad at you, right, lass? I can't see you caring about his sexual orientation or whatever the hell they're calling it these days."

"I don't," Melanie said. "Neither does Mom. But I don't know . . . Brian's always been moody. He has his spells, kind of like Mom, his blue periods, even his angry periods. When I heard him shout that he was a homosexual, some part of my brain clicked. I thought, oh, well, that's why. And now we know, and it's all out in the open, so everything will get better.

"But it didn't get better. Something went off in him. I mean, *went off,* and suddenly it's like he hates us. All of us. I don't know why."

Her godfather looked troubled. "You try talking to him?"

"I left six messages, then went over in person. He wouldn't answer the door."

"That kid just tries your patience."

"He probably needs more time."

Jamie didn't look convinced. "He shouldn't need time to know to treat his mom and sister with respect. Well, what's done is done. Has Harper said anything more about it?"

"You know this isn't the kind of stuff he talks about."

"Harper needs to pull his head out of his ass," Jamie declared, one of his favorite opinions about Harper. He said it without vehemence though. The two men went back too far to be hotheaded about their differences now.

"Dad's just conservative," Melanie said. "I imagine

not too many of his aging Republican cronies have ever had to deal with sons announcing that they're gay."

"Your son is still your son."

Ann Margaret placed two fingers over the gauze pad covering the needle on his arm. "So says the man who doesn't have one."

Jamie actually flushed. "Just mind your own business, you nosy little—"

Ann Margaret yanked the needle out of his vein. He made a silent O with his lips, then, every inch a chastised schoolboy, obediently lifted his arm above his head and held it there.

"You're doing great," Ann Margaret declared merrily, and Jamie gave Melanie a long-suffering look that declared he knew he'd met his match—but he still didn't want to hear about it.

Ann Margaret moved on to Melanie next, removing the needle, applying a Band-Aid.

"I think Harper is going to give soon," Melanie confided when both she and her godfather were allowed to sit up. She moved to Jamie's stretcher, where they sat side by side.

"You think?"

"I found him crying," she said quietly. "Late last week, on the sofa downstairs, when he thought no one was around."

Jamie glanced down at the floor, completely subdued. After a moment Melanie looked at him curiously.

"What do you want from him, Jamie? Dad was raised in the fifties, when men were men, women were women, and gays were freaks. I'm not saying that's right, but it's hard to undo a lifetime of thinking."

"You always were a good diplomat, Mel."

"It's not world politics, Jamie. It's *family*."

They both drifted into silence, and after a while their gazes turned to the glittering crowd.

Melanie picked out her father. He now stood in the

left corner of the living room, sharing a laugh with his rival at Mass General. William had arrived and waited at her father's heels. Like Harper, William Sheffield, M.D., prided himself on his perfect appearance. Tonight, though, he looked tired, worn around the edges.

Maybe trying to keep up with three women was finally taking its toll on him.

Melanie quickly pushed that thought away. Not her business anymore, not her problem.

She looked for her mother and found her at nearly the opposite corner of the room from her husband. Melanie's parents rarely kept each other company at parties, and not at all these days, with the situation with Brian causing a rift between them.

They were never the type to argue in public, however. They never even disagreed in front of their children. Discussions took place discreetly, late at night, when they thought Brian and Melanie were asleep, and a united judgment was then passed in the morning. For the most part, Melanie regarded her parents' marriage as solid, if stale. Even now she didn't worry about them. After all, they'd weathered far worse crises.

Presently Patricia set down her orange juice glass and started moving. She passed right by where Harper was standing. Melanie thought her mother would simply keep going, but her father reached out and stopped her with a touch of his hand to her bare elbow. It was hard to say who was the most surprised by the unexpected contact, Patricia or Melanie.

Harper's mood was definitely softening, for whatever he said to his wife, it made her smile. He murmured something more, his blue eyes sparkling, and she actually laughed, looking startled, looking pleased. She turned toward him fully. His long surgeon's fingers skimmed her collarbone before coming to rest on her slender waist, and she leaned toward her husband in a way Melanie hadn't seen in a long, long time.

Jamie shifted beside Melanie, and she realized he was watching her parents as well, his expression hard to read.

"It's going to be all right," Melanie murmured with renewed confidence. "See, the worst is over."

"Your mom looks great," Jamie said softly, and behind them Ann Margaret bound their pints of blood more briskly.

"She's attending her AA meetings diligently. She's a tough one, you know." Melanie glanced at her watch, then hopped down from the stretcher. "You in town a bit?"

"Coupla weeks, love."

"Tea at the Ritz?"

"Wouldn't miss it for the world."

"It's a date. Take good care of him, Ann Margaret. I'll catch you both a little later."

MELANIE HAD NO sooner turned down the back hall to the kitchen than she bumped into another guest. She glanced up to apologize and found herself looking at a short, balding man in rumpled streetclothes. She'd seen his overcoat earlier, she realized, heading down the hall, disappearing around the corner.

"Who are you?" she asked sharply.

The man grinned, but it wasn't friendly. "Larry Digger, ma'am. *Dallas Daily*. Unh-unh. Don't turn away from me, Miss Stokes. I've spent all night long waiting to catch you alone. Goddamn, you are one busy lady."

"You don't belong here, sir. This is a private function, and if you don't leave right now, I'm calling security."

"I wouldn't do that if I were you."

"Well, you aren't me," she said firmly. She opened her mouth to summon help. Suddenly the man's hand snapped around her wrist and he stared at her with an intensity that was startling. Melanie couldn't breathe.

Something was stirring in the back of her mind. Ripples in the void. *Not now, not now.*

"I know about your father," the man whispered intently.

"H-Harper Stokes?"

"Nah, Miss Stokes. I know about your real father, your *birth* father."

"What?"

He smiled. A smile of supreme satisfaction. "Follow me, Miss Stokes," he said calmly. "I'm gonna tell you a story. A little story about Texas and a serial killer named Russell Lee Holmes."

THREE

L ARRY DIGGER TUGGED Melanie into the foyer.
The Duvets, about to depart, gave them a curious look, and Melanie's lips formed an automatic smile. She was still turning the reporter's
words around in her head.

*I know about your real father . . . your birth fa-
ther . . .*

Digger twisted them away from the guests and
headed down the back hall. Two servers burst
through the swinging doors at the end. "Jesus Christ,
this place is overrun. How many rich people do you
know?"

"Do you want money? Is that what this is about?"

Digger jerked her toward the back patio, but it was
also filled with guests who gave them startled glances.
"Fuck this!"

He gave up on the house altogether and pulled her
across the street to the Public Garden.

The night was warm and humid, the air fragrant
with cherry blossoms and hyacinths, the gas lamps
soft. May was a gorgeous month in Boston, and people took advantage of it. Melanie could see young
couples nuzzling beneath maple trees, older couples
herding their children, other people walking dogs.

The park was active and well lit, so Melanie wasn't afraid.

Mostly she was confused. A dull throbbing had taken root behind her left eye, and she was thinking Russell Lee Holmes, Russell Lee Holmes. Why did that name sound so familiar?

Larry Digger stopped beneath a tree, shoved his pudgy hands in his trench coat pockets, and squared off against her.

"Russell Lee Holmes murdered seven children. They ever tell you that?"

"What?"

"Yep. That's what he did. Mean son of a bitch. Liked his children young and with curly blond hair. Kidnapped poor children mostly, white trash like himself. Took them to dump yards and messed them up like you wouldn't believe. I have photos."

"What?"

"Come on," Digger said impatiently. "Stop playing stupid. Russell Lee Holmes. Killed your parents' first daughter. Raped her and cut off her head. What was her name again?"

Oh, God, that's where she knew the name. Brian must have told her, or Jamie. Certainly her parents never spoke of that time.

"M-M-Meagan," Melanie whispered.

"Yeah, Meagan, that's it. She was the worst one, all right. Four years old, cute as a button. Your parents doled out a hundred thousand bucks for ransom, and all they got to bury was a headless corpse. Enough to drive a mother to drink—"

"Shut up!" Melanie had heard enough. "What the hell do you want, Mr. Digger? Because if you think I'm going to just stand here and listen to you take potshots at my family, you got another think coming."

"I want you!" Digger moved in close. "I've been following you, Melanie Stokes. For twenty-five years I've been trying to find proof of your existence, trying to find out if Russell Lee Holmes really did have a wife and child, because that son of a bitch wouldn't tell a soul, wouldn't even tell me on his execution day, the bastard. But I've kept looking. Russell Lee Holmes was front-page news when they got him, and he was front-page news when they fried his ass. And he's gonna be front-page news again when I announce that I've found his daughter. You know what, Miss *Holmes*—you got his eyes."

"Look, I don't know what your game is, but I was found in *Boston*. I don't have anything to do with some guy in Texas."

"I never said you grew up in Texas, just that your daddy died there—"

"After fathering a child in Boston? I don't think so."

"Oh, but I do. See, Russell Lee may have lived in Texas, but once he was arrested for murder, it was probably best for his wife and child if they got out of town. The newspapers were overflowing with accounts of what he did, you know—particularly the Stokes girl." Larry Digger rocked back on his heels. "He kidnapped her right from the nanny's car, sent a ransom demand, and raped and killed her even as your parents were struggling to raise the money. Very ingenious of him, you have to admit. I mean, there he was, coming up with ways to get *paid* for his work—"

"Goddammit." Melanie had definitely had enough. "I am *not* Russell Lee Holmes's daughter. You, on the other hand, are a crackpot. Good-bye."

Melanie took a step. Larry Digger snapped his hand around her wrist and held tight. For the first time Melanie was afraid. When she turned, however, the reporter said calmly, "Of course you're Russell Lee's daughter."

"Let go of my arm."

"You were found the night Russell Lee Holmes died," the reporter continued as if she hadn't spoken. "They ever tell you that? Yep, Russell Lee goes to the chair in Texas, and a little girl without a past suddenly appears in Harper Stokes's hospital. Awfully coincidental if you ask me. And then you gotta wonder—why was Harper even working that night? The man who killed his little girl is being executed, and he stays home to work? Kind of strange if you ask me. Unless he knows he has a good reason to stick around the hospital."

"I was drugged and abandoned in the ER," Melanie said slowly. "My father is a cardiac surgeon. That he came downstairs at all was purely a fluke—"

"Or good timing."

"Oh, for heaven's sake, how many men die a day in the U.S. anyway? A few thousand? A few hundred thousand? Want to tell me I'm their daughter too?"

She gave the reporter an exasperated glance and simultaneously yanked her arm free. Digger appeared unconcerned, fishing out a crumpled pack of cigarettes and pounding out a smoke.

"Come on, Miss Holmes. You honestly never wondered where you came from? You're not the teeniest bit curious?"

"Good-bye."

He smiled. "I know your family, Melanie. Your mom, your dad, your brother. I covered their story when Meagan was kidnapped, and I was with Patricia and Brian the night they fried Russell Lee Holmes. You don't want to listen to me, fine. You go inside and tell your mother that Larry Digger is here to see her. Didn't she just get out of rehab? I understand that since the death of her first daughter, her nerves have never been the same." Digger exhaled a plume of smoke right into Melanie's face. "What do you think?"

"You are a piece of shit."

"Ah, honey, I've been called worse." Digger flicked ash off the end of his cigarette. "How's Brian anyway? I remember him pressing his face to the glass in the witness room—you know, back then. When they fried Russell Lee, it was gruesome, just plain sick. Everyone closed their eyes and covered their ears. But fourteen-year-old Brian Stokes pressed his face against the glass and stared at Russell Lee dying as if he was trying to sear it into his brain. *Sear it,* mind you.

"I hear Brian's gay now. Do you think watching a man die could affect a man's sexual preferences? Just asking."

The last comment, so cruel in its casualness, struck Melanie like a blow. She had to close her eyes, and then she was so angry she couldn't speak. She wanted to hurt him. The intensity of the desire balled her hands into fists. But she was no match for him, fat and all, and they both knew it.

"I want you away from my family," she said finally. "Whatever it is you have to say, you say it here. If you honestly have a story, I'm sure a quote from a killer's child is worth enough to you to stay the hell away from them. Deal?"

Larry Digger pretended to consider it. He took another deep drag from his cigarette and looked at the park around them, but his beady eyes were already gleaming triumphantly.

"I like you," Digger said suddenly. "I don't like most people, Miss Holmes. But I like you. You not only have Russell Lee's eyes, you got his spine."

"I'm just so darn flattered," Melanie spat out, and Digger laughed.

"Yeah, you're a fine piece of work. So tell me, sweetheart, what's it like to suddenly get to live with so much money?"

"Oh, it's just as good as you dreamed, Larry, and everything you'll never have."

"Yeah? Too bad I'm going to ruin it for you." Larry Digger stubbed out his cigarette on the tree trunk and got serious. "The hospital," he said. "I think that's the key. Over a hundred hospitals in this city, and you just happen to end up at Harper's?"

"Coincidence."

"Maybe, but they all start to add up after a while. First we got the timing, Miss Holmes. You just happened to appear the night Russell Lee is fried for killing little kids. Then we got location. You just happened to be dropped at Harper's hospital and he just happened to have blown off an execution to be there. Then we got you. A little girl. Found perfectly clothed and in good health but nobody ever claimed you? All these years, not a single whisper from the people who must've taken care of you for nine years, bought you clothes, fed you, put a roof over your head, hell, even made sure you were found at a hospital, where you'd be in good hands. And then there's the matter of your amnesia. A healthy little girl who couldn't remember *anything* about where she came from, not even her own name. And all these years later, two *decades* later, you *still* don't remember. Seems strange to me that a nine-year-old child could appear out of nowhere, remember nothing, and be claimed by no one. Strange. Or planned."

"You know what they say, truth is stranger than fiction."

"Oh, that's a good one, Miss Holmes. Harper ever take you to a hypnotist? What about regression therapy or aromatherapy or whatever else quacks are dreaming up these days?"

"The doctors who checked me out said I was physically fine and that I'd remember when I was ready to remember."

"Come on, Miss Holmes, surely the great Dr. Harper Stokes had a few opinions on this subject. He coulda taken you to a hypnotist anytime and what would anybody have done about it? What would have happened? You would've remembered, that's what. And your family, sweetheart, doesn't want you to remember."

"Oh, this is *stupid!* All you have supplied are a bunch of coincidences. And your little scenario has holes you could drive a truck through. Plain and simple, my parents *loved* Meagan. No way would they knowingly have adopted the child of her killer. That doesn't make sense."

Larry Digger was looking at her curiously. "You honestly believe that, don't you?"

"Of course I do. What the hell do you mean?"

"Huh." He nodded to himself as if she'd just answered a very important question. Melanie shook her head, starting to feel more confused now, as if she were at the top of a very steep precipice and she'd just taken her first misstep.

The throbbing in her head was growing. Black voids were appearing in front of her eyes. She hadn't suffered from a serious migraine in years, but now she had the faint realization that she was dangerously close to vomiting.

"Maybe you had to know Harper and Patricia in Texas," Digger was murmuring. "Maybe you had to see them sitting up in their rich palace no fourth-year resident should be able to afford. Maybe you had to see them in Texas with their two kids, one so sweet, everyone loved her, and one already so troubled, half the moms on the block wouldn't let him play with their children. I'm getting the impression, Miss Holmes, there's a helluva lot about your family you just plain don't know."

"That's not true. It's not."

"Ah, Miss Holmes." Larry Digger sounded sympathetic, almost pitying. It confused her more than his vicious comments had. "Let me tell you something, Melanie, for your own sake. I didn't find you on my own, kid. I got a tip. An anonymous call in the middle of the night. Needless to say, reporters don't like anonymous tips, not even washed-up pieces of shit like me." His teeth flashed, then his voice turned horribly somber. "I had the caller traced the second time, Miss Holmes. Right back to Boston, Massachusetts. Right back to Beacon Street. Right back to *your house*. Why do you think that is, Mel? Why is someone from your house calling *me* about Russell Lee Holmes?"

"I don't . . . It doesn't . . . None of this makes any sense." The world tilted suddenly. Melanie sat down on the ground. She heard herself whisper, "But that was so long ago. . . ."

Larry Digger smiled. "You get what you deserve, Melanie Stokes. By the caller's own words, you get what you deserve."

"No—"

"How much of a person's temperament is genetic, Melanie Holmes? Are junkyard dogs born or raised? Are you really as polished and refined as your uptight adoptive parents, or does a little Texas white trash lurk beneath that surface? I already know you can be tough. Now, what about *violence?* Ever look at a little kid, Miss Holmes, and feel *hungry?*"

"*No!* No. Oh, God . . ." Her head exploded. Melanie grabbed her temples, pressed her forehead against her knees, and rocked on the grass.

From far away she heard Larry Digger chortle. "I'm right, aren't I? Twenty-five years later, I'm finally getting it ri—" His words suddenly ended in a yelp.

Melanie turned slowly. A white figure had joined them in the park. He seemed to have his hand clamped on Larry Digger's shoulder.

"She asked you to leave," the newcomer said calmly.

Larry Digger tried to push the man away. "Hey, this is private. Don't you got horse d'oovers to serve or something?"

"No, but I'm thinking of sharpening my knives."

The man tightened his grip even more, and Digger held up his hands in surrender. The minute he was released, he backed up. "Okay, I'll go. But I'm not lying. I do have proof, Miss Holmes. I have information, not just about your father, but your *birth mother* as well. Ever think of her, Miss Holmes? Bet she could actually tell you your real birthday, let alone your real name. Midtown Hotel, sweetheart. Pleasant dreams."

The man took a quick step forward at the sarcastic tone, and Larry Digger hightailed it out of there, his stained coat flapping behind him.

Melanie's stomach heaved. She celebrated Larry Digger's departure by spewing shrimp all over the grass and the man's glossy black shoes.

"Shit!" he yelped, leaping back awkwardly. He didn't seem to know what to do.

That made two of them. Tears of rage streamed down Melanie's cheeks. Her head was throbbing, and images added to the chaos in her mind. Blue dress, blond hair, pleading eyes. *I want to go home now. Please, let me go home.*

"Are you going to be okay?" A hand draped back her hair. "Jesus, you're burning up. Let me call an ambulance."

"No!" Melanie's fear of hospitals outweighed her fear of pain. She snapped her head up and promptly winced. "Give me . . . a minute."

Her savior was not impressed. "Jesus, lady. You go walking with a seedy-looking stranger—what were you thinking?"

"Nothing, obviously." Melanie pressed the heels of her hands against her eyes. The man was absolutely right, and she resented him for it. With no other choice, she finally risked opening her eyes.

It was hard to see in the dark. The gas lamp caught the man's features only in half wash, illuminating a square jaw, lean cheeks, and a nose that had been broken a few too many times. Thick dark hair, cut conservatively short. Lips pressed into a grim, unyielding line. She recognized his uniform. Great, she'd just been saved by one of her own waiters.

She closed her eyes again. Nothing like being caught at her worst by someone who could spread stories.

"Are you going to live?" the waiter asked sharply.

"Possibly. It would help if you'd lower your voice."

He seemed contrite for a moment, then ruined the impression with his next words. "You shouldn't have let him drag you off like that. That was a stupid thing to do. Did he want money?"

"Who doesn't?" Melanie staggered to her feet, needing to move, to just . . . move. Unfortunately the ground shifted beneath her, the trees bobbed.

The waiter had to grab her arm. "You keep trying to stand and we're going to have to start a suicide watch for you. Vision?"

"White dots."

"Hearing?"

"What?"

"Prescription meds, right?"

"In the house," she murmured, and tried to take a step. Her legs collapsed. The waiter caught her. She floated limply on his arm, suddenly beyond caring.

Please, please let me go home!

No, honey. You don't want to go home. It's not safe . . .

The man muttered something about foolish women, then swung her up in his arms. She leaned against his shoulder. He felt solid and firm and strong. He smelled like Old Spice.

Melanie buried her face against his neck and let the world slip away.

SPECIAL AGENT DAVID Riggs was not happy. First, because he wasn't fond of rescuing damsels in distress. Second, because he was going to take a lot of heat for rescuing this particular damsel.

"We're eyes and ears only at this stage. This is a very delicate investigation. Don't fuck it up."

Riggs was pretty sure Supervisory Agent Lairmore would consider following, intervening, and now carrying Melanie Stokes to be a fuckup. He was supposed to be shadowing her father. He was supposed to be overhearing Dr. Harper Stokes's confession of healthcare fraud that he would casually drop at his daughter's black-tie event, high on vodka tonics and friends. Uh-huh.

David shifted Melanie more comfortably in his arms and crossed the street. She was smaller than he would've guessed, having watched her dart around the house all evening like a firefly. She never slowed down and hardly even seemed to need a gasp of air. He'd watched her do everything from heft boxes of mangoes to mop up a spill. He'd also noted that she circled back to the living room half a dozen times to discreetly check up on her mother.

Now she was leaning her head against his shoulder in a way a woman hadn't done in a long, long time.

He didn't know what to make of that, so he turned his mind sharply to the file he had on the Stokes family and the few things it told him about Melanie Stokes. Daughter, adopted at the age of nine after being abandoned at the hospital where Dr. Stokes worked. A bit of a media buzz portraying her as a modern-day Orphan Annie. She'd graduated with a B. A. from Wellesley in '91 and was active in various charitable organizations. One of those I-want-to-give-something-back-to-the-world kind of people. Nine months earlier she'd become engaged to Dr. William Sheffield, her father's favorite right-hand man, then ended it a mere three months later without ever giving a reason. One of those my-business-is-my-business kind of people. She helped take care of her mother, who, as Larry Digger had pointed out, had never been the same since the murder of her first daughter. One of those you-mess-with-my-family-you-mess-with-me kind of people. Whatever.

Nothing in the files indicated that Melanie Stokes was the daughter of a serial killer, though David had found the reporter's list of coincidences extremely interesting. Then again, David couldn't decide what he thought of the reporter. For all his bluster, Larry Digger's hands had been shaking toward the end. The man had probably skipped his nightly pint of bourbon to make contact. No doubt he was drowning in it now.

Melanie moaned as the house lights hit them both.

"Don't throw up on me again," David muttered.

"Wait . . ."

"*Are* you going to be sick?"

"Wait." She gripped his jacket. "Don't . . . tell anyone," she muttered intently. "Not . . . my family. I'll pay you . . ."

Her eyes were clear. Big and earnest and a startling color, somewhere between blue and gray.

"Yeah, well, sure. Whatever you want."

She sank back down into his arms, seemingly satisfied. David pushed into the foyer and everyone spotted them at once.

"What's going on here?" Harper Stokes immediately strode toward them, William Sheffield in tow. Then Patricia Stokes came flying, sloshing orange juice on her designer dress.

"Oh, my God, Melanie."

"Bedroom?" David asked, and ignoring everyone's gasps and questions, headed up the stairs. "She mentioned having a migraine."

Harper swore. "She should have Fiorinal with codeine in the bathroom. Patricia?"

She darted ahead three flights and burst from her daughter's bathroom, pills and water in hand, just as David laid Melanie down on a rumpled bed. Immediately he was pushed aside by her family, Harper anxiously picking up his daughter's hand and checking her pulse. He took the water and held it to his daughter's pale lips to wash down the pills. Patricia followed with a damp towel, gently bathing Melanie's face. That left William Sheffield, who hovered self-consciously in the doorway. It wasn't clear to David why the former fiancé was even in the room.

"What happened?" Harper demanded. He checked

his daughter's pulse again, then took the towel from his wife and positioned it across Melanie's forehead. "Where was Melanie? How did you end up with her?"

"I found her in the park," David said. Apparently the answer sounded as vague to Harper as it did to David, because the surgeon shot him a look. David returned the stare.

Of all the people in the room, David knew the most about Dr. Harper Stokes—he'd spent the past three weeks compiling a file on the man. Considered a brilliant surgeon by many, he'd recently been anointed the top cardiac surgeon in a town known for its surgeons. Others alleged he was an egomaniac, that his zealousness to heal had more to do with the recognition it brought him than honest interest in his patients. Given the growing Hollywoodization of hospital surgery, David found that a tough call to make. Most cardiac surgeons these days were after fame or fortune. After all, there were NBA athletes courted less aggressively than a good, charismatic surgeon who could bring in the bucks.

The only thing different David could find out about Dr. Harper Stokes was his background. In a day and age when a surgeon's career track started at the age of eighteen with enrollment in an Ivy League college, Dr. Stokes's academic career was mediocre at best. He'd graduated from Texas A&M at the middle of his class. He hadn't gotten into any of the top twenty medical schools, having to settle for his local "safety school," Sam Houston University. There, he'd been known more for his upscale wardrobe and dogged work ethic than for a gift for surgery.

Oddly enough, the single event that seemed to transform Harper Stokes from average resident to surgeon extraordinaire was the kidnapping of his daughter. His personal life had disintegrated, and he had turned to work. The more chaotic the Stokeses' world became, the more time Harper spent in the hospital, where he did have the power to heal and redeem, and, what the hell, play God.

Russell Lee Holmes may have destroyed a family, but in a strange way he had also created one topnotch surgeon.

Recently the FBI had received three phone calls on the healthcare fraud hotline about Boston's number one cardiac man. Someone thought Harper's pacemaker surgeries were questionable. At this point in the investigation, David had no idea. Could be just a jealous rival blowing smoke. Could be that the doctor had come up with a way to make a few extra bucks— God knows the Stokeses lived high enough on the hog.

So far the only dirt David had found on the man was his penchant for beautiful women. Even that didn't seem to be much of a secret. He went out with his pieces of pretty young fluff; his wife kept looking the other way. Lots of marriages worked like that.

"But why was Melanie in the park?" Harper was asking with a frown, jerking David's attention back to the cramped bedroom.

Melanie answered first. "I wanted some fresh air. I was going to step out for only a moment."

"I happened to notice her leaving the house," David said. "When she hadn't returned for a while, I decided to see if everything was all right. I heard the sound of someone being ill across the street and found her."

Harper remained frowning, then turned to his daughter with a mixture of genuine concern and reproach. "You've been pushing yourself too hard, Melanie. You know what stress can do to you. You have to remember to monitor your level of anxiety. For heaven's sake, your mom and I would've helped you more if you'd just said something—"

"I know."

"You take too much upon yourself."

"I know."

"It's not healthy, young lady."

Melanie smiled wryly. "Would you believe I get it from you?"

Harper harrumphed but appeared honestly sheepish. He glanced at his wife, and the two of them exchanged a look David couldn't read.

"We should let her rest," Patricia said. "Honey, you just get some sleep, relax. Your father and I will handle everything downstairs."

"It's my job," Melanie tried to protest, but the pills were getting the better of her, making her eyelids droop. She made an effort at sitting up in the bed, but didn't even make it past halfway. Finally she curled up in a little ball in the middle of a big sleigh bed. She looked frailer than she had standing up to the reporter. She looked . . .

Patricia covered her with a quilt, then ushered everyone out.

"You just happened to notice Mel leaving the house," William Sheffield said as David brushed by him.

David calmly responded. "Yes, I did. Did you?"

The ex-fiancé flushed, glanced quickly at Harper for support, and when he got none, slunk away.

"Thank you for helping our daughter, Mr.—" Patricia paused in the doorway long enough to place a light hand on David's shoulder.

"Reese. David Reese."

Patricia kept her hand on his shoulder. "Thank you, Mr. Reese. Really, we are indebted—"

"Not a big deal."

She smiled, an expression that was sad. "To me it is."

Before David had to summon another reply, Jamie O'Donnell burst up the stairs, demanding to know what had happened to his Melanie. A trim woman with graying Brillo-like hair and nurses' whites was hot on his heels. Ann Margaret, David heard Patricia exclaim.

David used the opportunity to exit, then paused on

the second story landing to eavesdrop. O'Donnell was adamant about being informed. Ann Margaret insisted upon seeing Melanie. Harper uttered something sharp and low under his breath. David didn't catch it, but all four adults immediately hushed up. No more conversation from upstairs, just the sounds of four adults easing into Melanie Stokes's bedroom.

The hair was prickling on the back of David's neck. He hadn't felt this way in a long time. Not since that day he'd sat in the doctor's office, waiting for the final news, then saw the look on the M.D.'s face when he walked back into the examining room. At that moment David had known that life as he knew it—as his father knew it—was coming to an end.

There was no good reason for him to feel that way here. So far he had just a doctor, a family, and a drunken reporter. Nothing that sinister, nothing that promising as an investigative lead.

And yet . . . What was it Larry Digger had said?

He'd received his tip on Melanie Stokes's alleged parentage from an anonymous caller who declared that everyone gets what they deserve.

That was odd. Three weeks earlier, when the Boston field office had received an anonymous tip regarding Dr. Stokes's alleged illegal surgeries, the caller had also insisted that everyone gets what they deserve.

And David didn't believe in coincidences.

FOUR

THREE A.M. DAVID Riggs's shift as a waiter for the reception finally ended and released him into the streets of Boston. He was limping badly, his back feeling the strain even more than usual. Playing waiter was hard work. It meant he got to serve drinks, replenish hors d'oeuvre trays, and scrub his knuckles raw cleaning up. It meant he got to run all over hell and back, trying to be both a decent server and a diligent agent. Next time Lairmore asked him to go undercover, Riggs would nominate Chenney. Let the rookie lead the glamorous life.

Beacon Street was deserted now, the rich folks asleep in their town houses. Farther down, however, he heard the telltale rattle of a grocery cart on city sidewalks. Not all of Boston's residents were wealthy.

David kept walking, cutting across the Public Garden, where hours earlier he'd eavesdropped on Larry Digger and Melanie Stokes. He should probably call Chenney, see how the rookie was holding up. The new kid in the Boston healthcare fraud squad was a serious bodybuilder, one of those guys who look like a giant slab of meat. Big square head on top of a big square neck on top of a big square torso. When he walked, his bulging arms arced out to the side, like an ape. He was hard to take seriously, particularly when he introduced himself as a former CPA.

David still wasn't sure what he thought of the kid. It didn't help that Chenney had no training. The academy gave agent wanna-bes only a sixteen-week basic intro to white collar crime. The real plunge into the fun-filled world of MDRs, HMOs, unbundling, uploading, Part A versus Part B claims wouldn't happen until time and budget permitted Chenney to take specialized training through the National Healthcare Antifraud Association. Until then it was sink or swim, the Bureau's favorite way of seeing what rookie agents were made of.

Tonight Chenney was supposed to be trailing Dr. William Sheffield, but David had caught the anesthesiologist leaving the party after two A.M., and Chenney hadn't been anywhere in sight.

Either he was very, very good, or asleep on the job. David knew where he'd cast his vote.

He grimaced in pain, caught sight of an on-duty cab, and made his decision. At this stage of the investigation, nothing was moving that urgently. He and Chenney could catch up in the morning.

The ride home was long, and by the end David was curled up on the floor, his nostrils filled with the rancid odors of sweat and tobacco while his lower back convulsed and he writhed helplessly. He stumbled out of the taxi as soon as it pulled up to his Waltham apartment complex, shoved money into the cabdriver's hand, and staggered to his feet. He walked around the parking lot. Had to work the muscles, had to get them to relax. Movement was important, exercise the only way to keep what flexibility he could.

Your sacroiliac joints are inflamed, Mr. Riggs—that's the joint where your spine is connected to your pelvis—and that inflammation will start to spread up your back, causing increased discomfort. Exercise, ice, and nonsteroidal anti-inflammatory drugs are the key.

I was an athlete! I was supposed to be a major league pitcher! I know how to ice down. I know pain!

There's not much else we can tell you, Mr. Riggs. Ankylosing spondylitis symptoms vary intensely from person to person and are systemic. You may experience fever, fatigue, and digestive problems, and sometimes AS attacks organs such as your eyes, heart, and lungs. We can't predict how it will affect you personally. All we can tell you is that arthritis is chronic and those people who promise you a miracle cure are only trying to make a quick buck. You can still lead a full, satisfying life with AS, of course, Mr. Riggs, and there are many organizations out there to help you, but you will have to be more creative. Figure out the lifestyle that best works for you.

I have no life. I have no lifestyle. I am so damn tired.

The worst of the spasms finally passed. He kept walking anyway, though he wasn't sure why. Maybe because he'd gone so long without sleep, he'd forgotten how to do it. Maybe because he'd come to dread his bed, where he would start out in slumber and end up clutching his throat, gulping for air. He hadn't experienced that until two weeks ago. He didn't know if it was some kind of phase or if his arthritis had gotten worse.

And he didn't ask, because he was never sure if he wanted to know the answer.

He thought of baseball, the heady days of sweet sixteen.

Saturday afternoons, playing ball with his dad and his younger brother, Steven, talking about "the show," because Bobby Riggs had been a pretty good pitcher in his day—made it to the minors—and now looked at his sons with hope. Then out of the blue Heather Riggs had been diagnosed with breast cancer, and her husband and sons had come to the field just to take a break from the pain. Then young, beautiful Heather Riggs had died from the breast cancer, and they'd come out to the field because it was all they had left.

A father and his two sons whacking balls and sliding around bases, learning to communicate with each throw, hit, and catch. Cancer could take a loving mother and wife and rip a family apart. But baseball would never let you down. Baseball was as good as gold.

And so was David's arm.

David's arm had been the best of the best. David's arm could take him to the show.

At seventeen he'd been a Mass All-Star pitcher, and the pro-team scouts were already knocking on the door. He and his dad would stay up late talking about which major league teams had the best pitching programs for him, which place *they* would choose.

Then the nagging pain in his lower back wouldn't go away. He had problems running. Bruised tendon, they thought. Maybe he was outpitching his arm, needed to give it a break. David had to ease up. Steven took over for a while.

But David's back got worse and his shoulder got worse, and one day he was in a doctor's office being told his joints were too inflamed for him to continue pitching, while Steven was throwing his first no-hitter.

The Riggs men had never been quite the same since. David gave up serious baseball—pro teams didn't recruit young studs with health problems—and went to college instead. He didn't play baseball anymore. He left that to Steven, who did get a college scholarship but was never scouted by the pros. Steven had an arm, but he didn't have *David's* arm, and they all knew it.

Steven was now an assistant baseball coach at UMass Amherst, happily married with two great kids and maybe the next major leaguer. And since David couldn't be an all-star pitcher for his father, he'd offered up federal agent instead. He'd put away murderers, catch a serial killer, get a movie of the week. When he'd been assigned to the Boston office, he'd fantasized about exposing Boston's Mafia. He'd work undercover to expose the prominent crime families and have a showdown with the head don.

First year out of the academy, a chiropractor finally diagnosed David as having AS. His "bad back" would never get better.

The Bureau assigned him to white collar crime, where the biggest field danger was paper cuts from sorting through hundreds of boxes of subpoenaed files. David got good reviews each year for his "analytics," the Bureau's euphemism for being adept at speed-reading large quantities of gibberish while downing take-out Chinese. And he watched his academy classmates break up drug rings, foil terrorism plots, and get promoted first. Those were the breaks in the Bureau.

His back felt much better now. Did that mean it would let him sleep? Nearly five in the morning. Steven probably had a game today. He should drive over and watch. His father would be there.

David would probably go in to work instead. The cleanup at the Stokes house wasn't finished yet, and David needed the excuse to be around. It would give him a chance to learn more about Dr. Harper Stokes and Digger's strange allegations about his adopted daughter.

David walked into his apartment as the first rays of sun began to lighten the sky. Only two pictures decorated the walls. Fenway Park lit up at night. Shoeless Joe Jackson. Not much about the place to call home.

David cast off his clothes without turning on the light and slid into bed. Two more hours until the alarm clock would go off. He needed to sleep.

He stared at the portrait of Shoeless Joe instead.

"Remind me life isn't fair," he muttered to his idol. "And tell me it's okay, dammit, it's okay."

Shoeless Joe didn't reply. After a moment David rolled over and pretended to get some sleep.

FIVE

T FOUR A.M. Melanie bolted awake, a scream ripe in her throat and images blazing in her mind. Little Meagan Stokes chasing her with a bloody head. Little Meagan Stokes chanting *"Russell Lee Holmes. Russell Lee Holmes. You're just the brat of Russell Lee Holmes."*

Melanie climbed out of bed. Her breathing was hard, her hands were shaking. She could taste blood. She finally realized that in her instinctive effort not to make any noise, she'd bitten her tongue.

She rubbed her damp cheeks, took a deep breath. A minute more and she slid to her feet. Downstairs, she could hear the grandfather clock ticking. Other than that, the three story house was perfectly still.

Melanie moved quietly. Driven by an impulse she didn't care to examine just yet, she headed downstairs.

The living room was empty, the furniture reassembled, and the whole room cast in a soft glow from the gas lamps on the street.

She drifted toward the fireplace, feeling lonely.

Since her breakup with William, she'd had too many nights like this one, when she woke up to silence and roamed the house, looking for something she couldn't name.

Until he'd proposed to her, she actually hadn't thought too much about a family of her own. She had her parents to take care of, her brother to worry about. Her life was full enough. But then William had asked for her hand in marriage. She'd never been sure why. She'd said yes. She'd never been sure why. Maybe because at that moment she had a vision of herself as Cinderella living happily ever after with Prince Charming, and that vision had seduced her.

The hard facts of reality had emerged soon enough.

She didn't miss William though. What she missed, she supposed, was the dream.

She came to a halt in front of the fireplace. And her gaze turned automatically to the huge oil painting of little Meagan Stokes.

"First we got the timing, Miss Holmes. You just happened to appear the night Russell Lee is fried for killing little kids. Then we got location. You just happened to be dropped at Harper's hospital and he just happened to have blown off an execution to be there. Then we got you. A little girl. Found perfectly clothed and in good health but nobody ever claimed you? All these years, not a single whisper from the people who must've taken care of you for nine years, bought you clothes, fed you, put a roof over your head, hell, even made sure you were found at a hospital, where you'd be in good hands. And then there's the matter of your amnesia. A healthy little girl who couldn't remember anything *about where she came from, not even her own name. And all these years later, two decades later, you still* don't remember?*"*

"No," she whispered to Meagan. "I don't remember. I swear I don't."

But she wasn't sure anymore. The stirrings in her mind, the recurring black voids, the little girl's voice. How many times now? She'd tried to pretend it wasn't happening, that her mind wasn't beginning to open up and show her things she didn't want to know.

She already had a family. She didn't want to know about a serial killer or her birth parents or her first nine years. None of that mattered. The only thing that did was that when she'd been abandoned in a hospital without even a name, the Stokeses had stepped in and rescued her.

For God's sake, she would be *nothing* without the Stokeses. Nothing.

Twenty years ago, she'd been a little girl waking up alone in a hospital ER. The white, white walls. The scary needles and tubes. The bewildering, frightening faces of strangers.

Everyone assured her she would be all right. Everyone told her that her parents would show up at any time and set everything straight. She was well fed, well taken care of. Someone out there most certainly loved her.

A couple of days passed. Time spent in the peds ward listening to other little children whimper and be comforted by their parents. Melanie would roll over in her high, white hospital bed and stare at the blank wall, trying desperately to picture the mommy who would come one day soon to comfort her.

Social services took over, transferred her to a nearby hospice. No more talk about the return of her loving parents. Now everyone murmured about finding a good foster home instead. What about adoption? It would be one thing if she were a baby, she heard someone say, but since she wasn't . . .

Night after night, alone in a plain room, realizing more and more that no one was going to magically arrive for her. No one was going to take her home. No one could even give her a name.

Then Patricia Stokes came.

She appeared in the doorway in a pretty pink suit, saying she'd come to read Melanie a story. Melanie didn't say a word. She looked at the thin, beautiful woman with her sad, lilting voice, and had thought almost viscerally, *I want her.*

She'd thrown her arms around the pretty lady. She'd buried her face against her fragrant neck. *Tell me everything is all right now. Tell me I have a home.*

The beautiful Mrs. Stokes had read her a story about a fairy-tale princess. For reasons Melanie hadn't known, she'd cried at the end. Then she'd hastily dried her tears, given Melanie a yearning look, and quickly left the room.

Later, one of the social workers explained to Melanie that Mrs. Stokes had lost her four-year-old daughter years ago in Texas. It had been very tragic. Now the Stokeses were starting over in Boston and Dr. Harper Stokes and his wife were among the most generous people in the community. Really, a lovely couple. So sad what had happened, of course, but sometimes God knows best.

Melanie got it. The Stokeses were missing a little girl the way she was missing a family. Apart, they were all lonely. Together, they would fit.

The next time Patricia arrived, she thrust out her arms. In an instant Mrs. Stokes folded her into her embrace. She began to cry again. This time Melanie patted her back.

"It's all right now," she whispered solemnly. "I'll be your little girl and everything will be all right."

Patricia had cried harder.

Six months later the Stokeses brought Melanie home.

By the time she was twelve, Melanie was the only one who could make her overworked father laugh. She was the one who understood Brian and his black moods.

Then there were the really dark nights, when her brother stayed out late and her father worked late, when Melanie would go downstairs and find her mother staring up at the oil portrait of the four-year-old daughter who would never be coming home. The little girl Patricia had brought into the world and lost.

The little girl who, even though Patricia had Melanie, she still couldn't forget.

On those nights Melanie would lead her mother upstairs and into bed. Then she would sit with her mother in the silence and hold her hand, trying to help her simply get through.

It's okay, Mom. I'll take care of you. I will always take care of you.

Five o'clock. The grandfather clock chimed again, rousing Melanie from her memories.

She was still staring at Meagan Stokes, who beamed as she held out her favorite red wooden horse to whoever was watching her. Little Meagan, with the perfect blue ruffled dress, big blue eyes, and golden sausage curls. Bright Meagan, who, just three weeks after the painting was completed, would be dead.

And twenty years later the Stokes family was still trying to get over it. Melanie understood now that there were some wounds not even an earnest new daughter could mend.

She finally turned away. She curled up on the sofa and whispered, "But they're my family too, Meagan. I earned them. I did."

THE MAN HUMMED softly to himself in the dark room. Making a list, checking it twice . . .

Twenty-five years he'd waited. Thought about what he'd do, turned it over in his mind, refined it until it was absolutely right. Three weeks earlier he'd started the ball rolling with a single phone call. *First get everyone in the same town.* With Larry Digger's arrival just a few hours ago, the last of the players had arrived. *Now let the games begin.*

Twenty-five years ago such crimes had been committed, both big and small. Twenty-five years ago such sins had been tolerated, both big and small. He had always thought human nature would take care of everything in the end. Someone would break, someone would talk, maybe even Larry Digger would finally put the pieces together.

But year had passed into year, and everyone did absolutely nothing. Told nothing, asked nothing, remembered nothing, learned nothing. Everyone got away with it.

He had had enough. Now he was taking matters into his own hands. Starting with the list—the complete compilation of the crimes committed by each.

The crime of not telling. The crime of not knowing. The crime of not remembering. The crime of unconditional love. The crime of unrelenting cowardice.

The crime of never being enough of a man.

Then there came the worst crime, a crime so big, he could not come up with a name that could capture its full nature. It was hypocrisy and greed and selfishness all rolled into one. It was taking what other people had simply because they had it. It was heartlessness and it was worse—it was ruining people's lives and not losing a moment of sleep.

It was the one Real Sin, for he had often thought that the true heart of the devil was contempt.

He had not come up with the price for this sin. It needed to be special, it needed to be simple, and it needed to be horrible.

He returned to what he did have. Candles and feathers and ancient art. A child's toy and a child's dress. Cow tongues and pig hearts and a bushel of apples. An object that bobbed in a glass jar and was so gruesome, not even he could stand the sight.

A phone number.

His preparations were complete.

Time for the opening gift. He studied his list. He studied his pile. He made his decision: Melanie. Melanie, who had actually found happiness as the Stokeses' other daughter. Melanie, who, in all these years, had never done him the favor of remembering.

He got out his butcher's knife. He sharpened the blade.

He was ready.

Do you know the perfect crime?

I do.

_____

SUNDAY WAS A beautiful day, bright spring sun, gaily chirping birds. Melanie woke up to discover herself on the camelback sofa with waiter David Reese peering down at her. She sat up in a hurry.

"What the hell are you doing in my living room?"

"My job. What the hell are you doing sleeping here?"

"None of your business!" Melanie blinked owlishly. It was bright. Too bright. And noisy too. Screeching cars, shouting pedestrians, honking horns. She suddenly had a bad feeling.

"What time is it?"

"One-thirty."

"*Oh, my God.*" Melanie never slept past eight. Never. And now it was all coming back to her. The scene with Larry Digger, David Reese carrying her home, the bad dream, the long night in front of Meagan Stokes's portrait. And now David Reese again, still smelling like Old Spice and rattling her nerves.

He'd traded in his white waiter's tux for an old Red Sox T-shirt and jeans. In daylight she saw that he had brown hair with hints of red. Deep brown eyes with hints of green. A face closer to forty than thirty, weatherbeaten and hawkish. Intense, she thought immediately.

He took a couple of steps away from her, and she noticed a limp. He winced but covered up by pressing his lips into a thin line.

"I take it you're here for work," she said finally.

"We're dismantling the juice carts. It's a laugh a minute."

"I'm sure it is. Now, is there something in particular that dragged you out into the living room?"

"Tools. Harry was in charge and all he brought was a ball peen hammer. Not too bright, Harry."

She said briskly, "The tool kit is in the utility closet in the kitchen. Go look there."

David merely stuck his hands in his back pockets. "We searched the kitchen area already. No tool kit. Nice collection of lightbulbs though."

"Oh." She frowned. "Well, my father might have taken it out for something. Go ask him."

"Can't. Dr. Stokes left first thing this morning."

"What about María?"

"That the maid? Haven't seen her."

"Well, maybe my mother knows what my father did with it."

"Mrs. Stokes is gone too. She didn't want to be late for her spa."

"Oh, I forgot." Sunday was AA day. Her mother wouldn't be home until at least five. Which meant it really was up to Melanie to find the missing tool kit.

She rose to her feet, but David didn't seem to be in the mood to move. In fact, he appeared to have something on his mind.

She looked at him curiously.

He asked abruptly, "How are you?"

"Fine."

"Spending the night on the couch?"

"It's a very comfortable sofa."

"With a clear view of Meagan's portrait?"

"I came for the sofa, not the view."

"Uh-huh," he said. "Just because a man showed up last night and alleged that the murderer of Meagan Stokes was really your father. That your adoptive parents aren't as good or kind as you believe—"

"Oh, my God, you heard everything!" She had thought he'd arrived only toward the end. She hadn't realized . . . He'd never said . . .

She jabbed a finger at his chest. "How dare you! You stood there and *eavesdropped* on my life. What the hell did you think you were doing?"

"Checking to see if you were all right—"

"Dammit, *why did you follow me last night?*"

David shook his head, his voice ringing with disdain. "You walked out the door in the middle of your own party with some suspicious man administering a death grip to your arm, and you have to ask why I followed? Chrissakes, you looked like you were setting yourself up to get killed!"

"I can take care of myself."

"Lady, go tell that to my shoes."

Melanie flushed. Shit, she had thrown up on him. It was hard to argue with that. Before she could summon some smart retort anyway, just for pride's sake, he said, "I got a job to do. When you find the tools, yell for Harry."

"Fine."

"Fine."

He headed down the hall and Melanie thought good riddance. It was late. She needed to get on with her day. Then a fresh thought struck her and made her call him back. "Wait!"

Halfway down the hall, David halted grudgingly, giving her an impatient stare.

"Since . . . since you did hear everything . . ."

"Uh-huh."

"What . . . what did you think of Larry Digger?"

"I think he's probably a drunk," David said matter-of-factly.

She breathed easier. Yes, this was the opinion she

wanted—assurances that Larry Digger was full of shit. "It's a preposterous story."

"Lot of holes, like you said."

"Really." She waved her hand dismissively. "No parents in their right mind would give the child of their daughter's murderer a home. That's outrageous."

David nodded again, but now his gaze was hooded and hard to read.

"He's probably just after money," she said. "Thank you, Mr. Reese. I'll get those tools to you shortly."

"There was one interesting thing he did bring up," David said.

Melanie paled. "What?"

"Why now? If it's all about money, why didn't Larry Digger approach you or your parents years ago?"

Melanie suddenly had a chill. She rubbed her arms to chase it away. "It could have taken him a long time to come up with a story. Or maybe he didn't need money before."

"The phone call's interesting too. Why say that he'd traced the tip to your house? Why add that particular detail?"

Melanie couldn't answer. Would Larry Digger really try to be exact if he simply wanted money? Cons could be elaborate. But why now? Not earlier, when she would have been more vulnerable, more interested in the past.

She was still churning the questions over in her mind when David said, "I could help you with this."

"Pardon?"

"I used to be a policeman, all right? I got arthritis. Took me off the force, but I still have contacts. If you want, I could check out Larry Digger."

The limp, the twinges of pain he tried to hide, must be from the arthritis. And his having been a cop would explain why he had followed her last night. Everything about Larry Digger would have triggered his instincts. So he had followed and looked out for her.

Melanie found herself warming toward David Reese. But then she shook her head. "It's okay, I can take care of it."

"With all due respect, what do you know about a man like Larry Digger?"

"Well, for starters, I know I can check his story about the anonymous tip by looking through our phone bills."

David narrowed his eyes. "What about a full background search?"

"I'll call his employer. Newspapers in Texas."

"Know how many newspapers there are in Texas?"

Melanie smiled at him sweetly. "Then I'd better get right on it, shouldn't I?"

"Don't give an inch, huh? Don't ever ask for help?"

"Welcome to the Stokeses, Mr. Reese. We take care of our own."

"Yeah?" David gave her a hard stare. "Then why, when some tired old reporter was dragging you out of your own home, was a waiter the only one who noticed? What do you think of that, Miss Stokes?"

Melanie didn't have an answer.

Two cups of coffee later, alone in the dining room, Melanie watched the afternoon sun sift through lace curtains as she picked at a blueberry muffin.

"Maybe you had to see them in Texas with their two kids, one so sweet, everyone loved her, and one already so troubled, half the moms on the block wouldn't let him play with their children. I'm getting the impression, Miss Holmes, there's a helluva lot about your family you just plain don't know."

Why didn't she know more about Meagan Stokes or her family's life in Texas? In spite of her bold words to both Larry Digger and David Reese, that fact was beginning to trouble Melanie.

She'd always assumed that the subject of Meagan was too painful for her parents to discuss. Also, it was probably not a topic of conversation they wanted to share with their adopted daughter. In spite of what people liked to say, families with adopted children had different dynamics. The beginning was not natural or smooth, but held a closer analogy to dating—everyone wore their nicest clothes, practiced their best manners, and tried not to do anything that would make them look too foolish. Then came the honeymoon phase, when parent and child could do no wrong, since everyone was just so gosh darn happy to have one another. Then, if the adoption was successful, the family finally eased into the fifty-years-of-marriage stage. Comfortable, well-adapted, knowing each family member's strengths and weaknesses, and loving them anyway.

Melanie liked to think her family had achieved that final stage of familial nirvana, but now she had to wonder. If they were so comfortable with one another, why hadn't they ever spoken of Meagan? Why hadn't Melanie asked? Even if it had been painful once, it had been *twenty years* ago. Surely after two decades . . .

It's the past, she told herself firmly. It shouldn't matter.

But now she was no longer certain. Larry Digger's insinuations were taking root. The reporter was starting to win.

Melanie gave up on the muffin. She crossed the hall into her father's study, where she was immediately greeted by the sight of books piled everywhere. On the cherry-wood desk, on the red leather swivel chair, and on the floor.

Apparently, while she'd been out dealing with Larry Digger, the literacy ball had turned into quite a success. She should catalogue the books that afternoon, prepare them for inventory by the rare-book dealer on Boylston Street. There was a lot of work to get done.

Melanie opened up the mahogany file cabinet and

looked for a file marked Nynex. The good news was
that her predictably anal father did keep the phone
records each month. The bad news was that they had
not yet received the new bill covering three weeks ago.
Tomorrow she would call and request an early copy
of the bill.

That would take care of Larry Digger.

But what about her own past? Why *hadn't* her parents pressed to find out more? In the beginning they
had probably been scared. If they found her real parents, those parents could potentially take her away
from them. But it had been twenty years and they had
never once asked her if she had remembered anything.
They had never even asked her if she wanted to pursue things further. What about hypnosis or regression
therapy or things like that? Surely her father, as a
doctor, had thought about it.

But nothing was ever said, and Melanie was left
with the uncomfortable thought that for all the close-
ness in her family, there was a strange, unspoken rule.
Don't push too hard, don't say too much. Don't look
back.

*"I'm getting the impression, Miss Holmes, there's a
helluva lot about your family you just plain don't
know."*

And if you told them the same, she thought bluntly,
what would they say? She was no better, she liked her
privacy too. She'd never told her family the details of
what went on with William. She'd never talked about
the perfect first date, when he'd taken her walking
along the Charles and they had discussed greedily, almost feverishly, what it was like to grow up knowing
you'd been abandoned by your birth parents. She'd
never talked about the weekend three months later,
the perfect weekend when they had made love until
four in the morning. Later, getting dressed, her body
all languid and flushed from sex, Melanie had spotted
the lace bra stuffed beneath the mattress, the bra that
wasn't her own. She'd gone home knowing her en-

gagement would have to end but never mentioning a word of it to her parents. When the deed was finally done, she'd simply told them it hadn't worked out. No more, no less. Her parents seemed to understand, though she could tell her father was hurt. William had been his idea, after all.

No one spoke of it again, and Melanie liked it that way.

She had her past, her parents had their past. The more she thought of it, the less she found it sinister and the more she considered it basic human nature. Little secrets, little moments of privacy. That was all. Just because people needed their space didn't mean they'd conspired to adopt the daughter of a killer. That was absurd.

Larry Digger was absurd.

Tomorrow she'd get the phone bill. It would reveal no calls to Texas. Then they could all get on with their lives.

And the voids? The little girl's voice and cries to go home?

Melanie didn't have an easy answer for that one. She was twenty-nine years old. She liked her work, enjoyed her community, loved her family. Did she really care about where she came from anymore?

Was there ever a point in your life when you didn't?

Melanie sighed. She wasn't going to get much done in her current state of mind. What she needed was a good jog.

She went upstairs, her footsteps slowing as she saw her bedroom door. It was ajar; she could see the reflection of tiny flickering lights on the wood panel. Then the smell hit her. Gardenias, thick and cloying.

Melanie didn't own anything that smelled like gardenias.

Something . . . something was beginning to stir again. Shadows shifting in her mind. Ripples in the void.

She pushed open her door. Her bed came into view.

She'd left it rumpled in the middle of the night. Now the yellow sheets were drawn up, the handmade blue and purple quilt perfectly smooth. Melanie's bed was never made.

"María?" she whispered.

No answer.

Her gaze fell to the foot of her bed.

And all of a sudden the images exploded.

Little girl holding the red wooden pony. Little girl on the floor of the crude wood cabin, clutching her favorite toy to her chest.

"I want to go home," she whimpered.

"*Give me the toy, sweetheart. If you give me the toy . . .*"

"*I want to go home.*"

"*Meagan, stop pouting.*"

"*P-p-please?*"

"*GIVE ME THE PONY.*"

"*I want to go home, I want to go home, I want to go HOME. No. No, no. NOOOOO!!!!*"

Melanie ran into the hall. She was crying, falling to her knees, pressing her forehead against the floor, trying to get the images to go away. She didn't want to know. She didn't want to see.

Then she inhaled the scent of gardenias again, and the pictures resumed rolling.

Vaguely she heard footsteps pounding up the stairs.

"Hello? I thought I heard a cry . . . Melanie!"

She couldn't get her head up. She couldn't tell David Reese to stay away. It wasn't his business. No one's business but hers.

She lay there with her head pressed against the floor and distorted pictures flashed like lightbulbs in her mind.

Meagan, pony, cabin. Meagan, pony, cabin.

Who is in the doorway? Who is standing in the doorway?

What am I doing here?

I don't want to know, I don't want to know . . .

"Oh, God," David said.

Melanie looked up. He was staring into her room with an expression on his face she couldn't read. Maybe it was shock. Maybe it was pity.

She had to turn away, and then she whispered, "Don't let my parents see. My brother . . . my brother will know what to do."

She closed her eyes again.

Who is in the doorway? Who is standing in the doorway?

I don't want to know . . .

SEVEN

B RIAN STOKES HAD always known he was destined for a difficult life. From earliest memory, his moods had been cynical and bleak. His childhood was defined by endless gray nights, his father always working at the hospital while his mother sat stiffly on the sofa, regal in her loneliness. Sometimes Brian would play little games, cuddling up to his mother, giving her his most charming grin until she would finally smile and pull him into her sweet-smelling embrace. Other nights he was cruel, smashing vases and furniture, running screaming through the house until his mother would break down into tears, sobbing and crying and begging to know why he hated her so much.

At the age of six he didn't have an answer. He didn't know why he made his mother laugh or why he made his mother cry. He was mostly aware of a sense of guilt and insecurity. That something in the household just wasn't right. They would all hate him in the end, he thought. His father, his mother, his baby sister, Meagan . . .

Probably the only person he'd been good to in his life was Melanie, and lately he'd been mean even to her. He'd ignored her phone calls and other overtures. He'd removed himself to his South Boston condo, where he could hone his self-loathing to a razor-sharp edge.

Three months ago he'd lain in bed, wondering why he didn't just slit his wrists, then had thought of Meagan. Precious, beautiful Meagan. The way she used to hold out her arms and beg for piggybacks. The nights he used to run to her room just to watch her sleep, to keep her safe though he hadn't known from what. Not until it was too late.

Meagan, Meagan, I am so sorry.

He'd gotten out a box of razors.

And then he'd thought of Melanie. The way she'd looked the first time he'd seen her, the way she'd thrown her arms around him, the way she had loved him, simply loved him.

Melanie had brought life back into the Stokes family, and Brian could not fail her. If he didn't want to live for himself, then he would have to live for her.

He'd joined a support group. He was learning that he carried too much rage. He was learning that he had "conflicted" views of his family and "issues with real intimacy." He was learning he needed to figure out once and for all who he wanted to be. Not what his father wanted, not what his family wanted, but what he wanted.

Brian Stokes needed to learn to love himself. And he was realizing more and more that had less to do with his confusion about being a homosexual and more to do with his guilt over his baby sister's death. Twenty-five years later all those days in Texas were suddenly haunting him with a vengeance. Some nights he'd wake up in a cold sweat. Other times he'd wake up screaming.

Then there was the night Brian dreamed his own parents' death, and it made him happy. These days he did not trust himself to go home.

Then this morning, Jamie O'Donnell had called. Melanie was looking too pale, too worn around the edges, Jamie said flatly. She'd had a migraine last night and she had migraines only under extreme stress. Did Brian know what the hell was going on?

He didn't. He was concerned.

Then he got the call after two P.M. Some man who wouldn't give his name curtly stating that Melanie needed him. Brian didn't argue. He ignored his father's specific declaration that Brian Stokes was no longer welcome at Beacon Street and ran through two red lights in his haste to get there.

He still wasn't prepared for the scene in Melanie's room. He took one look at the old red wooden pony and the altar of lit votive candles and said, "Don't let Mom see that."

"Are you kidding? For God's sake, get in here and shut the door."

Brian entered the bedroom and shut the door. His sister stood across the room, still wearing pajamas though it was extremely late in the day. Her arms were wrapped around her waist. Tears stained her cheeks. The sight of her so obviously frightened undid him. Melanie was never frightened. Never.

"Melanie—" He took an automatic step toward her, then hesitated. She looked unsure of him, conscious of the gulf that had grown between them. That was fair, he decided. He was standing in this room and he was unsure.

Another awkward moment passed. She finally broke the silence.

"Brian, meet David Reese." She pointed to the only other person in the room, who was moving around with purpose. "David Reese is a former police officer," she explained. "He has contacts—"

"Former police officer?"

"Arthritis," David said curtly. Brian nodded; he'd noticed the limp. "I called in a friend, an active detective, someone who knows how to be discreet. Your sister is real hung up on being discreet."

Melanie was looking at Brian questioningly. He finally nodded his approval. He didn't know what he thought of David Reese, but he didn't know what else to do. He'd never seen anything like this before, and he didn't have any connections in law enforcement.

"Jesus Christ, what *is* this?" Brian finally burst out. "I mean . . . who would? How? Why?"

"Don't know yet," the ex-cop said. "We'll start with the what, which is forty-four votive candles scented with gardenias. One red wooden pony, a scrap of old blue fabric, some bloodstains. Note the arrangement of the candles. Someone's sending a message."

Brian turned slightly and gazed at the arrangement straight on. Shit. The flickering candles spelled one word. Meagan.

A distant memory returned to Brian. Baby Meagan on the floor. Brian grabbing her doll and ripping it apart. Meagan crying, not understanding. Brian shaking the stuffing all over the floor. *"You gotta be tough, Meagan, you gotta be tough."*

The distance between them yawned again.

"I got up in the middle of the night," Melanie said quietly. "I went downstairs. When I came back up . . . well, here it was."

"You were up in the middle of the night?" Brian asked sharply. "Melanie, it's been years . . ."

"Do you sleepwalk?" David Reese asked her.

But Melanie was gazing at Brian, and in her eyes he saw what he'd been most afraid of: hurt. He'd hurt her. When Melanie got up in the middle of the night, Brian was supposed to be there for her. He was the one who always woke up, always followed her downstairs to keep guard as she stared at Meagan's portrait. He was her older brother. It was his job.

"I don't sleepwalk," she said after a while. "Sometimes, I'm just . . . restless."

"Melanie . . ."

"Later, Brian. Much later."

David Reese cleared his throat, forcing their attention back to him. "Your mother could return home at any time, so we gotta get working here." Without waiting for an answer, he continued brusquely. "Let's start with the horse. It's the one from the oil portrait downstairs, isn't it? Meagan's horse."

"The chipped ear," Brian murmured. "I did that. I threw it against the fireplace. I was . . . angry. She had it the day she was kidnapped, but it was never recovered. At the time the police said Russell Lee kept it as a—what did they call it?—as a trophy."

"You never saw the horse again? Not even when they arrested Holmes?"

"No. Never."

"And the fabric?"

"I don't know." Brian studied it for a moment, not touching it but looking down at it. "It could be from her dress," he decided at last. "It's blue. But that was a long time ago, you know, and it's so . . . stained now."

"Was she found with her dress on?"

Brian glanced at his sister, hesitating. "Wrapped in a blanket."

David nodded. Meagan had been found in *only* the blanket.

"How did someone get in?" Melanie interjected finally. "We have an alarm system."

"Was it set?" David demanded.

"Of course it was set!" She looked at him dryly. "Come on, you're dealing with a family who knows exactly what can go wrong. You'd better believe my father sets the alarm each night."

"Huh." David mulled this over for a minute. "Who stayed the night?"

"Myself, of course," Melanie said. "Mom and Dad. María, the live-in. Also, we'd planned for Ann Margaret, my boss and friend from the Red Cross Center, to stay in the guest room—it's a long drive back to Dedham that late at night. I imagine that she did, but we'd have to ask María to be sure."

"Does your dad search the house before setting the alarm?"

"Why would he do that?"

"You had three hundred people in your house last night. Any one of them could've slipped unnoticed upstairs, and—"

"And simply waited," she finished for him.

"Shit," Brian said.

"There's got to be a connection between Larry Digger and this," Melanie said. "Maybe he sneaked in after we spoke. Maybe he found this stuff when he was following Russell Lee Holmes."

David shook his head. "Too subtle. How could a man dressed like him—smelling like him—slip unnoticed upstairs?"

"He got into the house the first time—"

"Wait a second!" Brian broke in. "Larry Digger? The reporter from Texas? Larry Digger was at *our house* last night?"

His sister smiled thinly, smiled tiredly, and then she told him.

Brian sat through the whole story stony-faced. He thought he should have a reaction. He didn't. The best he could come up with, staring at forty-four candles arranged in his dead sister's name, was fatalism. Texas was already back in his dreams, already messing with his mind. They couldn't move on, that was the problem. None of them had ever learned to move on, and now Russell Lee Holmes was going to get them in the end. Had they really thought something as simple as death could conquer a man like Russell Lee Holmes?

"Brian?" Melanie asked quietly. "Brian, are you okay?"

He touched his cheeks. Shit, he was crying. "And you didn't even call and tell me," he whispered.

"I called you today."

"Things have changed that much, have they, Mel?"

She looked at the floor. "You were the one who

went away, Brian. You were the one who decided to hate all of us."

She was right. Brian wanted to take her hand, squeeze it gently, remind her of the old times. He couldn't.

"Forget about Larry Digger," he declared rashly. "I'll take care of everything, Mel. I promise."

"No! That's not what I want, Brian. I can handle the situation."

"There is no situation! Larry Digger was a sleazy half-rate journalist then, and he's a sleazy half-rate journalist now. You are not the daughter of Russell Lee Holmes, and I will not tolerate someone approaching my baby sister with this kind of bullshit. This has nothing to do with you, Mel, nor should it."

Melanie's eyes turned hard. "*Nothing* to do with me? *Why?* Because I'm not a real Stokes? Because even after twenty years you still treat me like a guest—"

"Dammit, that's not what I meant. You know me better than that, Mel."

"No, I don't anymore! So you'd better explain what you meant, Brian, because as far as I'm concerned, all developments, attacks, and threats on our family—on *my* family—have everything to do with me!"

"It does not," he roared back. "With all due respect, you weren't part of this family when Meagan was kidnapped. Do you know that BOLO means Be On the Look Out for? Do you know that local postal companies will deliver hundreds of thousands of copies of a missing child flyer for free? That major airlines will carry them to airports all across the United States?

"*Do you know* how it feels to deliver ransom money and then just wait? Or what it's like when the police stop talking about recovery and show up with cadaver dogs? Or even better, what it's like to go to a morgue viewing room to identify the remains of a child? You don't, Mel. You don't know, because Meagan had nothing to do with you and that's the way we want to keep it!"

"Too late," she said crisply.

His sister stormed away from him toward David Reese. He was the older brother, dammit. He should be allowed to protect his sister if he wanted to. *And he did not want Melanie involved with Meagan.*

"It gets worse, Brian," his sister said. "I'm seeing Meagan Stokes, and I don't think the images are dreams.

"I think I'm finally remembering, Brian," she told him quietly. "And what I'm remembering is the last days of Meagan Stokes's life. When she was kept in a wood cabin. When she clutched her favorite wooden toy. When she still believed she would get to go home alive.

"And there's only one way I could know that, Brian—if I was also there. If I was with her. If I was *Russell Lee Holmes's daughter.* I'm sorry, but I think Larry Digger just might be right."

Brian suddenly started to laugh.

"Of course, of course," he heard himself gasp. "Evil never dies. It just becomes part of the family. Welcome to the real Stokes family, Mel. Welcome *home.*"

EIGHT

A PAGER WENT OFF. Brian returned the call, then announced he had to go to the "goddamn" hospital to see a "goddamn" patient. David took that to mean that he was still a little bit upset.

David and Melanie walked him down to the front door. Brian was muttering that everything was screwed, Melanie was murmuring that everything would be all right, and David was wondering when Chenney was going to show up. They'd just gotten Brian out the door with promises to keep him posted and blood oaths not to mention anything to his mother, when Chenney came trotting up the stone steps, juggling four heavy evidence kits and looking wired for action.

"You need to change," David stated brusquely to Melanie.

Melanie nodded, looking subdued. The exchange with her brother had obviously taken its toll, robbing her eyes of the fierce spark that had entertained David just hours before and leaving her looking bruised. Tough day for Melanie Stokes.

"I'll grab some clothes, change in the guest room," she murmured.

David's voice came out gentler this time, almost

soft. "Well, sure. We won't be up for a few minutes anyway. You know. Take your time."

He shrugged a bit, feeling awkward now for no good reason. Chenney was staring at him in disbelief, while Melanie flashed him a grateful smile that unnerved him a bit more. He wasn't that prickly, was he? He had manners. He'd even been raised to hold doors, pull out chairs, and chew with his mouth closed. He could be charming.

He scowled. He was losing focus.

Melanie disappeared upstairs, he turned to Chenney.

"What am I doing?" the rookie said in a rush. "What do I say? What's my cover? Do I need a badge?"

Christ, where did the academy get these kids?

"Chenney, you're passing as a cop. Use your real name and, for God's sake, real procedure when bagging the crime scene. Got it?"

Chenney nodded. "Got gloves, got bags, got fingerprinting kit, got vacuum. It'll be clean."

"You're golden."

"That's all? That's all I'm doing?"

"I know, it's not like the full-color brochure. You'll get used to it."

"I don't understand what this has to do with healthcare fraud," Chenney mumbled.

"That's why they pay us the big bucks."

"Lairmore know about this?"

David stiffened. "Not yet."

Chenney looked at him squarely, showing the first real spark of intelligence that David had seen. "He's not going to like this. Your position is becoming involved, now you have me running around impersonating a police officer, and none of this seems directly pertinent to the case. If this blows up . . ."

"I'll be sure to say none of it was your idea."

"That's not what I meant," Chenney protested, appearing honestly injured.

"Whatever. Upstairs, Chenney. We need to finish before the parents come home."

"Why?"

"Work now, debrief later. That's the drill."

David led the way up the stairs, knowing the kid was right about Lairmore and feeling even more tense. He needed to get Melanie talking about her family, particularly Dr. Harper Stokes. He needed to start tying this stuff together in a nice, clean case analysis.

Behind him Chenney lugged the heavy vacuum cleaner and fingerprint kit. "Well, if they're paying us the big bucks, why can't he afford a personality?"

Things smoothed out upstairs. David had to give the junior agent some credit. At the first sight of the altar with the now-extinguished candles and child's toy, Chenney settled right down, donning a pair of latex gloves and looking all business. By the time Melanie walked into the room clad in a nubby wool sweater and ripped-up jeans, he'd already started documenting the scene.

David made the introductions. He was aware of how young and fresh Melanie looked with her unmade-up face and clipped-back long blond hair. They caught Chenney up on the situation. He took a lot of notes, then they took a little field trip across the hall to Brian's room.

It seemed very dark, decorated in shades of forest green and deep burgundy. Brian hadn't lived in the house for ten years, but the big captain's bed carried the clear imprint of someone having sat on it.

"So the subject sneaked up here after the party, made himself comfortable, and waited for lights-out," Chenney deduced, then ruined the professional image by looking to David for approval.

"You're the cop," David reminded him with a bit of an edge. The rookie stood straighter, then looked at Melanie Stokes.

"Well, at least he wasn't trying to hurt you, ma'am," Chenney said.

Melanie was startled. "What do you mean?"

"If the guy was here all night, he could've come into your room anytime. But he waited until you left to make his move. Just look at the candles. Votives are good for about eight hours. They were nearly burned down to the base by two P.M. So we can assume he entered your room after four A.M.—when you had vacated the premises."

"Thank God for small favors," Melanie muttered.

Chenney shrugged. "The perp definitely didn't want to have a confrontation with you, ma'am. At this stage, he just wants to do his little displays. So you figure he sets it up while you're gone. Forty-four candles, the horse, the fabric. I'd say it took him at least an hour. So maybe he departed the house around six—"

"He couldn't depart," Melanie interrupted with a shake of her head. "That would set off the alarm system. Any opening of an external door, whether from the inside or outside, activates the system."

They all looked back at the bed. "So he set it up, lit it, and went back into hiding," Chenney said.

"Waited until someone got up and deactivated the alarm." David filled in the picture in his head and liked none of it. "Then he just sauntered out the front door."

Melanie was looking shaken again.

"There's another consideration," David mused out loud. "The subject was already in the house. He/she/it could've chosen any room for the display, but he went to Melanie's room, not her parents'. I'd say that makes you the target, not them."

Chenney seemed a bit taken aback by this blunt disclosure, but Melanie simply nodded. David hadn't thought she'd mind. From what he could tell, Melanie worried a lot more about her family than she did about herself.

"It's getting late," she said at last. "I'm surprised my mother hasn't come home as it is, so . . ."

Chenney took that as his cue. "I'm gonna need an hour or so. You start thinking of a plausible excuse for my presence, I'll start working through the scene."

"Thank you, Detective."

"No problem, ma'am!" Chenney left.

Melanie and David were suddenly alone. She crossed over to the large bank of windows, looking out over the Public Garden, where the cherry trees were in bloom and young lovers were walking hand in hand. With the fading sunlight catching her profile in shadows, she looked at once vulnerable and pensive. She looked lovely, David thought. Then he shook the thought away.

"We have a few more questions. You ready?"

"I made my brother cry."

"He's a big boy. He'll get over it."

"There is a shrine to a murdered child in my bedroom." Her voice rose a notch. "It's in my head, David. Dear God, it's in my head."

She pressed her forehead against the window, as if the contact might chase the images from her mind. She took a deep breath, then another. Her hands were shaking. David watched her weather the storm and didn't do a thing. After another minute she pushed herself away from the window and squared her shoulders.

"Well," she said briskly in that tone of voice he'd come to know well, "what's done is done. Detective Chenney will take care of everything and let me know what he learns?"

"He'll send the evidence to the lab. See what comes up."

"Like fingerprints, right?"

David arched a brow. "There won't be any fingerprints."

"You don't know that—"

"Come on. This guy spent hours staging a scene. He's not going to make a mistake that obvious."

She looked deflated for a minute, then bounced

back stubbornly. "Well, the detective will learn something."

"Maybe. Look, if you want answers, let's start right now. Lab work isn't everything. Most info comes from interviews, and we have just a few questions for you."

"You mean Detective Chenney has some questions."

"Sure, you can wait for Chenney, but he's gonna be in your room for at least an hour. By then it'll be six, your mom could be home anytime . . . I don't think you want to have this discussion then."

"Oh."

David pushed the advantage, not wanting to give her time to think. He strode forward brusquely. "We'll start with the standard drill. Get through it all in a jiffy."

Melanie still looked hesitant, but in the face of his curt determination, she finally nodded.

"We got a pretty good idea how the person got into the house," David stated. "Now we need to know why and we need to know who."

Melanie shook her head. "Other than Larry Digger, I have no idea who would connect my family with Russell Lee Holmes after all these years. My parents don't discuss Texas much."

"Why not?"

She gave him an exasperated look. "I imagine because it hurts like hell."

"Twenty years later?"

"Hey, Mr. Reese, when your daughter is kidnapped and murdered, you can get over it in twenty years. My parents haven't."

David grunted, sufficiently chastised. "Fine. Let's start with the altar, then—it tells us a few things. For starters, this was an intimate act. Not just in your house, but in your bedroom. Not just in your bedroom, but at the foot of your bed. Then there are the items themselves. The pony and scrap of fabric that appear to be from Meagan Stokes, the first daughter. That seems to be a very deliberate slight against you, the second daughter. Then there is the use of scented candles. Do you know much about the olfactory senses, Melanie?"

"You mean other than to smell?"

"There's more to it than that. The sense of smell is directly wired to the limbic system, which is one of the oldest parts of the brain. An important part of the brain too. It's the part that helps you love and helps you hate. And"—he looked her in the eye—"it helps you *remember*. Exposing someone to a strong fragrance linked with a certain time or place is one of the most effective ways to evoke a memory."

He saw that Melanie grasped his meaning immediately, because she sat down hard on her brother's bed. "The gardenias, the flashbacks. It was planned, wasn't it? Shit. It was *exactly* what the person wanted." She suddenly sounded furious. "I will not be manipulated in my own house. I will not!"

David regarded her curiously. "Did you say flashbacks? As in more than one?"

She looked cornered. "Fine, fine, I'd been starting to see little things. Not much. A black void, a little girl's voice. Nothing substantial."

"Uh-huh. When did it start?"

"I don't know. Six months ago."

"Six months ago. Of course."

"Of course?" Now she was scowling. "What do you mean, of course?"

"I mean six months ago was right about when your brother announced he was gay. Six months ago was right about when Boston's most perfect family started to fall apart."

"How do you know all this?"

"Caterers gossip," David said offhandedly. "Think about it. The Stokeses move to Boston, adopt a new daughter, and for the next twenty years life is just grand, right? Then comes Brian's announcement and things around here start to fall apart. Your father isn't speaking to him, right? Your mom is distraught over the situation and starts drinking again. And you suddenly start having flashbacks."

"It's not like that," Melanie protested. "One son coming out of the closet doesn't cause all that."

"Maybe not in most families," David said matter-of-factly, "but in a family with the Stokeses' history? Come on. You're a bright person, you can put this together. Your mom and dad have already lost one child. You have already lost a whole family. When your father practically disowned your brother, don't you think it hit all the same triggers? Didn't you and your mom and probably your dear old dad start to feel like everything was falling apart again? Old insecurities, old fears . . ."

Melanie looked haggard. "Jesus Christ," she whispered. "Why don't you just fucking cut out my *heart?*"

"I'm not trying to cut out your heart. But someone is trying to get you to remember."

"But why? Who?"

"Someone who knows what happened to Meagan," David said. "Someone who could recover the toy she had with her the day she died. Someone who knows enough about you, Melanie, to realize that the scent of gardenias would trigger a memory of Meagan."

Slowly Melanie nodded, following his train of thought. "Larry Digger," she said savagely.

"No. Larry Digger doesn't know shit. If he had proof, he'd already have written his story and sold it to the highest bidder. He wouldn't be messing around with votive candles."

"Russell Lee Holmes?"

"Executed and buried. Come on, you know who I'm talking about."

She was immediately defensive. "No, I don't! My family has nothing to do with this!"

"Larry Digger alleged that there was more to them than met the eye—"

"Larry Digger is a drunk!"

"Larry Digger knew them in Texas, which is more than you can say. Why was your father in the ER the night you were found? How is it that you can remember Meagan Stokes? You gotta have some connection with Russell Lee Holmes, and according to Larry Digger, your parents know that. Your parents didn't adopt a random little girl, but the daughter of Russell Lee Holmes."

"That makes no sense!" She'd risen off the bed. She was nearly nose to nose with him now, and neither one of them backed down. "My parents loved Meagan! They would not adopt the daughter of her killer!"

"How do you know? How do *you know?"*

He thought she was going to hit him. Maybe she thought she would too. The air had gotten too hot and too tense. Then her gaze dropped to his lips, and the air became tangled with other, unwanted emotions. Her lips thinned. She drew back furiously.

She said in a cold voice, "All right, David. Let's do it your way. My beloved parents really conspired to adopt Russell Lee Holmes's daughter. Maybe in a sick and twisted way they felt he owed them a child. I was drugged so I wouldn't remember where I had come from, and my father stayed in the ER, and *voilà,* everything went as planned. I got my new family, they got a new daughter. Everyone's happy. Right?"

"Yeah?" David was suspicious. He didn't think for a moment that she believed any of this.

"Then," she continued relentlessly, "twenty years later, they magically do what? Suddenly announce the truth? Or even more outlandish, plant an altar in my room in the dim hope that I'll remember and figure out who I am and what they did? Come on! First you're saying they conspired to adopt a killer's daughter, then you're saying they conspired to reveal their conspiracy. Give me a break."

David frowned. He said grudgingly, "That doesn't make much sense."

"No kidding."

"Unless—"

"No!"

"Unless it's just one person trying to reveal the truth. Think about it. Six months ago this whole family was turned upside down. There's a rift between your father and brother, a rift between your mother and father, and even tension between you and Brian. It seems to me that family loyalties and dynamics are shifting as we speak. Maybe that's the key. Maybe the last six months finally gave someone incentive to come forward with the truth of what happened all those years ago. It gave someone incentive to call Larry Digger. How about that?"

Melanie looked mutinous, she didn't have a quick retort. The last six months had changed everything, and she knew it.

"We should run through all your family members," David said.

"No."

"You do it with me or you do it with Chenney. Your mom could come home at any time."

"You know, you can be a real son of a bitch."

"Yeah, but I'm the son of a bitch who noticed when you were being dragged out of your own house by a seedy-looking stranger. And I'm the son of a bitch who came running when you passed out in your hallway. Not too bad for a son of a bitch."

His voice sounded more belligerent than he'd intended, and Melanie turned away, looking troubled.

"No," she said at last. "You're not bad."

He shifted from foot to foot, slightly mollified but also self-conscious. Popularity wasn't in his job description. Results were.

"We're a very private family," Melanie said after a

moment. "My parents have suffered enough. I don't want you to think of them as criminals."

"I know, I promise to bear that in mind. Now let's start with your father and brother. It's common knowledge that your father has cut your brother from his will. Maybe that made your brother angry, gave him an ax to grind?"

"Brian would not do this. I won't pretend that he and my father have an easy relationship, but if Brian wanted to hurt Dad, he wouldn't use Meagan Stokes—it hurts *him* too much. You saw Brian when he walked into my room. He's even more shaken up than I am. For God's sake, he just saw his little sister's toy from twenty-five years ago. The little sister I know he thinks he failed."

"He's an intense guy."

"David, his younger sister was *kidnapped* and *murdered*. He was nine when it happened, which is old enough to understand what's going on but not old enough to do anything about it. Meagan's murder was a traumatic chapter for this family, okay? If they were all perfectly well adjusted after that, *then* they would be odd."

David didn't comment. Personally he thought the Stokeses were a little beyond odd.

"What about your mom? Sounds like she didn't care for Harper's dismissal of her son. She resumed drinking—"

"Yes, which is a problem that started when Meagan was kidnapped! Meagan's murder hurt her worst of all, David. She's still trying to get her life together. There are nights I find her downstairs, touching that oil painting as if she can feel her daughter's cheek. There are weeks you can just see it in her eyes, that endless wondering of what she could've done differently or how she could've been a better mother. I know there are times she looks at Brian and me and is simply terrified. Don't pin this on my mother, David. She's already paid her dues."

"Seems the whole family's always looking out for her, a grown woman."

"We love her! We worry about her!"

"And you don't love your dad?"

"That's different. My father is capable of taking care of himself. My mom—"

"Is troubled," David supplied flatly. "Depression, drinking. Anxiety attacks. Patricia Stokes may be a great mom, even a loving mom, but she's not going to win a most stable person of the year award."

"My mom is a good woman, David. She loves us very much. She just . . . she just misses Meagan."

David arched a brow, holding Melanie's stare for a long time. So she meant what she said about her mom. David continued down the list.

"And your father? How does he feel about all this?"

"Oh, Dad is Dad." For the first time, Melanie relaxed. "He's a man's man, laughs when he feels like crying and would never go to the hospital himself unless the bone was protruding from the skin. Takes his role as a family provider very seriously and is positively intense about looking after our welfare—you know, the man's turf. You probably understand him better than I do."

"Does that include him disinheriting his own son?"

Melanie grimaced. "Dad's not good at admitting he's wrong." Then in a level voice, she said, "My father is a fixer, David. He fixes people, he fixes problems. Unfortunately, it's hard to fix emotions like grief and remorse and guilt. I know there are many things about my mom he just doesn't get, and Brian's announcement caught him totally off guard. In my father's world, your firstborn son *does not* announce he's gay. He just needs time to accept it. He really is a good father."

"He prides himself on his income."

"He does very well."

"Does he support the family too well?"

Melanie frowned. "I don't know what you mean."

David made a show of shrugging. "What does a Beacon Street town house like this cost? One million? Two million? And then there are the furnishings, the cars, the vacation homes. The artwork, the antiques, the silk curtains. Awfully nice life even for a doctor."

Melanie's guard was up now, her face shuttering. "I don't think my family's finances are relevant."

"Most crimes are committed for love or money. And Larry Digger commented that in Texas, your parents lived better than they should've."

"Larry Digger is jealous," Melanie said firmly. "That's all."

David waited, let the silence drag out. She didn't budge. Who knew what the Stokeses were really like? But David decided they had a helluva daughter in Melanie.

Or was that toughness courtesy of Russell Lee Holmes?

Shit. David had just given himself the chills.

He returned to the Stokes family members and friends. "What about William Sheffield? How did you two meet?"

"He works with my father. Dad brought him home for dinner." Her lips curved dryly. "Oh, the conspiracy."

"I heard him talk last night," David commented. "Sounded like he was from Texas, which makes a lot of former Texans in this house."

"Sure. That's why he and Dad originally started talking. Two expatriate Texans in a Boston hospital. If you ever moved to Texas, you'd probably befriend the first Bostonian you met."

"Yeah, but would I marry him off to my daughter?"

Melanie stiffened. "That's ancient history."

"Does that mean he ended it and not you?"

"The ending," she said in a steely voice, "was mutual."

"How mutual?"

"I found him in bed with another woman, David. That pretty much seemed a hint."

David was startled. Weasely William Sheffield cheating on Melanie Stokes? Christ, he was even dumber than he looked.

"Bitter?" he asked more intently than he'd wanted.

"Nope. The ending was inevitable. We never should have become engaged to begin with."

"Then why did you?"

She shrugged. "He was an orphan too. I thought that gave us something in common. Or maybe it was simply because he asked, and if you've been abandoned once, having someone say they want to spend the rest of their life with you is irresistible. We both realized our mistake soon enough, particularly once he started telling me I didn't count as an orphan."

"Huh?"

"I had been adopted," Melanie said dryly. "I had been given a family, a rich family. After a while it became clear that that ate away at William. Of the two of us, he'd been more wronged by life, so life, and especially me, owed him something. Let's just say I'm not very good at owing anyone anything."

David almost smiled. Yeah, he couldn't see her answering to William Sheffield's beck and call. The stupid little prick. He cleared his throat, struggling once more to get back to business.

"Did anything seem off to you with William last night? Did he seem pale? Preoccupied?"

"He works hard."

"Any harder than usual lately?"

Melanie took a minute to answer. "I don't think so. Generally he's assisting my dad and my dad's workload hasn't been heavier than usual. But I did think William looked as if something was bothering him."

"Then maybe we should check into it."

"He doesn't have anything to do with Meagan—"

"He's involved with your family now. He spends

time in your house. Maybe he learned something from
your father and hopes to capitalize on it."

Melanie sighed, but she didn't argue. He could tell
that doubts were beginning to wear her down.

"What about the Irishman who was here? Jamie
. . . Jamie . . ."

"Jamie O'Donnell. He's my godfather. He wouldn't
have anything to do with this."

"What's his connection to the family?"

"He and my parents go way back in Texas. They've
known each other for forty years. He was best man at
their wedding."

"He's business partners with your father?"

"They do some deals every now and then. To tell
you the truth, I'm not sure how Dad and Jamie first
met. I know Dad's parents lived in the suburbs,
whereas Jamie pretty much grew up alone—in cardboard houses, he likes to say. They both built themselves up, Jamie as a businessman, my father as a
surgeon. I think they respect that about each other."

"And O'Donnell knew Meagan?"

Melanie's gaze softened. She clearly had a soft spot
for her godfather. "The situation with Meagan broke
Jamie's heart. You want to know why my parents love
him so much? Because he viewed the bodies for them,
David. He told me about it once. When a child is
missing, someone in the family must take responsibility for viewing bodies that match the age and general
description of the child. That was Jamie's job. He
went from morgue to morgue all over the South, viewing remains of four-year-old girls that fit the description of Meagan Stokes.

"He told me once that he still sometimes dreams of
all those little girls, wondering if they ever did find a
home, ever ended up buried by people who loved
them. Or if they all just ended up in potter's field with
only a number for identification. Sometimes I think
losing Meagan affected him even more than my father. Most likely they just show it differently."

"And the other woman?" David pressed. "She came up with him, wearing nurses' whites."

"Oh, that's Ann Margaret."

"She spent last night here too, you thought."

"Yes. She's my boss at the Dedham Red Cross Donor Center. I've been volunteering there for ten years now, so she's come to know all of us."

"Sounded to me like she had a Texas drawl too."

Melanie rolled her eyes. "Yes, she lived there decades ago. She's been in Boston forever now. And that's totally random. She wouldn't even have been in the house if I hadn't started volunteering at the Red Cross Center."

"Huh. I kind of thought there was something between her and your godfather."

Melanie faltered. "Actually I kind of thought there might be something too. They've seen each other many times at the various functions I've organized. They could be *involved,* I guess. I don't see how it's anyone's business but theirs."

"Why wouldn't they tell you if they were seeing each other? What do they have to hide?"

Melanie shook her head. "Since when does exercising the right to privacy mean hiding something? Ann Margaret of all people has nothing to do with Meagan Stokes. None of the Stokeses even knew her back then. Let's not be too ridiculous here."

"Are we being so ridiculous?" David asked bluntly. "What exactly was the situation with Meagan Stokes? Do we really know what happened twenty-five years ago? There is the red wooden pony in your room along with a scrap of fabric that, according to your own brother, shouldn't still exist. Larry Digger is claiming he got phone calls about Russell Lee Holmes from your own house. *You* are starting to remember Meagan's last days. Seems to me that everything right now is up for grabs. Whatever we thought we knew about Meagan Stokes, we don't. Whatever you thought you knew about your past, you don't. And whatever you thought you knew about your friends and family, you don't."

Melanie's face had paled.

"Someone's leaving a murdered girl's toy in your room. Now is not a good time for assumptions."

"Do you believe in ghosts, David?"

"Not at all."

"What about fate or karma or reincarnation?"

"Nope."

"Do you believe in anything?"

David shrugged. It wasn't a question he'd contemplated in a long time, but he found he did have an answer. "I believe Shoeless Joe Jackson should be in the Baseball Hall of Fame. And I believe what's going on here has nothing to do with Russell Lee Holmes. Instead, it has to do with your family. And you, Melanie, need to be careful."

She smiled wanly, her finger plucking at the edge of her brother's bedspread. She looked like she was going to say something, then she just closed her mouth.

After a moment she looked up at him. "Thank you."

David hadn't expected gratitude. He didn't know what to say. He studied the floorboards. Old. Thick. Solid. Chenney was probably almost done, he thought. They should both get moving. He remained standing where he was. Then his hip locked up on him and he had to shift position, rubbing absently at his lower back.

"Does it bother you a lot?"

"What?" he asked distractedly. *Someone tips the Bureau about Dr. Stokes committing healthcare fraud, while also tipping Larry Digger that Dr. Stokes's adopted daughter might be the child of Russell Lee Holmes. What's the connection?*

You get what you deserve.

So which one of the players feels that the Stokeses had not gotten what they deserved? And why do something about that now?

"The arthritis."

"Huh?"

"You're rubbing your back."

"Oh." He immediately dropped his hand to his side; he hadn't realized what he'd been doing. "I don't know." He shrugged self-consciously beneath her steady stare. "Some days are fine, some aren't."

"Are there things you can do for it? Exercises, medication, ice packs?"

"Sometimes."

"But it cost you a dream, didn't it?" she asked softly. "Of being a cop."

He was not prepared for her to come so close to the truth, and then he was struck with something akin to claustrophobia. He felt the sudden need for space. The sudden need to retreat. Hell, to hide in some deep, dark cave where no one could look at him too closely and see that he was afraid these days. He was afraid of everything—his future, his health, his career—and it shamed him.

"I need to get back to work," he stated emphatically. "You know caterers. Job's never done."

"Sure." Melanie rose off the bed. The room was nearly pitch black now. Night had fallen on them so quietly, they hadn't even thought to turn on the light.

She was regarding him steadily. Too steadily, he thought.

"David," she said. "Would you be willing to do one last favor for me?"

"I thought you didn't accept favors—"

"I want to see Larry Digger. First thing tomorrow."

Shit. David shook his head. "He's not a reputable source."

"But he's the best I have and you're the one who just said I have to start questioning everything. I want to speak with him, David. If need be, I'll go alone." She spoke in that level tone of voice again. That non-negotiable tone of voice.

"All right," he said heavily. "Ten A.M., out front."

Melanie smiled. She crossed the room. She brushed his hand briefly, a small token of gratitude, nothing more. Then she disappeared down the hall, where the sickly scent of gardenias remained thick.

NINE

B Y SEVEN P.M., David and Chenney had cleared out of the Stokes household and headed in their separate directions. Night had fallen, warm and lush, a perfect spring night in a city that weathered such long, cold winters, it knew how to appreciate spring. So far David was spending his beautiful spring evening parked on the east end of Storrow Drive, waiting for petrified tourists to battle their way to Faneuil Hall. He'd headed home to shower and change his clothes. There, he'd consulted Shoeless Joe, who didn't have any stellar advice. Shoeless was best at baseball and dry cleaning. Healthcare fraud, cool blondes, and twenty-five-year-old homicide cases were out of his league.

David had decided he'd do more research on the Stokes case at the office. Not that he had big plans on a Sunday night.

Not that he could get the image of Melanie Stokes out of his head.

Now his twenty-minute commute was turning into a sixty-minute Boston marathon. On Storrow Drive, the out-of-towners were paralyzed, hunched over their steering wheels with the nervous looks of scared jackrabbits. The taxi drivers, on the other hand, were cutting in front of every Tom, Dick, and Harry, blar-

ing their horns and turning the four-lane traffic jam
into an even larger snarl. They didn't call Boston drivers assholes for nothing.

David should just get an apartment downtown.
Agents made good money, and it wasn't like he had a
wife, two point two kids, and a black Lab to support.
He could get a decent place on Beacon Hill. Save himself a commute that most Boston drivers turned into
blood sport. Be able to walk to work whenever he
wanted. End up in the office all the time.

Oh, yeah, that's why he stayed in the 'burbs. 'Cause
otherwise he'd be living in One Center Plaza.

A cab that was twisted across two lanes finally decided to give up one and they all eked forward.

The in-line skaters were still out, joggers too. In the
pedestrian river park that ran along Storrow Drive,
soft city lights illuminated college students in cut-off
shorts playing night Frisbee while J. Crew–clad yup-
pies walked overbred golden retrievers. Behind them
flowed the Charles River, which hosted Harvard's
crew team as well as many other pollutants. One year,
former governor Weld dove into that water during the
election race to prove it really wasn't as bad as it
looked. They'd be testing him for cancer for years to
come.

It took Riggs another twenty minutes to make it the
last two miles to the office. Another lovely evening
spent driving Boston-style.

The FBI occupied floors four through eight of One
Center Plaza in downtown Boston. Visitors got to
enter at the midpoint—floor six—and the healthcare
fraud squad got to go straight to the penthouse suite
on floor eight. The view wasn't half bad.

David walked through a sprawling turquoise space
that had been remodeled more times than most agents
could count. City lights glimmered through the wall
of windows, the only illumination in the dark, empty
space. Caseloads must be very light right now if David
was the only one burning the Sunday-night oil.

He finally came upon the wall panel, snapped on the overhead lights, and blinked owlishly. Dark, crouching beasts metamorphosed into tongue-shaped desks rimming the perimeter. Hunched backs became computers sitting on top of desks. Monsters transformed into piles and piles of subpoenaed records. Welcome to Riggs's world.

He headed to his desk, automatically avoiding the holes in the floor where pipes had been ripped out in yet another expansion of the limited office space. The Boston field agency was among the fastest growing in the Bureau, having gone from old-fashioned offices to compact cubicles to the current one big turquoise-carpeted space where they could all openly and freely exchange ideas. On slow days agents amused themselves by dropping pennies down the old pipe holes and listening for the landing.

His message light was blinking. David popped up the receiver while rubbing his lower back and dialed in. He had received two messages since checking in at noon.

"David, it's your dad. Thought we'd see you today. Guess you had to work. Steven's team did well, won four-three though not through any help from his pitchers. Bad batch this year, he's at his wits' end. I think he should make his starter sit out altogether—the boy's a head case—and bring up this freshman, James, who has a superb arm. They'd pay for it this year, of course, but in the long run—"

David fast-forwarded through that message until he came to the second one, left by Chenney.

"I'm at the lab. They're PO'd we didn't use an official forensics team and snarling that we probably contaminated evidence. I told them to get over it. Hey, we gotta catch up. I'm confused as hell 'bout the case. Plus, I never told you about my morning surveillance. I started at the hospital watching Sheffield like you said, but he left with the flu. Then I spotted Harper leaving the hospital with Jamie O'Donnell. . . . I did try to call you first, Riggs, but you never turn on your beeper, you know. So I made a judgment call, whether you like it or not. Call me when you get a chance."

Shit. David would bet money that Chenney had gone with Harper and Jamie O'Donnell because watching them seemed more exciting than sitting outside the house of a sick man. The kid still had so much to learn about what constituted "real" work. It's not the glamour, Chenney. It's results.

He dialed the rookie's cell phone. No answer, so David left a message to meet him at the Massachusetts Rifle Association at ten P.M. That gave David ninety minutes to kill.

He requested a copy of the Meagan Stokes case file from the Bureau field office in Houston. Then he called the Houston PD for a copy of their case file as well, as they had had primary jurisdiction. The Bureau case file would focus on the kidnapping aspects and any profiling if it was done. The PD case file would have the nitty-gritty, including the evidence trail. David wanted to find out if Meagan's red pony really had been recovered and had been sitting in an evidence locker all these years. That still wouldn't explain the full magnitude of the scrap of blue fabric, but David hadn't even told Melanie or Brian about that yet. He wanted more time to think about it himself.

David journeyed down to the Bureau's research center and booted up the machine. It took a few minutes for the computer to warm to life. He used the time to prop up his leg awkwardly on the desk and bend over it to stretch out his back. The Bureau had research agents who could look up anything an investigator was willing to write down on the forms, but David liked to do it all himself. Skimming files, narrowing searches, made him think. And sometimes the information he needed in the end wasn't what he'd started out looking for, but what he'd found along the way.

He started his search with Melanie Stokes. September 1977 was the magic date. The *Boston Globe* carried a small human-interest story on a girl, approximately nine years old, who'd mysteriously appeared in City General's ER. The girl had been drugged with morphine and had suffered an allergic reaction. To date, no one had come forward to claim her.

A week later, he found a small update. The girl, who could identify herself only as Daddy's Girl, had been given a clean bill of health and turned over to Child Services. She was in good condition and showed no evidence of abuse. She had no memory, however, and an extensive picture campaign had yet to yield results. A black and white newspaper photo appeared beside the text. Young Melanie Stokes looked plump, her hair was straight and limp, her features undistinguished. Certainly not the most beautiful little girl in the world, but there was something about her face— something yearning, he thought.

A few months later a significantly larger story appeared. "Real-Life Orphan Annie Finds Daddy Warbucks." The *Boston Globe* carried a feature article on "Daddy's Girl" going home with Dr. Harper Stokes and his wife, Patricia, who had started formal adoption proceedings. A social worker reported that Patricia had given Daddy's Girl a new name.

"The little girl asked Mrs. Stokes why she didn't have a name. And Mrs. Stokes said of course she had a name, they just had to find it. Then our little sweetheart asked Mrs. Stokes if she'd give her a name. Mrs. Stokes became very teary-eyed. It was really touching. She said, 'How about Melanie? It's the most beautiful name I know, and you're the most beautiful girl I know.' Ever since, Daddy's Girl will reply only to Melanie so that's what we call her. I think it's really great that she finally has a name. Of course, now she wants a birthday."

Another source, who wished to remain anonymous, disagreed that Melanie was such a great name. "Personally I think it's a little sick. I mean, it's just so close to Meagan. It can't be healthy for any of them."

David thought that woman might have a point. Melanie got a name, Melanie got a great house, but she'd also gotten to grow up literally staring at a portrait of the first daughter. The murdered daughter.

Seemed spooky to him.

David switched to looking up Russell Lee Holmes. Here he found some information that was much more interesting. He read so intently, he was almost late to his meeting with Chenney.

"WHY ARE WE meeting at a gun club?" Chenney asked a little after ten as David unlocked the doors leading to the cavernous indoor shooting range.

"Because I think better shooting." David shoved the doors open and they walked into the empty room.

"Oh," Chenney said as if he understood. The kid was addicted to weight lifting, so maybe he did.

David had been a member of the MRA all his life, first through his father, then on his own. For most of his childhood, if he wasn't playing ball, he was sitting in the club lounge, listening to cops talk about the screwed-up legal system and the age-old rule to shoot first and ask questions later because it was "better to be tried by twelve than buried by six." By the time David was sixteen, he knew almost as much about police procedure as he did baseball. And he was just about as good with a gun. In the club's trophy case were a few plaques and honors that were his own.

"Holy shit!" Chenney said as David opened his gun case and started unpacking. "They told me your father was a custom pistolsmith, but I had no idea! Can I hold it?"

David shrugged, handing over his Beretta to Chenney while he dug out eye gear and a box of bullets. People had been shooting earlier in the day. The air was acrid with the lingering odor of gunpowder and oil.

"My God, this sucker has radioactive sights! I've only ever heard of them."

"My dad," David said simply, and pulled on his goggles. His gun was a souped-up hot rod these days, ready for a shootout with several AK-47–carrying drug lords. He kept telling his father the customization wasn't necessary. His father kept saying "uh-huh" and doing it anyway.

"Oh, my God, you have . . . everything!" Chenney was twisting the gun all around in his hand. "Check out this hand-metal checkering. Forty lines per inch. Gorgeous! He had to use a magnifying glass for that, huh?"

"Dad's an artist."

"Ambidextrous safety, dehorned, custom sights. Sheesh." Chenney pointed it down the shooting gallery and dry-fired. "Five-pound trigger, accurized, I'd bet. Now, that's a gun." Chenney handed over the semiautomatic with reluctance. He gazed at his own Glock with the expression men got in rest rooms when they realized the other guy's penis was bigger than theirs.

Then he seemed to get over it. Both of them slid out clips and loaded. "Oh, yeah," Chenney said after a second, "your brother was a pitcher, right?"

David stilled, then pushed the third bullet in. "Yep."

"I know he's a coach now, but he must still keep his arm up."

"Yep."

"Cool. I belong to a league, see. Bunch of guys, mostly feebies, bureaucrats. I'll tell you honestly, our pitcher sucks. If we don't find a new guy, we're in for a rough summer. So I heard from Margie that your brother was this great pitcher. Pitched for UMass, led them to a division title. He must be pretty damn good—that's a tight division."

David focused on getting the fourth bullet in. "It's a tight division."

"We want him!" Chenney exclaimed. "He's just what we need—a ringer to strike out a bunch of over-the-hill cops who spend way too much time at Dunkin' Donuts. Will you set it up for me?"

"A ringer, huh?"

"Yeah, the best pitching arm around."

"Sure," David said. "I'll set it up for you."

David finished loading his clip. He slid it into place. He swallowed twice. Then he peered down his finely accurized sites and said, "You left Sheffield today, didn't you? This morning. You abandoned your target for a more interesting party on the block."

Chenney flushed. "You'll be glad I did. I overheard some interesting stuff."

"Chenney, don't ever leave your target. If you're following someone, you're following someone—"

"He was sick! I watched him stagger out of the hospital looking pale as a sheet. Shivering and sweating. He told the unit head he had the flu and they sent him packing. Trust me, once Sheffield made it home, he wasn't going anywhere."

"Chenney," David repeated firmly, "don't ever leave your target. If you're following someone, you're following someone. Got it?"

"All right, all right." Chenney put on his goggles, not looking happy at the dressing-down. By mutual agreement they set up the first targets the customary twenty-one feet back and ran through one clip.

The rookie shot aggressively. He lined up fast, fired fast, and screwed his face into an ugly expression that would've made Clint Eastwood proud. He put most of his bullets through the inner two rings, but when they brought in their targets, Chenney could barely pass a pencil through the single hole made by David's twelve shots.

"Twenty-one feet's too easy," he grumbled. "Average distance for a law enforcement conflict, my ass. You ought to be prepared for anything."

David shrugged, tearing down the paper and clipping up fresh targets. "So what did you learn, Chenney? What made Harper Stokes and Jamie O'Donnell seem so interesting?"

"Hey, something's up," the rookie stated immediately. "I followed Harper and Jamie O'Donnell to some ritzy golf course. With a bit of encouragement, management let me hang out at the bar, where I could hear everything O'Donnell and Harper were saying over their lemonades. Harper, he downs an entire glass without saying a word. Then he simply turns to O'Donnell and out of the blue states, 'I got a note.' "

"A note?"

"Yeah, he told O'Donnell he found it on his car this morning. It said, 'You get what you deserve.' He looked O'Donnell right in the eye, rather intense like, and asked him what he thought it might be about.

"O'Donnell looked at him for a minute, also real quiet, like they were having some kind of subtle pissing war, then said, 'Annie's been getting phone calls.' "

" 'Annie's been getting phone calls'?"

"Yeah. He said someone's been calling this Annie person and hanging up. She assumed it was some prankster. But you could tell they weren't so sure. Then Harper said, 'Larry Digger's in town.' O'Donnell seemed a little surprised. He shrugged. And Harper said, 'Josh gave me a call. Apparently Digger contacted him with a few questions about Melanie. Why do think that is?' O'Donnell just shrugged. He said, 'Who knows why Digger does anything? Maybe the whiskey dried up in Texas.'

"Harper grunted. You could tell he didn't buy it. But he didn't say anything more and neither did O'Donnell. A few minutes later they started playing golf, but I'll tell you, something wasn't right. They were tense and pretty quiet the whole nine holes. And they played *fierce,* you know what I mean? This wasn't two guys out having a leisurely Sunday tee time. They went after each other as if out for blood. Really weird relationship there. I don't think they're going to donate kidneys to each other anytime soon. Do you think this has something to do with the scene in Miss Stokes's room this afternoon?"

David looked at the rookie incredulously. "Yeah. I think it does."

"I knew it." Chenney beamed. "So it's not such a bad idea that I left Sheffield, huh? I learned something in the end. I did." He faltered. "So what did I learn, Riggs? What the hell is going on?"

"Ain't that the question," David muttered. He sent the targets back fifty feet, donned his earplugs and goggles, and started firing. After a moment Chenney joined him.

Spent shells gathered on the shooting bench and bounced on the floor. Nine-millimeters spit a little fire from the side vents, making it hot, making it loud. Chenney went after his target like hell on wheels. David was slow and rhythmic, performing a motion he'd done so many thousands of times, it was as natural to him as breathing.

Harper and Jamie O'Donnell. And Annie? Ann Margaret, most likely. Ann Margaret getting phone calls, though Melanie swears she has no real ties to the family. So what's the thread through all of this? What the hell is going on?

It came to him as he cleared the last shot. He ejected his clip, opened the chamber, and set his gun down with the barrel still pointed along the shooters alley. As he drew off his plastic goggles, Chenney retrieved the targets.

At fifty feet David's cluster had expanded slightly within the bull's-eye. Chenney's was getting ragged, his last few shots dropping down due to his haste. While Chenney scowled, David calmly filled him in on the events from last night, starting with Larry Digger and the reporter's allegation that Melanie Stokes was the daughter of Russell Lee Holmes.

"That's nuts," Chenney declared at the end. "No parents are going to knowingly adopt the kid of a murderer. And even if they did, there's no motive for them to alert someone to that fact now. You know what I think it is?"

"I'm almost afraid to ask."

"A smear campaign!"

"A smear campaign?"

"Yeah, against Harper Stokes. Think about it. First we get an anonymous tip that Harper is committing healthcare fraud, allegedly inserting pacemakers into healthy people. So far we haven't found evidence of anything, so who knows? Then Larry Digger gets a call, allegedly from the Stokes house, that Harper's daughter is the child of a murderer. Harper Stokes has a bit of an arrogance rep and he's successful. Maybe some underling is out to get him, or a rival cardiac surgeon. They're striking Harper where it would hurt most—his reputation."

"I don't think so."

"Why not?"

"Because of Harper's reaction to the note. He didn't just dismiss it the way you would if it was some random thing you found on your windshield. Instead, he asks O'Donnell about it, and O'Donnell doesn't have anything to do with Harper as a surgeon. Then Harper's next words are that Larry Digger is in town—Harper himself is connecting the note to some petty journalist he knew twenty-five years ago. And how does O'Donnell react to all that? He comments that Annie is getting phone calls."

"Who is Annie?"

"Ann Margaret, I believe. Melanie's boss at the Dedham Red Cross Donor Center."

"What does she have to do with all this?"

"She's from Texas."

"Texas?"

"It's the common denominator," David said patiently. "All these people are from Texas, and we know what happened in Texas."

"We do?"

"Meagan Stokes, Chenney, four-year-old Meagan Stokes. That's what Harper Stokes and Jamie O'Donnell were talking about. Harper's first response: *Larry Digger is in town . . . asking about Melanie.* And O'Donnell trying to dismiss Digger but obviously not completely convinced himself as to what Digger is up to. Well, Larry Digger is in town looking for dirt about what happened twenty-five years ago. No matter which way you spin it, we come back to the homicide of a four-year-old girl."

"But that's a closed case. They fried the guy. End of story."

"So you'd think. But here's a news flash. I pulled up some information on Russell Lee Holmes before I came, and you know what? Good old Russell Lee was never *convicted* of murdering Meagan Stokes."

"Huh?" Chenney was confused.

"Russell Lee was convicted of killing six children, but Meagan wasn't one of them. The police didn't have enough physical evidence to make the case. It was only later that he admitted to Meagan's killing, a confession he made to Huntsville beat reporter Larry Digger."

"Shit. You don't think . . ."

"I don't know what to think yet. But I got a lot of questions about what happened to Meagan Stokes. And I have a lot of questions about exactly who is sending these little messages, and what it is the sender thinks everyone deserves."

"We're beyond healthcare fraud, aren't we?" Chenney pressed. "Meagan's toy, the scrap of fabric, the notes that these people need to get what they deserve. We're looking at homicide, aren't we? A twenty-five-year-old homicide." Chenney didn't sound glum about this development but excited.

"Yeah," David muttered with less enthusiasm. "Maybe."

He reloaded his gun, his mind still preoccupied. He got ready to shoot, and he said quietly, "Did you notice anything weird about the scrap of blue fabric in Melanie's room, Chenney?"

"Not really. It was old and bloodstained. Probably twenty-five years old. The lab will sort it out."

"The fabric probably is old," David informed him. "But that blood was not. As a matter of fact, I'd say the blood was about eight hours old."

"Huh? That doesn't make any sense."

David turned toward him, the hard lines of his face even harsher beneath the fluorescent lights. "You ever play games, Chenney?"

"Yeah, baseball, basketball, football."

"No, strategy games. Chess, bridge, hell, D&D."

"Well, no." The rookie looked bewildered. "What does that have to do with anything?"

David turned back to the targets. "We are in a game now, Chenney. The anonymous tipster, he dragged us in for some purpose only he knows about. Then he dragged Larry Digger in the same way. And now here we all are, players on the board, while he tosses the dice. Sends notes to some people, an altar to someone else, phones still others."

"But why?"

"I don't know yet. Off the top of my head, I'd say something more happened twenty-five years ago. Something that affected a key group of people, something they've all done a great job of hiding. But this tipster, he's upset now, he's tired of the quiet. He wants everyone finally to get what they deserve. And he seems willing to go to great lengths to make sure it happens."

Chenney pondered this in silence. "Are we talking some kind of nut?"

"I don't know."

"The altar, that seems to be the work of a nut."

"Maybe. But why would a nut call the FBI? What would a fruitcake want with the Bureau?"

"A job," Chenney said with a ghost of a smile. But then he sobered up again. "Yeah, I don't like the call to the Bureau. The crazy ones want vengeance, not justice. You think this tipster really is telling the truth? That Harper Stokes is committing fraud, and he and his wife knowingly adopted the daughter of a serial killer?"

"I don't know."

"Riggs, what the hell are we supposed to *do?*"

David donned his ear protection again, then the goggles. "First thing tomorrow, pull all the files on William Sheffield, going back to Texas. Then do the same with Ann Margaret and Jamie O'Donnell. I want to know exactly how each person got involved with the Stokeses. I want to know exactly how or if they met Meagan Stokes and if they were questioned by the Houston police twenty-five years ago. I want to see *financials* going back as far as your little heart can imagine. You cover the friends and I'll do the same with the family. We shake the tree hard enough, something will fall out.

"And then we move on it." David finally smiled, but it was savage and grim. "I fucking hate games."

He picked up his gun. Adopted the target pistol stance, sighted the red rings twenty-five yards away. His hand shook slightly; the 9mm was heavier than the .22 target pistol that earned him the NRA ranking of distinguished expert back in the days when everything he touched had turned to gold. Back in the days when there had been nothing young, virile David Riggs couldn't do.

He thought of Melanie Stokes again, the way she'd touched his hand.

He thought of Chenney, *So I heard from Margie that your brother was this great pitcher . . .*

He thought of the pain in his back that was slowly

and steadily getting worse. He thought of the illness that had no cure.

He fired off three shots, fast and smooth. Chenney drew in the target. The single hole through the bull's-eye was nearly perfect.

"Shit!" Chenney said in awe.

David just turned away and began picking up the spent shells.

T E N

ELEVEN P.M. While David Riggs picked up spent shells in the shooting range, Melanie roamed the three stories of her home, looking for anything that might give her peace of mind. She'd opened all the windows on the third story and turned on a fan to air out the cloying scent of gardenias. She'd cleaned her room, hanging up clothes, tending her plants, straightening her drawers. She'd showered, letting the water pummel the tight muscles of her neck.

By the time she emerged from the bathroom, it was easy to believe the afternoon had never happened. The altar had been a figment of her imagination. The images in her head merely a particularly bad dream.

She was in her home. She was the beloved daughter of Patricia and Harper Stokes. Nothing could touch her.

Melanie sat on the edge of her bed and had a good cry.

She wasn't prone to sobbing. She hadn't cried when she'd ended her engagement with William. Tears embarrassed her, made her feel weak, and she didn't like that. She was strong, she was capable, she was in control of her life.

But tonight she cried hard. It finally dissolved the

horrible knot in the pit of her stomach and eased the ache in her chest. It cleared her mind, and that allowed her to consider the afternoon objectively for the first time.

She discovered that she was frightened and rattled after all. She wasn't afraid of the altar or the person prone to such petty acts. She was frightened, however, of the consequences. What if she truly was the daughter of Russell Lee Holmes? If her father had dismissed a birth son for his sexual preferences, what in the world would he do to an adopted daughter who turned out to be the child of a killer?

She was not so strong and noble after all, Melanie decided. She wasn't keeping Digger's allegations from her parents to protect them. She was keeping them from her parents to protect *herself*. Because she had no intention of doing anything that might alienate her family. Because even at the age of twenty-nine, abandonment issues were a bitch.

Melanie finally trudged downstairs, entering the sterile world of the stainless steel kitchen, and brewed herself a cup of chamomile tea. She added a bit of honey, a squeeze of lemon, then retreated to the dining room. The grandfather clock in the foyer chimed once to signal half past the hour.

Eleven-thirty P.M. Her mother should have been home hours ago. Her father too. David was right. Her family was fractured, her father disappearing more and more, her mother battling the gin, and her brother AWOL. Whom was she trying to kid? The Stokeses were a mess.

She thought to hell with it all, and headed for her father's study. The books were there. She needed to catalogue them. She should've done it hours before. She was being lazy and remiss. Now it was time to focus, time to get to work.

She pulled out a piece of paper from her father's desk and got busy. One book down, a hundred more to go. She got up, headed into the foyer, and checked the alarm. It was set and tested active.

She returned to the study, made it through five more books, then had to check the windows. The alarm system would tell her if any zones were trespassed, of course. But she had to make the inspection anyway before she could convince herself to return to the study.

She finished her chamomile tea and settled into work mode. Title, author, publisher, date of copyright. Number, catalogue, move on. Work was important, and she was good at her job.

Larry Digger. Why approach her now? What did he really want from her? A story of the year or a quick buck?

The altar in her room. Who would do such a thing? What message was being sent? That she wasn't Meagan Stokes? That she couldn't replace her parents' first child? She knew that well enough herself, thank you very much.

David Reese. Waiter, former cop. Fascinating hands. She'd noticed them earlier. Long, deft fingers. Broad, calloused palms. Hands you could depend on. A face, however, that needed to learn how to smile.

"What are you going to do, Mel?" she murmured to herself in the empty house. "What are you going to do?"

She didn't know. When she'd first inhaled that scent of gardenias and the images had exploded in her mind, they had seemed so real, so genuine, that a part of her had thought, this is it, I am Russell Lee Holmes's child. But in the aftermath she found it easier to retreat behind doubts. There could be another explanation. Maybe she just had weird associations with gardenias. Maybe she was simply too susceptible to Larry Digger's innuendo.

But the altar in her room, with Meagan's toy, a bloody scrap of old fabric, and forty-four gardenia-scented candles arranged to spell a dead child's name . . .

Melanie didn't have an explanation for it. According to her brother, Meagan's toy should not still exist. According to her own desires, she should not be able to remember a shack inhabited by a murdered child. According to her world, a trespasser should not wait in the bedroom across the hall from hers late at night, simply to mess with her mind.

But the altar existed. It was real. Someone was trying to send a message about something, and she had to take that seriously. She should ask questions of Larry Digger, she supposed. Do research on her own. See what the police found out. Maybe someone was just angry with her and her parents and trying to shake things up. She would have to get to the bottom of it, if not for her family's sake, then for her own.

The house security system sounded a warning chime. Melanie stilled, then heard the telltale beep of someone entering the entry code into the front alarm box. Another beep as the alarm was rearmed. Seconds later footsteps sounded down the hall, then her mother poked her head into the study.

Patricia wore a long, black wraparound coat and a pillbox hat. The makeup was smudged around her eyes, and she looked as if she'd had a very long day. Generally she returned from her AA meetings looking flushed and revitalized, armed with her twelve steps and ready to take on the world. Not tonight.

She stepped into the room with her fingers nervously fiddling with the top button of her wrap and her gaze studiously avoiding her daughter's.

"Hey," Melanie said at last. "You're home late."

"Hi, sweetheart." Her mother smiled belatedly, struggled harder with the top button of her coat, and finally got it undone. She draped the wrap over a pile of books by the door, plopped her hat on top of it, then finally crossed to Melanie for a brief kiss on the cheek. Her lips felt cool. Melanie caught the scent of stale cigarette smoke mingled with Chanel No. 5, and stiffened.

Her mother smelled as if she'd been in a bar.

Automatically, helplessly, she started searching for signs. The smell of mouthwash used to cover gin and tonic. A slight swaying. Overbright eyes, anxious chatter.

Her mother's hands were shaking, her expression tremulous. Other than that, Melanie couldn't be sure. It could be just one of those days for her mother, or it could be worse. In the past six months it had become so hard to tell.

Her mother pulled back, seeming to inspect the piles of books.

"Is your father already in bed?" she asked brightly.

"He's not home."

Patricia frowned, picked up an old book. "Well, he's out rather late for a Sunday. Probably checking up on some important patient."

"Probably."

Her mother set down that book. Picked up another. Her back remained to her daughter. "How is your migraine, honey?"

"Fine."

"Relaxing day?"

"Sure," Melanie said quietly. "Sure."

Patricia turned. She dropped the book she was holding almost forcefully, almost angrily, and the sudden display of emotion sounded Melanie's alarm bells once more.

Patricia's chin was up. Her blue eyes were beginning to glow. She appeared defiant, and that made Melanie's heart sink. Oh, God, so she'd been out after all.

Her mother simply wasn't that strong. Her life had so many demons, so many dark moments . . .

And then Melanie found herself wondering why. It had been twenty-five years and yet she was still so troubled. *Just what had she done?*

"I'm not drunk," her mother announced abruptly. "Oh, don't bother to deny it, Melanie. I can see in your eyes that you think I've been drinking. Well, I haven't. It's just been . . . it's just been one of those days."

"So you had only one drink instead of four?" Melanie's voice came out sharper than she intended. She bit her lip but couldn't call the words back.

"Sweetheart, I'm telling you, I didn't have a drink—"

"Then where have you been all day? It's nearly midnight!"

"I've been out."

"Out where? Come on, Mom, out to what bar?"

Patricia drew herself up haughtily. "I wasn't aware that I had to explain myself to my own child."

"That's not what I meant—"

"Yes, it is. You're worried, and when you worry, you mother all of us. And we let you, don't we, Melanie? I've been thinking about that tonight. How much your father and I depend on you to take care of things. How much *I* depend on you. For God's sake, we let you work yourself to a point of vicious migraines. What kind of parents do that?"

Patricia crossed the room, taking Melanie's hands and looking at her with an urgency that confused Melanie, caught her off guard.

"Oh, God, Melanie," her mother cried. "If you could've seen yourself last night, having to be carried back into your own home by some stranger. You looked so pale, so fragile, and I realized for the first time what I'd been doing to you. I've been so lost in my own confusion, my own pain over Brian, I'd never thought about yours. You just seem so strong, I take it for granted. So I turn to you, pile it on. And you're such a good girl, you never complain. But it's not fair of me, and at my age I ought to know better. For chrissakes, when am I going to take care of myself?"

Melanie opened her mouth. She had the strange sensation of being in quicksand.

"I . . . I don't mind."

"Well, you should."

"Well, I don't. I honestly don't."

"And I'm telling you that you should! Melanie . . ."

Patricia took a deep breath. For a moment she appeared impatient and almost furious. Then she looked frightened and, at last, fatalistic, as if something else had happened, something she wasn't prepared to share yet but they would all know about in the end.

Jesus Christ, what was this all about?

Patricia said more quietly, "Melanie, have you ever had a turning point in your life? I know you're only twenty-nine, but have you ever felt yourself at a crossroads, when suddenly all of life was murky, and even though you can't see the landscape and you're not sure where you're going, you know you must take a step. And that this will be an important step. This will be The Step."

Melanie thought of the past twenty-four hours. She said, "Yes."

"Good." Her mother clutched her hands more tightly, her eyes beginning to burn again. "I had a turning point today, Melanie. I've had them before— I'm fifty-eight years old after all—and to tell you the truth, I've blown all of them. Stepped the wrong way every single time. Gone back instead of forward. But I think I finally did it right, Melanie. Because I thought of you."

"Mom?"

"I found myself in a bar tonight."

"Oh, God, I knew it. Why? What happened?"

"It doesn't matter. I went to a bar. I contemplated ordering a drink. I was so rattled, I was thinking, why not? Once you've fallen off the wagon the first time, it just doesn't seem so far to fall. We all have our patterns, and this one's mine. When I'm frightened, I head for the booze. I'm overwhelmed, sad, depressed, I head for the bottle. But then I thought of you, Melanie. How you looked last night, flattened by a migraine and still not wanting to worry us. How much you take inside yourself when you shouldn't have to. How you love me even when I do all the silly things I do. How much you love all of us when I know there are times we are far from lovable.

"And I thought . . . I thought I couldn't have a drink and still face you. I just couldn't." Patricia's voice grew soft. "Melanie, do you even know how much I love you? How you are such a godsend to me? The last six months, you have held me together. I don't think I could've made it without you. I want you to know that. I want you to know, to really know, how much I care."

Melanie couldn't speak. She held her mother's hand, feeling touched, but, heaven help her, also suspicious. Her mother never spoke like this. None of them did.

She was thinking of Larry Digger again, wondering if he had gone back on his word and approached her mother, if that was what had rattled Patricia Stokes. And then she was thinking how odd it was that they were having a conversation about how much they cared while both of them were purposefully keeping huge chunks of their day to themselves. It was like exchanging compliments on hairdos while wearing hats.

And then she wondered how much of the Stokes family was based upon that, lies of omission carrying back to the sunny days of Texas.

Her mother let go of Melanie's hands. She picked up a pile of books and set them on the floor. Now that she'd said what she wanted to say, the intensity had drained out of her face. She looked more settled. Whatever need she'd had, she'd fulfilled it, at least for then.

"Here," she said firmly. "Now that I've filled your

head with too much stuff, let me help you. Your father's right—you're working too hard."

"Mom?"

"Yes, darling?"

"I love you too."

"Thank you," Patricia whispered softly, and smiled back, looking happy. She picked up a book and got to work.

Thirty minutes later the front door banged open. The alarm chirped. Both women jumped, then flushed self-consciously, sharing a nervous laugh neither cared to explain. Harper came striding into his study in green hospital scrubs, one hand tucked behind his back, the second hiding a yawn. He halted and regarded them both curiously, clearly not expecting to find either awake.

"I thought I saw the light on. What are you two ladies still doing up?" He gave his wife a kiss on the cheek, then hugged his daughter. "Sweetheart, feeling better?"

"Right as rain," Melanie said. He checked her forehead and pulse anyway. After migraines, he always tended to her as if she were a patient.

"Better," he finally declared, "but you still need to take it easy. Here, maybe this will help. I was going to give these to you and your mom in the morning, but as my two favorite women are still up . . ."

Harper pulled out his hidden hand and produced a small bouquet of flowers and a box of chocolates. Four sunflowers, treated with purple dye until they were a rich magenta color. Very striking, and offered at only one of the more tony florists on Newbury Street. He handed them to Patricia and she flushed, giving her husband almost a shy glance.

Her father was definitely working hard at making up for past mistakes, Melanie thought approvingly. Not bad at all. She got a small box of champagne truffles. Teuscher. Flown in from Switzerland twice a week. She approved of that peace offering as well and promptly helped herself.

Her father pretended to check the pulse on her wrist again, then swiped a chocolate. She had to laugh. On impulse, she hugged her father again, and even more unexpectedly, he held the embrace.

"You should get upstairs," he said after a minute, his voice a little gruff. "You need rest, young lady."

"Why don't we finish up tomorrow," her mother said lightly. "I can help you out in the evening, and we'll get through them in no time."

Melanie was tired. But then she found herself thinking of her room again. Her room and the altar. Her room that had been entered in the dead of night while the rest of the house slept.

Melanie gazed longingly back at the books.

Her father would have none of it. Ever the fix-it man, he took her arm and led her and her mother upstairs.

Nighttime rituals came smoothly. Her father set the alarm from the second floor landing. Her mother kissed her cheek. Her father gave her a hug. Melanie murmured good night. Her father told her to sleep in. She said she had a meeting at ten. Her father said he had surgery at eleven, her mother commented she was due at the children's hospital to read at eleven as well. The beginning of a new week at the Stokes household.

Her parents disappeared inside their bedroom. Melanie just caught her father asking her mother how her day was. Patricia did not say anything about turning points. She simply said, Fine. And yours? Fine. She imagined them climbing into their separate sides of the bed, continuing the same polite conversation until both fell asleep.

Then she thought of David Reese and wondered if he would stick to his side of the bed. She doubted it. He struck her as the intense, silent type. Sex would be hot, slick, and fierce. Few words before and after, but what a ride in between. Something twisted low in her stomach, made her sigh. Yearning. Hunger. Pure sexual frustration.

She was lonely these days, she thought, and smiled wryly. Why else would she spend so much time trying to convince herself she had the perfect life?

Melanie reached the third floor. She inspected Brian's empty bedroom from the door. Tonight, no intruders lingered. Only then did she finally, reluctantly, go to bed.

Her dreams were the standard anxiety dreams. She was in her first year at Wellesley, sitting down to take a final exam and realizing at the last minute she'd forgotten to study. She didn't understand the questions. Oh, God, she couldn't even fill in her name.

Then she was in an elevator shaft plummeting down.

Then she was suddenly in the hospice where she'd stayed when she was nine years old, eagerly waiting for the Stokeses to take her away. Except this time they walked right past her. This time they picked up a new girl with perfect sausage curls and walked out the door.

No! No! she cried in her dream. *You're my family. My family!*

At the last minute, fourteen-year-old Brian Stokes looked at her. "Did you honestly think you couldn't be replaced? Just ask Meagan."

The hospice spiraled away. She ran through black voids, utterly lost, calling and calling for someone to see her, to tell her her name. She couldn't bear not to know her own name. And the blackness went on and on and on . . .

Suddenly she was cocooned in a warm embrace. Solid arms, low, gentle voice. *Shh, it's okay, love, it's okay. I'm here for you. I will always be here for you. Even if you never remember . . .*

Melanie stirred. In her sleep she whispered a name.

It was the closest to the truth she ever came until it was too late.

ELEVEN

MONDAY MORNING PATRICIA watched her husband read the *Boston Globe*. After all these years, she knew exactly how Harper would read the paper—starting with the business section, where he would check his stocks and on a good day smile and on a bad day frown but never actually announce anything because he always kept the financials to himself. Then he would move on to the local section, first skimming it for any articles pertaining to himself or City General, then reading the articles in depth. After Boston news, he moved to national, then international, slowly expanding his circle of interest to include the things not immediately relevant to himself.

He had once told her that it was important to be well read on all subjects so you could make intelligent conversation at work. Though he'd never expanded upon that statement, she'd understood all the things that were left unsaid. Harper came from blue collar stock. People who did not debate national news or attend black-tie parties or hobnob with political movers or shakers. People whose biggest dream was someday landing a government job that would provide enough of a pension to support fishing in their old age.

Harper, of course, had dreamed big. From the very beginning he'd bought the right clothes, trimmed the calluses from his hands, and done his best to appear even more upper class than the people who were born into it. Even though he'd been a struggling med student, no one had questioned his roots.

Patricia suspected that Harper also thought this facade was important to her, because she'd grown up in the lap of Texas oil luxury. He would never have it be said that she married beneath her or that he provided less for her. Love and money were intrinsically tied in his mind.

Patricia respected that. She admired it. Harper fit the model of man she'd come to know so well: conservative, hardheaded, firm. She supposed that's why she loved him so much. No matter what he did, he was familiar to her. His shortcomings were her father's shortcomings, his strengths her father's strengths. His brand of caring, her father's brand of caring. There were never any surprises, and in her later years she appreciated that.

Once, when she'd been just a child, she'd thought marriage would be about roses and candlelight and never-ending romance. Her husband would always be dashing and passionate. She would always be beautiful and sweet sixteen. Life would be taken care of for her; she would never be lonely or frightened.

Of course marriage didn't work that way. Sometimes, on the bad days, when it required effort just to open her eyes and swing her legs out of bed, she wondered what she was still doing with Harper. What kind of woman stayed with a man who first pursued her with obsession and now hadn't touched her in years? What kind of woman stayed with a man who'd looked at her the way Harper had looked at her the day Meagan's body was identified, as if she was the worst form of life on earth, as if she'd done something even crueler than kill her own child?

On her strong days, however, she acknowledged

that this was simply what marriage was about—perseverance. She and Harper had survived the grueling demands of a surgeon's career even as Harper's fellow residents divorced in a giant tidal wave. They had endured the loss of their child when the divorce rate for such couples was over seventy percent. Long after their friends had remarried and divorced for the second time, they were making the decision to adopt a little girl. They had raised their children together. Gotten them through college. Seen them ensconced in their chosen careers.

Their marriage may not be a honeymoon anymore. It may even be more about companionship—which she knew her children, even Melanie, didn't understand—but it was also about having a history. Knowing each other so well. Growing together. Accepting each other.

Weathering life together. Simply weathering it.

The past six months had certainly put that to the test. Since the scene with Brian, Patricia had found herself unhinged in ways she couldn't discuss with her husband, or even with Melanie. She would find herself lying in bed, listening to Harper's snores far away, and thinking of the bottles of gin that beckoned in the parlor, the sweet oblivion she often remembered as a lush, ecstatic dream. Other times she would find herself going downstairs and staring at Meagan's painting, beautiful, happy Meagan, who'd trusted her mother to banish the monsters that hid beneath the bed.

Then, in the brief period when she had given in to the lure of gin and tonic, she'd reached some new level of being permanently off kilter, where she would wake up at four A.M. and race to Brian's room, convinced he must be there though he hadn't lived at home since he was twenty-four. She would yank out drawers like a woman possessed, searching for old clothes she could hold against her and inhale the scent of her son's skin. And when she failed to find any trace of him still imprinted in the room, when it began to seem that Harper had wiped her firstborn child from the face of the earth, panic would rear its ugly head, and aided by alcohol, devour her alive.

Suddenly she would be desperate to find Meagan. *Meagan darling, where are you? Come home to Mommy. Please, come home.*

The cop would materialize beside her in Brian's darkened room. "At least she didn't suffer, ma'am."

Her head was cut off—she suffered!

Next, the blue-suited FBI agent would step through the window. "There was nothing you could do, ma'am."

I shouldn't have left her with Nana. Why did we hire so much help?

Finally, the burly sheriff would slide from beneath the bed, chewing a big plug of tobacco to cover the fact he'd just been ill. "Well, ma'am, at least now you know. It's better to know."

My baby is never coming home. My baby has no head. Would you look at what he did to her hands? Oh, God, oh, God, why am I still alive? Why couldn't you just kill me? Please, please just kill me . . .

Curled up on her son's bed twenty-five years later, she would imagine herself sitting on the grass outside the woods where the cops were working. She would hear the buzz of the flies and smell the overripe scent of decay. She would open her mouth to scream and laugh instead. Just laugh, laugh, laugh.

"It will get better, lass. Somehow, it will get better." Jamie had told her that.

But it had gotten worse. For the next five years her life simply spiraled away.

From pushing a new life from her body to picking out the tiny white coffin for a closed-casket funeral, because there wasn't enough left of her four-year-old daughter for a viewing. From active mom to screaming, raving lunatic, turning away from her son, refusing to acknowledge his existence because children just broke your heart. From dutiful wife to frozen, inconsolable human being, refusing Harper's tentative overtures, knowing he blamed her for what happened to their daughter, knowing that he was despite that making amends. Realizing she no longer cared.

A chill had moved over her, until she didn't belong to herself. She shut down, picked up the bottle of gin, and embraced the fog that blanketed her like the softest caress. She lived for the fog, she loved the fog. It was the best lover she'd ever had, and she fell graciously into its arms, smoothing it like a handful of rich soapsuds over her bare, aching breasts. She rolled languorously through the days, not thinking, not feeling, not existing, because then the pain would be too much.

Just kill me, just kill me. Why aren't I dead?

Her father had demanded she stop drinking. Her husband had checked her into a rehab ward, seeking as always a scientific solution to her emotional ills. None of it mattered. She hadn't cared what they thought, she hadn't cared what they wanted or that her son was turning into a somber, hard little man, incapable of smiling. She hadn't cared about anything.

Then Harper, dazed, overwhelmed, workaholic Harper, had done the unexpected. He'd moved them all to Boston, where images of Meagan could no longer torture her or Brian in the halls. And in a single defining moment, the kind of moment that gave her faith in him and hope for their marriage, Harper had brought her to see "Daddy's Girl."

Patricia had taken one look at Melanie, small, earnest, blue-eyed Melanie, and everything in her had given way.

She fell in love again. The ice cracked, the fog receded. She wanted to hold this little girl so badly, it was a physical ache. She wanted to take care of her troubles, she wanted to tell her it would be all right. She wanted beyond all reason to keep her safe.

She loved little Melanie for being little Melanie. She loved the way she endured the unknown, the way she tried to make people smile. She was strong. She was spirited. She was earnest. She was everything Patricia had always wanted to be but had never quite managed. She was Patricia Stokes's hero.

For Melanie, Patricia had pulled herself together. For Melanie, she'd started to love Brian again, to give him the attention he desperately needed, to give him back his mother. For Melanie, she'd even started loving her husband again, because just when she'd thought there was nothing left between them, he'd given her this most precious gift: a second daughter and a chance to make things right.

The night Melanie came home, Patricia had slowly stripped off her clothes and for the first time in five and a half years, she'd crawled into her husband's arms. Harper had even accepted her, though she knew there had been other women in between and she knew his heart had not completely melted like hers.

When the short physical period ended, she understood. Harper would never love her the way he once had. He would not worship her or pursue her as he'd done in the very beginning. He would not look at her with the same urgent passion.

He would accept her. He would take care of her. But he would not forgive. In Texas, forgiveness was women's work.

Now Harper set down the business section. He picked up the metro news. For a moment she had a glimpse of the face she'd known for thirty-eight years, his eyes still as blue, his jaw still as square, his hair still as thick and golden.

Even at the age of fifty-eight, he looked like the man who had turned her head away from Jamie O'Donnell and swept her off her feet.

She sectioned out another bite of grapefruit.

And unbidden, the memories came back to her—of Texas nights, hot and humid, when the three of them had thought they could take over the world, Jamie so strong, Harper so charming, and Patricia simply so beautiful.

Harper's nothing but a handshake and a smile, lass. He's obsessed with image, not substance. You can do better than him.

He understands me, Jamie.

Why? Because he wears the right clothes, gets a good manicure? Because he'd sell his own mother for an invite to the right party?

Exactly, my love. Exactly.

"I'm sorry, Meagan," she mouthed to her grapefruit. "I am so sorry."

Harper lowered his paper. "What?"

"I'm worried about Melanie."

Harper promptly set down the paper. "She's been working too hard," he said seriously. Health was his domain, and he'd always been very worried about Melanie's, especially her migraines. "She's got to learn to slow down."

"I've been trying to help her," Patricia said, then shrugged delicately. She couldn't get her daughter to slow down any more than she could her husband.

As if reading her mind, Harper said, "What if we all went on a vacation?"

"Pardon?"

"I mean it, Pat." He leaned forward, sounded earnest. "I've been thinking about it for weeks now. I've always said someday, when I retire, we'll travel everywhere. Well, hell, I'm not getting any younger. None of us are. Maybe it's time to finally be impulsive. Take our children and cruise the world. What d'you say?"

Patricia couldn't say a word. With shaking hands she set down her silver spoon. Cruise the world. Just like that. In her wildest dreams her husband never said such things.

She searched his gaze warily, looking for something she couldn't name. She wondered if her husband knew that even after all these years, she loved him.

Even when he put his job before the family. Even when he went out with those silly young twits, then came home and kissed her dryly on the cheek. She wondered if he knew how patiently and quietly she was waiting for the day he did retire and he would belong to her again. Then maybe they could recapture what they'd shared so briefly in those first hot days of Texas. Then maybe they could finally leave all the mutual mistakes, and mutual sins, and mutual regret behind, and start fresh.

Didn't people always say it's never too late for new beginnings?

"Would you . . . would you leave the hospital?"

"Well, not *leave it* leave it."

Patricia ducked her head so he wouldn't see her disappointment. "A vacation, then? Like a week or two?"

"Longer. Maybe four months, six months. Hell, maybe I could be really wild and take a leave of absence."

A leave of absence. That got her attention again. She didn't know whether to be thrilled or suspicious. She did her best to sound interested. "Really? When?"

Harper said matter-of-factly, "I was thinking next week."

In the sudden quiet of the patio, Patricia was certain her husband would be able to hear the pounding of her heart. Next week. Harper never moved that fast. He never did anything as dramatic as take a leave of absence from his career.

Oh, God, it wasn't about Melanie or romance after all. He knew. Her husband knew.

The note, sitting in her car after the AA meeting. Inside her locked, alarmed Mercedes, placed on the driver's seat.

Five words, cut out of a magazine. Simple. Knowing. Chilling to the bone.

You get what you deserve.

In the cold moment that followed after she read the

note, her heart beating like a trapped bird in her chest, Patricia had experienced a horrible instance of prescience, where the past blended with the future and there was no way she could stop it. Don't hurt her, she'd found herself silently begging. Don't hurt Melanie. I was good this time. I swear, I swear, I have been so good.

"Pat? Come on, I thought you would be pleased."

"Six months," she murmured, keeping her gaze on the table. "Somewhere far away. Would we take Melanie?"

"Yes."

"Would we   would we take Brian?"

Harper hesitated, then slowly he nodded. "But not any lovers. I'm trying, Pat. Jesus, I'm trying. But I'm not ready to go that far."

"The whole family," she murmured. "Going away. Someplace far. They would need more notice than a week, sweetheart. That's awfully short."

He remained firm. "Hey, if I can find a way to get out of the hospital, so can they."

"So next Friday?"

"Yes. Next Friday."

She should push more, she thought. Demand to know why. She was too afraid of the answer. She whispered, "All right, darling, all right."

María appeared in the doorway. "Dr. Sheffield here for Dr. Stokes."

Harper looked surprised, but then he rose and placed a quick kiss on his wife's cheek. Patricia had placed the sunflowers on the patio table that morning. He touched one magenta petal. "It'll be all right," he told her softly. "You'll see."

He strode out of the room. Patricia was alone with her half-eaten grapefruit. She wasn't sure what had just happened. The spur-of-the-moment vacation for no good reason. Her own desperate willingness to play along.

Secrets, she thought. Hers. His. And last night she

suspected Melanie had them too. There had been too many long pauses in her daughter's speech. Too many guards on her eyes. Melanie always had kept too much to herself. Did she really think her parents hadn't figured that out?

You get what you deserve. You get what you deserve.

Oh, Jesus God.

Patricia felt exhausted. She could barely lift her spoon or summon the energy to eat. Life was spiraling away on her again. Her breath was coming too quick and fast. An anxiety attack. At her age you would think she would know better. She didn't.

She went in search of her daughter. If she could just see Melanie, just know that her little girl was all right, not kidnapped, not murdered, not dead, it would help. If she could reassure herself that this was the present and the past was truly the past and long dead . . .

But Melanie was nowhere in sight. At ten-thirty in the morning Patricia Stokes crawled back to bed.

She knew she should be stronger. Today she wasn't.

MELANIE WOKE UP late again, then had to scramble to be ready by ten. She yanked a dress over her head while dialing Ann Margaret to tell her she wouldn't be at the donor center today. She wasn't feeling well. Maybe a touch of the flu. Ann Margaret was sympathetic. Don't worry, dear. Get lots of rest, dear. You know how much we worry about you.

Melanie went downstairs feeling about two inches tall. She hated lying and was doing too much of it these days.

She burst out the front doors eight minutes after ten. David Reese was waiting across the street, leaning against a cherry tree, his legs crossed, his hawkish face showing impatience. He looked as if he hadn't slept a wink the previous night, and the moment he spoke he sounded in a sour mood.

"Was that William Sheffield who just walked into your house?" David asked as a form of greeting.

"Yes. He probably has some meeting with my dad." She was fidgeting with the strap of her purse, trying to get it to stay on her shoulder, but apparently David had had enough of waiting. He pushed away from the tree and immediately started walking.

"Do they always meet at your house?"

"Well, no, not always."

"Why this morning?"

"I don't know. I just caught the tail end of things as they walked into the study, but William was upset. Sounded like his house was broken into last night."

David came to an abrupt halt. "*His house* was broken into? Like yours the night before?"

Melanie saw where his thoughts were heading and immediately shook her head. "I'm sure this has *nothing* to do with our house. William has a slight *bingo* problem, you know? No doubt he got a little over his head again and a few creditors decided to help themselves. That's what Dad was grumbling when he showed him into his study. 'Well, William, what do you expect?' I guess the intruder even left a note."

David grabbed her arm. The intensity in his eyes caught her off guard. "A note? What kind of note?"

"I . . . I don't know. I didn't hear that much."

"Did you hear William say something was actually taken?" David demanded. "Did he actually complain about losing money?"

Melanie tried to remember. She honestly hadn't paid that much attention. "I think he did deny it; he said he'd won last night. But my father didn't believe him. Said his record spoke for itself."

"What about the note?"

"He just kind of went, 'Well, if it was just a creditor, why the hell would he leave a note? Creditors take money, not write poetry.'" She paused. "Basically, William was upset and my father was trying to calm him down. End of story."

David was still frowning, but he finally let go of her arm. "I'd like to know what the note said."

"*Why?* What could possibly be so important?"

" 'You get what you deserve,' " David said. "Isn't that what Digger's caller told him?"

"Oh." Melanie had forgotten about that. She considered it for a moment, then shook her head. "William's just an associate of my father's. He has enough problems of his own."

David let the matter drop. They both resumed walking.

The morning was bright and sunny, not a cloud in the sky and not a tourist-free space on the tree-lined street. Men in double-breasted blazers window-shopped at Armani's, while college coeds with pierced navels walked into Ann Taylor and coffee shops. She and David wove their way through the throngs. The hotel was only fifteen minutes away by foot.

Melanie finally looked at her silent companion. David had dressed up for the occasion in black slacks and sports jacket. Brooks Brothers would be her guess. Looked nice on him. Very nice.

They went four blocks down Newbury before Melanie's nerves couldn't take the silence anymore.

"Did you have a relaxing evening?"

"Dandy."

"You're limping less today."

"Lucky me."

"You're not much for conversation, are you?"

"I grew up in a household of men. Mealtimes were for chewing."

"I bet. So what happened to your mother?"

"Cancer."

"I'm sorry."

"So was she."

Melanie refused to be fazed. "So then it's just your father and . . ."

"One brother. Younger." He added, "Steven. Currently married, two children, baseball coach at Amherst. Good pitcher. Better?"

"A regular speech," she assured him, and thought he might have smiled.

They crossed over to Boylston Street, passing the Pru Center, where the Stokeses did all their shopping, then turned at the Shari Theater, where Melanie had watched the re-released *Star Wars* trilogy in a single afternoon. The hotel was nearly in sight.

"You didn't call Larry Digger, right?" David checked.

"Of course not—"

"Good. I want to catch him off guard, before he has a chance to perfect his story. What about your parents? What did you tell them last night?"

"Nothing—"

"And your brother? Hear anything more from him?"

"No."

"He didn't even call?" David seemed surprised by that. "So much for the protective-older-brother act."

"Brian's one of those people who require a lot of space. He'll call when he's ready. He will."

"Always the diplomat, huh?"

She looked him in the eye. "Don't knock it until you try it."

"Touché," he said. "Touché."

They arrived at the First Church of Christ, Scientist, just a block from the hotel. Melanie watched shouting children splash in the long reflecting pool. God, it was a beautiful day.

A moment later she followed David into the Midtown Hotel.

THERE WEREN'T MANY people in the lobby. One man was buried behind a newspaper in the corner, while an exhausted mom tried to rein in two racing children. The counter was manned by a short, pert redhead whose eyes lit up at the sight of David. She managed to ring Larry Digger's room while giving David a blatantly suggestive glance.

Melanie decided she didn't like the redhead much.

David himself barely seemed to notice her. A mood had swept over him upon entering the hotel. His face was shuttered, but his hooded eyes were observant. He stood differently, up on the balls of his feet with his left leg back for balance. He was on alert, Melanie finally realized. Studying the lobby, its occupants, its exits. He was preparing for Larry Digger.

The redhead got off the phone with Larry Digger and pointed them down the hall, giving David a last generous pout. He turned away without a backward glance.

They found Larry Digger waiting for them at the door to his room, his face smug, then faltering when he saw David.

"Who the hell are you?" Digger demanded.

"Your helpful hardware man," David said. He led Melanie inside, then kicked the door shut with his foot and stood, arms across his chest.

"Shit, you're the waiter." Digger turned to Melanie. "Why the hell did you bring him? This is between us."

"I want to see your proof, Mr. Digger. Mr. Reese offered to escort me. Now, do you want to talk, or should I leave?" She sat on the edge of a chair, making it clear she was ready to get up again at any time.

Digger looked at David unhappily. "Can't you at least wait in the hallway?"

David did Melanie the favor of answering. "No."

Digger gave up, pacing the small room. He was wearing the same pants from last night but a fresh shirt. There was no evidence of a suitcase in the room, just one worn duffel bag and a pile of notebooks on the bedside table. A tape recorder rested in the middle of the bed, the top open and gaping hungrily.

"You can start talking anytime," Melanie prodded him. "That is, if you have anything useful to say."

Digger stopped pacing and gave her a belligerent gaze. "Oh, no, that's not the way this is going to play out. You want your proof, you have to answer *my* questions first. That's the way it works."

"Why? At this point I'm still not sure you're telling the truth. Maybe you're making this all up for money."

"And that's such a sin? Jesus, what would you know? Living in that town house, every need taken care of, every wish fulfilled, and what did you do for it, sweetheart? What did you ever do to deserve the life you lead?"

Melanie's lips thinned; his comments struck too close to home. "I was lucky," she said stiffly. "So far, much luckier than you have ever been."

"Well, doesn't that just make you special? Hey, for your information, I don't even need you anymore. I've talked to the intern who found you at the hospital. I've gotten in touch with the social workers assigned to your case—"

"What about Harper and Patricia Stokes?" David asked from the doorway. "Did you contact them?"

"Not yet, but since Melanie's not cooperating . . ." Larry Digger made a show of shrugging, but his gaze was shrewd. He leaned against the bureau and eyed them both.

"I figure I can write this up by end of week," he announced. "Auction it off to the highest bidder, with or without a quote from Miss Holmes. Welcome to journalism in the nineties."

"Then it is about money. When all is said and done, you are simply after a buck. Well, that answers my question. Good day, Mr. Digger, and good riddance." Melanie shook her head in disgust and stood.

Digger grabbed her arm. Bad move. David immediately strode toward him.

"Oh, what are you gonna do, gimpy?"

David's face turned to stone, and Melanie felt the hair prickle at the nape of her neck. David Reese was angry, a deep anger that made him dangerous. At that moment Melanie had no doubt he could inflict as much or as little damage as he intended.

The reporter was not a dumb man after all. Very slowly he brought up his hands. "Hey, hey, hey, we've gotten off track here. We all want the same thing. I'm sure we can work it out."

David relaxed just slightly, but his gaze held a warning. Digger tried to plead his case to Melanie instead.

"It's not about money," he said sourly. *"It isn't."*

"Sure it is."

"Goddammit! Don't you think I'm tired of chicken-shit tabloid journalism too? I have a *real* lead, Melanie Stokes, whether it violates your precious little world or not. And I intend to write a *real* story whether you like it or not."

"Tell me the truth," Melanie said curtly. "Tell me something convincing."

Digger crossed to the bedside table and picked up a handful of ragged papers. "You want your truth, here it is. *This* is the story of Russell Lee Holmes and the woman who bore his child."

"How do you know?" Melanie pressed. *"How do you know?"*

Digger was silent for a moment. He seemed to be contemplating his options. Maybe his greed was warring against what appeared to be his genuine pride in a job well done. Maybe he just wasn't sure how seriously to take her. Then he spoke.

"Russell Lee Holmes had a tattoo on his upper arm. This was all documented when he was arrested. The tattoo said 'Trash loves Angel.' Now, Trash is Russell Lee's nickname. He wouldn't tell anyone who Angel was, just said he wasn't 'no fuckin' virgin.' But, unfortunately for him, Russell Lee sometimes spoke in his sleep. He liked to say the name Angel. And every now and then he'd have these little conversations with his baby—with his own kid.

"Even before they brought him to the electric chair, I started looking into it, trying to find his wife and child. I wanted to know what it was like to be married to Russell Lee. You know anything about child molesters, Miss Stokes?"

She shook her head.

"There are several types. You can be either a preferential child molester—meaning you really do prefer children—or a situational molester, which means you'll turn to children if they happen to be around, but adults will do just as well. Make sense?"

Melanie nodded, though she wasn't sure something so horrible could make sense. Larry Digger continued more enthusiastically now, warming to his subject, pleased to show off his research.

"Most child molesters are situational offenders," he said. "They fall into four categories—repressed, morally indiscriminate, sexually indiscriminate, and inadequate. A repressed guy will molest his own children versus risking approaching anyone else. He's not only a sick son of a bitch, he's basically a spineless bastard as well. The morally indiscriminate, on the other hand, is a true equal opportunity monster. He'll rape his children, he'll rape his neighbor's children, and then to top it all off, he'll rape his wife and his neighbor's wife. He has no conscience at all, and preying on kids is just part of the fun. Then we got the sexually indiscriminate. He'll prey on anyone too, but for a different reason. He's sexually bored, likes the risk, the sense of adventure. What do you think is worse, Melanie? Preying on your kids because you can or preying on your kids because you have nothing better to do with your time?"

He didn't give her a chance to answer, which was just as well. Melanie suddenly had a feeling where the reporter was going, and it was a freight train straight to hell.

"The fourth type is the inadequate," Digger announced. "He's a loner, probably has no adult relationship to fulfill his needs, and in the end lures children he knows or has easy access to, because they are nonthreatening and he knows he's a wimp and not capable of much. So there you go, four types of sickos. Wanna cast your bet as to which type fits Russell Lee Holmes?"

"Morally indiscriminate," David said without hesitation. "Has no conscience or sense of remorse about his actions. He didn't even repent when sitting in the electric chair."

Digger nodded approvingly. He looked Melanie in the eye.

"There's another defining characteristic of the morally indiscriminate offender, a neat little twist that'll just chill your heart. He'll not only turn on his own children, but he'll have children *just so he can have them to turn on*. So he has property at home. So he has all the access a godlike creature such as him is entitled to. I want to find Russell Lee Holmes's wife because I want to ask her what it was like to realize she'd been used by her own husband to produce his next victim."

Digger's voice turned soft. "Do you understand yet why you were given up by your own mother, Miss Holmes? Why you might have been spirited as far away from Texas as possible? Why your birth mother has never made any attempt to claim you or acquaint you with your past? Do you understand yet why you had been brought into this world?"

Melanie was having a hard time breathing. A fresh migraine was taking root behind her eye. The shadows were shifting in her mind again, revealing glimpses of a time and place she didn't want to know. The wooden shack. The little girl, clutching her favorite toy and staring right at her, not knowing yet what her fate would be.

"You still haven't given any proof," she said

roughly. "You've only established that Russell Lee Holmes was evil. I got that. So his wife had motive to give her child up for adoption. I got that too. But you still haven't said anything to convince me that I'm that child. Come on, how in the world would some poor woman in Texas get her child to a Boston hospital ER?"

"Honestly, I don't know. But I can still give you your connection. See, I tracked down the midwife who had the honor of delivering one Baby Doe to none other than Russell Lee Holmes and his wife. Of course, she didn't know who they were then. Interestingly enough, Russell Lee used aliases for himself and his wife even before he began his dirty deeds.

"But when Russell Lee's pictures suddenly became front-page news, the midwife figured it out. And then, when she's still trying to figure out if she should say something about it or not, a man appears in her doorway.

"He offers her a large sum of money to forget all about Russell Lee Holmes's child. He tells her if she ever says a word, there will be consequences. *Dire* consequences. Now, this is the kind of man you don't mess with. So the midwife agrees. She doesn't take the money—she's got a little bit of an attitude about pride in her job and all that—but neither does she ever say a word. The identity of Russell Lee's kid remains safe with her long after Russell Lee goes to the chair."

Digger smiled. It was the only warning Melanie got. "Hey, Miss Holmes, the man who approached the midwife was Jamie O'Donnell. Now, if this has got nothing to do with you, why does your godfather care about Trash's first kid? Why is he showing up on the porch of some little old midwife and threatening her life if she can't keep a secret? You wanna tell me?"

Melanie's stomach plummeted. She didn't have an answer.

"Did you . . . did you contact Jamie? Did you ask him that?"

"Jamie O'Donnell? Shit, you're a few cards short of a full deck. The man runs guns, for God's sake. He knows people, he's hurt people. No way in hell I'm going near him."

"*What?*"

Larry Digger blinked at her shocked tone. "Lady, don't you know *anything* about your family?"

Melanie was dazed. Her godfather imported small gift items. Wooden boxes from Thailand, figurines. He traveled a lot. That's all.

"What about this Angel?" David asked. "You found her?"

Digger shook his head. "No. Like I said, the woman used an alias and the midwife knew only the fake name. I asked for a description, but it was too generic to help. Russell Lee didn't leave any personal documents behind, and even his lawyer is a tight one on the subject. Client-lawyer privilege carries to the grave and all that crap."

Digger stared at Melanie. "*You* must have lived at least a few years with your birth mom. Now, I know your memory isn't all it's cracked up to be, but a mom is a mom. She's gotta be in your mind somewhere. A little bit of hypnosis, regression therapy, whatever, I can reunite mother and child. Now, how is that for a story? What d'you say, Miss Holmes? Wanna meet your *real* mom? Wanna hear your *real* name? It'll be fun."

Knocking sounded at the door. "I ordered breakfast earlier," Digger said. "Never come between a man and his fried eggs."

David stepped toward Melanie. Digger opened the door. Two sounds emitted—short, popping crackles, like potato chip bags bursting open. And Digger collapsed where he stood, blood bubbling from his chest.

Melanie found herself looking at a dark-haired man wearing a poorly fitting hotel uniform and a very large gun.

He took aim again.

"Get down!" David roared, leaping toward her and sending them sprawling behind the bed. Two more pops. Bullets sailed just above their heads.

As she watched, David reached beneath his nice sports jacket and pulled out a gun.

"FBI," David Reese yelled. "Drop it!"

TWELVE

THUNDER ERUPTED SUDDENLY from David's gun. Three pops followed, sending one bullet flying past Melanie's ear. She cringed, and then David's gun roared once more.

"On the count of three," David commanded.

"What?" She couldn't hear through the ringing in her head.

"On the count of three, *run*."

Pop, pop.

"One. Two. THREE!" David sprang up firing. *"Now, now, now!"*

Melanie crawled two feet before she could get her legs beneath her. Still firing with one hand, David pushed her, and she bolted out from behind the bed.

The shooter was fleeing down the hall, carrying Digger's notes and leaving a trail of blood behind him.

Melanie took off in the opposite direction. David Reese was right behind her.

"Everyone down! Shooter in the building! Press the alarm, press the alarm!"

People flattened like pancakes. Two women screamed. Melanie kept running through the lobby and the doors into bright blue sunlight and Copley Street.

She made it halfway up the block before a strong arm whipped around her waist and snapped her to a halt. She screamed, he stuffed a hand in her mouth and yanked her into a doorway. She started fumbling for her mace.

"It's me, goddammit, it's me. Calm down!" David's skin was pale, his hair spiky with sweat. She couldn't see any sign of a wound, but he was breathing hard and he looked as if he was in a lot of pain. Maybe ducking up and down and shooting firearms weren't good for his back. If he did have a back problem. If his name was David Reese.

She tried to shove away from him. He locked his arm around her waist more firmly.

"Who the hell are you? What the hell are you do-ing?" she yelled, still pushing hard.

"Trying to keep you out of the line of fire," David bit out. "Do you think a guy like that has qualms about shooting you in the back?"

She almost wiggled free. He caught her again. "I don't know what I know about a guy 'like that.' I've never been shot at before!"

"Well, neither have I, so shut up and let me think."

Sounds had erupted on the streets. People shouting. Cars honking, then screeching to a halt. The shooter was probably bolting from the back exit of the hotel. After another moment David loosened his grip and looked out into the street.

"Shit." He turned on her angrily. "Don't you real-ize who that was?"

"No," she spat out. She took advantage of his re-laxed grip to try to yank away. "Dammit, let me go!"

"Jesus Christ." He half released her, half covered her mouth. Bad move. She bit him. This time he let go, but his eyes were burning.

Down the street, sirens finally split the air, and two cop cars came barreling into view.

"That was the guy reading the paper in the lobby," David growled. "The guy who watched us walk into

Digger's room, and instead of turning away, came in after us. Now, why the hell would someone do that?"

"Are you really with the FBI?"

"Yes."

"You lied to me!"

"Well, you got your revenge, because that guy wasn't firing blanks and he wasn't shooting for show. Now would be a good time for you to answer more questions, starting with the complete list of everyone who would want you dead!"

LATER, DAVID REESE took her back to the hotel room which was now swarming with police. He introduced himself as Special Agent David Riggs of the Boston office FBI and promptly launched into a steady stream of questions, as if caterers turned out to be undercover agents every day.

Melanie stared at Digger, unable to look away. He had a large hole in his chest and his blood was everywhere. It carried a warm, rusty scent and was underscored by the smell of feces and urine. David explained that death caused the bowels to relax and release their contents. Melanie hadn't known that.

A Boston homicide detective arrived. Clad in a dapper double-breasted suit, his pitch-black hair slicked back and his face freshly scrubbed, he introduced himself as Detective Jax. He looked like he ought to be in a one-hour cop drama. He gave Melanie a slow once-over, offered her a seat and a cup of water, then got down to business.

"Nine millimeter," the detective told David as he dug bullets out of the drywall with his pocketknife. He dropped them into a plastic bag.

"A Beretta," David said. "Can't mistake the sound."

Jax pointed at the floor, where a trail of dark red drops led toward the hall. "His?"

"Got his hand. Slowed him down a bit, but not

much. Tough son of a bitch. I hate that trait in assassins."

Jax grinned. He finished collecting bullets and moved on to Digger's open duffel bag. "Two pairs of underwear, both dirty. Two white shirts, not really white. *Three* brand-new bottles of JD. A man with priorities, I see."

"He didn't seem that bad when we talked to him. Tox screen will tell the story." David nodded at the cleared bedside table. "The shooter grabbed Digger's notes before taking off. Not an easy maneuver with shots being fired, so my guess is that was part of the deal. Two dead people and all the reporter's information."

"Two dead?" Melanie spoke up. "Why two targets? Only Larry Digger was shot."

David answered her. "The receptionist said the shooter was here all day yesterday. She simply assumed he was a friend of one of the guests. Then he showed up again this morning with the newspaper. So the guy is on day two of a stakeout when we showed up. He watched us head for Digger's room, then, according to the receptionist, he got up, made a call from his cell phone and disappeared to the basement, where he must have snatched the uniform."

Melanie's eyes widened. The Boston detective shared her concern.

"This guy walked into the room with a silenced Beretta, knowing *all three* of you were in it?" Jax said.

"No one knew I was Bureau," David stated matter-of-factly. "And no one knew I was coming. My guess is, that's what the phone call was about. Whether the shooter should proceed with an unexpected *third* person present."

"Versus the original targets of Larry Digger *and* Melanie Stokes."

"You figure the shooter was told it would only be a matter of time before Melanie met with Digger. So he waits—two for the price of one. Harvard MBAs aren't the only ones worried about efficiency in the work-place anymore."

Detective Jax shook his head, working a toothpick in the corner of his mouth as if it were his last ciga-rette. "That guy had to be bumming when he realized you were a Feebie. So much for quick and easy."

David finally cracked a ghost of a grin. "I'd like to think so. It may be the only good thing to come out of this day."

His gaze flickered to Melanie. She got it. Good ol' David Riggs was lamenting the loss of his cover. Now he'd have to explain why a G-man was posing as a caterer. That would be an interesting conversation. She was already sharpening her claws for it.

"Well, hope you don't have any travel plans, G-man," Detective Jax said, " 'cause this is our juris-diction and we're going to have *lots* of questions for you."

"I got my case to run too."

"Which will be my first question—"

"Detective, don't bother."

"Sooner or later—"

"Then find me later."

The two men exchanged steely glances. Finally Detective Jax granted David the first round of the pissing war, shrugging a little and switching the tooth-pick to the other corner of his mouth.

They decided to notice Melanie again, leading her out of the room so the photographer could shoot an-other roll of film. Someone in a white coat was run-ning a tape measure between Larry Digger's body and the open door, while the medical examiner arrived and began a preliminary examination of the scene. The business of death, Melanie discovered, took a lot of people to complete.

"We want you to come downtown now, ma'am," Detective Jax said. "We have a sketch artist we'd like you to work with so we can start circulating a picture to local doctors. Maybe the guy went in search of a little love and tenderness for his hand."

"I want to go home," Melanie said flatly.

The two men exchanged looks. "We'll talk about that downtown," David said, reaching for her arm.

"I don't think so. Last I knew, I wasn't under arrest, *Special Agent*. Which means I can do whatever I want. At this point I'm going home."

"Melanie, just listen to me for a minute—"

"Listen to you? *Listen to you?*" Her control began to unravel. "I don't even know who you are! Why were you at my house Saturday night. Did you know about Larry Digger ahead of time? Did you think he would show up? Or does this have to do with more than him? *Oh, my God.* Who are you really investigating? You used me!"

David managed to grab her arms. "Downtown, Melanie."

"No, I will not—"

He snatched a raincoat, covered her head, and dragged her toward a patrol car. Suddenly she was bombarded by the sounds of snapping cameras and four TV personalities competing for a story.

"Officer, Officer, do you have any leads?"

"What's the motive? Is this Mafia related?"

"Is she a witness? Or a suspect? Come on, give us a statement."

"Duck your head," David said calmly. "In you go."

He stuffed Melanie into the backseat, and seconds later the car was pulling away. The cameras continued frantically snapping last shots in preparation for the eleven o'clock news.

Larry Digger had finally gotten his dream, Melanie thought. The aging reporter was officially front-page news.

THIRTEEN

"I JUST NEED TO change clothes and grab my things," David announced nearly five hours later as he walked into his apartment and tossed his keys onto the couch. Melanie remained standing in the doorway, still so angry, she didn't trust herself to speak. She wanted to skin David Riggs alive. She wanted to stake him to a hill of red fire ants and cover him with honey.

If she wasn't so angry, she would be afraid.

"You're the target of a hired hit, Miss Stokes. Furthermore, you've seen the assassin, so he definitely can't let it go. We simply can't guarantee your safety if you return to your residence at this time."

Special Agent Riggs, who seemed to have taken personality lessons from a brick wall, had announced that he would watch her. They'd go to his apartment and pick up his things. They'd buy her some things. He'd take her to a hotel for the night. Problem solved.

Detective Jax hadn't even looked at her. Said if the FBI had the resources to spare, it was fine by him. So nice to finally learn her place in the world.

"It's not exactly Club Med," David muttered now, snatching up various items of clothing strewn across the floor. "I'm not home much."

"No kidding," she said sourly.

The color of David's apartment was hard to determine as most of the space was covered by clothes, magazines, and paper. Wadded napkins had been tossed on the parquet floors. A pile of unopened mail lay on the dining room table. Mounds of paperwork nearly obscured the laptop on an old oak desk. The place didn't have a stick of furniture that looked new or a plant that required care.

At least he'd hung two pictures. One was of Fenway Park at night, while the other was of some guy in an old-fashioned baseball uniform. There was also a line of baseball caps hanging on one wall and at least two baseball bats. Then there were the four movies piled on the floor next to the VCR: *Bull Durham, The Natural, Field of Dreams, Eight Men Out.* Apparently, the apartment had a theme.

Melanie sniffed suspiciously and turned back toward the sidewalk. "I'll wait outside."

"I wasn't expecting company." David scowled, then swiped up another towel. "Close the door, gimme a minute. It's not as bad as it looks."

"I don't think that's possible." But Melanie returned to the foyer and shut the door. Not a good move. The room was instantly cast in darkness. Her stomach rolled. Images of bloody Larry Digger pressed against her mind, and she felt suddenly very tired.

She pulled back the vertical blinds, seeking the reassurance of sunlight. David crossed the room and jerked the blinds shut.

"You're not really getting this whole notion of protective custody, are you?"

"There's nothing back there but woods."

"Someone can climb a tree and shoot you."

"Open your blinds, *Agent Riggs,* or I'm going to puke."

David pinned her with an intent gaze, but then it softened. "You all right?" he asked roughly, as if he wasn't used to being kind.

"Stop it," she ordered immediately. "No playing nice."

"I'm not playing—"

"Of course you are! You lied to me. You still haven't told me what's going on and you're keeping me from going home."

"I'm not the enemy. Jesus Christ, I just dodged bullets for you!"

"*For me?* Hah. You've been following me with your own agenda the whole time." She jabbed a finger into his chest, her temper building dangerously. "Give me some answers, David Riggs. Why were you at my house Saturday night? Who really was *Detective* Chenney? What the hell are you investigating and *what is going on?*"

"I don't know, goddammit. I don't." A warning gleam had come into his eye.

Melanie ignored it, leaning closer, angling up her chin. She wanted a fight, she realized. She wanted something other than helplessness and fear. And she wanted some reaction from him. Because she'd *liked* David Reese the waiter. He had seemed an ally of sorts, and it was pitifully true that these days she didn't have very many of them.

"*If this has nothing to do with you, Melanie, why does your godfather care about Trash's first kid?*"

David turned away. "I want out of these clothes," he announced curtly. "You probably need to change as well. Then we'll eat, and *then* we'll talk."

"Will you answer my questions?" she called after him.

"Only if you ask nicely."

"I reserve the right to be as nasty as I want—"

"No fucking kidding," David muttered, and disappeared into his bedroom. Two minutes later he was back in the hall, having exchanged his slacks and jacket for jeans and a gray sweatshirt, its sleeves pushed up. His dark hair was tousled, and he sported a five o'clock shadow to go with his glower.

He no longer looked like an FBI agent but like a red-blooded man. Dark hair smattered the backs of his hands, tendons wrapped around his forearms. Broad chest, narrow hips, grimly set jaw. A man used to control. A man who did things on his terms. Few friends. Fewer loved ones.

And, dammit, *that* was a type she knew too well. Her father running her life, Brian trying to protect her, William hoarding his secrets. Her godfather too.

David took a step forward and she caught a glimpse of the limp he was trying to hide. His expression remained shuttered. His hands fisted at his sides. Even in pain, he gave nothing away. Even in pain, Special Agent David Riggs shut her out.

He tossed her a pair of sweats.

"You change, I'll order the pizza."

Melanie nodded. Then, much to her horror, she burst into tears.

DAVID FETCHED A large pepperoni pizza and two dinner salads from Papa Gino's on the corner. He was back in his apartment in less than five minutes, and they sat down at his recently cleared dining room table.

Melanie seemed to have shrunk while he'd been away, her petite frame nearly swallowed by his old black sweat pants and red T-shirt. And she looked pensive.

The crying jag had obviously embarrassed her. It had scared the crap out of him. He didn't know what to do when women cried. Hell, he didn't know where to look. He'd felt out of his league, the way he'd felt since he'd driven Melanie to his apartment and realized he couldn't remember the last time he'd brought a woman home. It had been a long time ago. Back in the days when he could sleep through the night without his muscles locking up and making him gasp for air. The kind of experiences a man really didn't need to share.

They ate in silence for ten minutes.

Then Melanie said, "All right. Begin."

David took his time to finish chewing a bite of pizza. "You ask first. I'll see if I can answer."

"Oh, well, that certainly promises clear and coherent communication."

He grinned. "I'm a G-man. We're famous for clear and coherent communication."

Melanie thinned her lips disapprovingly. "Are you really with the FBI?"

"Yes."

"Do you really have arthritis?"

His jaw tightened. "Yes."

She gazed at him curiously. "They don't mind?"

"I can fulfill the duties required of the job."

"But aren't there physical tests—"

"I passed."

"And wouldn't other agents worry about being partnered with someone who—"

"I like to think that my sparkling personality more than compensates for such concerns."

Melanie rolled her eyes. "So what do you do?"

"White collar crimes."

"Like fraud cases, banking, money laundering?"

"There you go. The glamorous life."

"I see." She gazed at him levelly, and he suddenly saw the killer instinct spring to life in her eyes. "So that story about how you were a cop and then got arthritis . . . That was just a load of crap designed to earn my sympathy and make me easier to manipulate? Wasn't it?"

"I needed a credible reason for you to let me help—"

"Why not the truth? Or are agents famous for lying as well?"

"Yes, ma'am," he said in a steely voice. "We sure as hell are."

She leaned closer. "What about *Detective* Chenney? Bureau as well?"

"Yes."

"And the whole display of bagging the scene in my room? The candles, the toy horse, the questions you made me suffer through—"

"Bags are at the crime labs, information is being processed. It's a real investigation, dammit. I am trying to help you."

She nearly laughed in his face. "Then tell me what you were doing at my house, Agent. Finally give it to me straight."

David took another bite of pizza. Then he helped himself to a drink.

"I was investigating Dr. William Sheffield," he said, gambling that William's betrayal would have cost him Melanie's loyalty. "His *bingo* problem has led him to take loans from some very questionable sources and gained our interest."

Melanie looked suspicious. "Then how did you end up following me?"

"You have a history with the man. I couldn't be sure what your exact involvement with him might still be. Then you left the party with someone who obviously didn't belong."

"You thought I was making a payment for William? Oh, please, I wouldn't give him water in a desert."

"Of course."

Melanie sat back. He supposed he'd passed round one, because the intensity had drained from her face. Now she looked confused, then troubled. "If William was your subject, why get involved in my case?"

"I think your life is in danger."

"I think you're right. But why?"

"I started researching Russell Lee Holmes. I also requested the Meagan Stokes case file just out of curiosity. I haven't received the full case file yet, but I've gotten to read enough newspaper accounts to realize that there are a lot of unanswered questions about

Meagan Stokes. For example, did you know that Russell Lee was never convicted of murdering Meagan Stokes?"

"What?"

"He confessed only after he was already convicted of six counts of first degree murder. The police never made the case because they never had any physical evidence tying him to the crime. Your brother is right, that horse, that scrap of fabric in your room—they were never found twenty-five years ago. So where did they come from? Who would still have a toy last seen with a murdered child?"

Her eyes, those startling blue-gray eyes, went saucer wide.

"You think someone else murdered Meagan Stokes."

"Maybe, maybe not." He shrugged, but then his hunch got the best of him again. He leaned forward. "There was a ransom demand in Meagan's case, did you know that? Russell Lee didn't do that with anyone else. And it doesn't fit with him or his MO. How would an illiterate, uneducated man fashion a ransom note? That alone suggests that either it wasn't him, or there was someone else involved. An accomplice. Maybe someone close to the family who would know its schedule."

"You think someone in my family helped Russell Lee Holmes kidnap and murder Meagan Stokes!"

"I think something really bad happened twenty-five years ago, and it wasn't the fault of Russell Lee Holmes. That's what I think."

Melanie looked like she was going to hit him, and then for a minute she simply looked scared. She picked up her soda and took a long sip, her hands shaking.

David got up and cleared the pizza box from the table. When he sat back down, she'd composed herself once more, her face still pale but her shoulders square and her expression resolute. She said, "All right, Agent. Tell me your theory. Tell me exactly what you think is going on."

So he did. "Something bad happened twenty-five years ago to Meagan Stokes, something that involved more than Russell Lee Holmes. That's why the police never found more physical evidence. That's why it's possible that Meagan Stokes's toy and dress fabric appeared in your room. And whatever it is that occurred, it involved your family and friends. For twenty-five years they've kept quiet. They let Russell Lee Holmes go to the execution chamber and got on with their lives. But now someone else has entered the picture. Someone who's suddenly shaking things up.

"This person calls Larry Digger with a tip on how he can finally find Russell Lee Holmes's child. This person creates the altar in your room, sending a message about you trying to replace Meagan. This person is also sending notes."

"What notes?"

David hesitated, forgetting she hadn't known and worried he'd just tripped himself up. "Ah . . . your father got a note."

"When?"

"At the party. After you had your migraine. I overheard your father and Jamie O'Donnell talking. Your father said he found a note on his car. It said the same thing Larry Digger's caller said. *You get what you deserve.*"

Melanie was staring at him incredulously.

"Your father also knew Larry Digger was in town," David continued rapidly. "He mentioned it to O'Donnell, who said that someone named Annie was getting phone calls. Now, who do you think Annie is?"

"Ann Margaret? You think he means *Ann Margaret?*"

"She's from Texas, just like the rest of them. Now we know your father knows something and O'Donnell knows something and Ann Margaret knows something. Who else is from Texas, and who else is talking about receiving notes?"

"William," she whispered.

"There you go. That just leaves your brother and your mom. Your brother seemed as shocked as you were about the altar in your room. But what about your mom? Notice anything unusual with her?"

Melanie sighed. David took that for a yes.

"Last night. She came home late, nearly midnight. She said she'd been to a bar, told me how much I meant to her. But . . . but I could tell she wasn't actually saying what had rattled her so much. And she was speaking too urgently, as if it was suddenly extremely important I understand how much she cared about me. You know, the way someone might speak if they thought something bad was about to happen. Something . . . final."

David nodded. "So there's theory number one. Something more happened to Meagan Stokes. It involves all of your family in one way or another. And somebody else knows now. This person is rattling everyone's chains, bringing out all the skeletons. Which brings us to theory number two."

He said quietly, "You are theory number two. Whatever happened twenty-five years ago, you hold the key."

"My amnesia. The lost nine years . . ."

"Exactly. Larry Digger couldn't find Russell Lee Holmes's wife on his own, but he was betting you could help him. If we assume that you are Russell Lee Holmes's child, think of what could be locked up in your mind. Certainly someone seems to believe you know something important. Hence, the scented candles and objects you might know in your room, put there to trigger a reaction—"

"But I didn't remember anything clearly."

"Not yet, but you might. Therefore, you, like Larry Digger, have become a threat."

"Larry Digger was getting too close," Melanie said

slowly, filling in the pieces. "He honestly did have a lead, he was making progress. So someone, still trying to cover tracks, orders him killed. I might remember, so I'm a target too. But that makes no sense. If someone is pushing people to get at the truth, why order assassinations on Larry Digger and myself?"

"It's not the same person who ordered Larry Digger and you shot. It was someone else. This person wants the truth exposed but for whatever reason can't just announce it on his own. Maybe he has no credibility, maybe he's ashamed, mentally disturbed, I don't know. So he's trying to get at things in an underhanded way. However, he's also scaring the shit out of everybody. Think about it. Your family and friends have done very well for themselves. If the truth about the past came out now . . ."

He let the words trail off meaningfully, and once again Melanie understood.

"You think someone I know hired that hit man. Hired the hit man to kill Larry Digger, swipe his research, and eliminate me as well. Extinguish whatever clues might be locked in my mind. Erase, once and for all, any trace of what happened to Meagan Stokes. Christ . . ."

Melanie grew silent, grew haggard. She whispered, "It's a war, isn't it? Someone is trying to expose a secret no one else wants exposed. And I'm just the person in the middle, the adopted child who might hold the key to the truth behind a little girl's twenty-five-year-old murder. Oh, Jesus Christ, at this point, whatever is in my head, I don't want to know!"

"I don't think you'll have a choice."

"I always have a choice," she said firmly. She got up from the table, wiped it, washed her hands, paced, then sat down.

"I probably am the child of Russell Lee Holmes," she murmured. "The memories of the shack. The notes . . ."

"We could look at having Holmes's body exhumed

and do a DNA test. That would resolve it once and for all."

She nodded absently. "There are just so many inconsistencies. Why would my parents knowingly adopt Russell Lee's child—"

"Maybe they don't know. Maybe Jamie O'Donnell arranged it."

"How, by dumping me at a hospital and assuming Patricia and Harper Stokes would magically adopt me?"

"Whose idea was it to adopt you, Melanie? Did they ever tell you who suggested it first?"

"My mother," she said instantly. "She and I . . . we just sort of *clicked*."

"There you go. And it wasn't a random dumping. Your father did work there and was in the ER. Seems a fair bet that he'd hear about you, come see you for himself, maybe bring his vulnerable wife, who is hungering for a little girl . . ."

"Still leaving a lot to chance," Melanie muttered.

"Fine. Spin it the other way. Your parents did know you were the daughter of Russell Lee Holmes. They agreed to adopt you for reasons we still don't understand, and provisions were made. The night Russell Lee was executed, you're dropped off at the hospital where Harper Stokes just happened to be on duty while the rest of his family was in Texas watching an execution you would think he'd also want to see." He paused. "Larry Digger had a point about the coincidences. One or two is happenstance, but three or four?"

Melanie's gaze dropped to the table. She rapped on it with her fingers many times. But then she looked up, and there was a clearness in her eyes David hadn't expected. It nailed him in the solar plexus, made him conscious of her golden hair and citrusy perfume and those haunting eyes. . . .

She said quietly, steadily, "But even then . . . I still don't believe it, David. I don't. My parents didn't just give me a home, they've been *good* parents. Not reluctant, not grudging. Whatever I've needed, whatever I've desired, they've given it to me. If you assumed they were in on 'it,' whatever it might be, wouldn't they be resentful? Wouldn't human nature dictate that every time they saw me, they saw the man who killed their daughter? I don't care what that damn altar was trying to imply. I'm not a second-rate daughter. *My parents* have never let me *be* a second-rate daughter. That's the kind of people they are, David. That's my family. It must be relevant that I love them so much, and they love me."

"Hey, family is family," he tried. "Sure you care—"

"Somewhere out there I have a birth mother," Melanie interrupted. "I have a real name, a real birthday. If you believe Larry Digger, I could be on the verge of what every adopted child dreams about—discovering her birth parents. But I don't care. I'd give it all up, David, just to have my family back the way it was. I love them. I have always loved them. I will always love them. That is how I feel about my family."

David didn't answer right away. Faced with Melanie's earnestness, a trait he himself lacked, he studied the floor and the scuff marks made from all the long nights he'd spent pacing it.

"Loving wives take home abusive husbands all the time," he said finally, quietly. "They get strangled for their trouble. Loving parents bail their troubled kids out of jail and give them a second chance. Then they take a bullet to the head while they're sleeping one night. Love doesn't have anything to do with it in the end. It can't save a person's life. Just ask Meagan. I'm sure she loved your parents too."

He strode to the bedroom door, intent on grabbing his duffel bag, but Melanie caught his arm. He stopped but didn't look at her. He didn't want to see tears on her pale cheeks. For all his big speech, he wouldn't be able to handle that, and he knew it. He suddenly hated the fact that he always sounded so harsh.

"I gotta pack a bag," he grumbled. "We should go."

And she whispered, "My family is all I have, David. Please don't take them away from me. Please."

He pulled his arm free and walked away.

FOURTEEN

FTER DAVID DISAPPEARED into his bedroom, pointedly closing the door behind him, Melanie wandered the living room, rubbing her arms. Ever since the shooting of Larry Digger, she couldn't seem to get warm.

Now her head was filled with conflicting images. Her big, burly godfather whom she adored. Her strong, silent dad who'd always been there for her. Her fragile, tremulous mom, whom she loved beyond reason. Brian, her hero. Ann Margaret, her friend.

A person capable of harming Meagan Stokes. A twenty-five-year-old cover-up.

She tried to tell herself it was all a crazy mistake. Logic gone awry, conspiracy theory run amok. But her mind was too rational for her own good. She couldn't dismiss the altar and the pieces of evidence in her room. She couldn't dismiss Larry Digger's body and the shooter who had aimed right at her. She couldn't dismiss David's point that the police had never found any physical evidence tying Russell Lee Holmes to Meagan Stokes.

Melanie didn't know what to do. She was tired, frustrated, and overwhelmed. She longed desperately for the comfort of her own home, and for the first time feared it as well. She wanted to hear her mother's reassuring voice. She had no idea what she would say. She wanted her family. She was beginning to feel as if they were all strangers.

What were they so afraid of?

Nine o'clock on a Monday night. Melanie didn't have answers, so she took the low road and sought distraction instead. David's apartment boasted a bookshelf crammed full of cheap metal trophies. One had a plastic guy on top that seemed to be pointing a gun. The dust-covered brass plate declared the owner to be the Junior Champion, .22 Target Pistol 25 feet.

Tucked between it and six others were a collection of well-thumbed gun magazines and patches and bars still in their wrappers. Marksmen, Distinguished Expert, one said. So David Riggs was not only a loner but a gun aficionado as well. That didn't surprise her.

But the largest trophy turned out not to have a thing to do with guns. It was pushed all the way in the back, as if David couldn't decide whether to be proud of it or not. A baseball player was poised on top, bat positioned on its dusty shoulder. The brass plate at the bottom was worn, as if thumbed over and over again. The letters faintly proclaimed: Mass All-Star Champion.

She moved on to the picture of the baseball player on the wall. *Shoeless Joe Jackson* was scrawled across the lower right-hand corner. The name sounded vaguely familiar to her.

She looked at the picture of Fenway Park, then returned to the bookshelf and found a scrapbook.

The first picture was old, the edges crinkled, the color yellowed. The woman was young, dark hair neatly curled under at her shoulders, warm, intelligent gaze looking straight into the camera. David's mother, Melanie realized; she had passed on her rich hazel eyes to her son. She looked like a strong, sensible woman. The kind who ran a tight ship.

She disappeared from the scrapbook much too soon. The split-level ranch house with its olive-colored carpet and brown linoleum disappeared as well, the family portraits becoming a thing of the past.

David's mother died, and his scrapbook became about baseball.

Here was David Riggs, age eight and decked out in a Little League uniform. Here was ten-year-old David with his whole team. Here was David, with Steven and Bobby Riggs posed on a baseball diamond. Here was Bobby Riggs tossing balls to his sons, who were now taller, leaner.

Certificates appeared in the scrapbook, announcing pitching achievements. First no-hitter. Lowest number of hits allowed in a season. Best E.R.A. Then came the newspaper articles. "Promising Young Pitcher in Woburn" "Woburn High Grooming Best Ever" "The Major League Recruiters Arrive in Town—All Know They Are Eyeing the Riggs Boy."

And the pictures . . . Pictures of Special Agent David Riggs Melanie would not have thought possible. No grim expression or lined face. He beamed in color photos, posing enthusiastically with his glove, then in mid-pitch. He played with the camera. He winked at the crowd. He was the hometown hero and the photographs documented it diligently. Young David Riggs, who was going to go to the pros and make Woburn proud.

Young David Riggs, arching up on the pitcher's mound to catch a ball, his face so earnest, so intent.

Next shot. The ball in his glove, his body descending from the sky, and his face beaming with joy.

Next shot. David holding up the ball, showing it to his father, who was screaming on the sidelines. For you, Dad, his expression announced. And Melanie could read Bobby Riggs's reply in his exulted look, his parted lips. *That's my boy,* the father was screaming, *that's my boy!*

Melanie hastily closed the scrapbook. She had intruded too far. These were private photos of a private time that had come and gone. This was David with his family, and David with baseball, which seemed to be an even more personal relationship. She should've let it be. Everyone deserved their walls.

Of course, she opened the scrapbook and looked again.

God, he was magnificent when he was happy. The passion, the fire. She could see how that would make him a good federal agent, but as a baseball player . . . wow.

And then Melanie entertained the worst of all female fantasies—she wondered if she could make him smile like that, if she could fill his eyes with such primitive joy. If she could heal a man and make him feel whole.

This time she closed the scrapbook more firmly, then tucked it back in its place on the bookshelf. The images were emblazoned in her mind. She did her best to tuck them away as well.

The bedroom door was still closed. She passed by closely enough to realize that he was talking in there. Phone call. To whom? Then she had another thought. Whatever he was saying, it probably had to do with her case. Which was her life. Which was her business, dammit.

Melanie cupped her ear against the wood. She could hear every word.

David was giving someone a thorough dressing-down. "Sheffield did not just stay home all night, dammit. He told Melanie's dad he won last night, which means he was out gambling. And apparently while he was out gambling, someone broke into his house. We're not even sure if anything was taken, but they left a note. Now, I want to know what the note said!

"Yeah, Chenney. Do you understand now why sticking to your target is so important? Is this getting through to you yet? Just because people go home sick doesn't mean they stay home sick.

"Look, I wasn't sure what I thought of this either in

the beginning. The case did seem far-fetched. But we've moved way beyond coincidence at this point. We know Harper Stokes got a note. Melanie believes her mother may also have gotten a note. Now, I can't be sure, but I'm willing to believe someone played a game at Sheffield's house as well. We need to know exactly what happened there.

"No, don't break into his house. Go through his trash. It's much simpler.

"Okay, it's also messier, but that's the glamorous life. Sheffield works tonight, right?

"Yes, I want you on his tail. And stick this time, even at work I'm getting very curious about the hospital angle. So far our anonymous tipster seems to know exactly what he's talking about, so we may have much more of a fraud case than we thought.

"Yeah, yeah, yeah, I know you don't know anything. God, they gotta start getting you guys more training. Well, do you have a pen and paper? I'll give you a lesson for the day.

"Okay, pretend for a moment that our tipster is correct and they are installing pacemakers in healthy patients. Now, no single doctor or healthcare professional, no matter how brilliant, can summarily recommend a pacemaker. A cardiologist would have an opinion. The cardiac surgeon too. Then there's the ER docs who admitted the case, the nurses who attended the patient, and the anesthesiologist who would be monitoring all the patient's vitals and administering meds during surgery. All these people examine the patient, update the chart, and know what is going on. And that's assuming the patient never asks for a second opinion. Lots of people do, which means a whole new round of doctors reading charts and offering opinions.

"So first off, it can't be as simple as faking a chart or misdiagnosing. Hospitals are set up exactly so that kind of situation can't happen. Given that, our suspects are going to have to find someone who at least exhibits symptomology. Probably a patient who comes into the ER as a "chest pain—rule out MI" admit, which means a person suffering from chest pains that they want to make sure isn't a myocardial infarction. A heart attack, Chenney. Myocardial infarction equals heart attack.

"Now, following protocol, most ERs will slap an EKG on the patient, snap a chest X ray, as well as draw six to seven vials of blood to test for cardiac enzymes. But some of these enzymes can take twelve to thirty-six hours to show up, so even if the chest X ray is clear and the EKG good, a hospital will generally keep the patient for a day or so for observation, particularly if there is a history of heart problems in the family and the person appears at risk—overweight, high blood pressure, and so on. Now, City General has a notoriously aggressive cath lab, so their ER docs also send the patient to the cath lab to shoot the coronary—check for blocked arteries.

"In the cath lab they have to feed a catheter through the femoral artery to inject the patient with dye. They'll heavily sedate the patient for the process, then send the patient to ICU for recovery and monitoring. They're also going to keep the patient under sedation because they don't want him or her to wake up in the middle of the night and pull out the catheter. So that gives us our first 'opportunity' for nefarious deeds right there.

"At night in the ICU, the nursing staff is generally spread thin and focusing on the more critical cases. You have a recovery patient who is drugged and certainly not going to notice what's what. Someone could easily slip into a room, inject a patient with a drug or tamper with the EKG, and probably escape with no one the wiser.

"Ask around, Chenney. Have people seen Dr. Sheffield roaming the ICU a lot? That might tell us something right there.

"No, I don't completely understand what healthcare fraud has to do with Meagan Stokes, only that our tipster seems to know more than we do. Anything back from the lab yet?

"Two types of blood? Really? Jesus." David sighed. "This case just gets weirder and weirder. Other findings?

"Yeah, I know it's too soon, I'm being an optimist. Okay, have them do a DNA test. I imagine one kind of blood is probably Meagan Stokes's. As for the other, I haven't a clue. Has the Meagan Stokes case file arrived from the Houston field office yet?

"What do you mean, they said the case file is unavailable? It's a twenty-five-year-old closed file. It's gotta be sitting in the archives.

"A case file can't be just 'out.' The Bureau isn't a library, for God's sake.

"Shit, someone is yanking our chain. Okay, what about the Houston PD? Did they fax over their case file? Uh-huh. Give me a rundown.

"Life insurance. On two children. One million apiece. Shit. What kind of parents insure their children for a million bucks? Then again, it does explain a town house on Beacon Street.

"No evidence from Meagan ever found? Yeah, that's what I thought. Okay, when I get to the hotel tonight, I'll give you another call and have you fax the file over. Don't worry about Lairmore. I'm the lead agent, so I'll take the heat. Most likely he'll chew my ass tomorrow morning sharp, then we'll all get on with our lives. You all set with Sheffield tonight in the ICU?

"I know you're tired, Chenney. So am I. Unfortunately, whoever the hell is doing this seems to be in a rush to make up for lost time. We had Larry Digger showing up on Saturday, the altar assembled for Sunday, and a paid assassin appearing on Monday. God knows what's happening right now as we speak. We're just going to have to deal for a bit.

"I'm watching Melanie Stokes tonight.

"I know, I get all the great jobs. Enjoy tagging Sheffield. Bye-bye."

Melanie scurried for the sofa. The bedroom door swung promptly open and David came striding into the room, scowling and looking preoccupied.

"The lab hasn't had enough time for in-depth analysis," he stated without preamble, "but we do know there were two types of blood on the scrap of blue fabric in your room. They'll run some more tests."

Melanie nodded. David didn't offer anything more. He was standing in the middle of the room with his hands on his hips and his mind a million miles away. He was tired too, Melanie realized. There were fresh lines around his mouth and at the corners of his eyes. His skin was drawn too tight, making him look especially harsh and stern.

He crossed the room to his answering machine. The message light was blinking and he punched play. Then he strode back into his room for his duffel bag while the tape rewound. He'd just returned to the living room when the first message began.

"Hello, David, this is your dad. Still haven't heard from you. I guess the Bureau is keeping you busy? I'm reading now about some new methods for accurizing. Want to bring your Beretta in? I have some things I want to try out." Bobby Riggs's voice petered out awkwardly. Melanie could hear the man swallow. "Ah, well. Just thought I'd see if you were in. No big deal. Give me a call if you have a chance. I got tickets to the Red Sox—or . . . ah, hell. It's been a while, David. Just call sometime."

Melanie looked at David. His face was still a mask. The next voice came on.

"Riggs, check your goddamn voice mail. I have a message that you've been involved in a shooting. I got a Boston police chief talking to me about homicide. What the hell happened to eyes and ears only, Riggs? And what happened to procedure? When one of my agents discharges his weapon, I *do not* expect to hear about it from Boston P.D. In case you're still ignoring the voice mail, I want you in my office oh-seven-hundred tomorrow! And bring a damn report with you!"

The call ended abruptly. David merely smiled.

"That was my boss," he said easily. "Guess I won't be getting that corner office after all."

A clipped professional voice came over the tape. "This is Supervisory Special Agent Pierce Quincy from Quantico. Sorry to call you at home, Agent Riggs, but I was notified today by the Houston field office that you were requesting the Meagan Stokes case file. I would like to know why you are requesting this particular case file. You can contact me at   "

He rattled off the number. Melanie looked sharply at David, who had gone perfectly still.

"Shit," he said after a moment, belatedly scribbling down the phone number. "What the hell is this all about?"

"He said you requested the file."

"Well, no kidding. But first Houston tells me the file is unavailable, now I have Quantico calling me at home to follow up on my request in less than twenty-four hours. Why does everyone suddenly care so much about a closed case file? And, especially, why Quincy?"

Melanie looked at him blankly. "Would you like to translate for those of us who are merely personally at risk and not the trained professional?"

David shook his head. He still looked confused. Actually, he appeared nervous. He finally walked into the kitchen, grabbed a bag of frozen carrots, and slapped it onto his lower back. "You haven't heard the name? He was involved in the Jim Beckett case last fall."

"The serial killer who escaped from Walpole?" Melanie had heard of that case. There was probably no one in New England who hadn't locked their doors and windows when the former police officer and killer of ten women had broken out of Walpole. In his brief time of freedom, Beckett had managed to cut a broad, violent swath. She didn't even remember how many people he had killed in the end. It had been a lot.

"Quincy did the original profile," David muttered. "Served as the FBI consultant when the case team reassembled and was instrumental in plotting strategy. Beckett murdered an FBI agent, you know. There was some question about her role at the time, but Quincy stated she died in the line of duty, and if Quincy says she died in the line of duty, then trust me, all the bureaucrats have her listed as dying in the line of duty. After helping catch Beckett, he's violent crimes official expert *du jour* and about as politically untouchable as one gets in the Bureau. Basically, God himself just called about Meagan Stokes."

FIFTEEN

"WHY WOULD THIS expert call about Meagan?"

"There's only one way to find out." David held up the number.

Melanie faltered. Her chin was up, her shoulders square. Some part of her wanted to be strong enough. This was her family, and she would do anything for her family. She *owed* it to them.

The rest of her was feeling bruised and battered. She wanted the truth, but she feared it just as much. The truth did not always set you free. Sometimes it bound you to dark, bloody deeds and cost you the people you loved.

"Why don't you go into the bedroom," David suggested. "You can rest while I handle the phone call."

"No. I'm ready."

"You've had a long day."

"It's my family, David. I want to."

He was quiet for a moment, then he shrugged. But his look was different. More understanding, she thought, and that undid her a little. Heaven help her, but if David Riggs turned kind now, she would most likely fall apart.

He turned away before the moment became something neither one of them was prepared to handle.

He set up the speakerphone on the dining room table and they both took a seat. Though it was after hours, they got Supervisory Special Agent Pierce Quincy on the first try.

"This is Special Agent David Riggs returning your call." David hit a button on his phone base. "Just so you know, you're on speakerphone and Melanie Stokes is also in the room."

"Good evening, Ms. Stokes," Quincy said politely, then added to David, "Why is she part of this call?"

"I'm in the middle of a case that concerns her," David said tersely, "and it was for her that I requested information on Meagan Stokes. Why are you involved? Isn't this a closed case?"

"Yes. Thus, I was equally surprised to find a field agent from Boston requesting this information. According to your file, you work with white collar crimes."

David tensed and Melanie got the distinct impression she was in the middle of a pissing war where information would be doled out only in hard-to-earn pellets. As the junior agent, David got to go first.

"My complete involvement in the case isn't something I want to discuss right now," he said curtly. "But to get the ball rolling, Melanie Stokes is Harper and Patricia Stokes's adopted daughter. Two nights ago a reporter named Larry Digger—"

"The *Dallas Daily* reporter?"

"That's the one. He showed up and alleged that Ms. Stokes was the daughter of Russell Lee Holmes. Yesterday she found a shrine at the foot of her bed. It contained one red wooden pony, presumably Meagan Stokes's toy, a scrap of blue fabric presumably from Meagan Stokes's dress, and forty-four gardenia-scented candles spelling out the name *Meagan*. Then today Larry Digger was shot and killed. Now, why do you have the Meagan Stokes file?"

"Forty-four candles?" Quincy murmured. Melanie

could hear scratching sounds as he made notes. "Confirmation on the toy and fabric scrap?"

"At the lab now. Brian Stokes, the brother, has made an initial ID."

"Interesting. I don't see any mention of the police ever finding the red wooden pony or the blue dress. On the other hand, many items from the other victims were recovered from Holmes's cabin."

"Why do you have the file?"

"Down, Agent," Quincy said lightly, earning a fresh scowl from David. "I'm sorry if I sounded too intense on the message, but I just started researching Russell Lee Holmes as part of an internal project to develop our intellectual capital—"

"What's that?" Melanie whispered to David.

"He's researching Russell Lee Holmes to add his profile to the violent crimes database of information," David translated. "The Beckett case must have been something else, because the Bureau usually encourages internal projects only when they decide an agent's one wick short of meltdown."

"The more you deal in death, Agent," Quincy said quietly, "the more you learn the value of stopping and smelling the roses."

It sounded to Melanie as if the older agent spoke less out of wisdom and more out of regret. She began to like Supervisory Special Agent Quincy.

He said, "Special Agent Riggs is correct. In the violent crimes division, we maintain an entire database of information we've gathered from murderers, rapists, all the people you wouldn't want to invite over to your mother's for dinner. It is by analyzing and comparing these cases, these offenders, that we have been able to come up with the common traits and behavior characteristics we use to profile.

"As part of my project, I proposed that we go back and analyze famous historic cases. Last month I turned to Russell Lee Holmes. Imagine my surprise when halfway through this process I received a call about one of the files.

"Do you know much about the Meagan Stokes case, Ms. Stokes?" Quincy asked.

"It's not something my family talks about."

"Do you have any theories as to why Larry Digger approached you?"

"I was found in the hospital when I was nine. I don't have any memory of where I came from. That makes me an easy target."

"We've covered this ground," David said impatiently. "There are some reasons to believe Larry Digger's allegations. That's not why I requested the Meagan Stokes file."

"Then why did you request the file?"

"Because I'm not blind, deaf, and dumb," David snapped. "Because I can read between the lines, and just as you've probably concluded in the last few weeks, there are a lot of reasons to doubt that Russell Lee Holmes killed Meagan Stokes."

Even though she'd heard this theory once before, Melanie still found it jarring. Hundreds of miles away, however, Quincy did not seem startled.

"Very good, Agent. I have spent two weeks trying to figure out what to do. After all, there is no statute of limitations on homicide, and I am almost one hundred percent certain that Russell Lee Holmes did not kill Meagan Stokes."

"He was innocent?" Melanie asked.

"I would not say he was innocent," Quincy calmly corrected her. "I believe he did kill six young children. I doubt, however, that he kidnapped and murdered Meagan Stokes."

"Russell Lee Holmes was never tried for Meagan Stokes," David reviewed. "He was convicted of killing six other children, and confessed to Meagan's murder only later, after he'd been found guilty. He made that confession to Larry Digger."

"Why do you believe he made the confession?" Quincy asked David like a teacher quizzing a student.

"Because he was already sentenced to death. What was one murder more?"

"Hold on," Melanie protested. "Even if it didn't cost him anything, why would Russell Lee Holmes do someone a favor by confessing? He's not exactly a nice guy."

"I don't think he did it for nothing," David said, and for the first time, he wouldn't meet her eye. "I think he may have been given an offer he couldn't refuse."

She didn't understand. They had just had this conversation. Why hadn't he said this then? What new warped theory was cooking in that head of his?

"I think," David said slowly, "we just figured out why your parents may have knowingly adopted the child of a murderer. He covers their sin."

Melanie stopped breathing. She had the strange sensation that David's apartment was tilting and she was plunging headlong into the abyss.

"Melanie?" David asked quietly. She managed to turn her head. He was looking at her with genuine concern. It turned his eyes gold. Both gentleness and anger brought out the gold. Why had she never realized that before?

She suddenly wanted him to hold her, to feel those arms around her again the way he'd done the first night, when he had carried her away from Larry Digger, and the scent of Old Spice had made her feel safe.

Melanie looked down. She worked hard at getting the next breath, then the one after that. Slowly the knot eased from her chest, the pressure easing slightly.

"Why don't we take this one step at a time," Quincy said reasonably. "You've drawn some interesting conclusions, Agent Riggs, but you're new at this and don't have all the information yet. Ms. Stokes, are you certain you want to be part of this discussion?"

"Yes," she said hoarsely. "Yes."

Quincy began almost gently.

"In 1969, when Russell Lee Holmes kidnapped his first child, Howard Teten was just beginning to outline the techniques we call profiling. Without a framework for approaching such crimes, the local police and FBI handled the Russell Lee Holmes case merely as a murder investigation. They focused on *how* the crimes were committed, the modus operandi, instead of *why* the crimes were being committed—what need was driving the killer's behavior. This is an important distinction, Ms. Stokes, for a serial killer's MO can change over time. Maybe he switches from binding to drugging victims, but a killer's need, *control and domination of women,* will not change. This is called the killer's 'signature.' It will be the same at every single killing, from the first to the thirtieth, even if everything else about the crime seems different.

"In 1969, however, the police did not understand this principle of a killer's 'signature.' They mistakenly attributed a murder to Russell Lee Holmes based on a superficial MO, since they lacked the tools to analyze deeper, more significant issues of his pathology.

"Russell Lee Holmes hated poor white children. Are we clear on that?"

David nodded. Melanie managed a small yes.

Quincy continued. "Russell Lee Holmes never advanced beyond the fourth grade and was illiterate. He held a slew of menial jobs, was known for his nasty temper, and his last job review simply stated: 'He likes to spit.' Most likely Russell Lee Holmes hated poor white children because a very deep, very real part of Russell Lee Holmes hated himself. And he acted upon this hatred pathologically, picking out small, vulnerable girls *and* boys because in the most elemental way, he was trying to destroy his own roots. Russell Lee Holmes did not suffer from a conscience. He did, however, possess a great deal of rage.

"Now, as an illiterate, unskilled man, Holmes

could not exercise his rage in a sophisticated manner. The six murders were clearly blitzkrieg attacks. Holmes entered poor areas, which were undoubtedly familiar to him and in which he undoubtedly blended in, and simply snatched whatever child was easiest. Later, the police identified the shack he used to perform the worst of his crimes."

"It was out in the woods, wasn't it?" Melanie whispered. "Single room. Tightly constructed, not even a draft. The windows are dusty though, I can't see out. And cracked halfway across. I watched the spider walk along that crack."

"Ms. Stokes," Quincy said carefully. "I happen to have pictures of the shack in front of me, full color crime photos. I'm not sure what you are describing, but Russell Lee Holmes's shack had no windows. It was a simple, handmade structure, and I assure you, it had plenty of drafts. Several of the floorboards even came up. Beneath them was where the police found his stash of 'trophies.' "

Melanie stilled. "It's not . . . I'm not picturing Russell Lee Holmes's shack?"

"Absolutely not."

She looked at David. "Then maybe, maybe I wasn't there. Maybe I'm not—"

"Or Russell Lee Holmes kept Meagan someplace else."

"Or Russell Lee Holmes was not involved," Quincy said.

"Then why would I be in the room, seeing Meagan?" Melanie addressed David.

"I don't know. Maybe Meagan was kept in a different location, and for some reason you were also held there."

"Ms. Stokes," Quincy said, "when you say you can picture Meagan Stokes, what exactly do you mean?"

Melanie couldn't bring herself to answer. She looked to David for assistance.

"She's recently started to remember things. That's

one of the reasons we believe Larry Digger may have been telling the truth. Melanie seems to have some memories of being shut up in a one-room cabin with Meagan Stokes."

"What else do you recall?"

"That's all."

"But you've just started remembering, correct? Think of the images that must be in your mind. There are so many things we could learn from you, particularly about the Meagan Stokes case. Would you be willing to come here? I know some expert hypnotists who could work with you."

Melanie almost laughed. "Oh, yes, everyone seems quite fascinated by the 'potential' of my mind." Her lips twisted. "Except me, of course."

"Hypnotism, Ms. Stokes. In a controlled environment. I promise we'll take good care of you—"

"No, thank you."

"Ms. Stokes—"

"I said no thank you! For God's sake, it all happened twenty-five years ago, and I *do not* want to remember dying children!"

Quincy was silent, probably disappointed.

"Of course," he said at last. "Then let's review what we know based upon the police notes. So Russell Lee Holmes hated poor white children. He kidnapped them, he tortured them in his private cabin, and when he was done, he strangled them with his bare hands, another symbol of someone performing a deeply personal act of violence. He disposed of the bodies randomly, dumping them naked in ditches, drainpipes, and open fields. Again this fulfilled his need to denigrate the children, to cast them aside as proverbial rag dolls not worthy even of protection from the elements.

"In short, in every act he performed, he revealed his hatred of youth, poverty, and weakness. He revealed his hatred for himself. And then we get to the Meagan Stokes file."

"She wasn't poor," David said. "There was a ransom demand. And her body was buried in a forest, not dumped. It was decapitated."

"She was in the nanny's car," Melanie murmured, "parked in front of the nanny's mother's house. I thought that was considered a poor neighborhood."

"It was a lower income neighborhood," Quincy said carefully, "but I would still categorize it as up from Holmes's usual hunting grounds. And then, the victim profile doesn't fit. Meagan was well dressed, well groomed. She sat in a nice car and played with an imported toy. She was bright and well spoken. If Holmes was acting out a primarily self-destructive act, there should've been nothing about Meagan Stokes to trigger his blood lust. There should've been nothing about her that would've reminded himself of him."

"Maybe it was revenge," Melanie said. "The other children he hated because they were like him. He killed Meagan because she was above him."

"Possible, Ms. Stokes, but not probable. That is a distinct change in motivation, and it's rare to see a change in a serial killer's pathology. Now, in some cases, a killer may snatch a different type of victim because the desired target is not available. He prefers young, twenty-something blond women, but when the blood lust got too high, the killer 'settled' for a thirty-something brunette. But in that case the killer's need, hurting women, was not that particular and thus it was still fulfilled. For other killers, however, the victim profile is intrinsically tied with their signature. They don't want to just hurt women. They need to hurt 'loose' women, so the killer would never substitute a mother of three for a prostitute, even if the mother of three was more convenient. That crime wouldn't fulfill their need. For these men, finding the right target is like falling in love. They describe spending weeks, months, years, looking for the 'right one.' They start with the physical—in Holmes's case, young, undersized, dirty, and poor. And then they simply see her. The one who moves something in their chests. The one who makes their palms perspire. And they know—this one will be their target.

"Russell Lee Holmes falls into this group of men, and looking at the victim profile, I am not convinced there was anything about clean, vibrant, upper-class Meagan Stokes to evoke blood lust in Russell Lee Holmes. To put it colloquially, she was not his type."

"There are all the other factors," David interjected, looking at Melanie. "Such as how did an illiterate man fashion a ransom note?"

"Excellent point, Agent," Quincy said approvingly. "I have a copy of the ransom note in front of me. As the police argued in 1972, it is a very crude note with the words cut out of newspapers and the grammar incorrect. It was hand-delivered to the hospital where Harper Stokes worked, which was clever but simple. All of this fit their image of Russell Lee Holmes. However, if you break the note down, that argument does not hold. The words are too precisely placed for an uneducated, angry young man. There is no glue leaking from the edges, indicating a great deal of precision. Finally, there are no prints, no postmark, not even saliva used to seal the envelope. Whoever created this note was patient, intelligent, and very savvy about police procedure. None of that fits with what we know about Russell Lee Holmes."

Melanie got up and shakily ran a glass of tap water in the sink. "Then why can I picture Meagan in that shack? If she wasn't kidnapped by Russell Lee Holmes, why would she be there?"

"I'm not sure, Ms. Stokes. I'm honestly very curious about your 'memories' and what they might mean for the Meagan Stokes case. My overall impression is that it was a copycat crime deliberately set up by someone who knew something of Russell Lee Holmes's activities and who set out to emulate them, not out of neurosis, but out of a rational desire to cover up his or her own crime. When Meagan was kidnapped, it was already suspected that the children were kept alive and hidden away, so perhaps a shack was chosen to ensure that the crime fit as much 'physical evidence' as possible. In 1972 that was certainly enough to fool the local police and FBI.

"But as I mentioned before, profiling takes us beyond mere physical imitation of crimes to the underlying motivations and behavior. Once again, the Meagan Stokes case does not fit with Russell Lee's motivation. Which brings me to the final, overwhelming factor in my mind—the disposal of her body.

"All of Russell Lee Holmes's victims were stripped naked and dumped. Except for Meagan Stokes. She was naked, but her body had been wrapped in a blanket. She was not dumped, but carefully buried. She was also mutilated, her hands and head cut off. Are you familiar with decapitation, Agent Riggs?"

"What do you mean?"

"Decapitation generally happens for two reasons. One is logical. The cleverer criminals, generally psychopaths who are actively seeking ways to cover their footsteps, will remove the head of their victim to make identifying the body difficult. They will also cut off hands in some cases."

David said, "But we've already established that Russell Lee Holmes isn't exactly clever or logical. So what's the second reason?"

"Emotional. Sometimes, if a murderer feels guilty about a victim, suffers remorse or shame, he will mutilate heads or hands to depersonalize the crime. Decapitation can be an indication that the victim was close to the killer."

"Oh, God," Melanie said, already knowing what was coming next.

"In conclusion," Quincy said quietly, "the body was covered by either someone who was very careful, or by someone who truly cared."

"The parents," David filled in, then added almost savagely, "for the money, right? The million bucks."

Melanie looked at him, startled. "What?"

"Harper and Patricia Stokes had million-dollar life insurance policies on both of their children," Quincy provided calmly. "In fact, before Russell Lee Holmes confessed, the police were actively investigating Harper Stokes. The seventies were a tough time for him. He had lost quite a bit of money on various speculative deals, and without that life insurance policy he may have been forced to declare bankruptcy."

"You do not murder your own child for money!" Melanie shouted. "Not . . . not even for a million dollars! And if both of them were insured, why Meagan? Why not Brian? Oh, God, why not Brian?" She bowed her head, even more horrified. Of course Brian had probably thought of that before. Most likely her moody brother had spent most of the last twenty-five years thinking *Why not me?* And he had always been resentful toward their father, almost hateful. Had he known? Had he suspected? *Oh, Brian . . .*

"Wouldn't you just fake the kidnapping?" she cried. "Couldn't they have just faked Meagan's disappearance, held her in a shack, and collected the ransom money from the bank or whatever? That would fit with what I know—"

"Except how would they explain the money," David said softly. "If Harper and Patricia Stokes suddenly had a hundred thousand dollars, people would get suspicious. If they had lost their daughter, however, and received the life insurance, then everything was explained."

"Except their daughter is dead. They wouldn't do that. I know them, David. They are my parents and I swear to you they couldn't do something as sick as murder their four-year-old daughter for money."

"Ms. Stokes," Quincy interjected somberly. "I know you don't want to hear this, but based on what I've seen here, I think Meagan Stokes was decapitated out of guilt. She was buried out of remorse. And she was wrapped in a blanket out of love. Ms. Stokes, in only three other cases have I seen a child's body so carefully swaddled and buried. In all three of those cases, the killer turned out to be the child's mother."

"Oh, God."

"Serial killers do not have a need to cocoon their corpses in soft blankets. Protecting a child, however, even when it is too late, even when it is out of guilt, is a trait that is distinctly maternal. At this point, based on what I have read, I would reopen this case, Agent Riggs and Ms. Stokes. I would look at the family members very carefully. I would examine everyone's motives and exactly what was going on with the family in the summer of 1972, including all friends and relatives. And I would start with Patricia Stokes."

SIXTEEN

THE WALTHAM SUITES was a decent hotel. The two-bedroom accommodation was decorated in shades of blue and mauve with that fake cherry-wood furniture so many New England hotels favored. One bedroom was upstairs in a loft area, the other was downstairs across from the kitchenette. David placed his duffel bag in the lower bedroom—closest to the door—while Melanie roamed the living room, her complexion still the color of bone.

At the drugstore by David's apartment they'd gotten her some basic toiletries. The pharmacy chain didn't carry any clothes, so Melanie remained stuck with David's old T-shirt and oversized sweats. They made her appear small, particularly now as she stood at the dark window with her arms around her waist and her gaze focused on a moonless night. Outside, cars raced down the interstate. Headlights washed over her face briefly, illuminating her eyes.

"Well," David said at last, "what do you think?"

"It's fine."

He waited for her to say something more, but she didn't. David wasn't sure what to do. Ever since the discussion with Quincy, Melanie had slid deeper and deeper inside herself. Her eyes had taken on the flat look of a war veteran, her lips compressed into a bloodless line. She'd hit the wall, he figured, and now would either bend or break. Unfortunately, he couldn't figure out which, and it was beginning to scare him.

She turned on the TV. A brightly dressed anchorwoman gazed somberly at the camera while reporting, "Shots broke out in downtown Boston earlier today." Footage of the outside of the hotel filled the screen. People were gawking at the door. A few tourists were taking pictures. Little was known, and the ten-second report wrapped up without saying much of anything.

Melanie turned off the TV. She picked up a magazine, flipped through it, set it down. Next, she picked up an ashtray. Her hands were trembling. Christ, she had small hands. He couldn't imagine her shut up in some shack with the likes of Russell Lee Holmes.

David set his laptop down on the dining room table. He planned on working most of the night, doing more research, catching up on his paperwork. At seven A.M. sharp he and Chenney had to meet with Supervisory Agent Lairmore. The discussion wouldn't be pretty. Lairmore liked things neat and clean, investigations run like paint-by-number kits. That his healthcare fraud agents were now chasing a twenty-five-year-old homicide would not amuse him.

David walked into the kitchenette, tossed his supply of vegetables into the freezer, then hesitated.

His back hurt. Shit, it *throbbed*.

He wasn't sleeping enough, and he was under stress. He was shooting guns again, and recoil always did him in. Truth of the matter was, the Bureau had done the right thing by assigning him to white collar crime. He couldn't go racing down dark alleys in the heat of the moment. He couldn't leap tall buildings in a single bound. He did have a medical condition, and it was growing worse.

His life now boiled down to three fun-filled options each night: carrots, cauliflower, or broccoli?

He went with cauliflower, stuffing two bags in the back waistband of his jeans. When he walked out of the kitchen, he looked like an idiot, and he knew it.

Melanie was no longer on the couch. She'd returned to the window and had her hands pressed against the glass. There was something about her profile, haunted, stark, resigned, that sent him reeling.

David had a crazy flashback. He was nine years old, and his mother had finally come home from the hospital. She was lying on the couch in the living room with him and his dad and Steven around her. His dad and brother were smiling rigidly. Dad had explained it to them earlier—their mom was dying. Nothing more to be done. Now they must be strong for her. As strong as strong could be.

His mom ruffled his hair. Then she stroked Steven's cheek as if he were still a baby. Then she looked away, her gaze steady, accepting, and so racked with pain, it had socked the breath right out of David.

They were all trying to be brave for her, he'd realized at the age of nine, when really his mother was the brave one. They were trying to be heroes, when she already was one. Oh, God, his mother was a magnificent woman!

And a heartbeat later the cancer took her away.

David snapped back to the hotel room. Grown man, not a kid. Frozen vegetables strapped to his back. That familiar ache tightening around his ribs.

He wished he could stand more like a man for Melanie Stokes. *Goddammit* . . .

"You should get some sleep," he said tersely.

She turned toward him, her face expressionless. "What are you going to do?"

"Work. Tomorrow I got a meeting with my boss, then I'll follow up with Detective Jax. It'll be a busy day."

Melanie frowned. "And what am I supposed to do?"

"Stay outta sight, of course. Relax a bit. Sit back and smell the coffee."

"Sit back and smell the coffee?" She arched a brow, her voice picking up, her cheeks turning red. Maybe he shouldn't have sounded so flippant. "*Sit back and smell the coffee.* Oh, sure. In the last two days I've learned I probably am the *fucking* child of a *fucking* murderer, adopted by other *fucking* murderers to cover their own *fucking* tracks. Sure, let me spend the day with Juan Valdez. That sounds *fucking great!*"

David leaned back. Then his own temper sparked. So he didn't know all the right things to say. He was just a guy. An overworked, unappreciated, sexually frustrated guy.

"I'd take you to the office," he informed her coldly, "but the Bureau doesn't have day care."

Her eyes went wide. The pulse point on her neck began to pound. Her hands formed into tight fists, and the frustration ripped down her spine in a long, violent tremor.

He was suddenly breathless.

Melanie wanted to fight, he realized. She wanted to yell, she wanted to scream, she wanted to run. He could feel it all there, broiling, clouding her eyes.

Saint Melanie. Charitable Melanie. Perfect daughter, perfect sister Melanie. For the first time he got it. All the little bits of her—the angry parts, the resentful parts, the fearful parts—she swallowed back down because she was the adopted daughter and she couldn't afford to make waves. She couldn't afford to be less than Meagan.

Shit, he suddenly wanted to kiss her. He wanted to close the space between them, take her lips, and feel all those emotions explode beneath him. Wild Melanie. Hurt Melanie. *Real* Melanie. Fuck. He wanted the *honesty* of it, and that was the biggest lie of all.

"I want to be alone," she said abruptly.

"Still hiding? Still going to smile and pretend it's all right?" He took a step toward her.

"You're one to talk," she said, bringing up her chin. She was trying to look blasé, but he could tell she was pissed. Her cheeks were red and her eyes overbright. She looked gorgeous.

He took another step and she shook her head.

"No," she said fiercely. "Dammit, just *no*. I don't care how you look or if you smell like Old Spice. I don't care if it's been months since I've had sex. I don't care if fucking you would be a helluva lot better than thinking about Russell Lee Holmes—"

"So you've thought about it." His tone was blatantly triumphant, unforgivably smug. She looked mutinous.

"Of course I did. You picked me up that first day. Carried me. Made me feel safe." Her voice faltered. She made a wistful sound, and it lured him closer, made him hold his own breath. Then her lips thinned and she recovered herself with a vengeance. "But that wasn't real, was it, David? Not an act of kindness at all, but a federal employee doing his job. And you *lied* to me. I am so *tired* of everyone lying to me!"

"I did my job by covering my identity. Not all lies are created equal."

She laughed harshly. "Splitting hairs, that's what it boils down to. Splitting hairs. Oh, my God, my mother."

She sat down on a chair. David said to hell with it and went over to her.

She was stiff, resistant. He curved one arm around her, figuring if she belted him, it was his own fault. But she didn't hit him. She made a sound, the sound of surrender, then strong, capable Melanie Stokes buried herself in his arms.

Ah, Christ. She was so small, hardly made a dent against his chest. And all that silky blond hair and the soft citrusy scent. He did want to keep her safe. Lord help him, he wanted to be her hero.

He pulled her onto his lap and rocked her against him.

She did not cry. He figured she wouldn't. Instead, she fisted his sweatshirt, burying her face against his throat. He placed his cheek on the top of her head and wrapped his legs around her.

"I love them," she whispered. "They're my family and I love them. Is that so bad?"

"No," he said roughly. "No."

"They gave me everything I ever wanted. They played with me, they loved with me. They went to *garage sales* with me, for heaven's sake. The Stokeses at a garage sale. Surely that couldn't all be a lie. Surely."

"I don't know. I don't."

She gripped him tighter. And a heartbeat later she murmured, "I'm nine years old again, waking up in the hospital with all these lines and needles sticking out of my body, and this time there is no one to bail me out, David. This time there is no one there."

"Shh," he told her again and again. "Shhhh."

She started to cry. After a minute he kissed the top of her head. Then he kissed her harder, smoothing back her hair, kissing the tears from her cheeks. And then he was kissing her neck, her forehead, the curve of her ears. Anything but her mouth. He knew, they both knew, he couldn't kiss her mouth. Don't cross the line, don't cross the line.

She angled her head up and he grazed the corner of her lips, the tip of her chin, the point of her nose, the dimple of her cheek.

"More," she whispered, "more."

So he kissed her throat, small, nuzzling kisses, like they were hormone-enraged teenagers necking on the sofa. He drew her lobe between his lips and sucked. She sighed and shifted restlessly on his lap. He nipped her ear. She wriggled against his erection, and now they were both breathing very fast.

Her neck. She had a long, sexy neck. Her cheeks,

smooth as silk. He followed the line of her jaw, and then, as if drawn by a magnet, his lips were at the corner of her mouth again. He could feel her breath coming hard. Feel her tension, the tight moment of total anticipation. A slight turn, by either one of them, and the kiss would be had. Her lips beneath his. Her mouth opening hungrily. The wonderful, satisfying flavor of Melanie Stokes.

He could feel her shuddering. God, she was tearing him apart.

Slowly, very slowly, David drew back. They both sighed and it said enough.

He was the agent building a case against her father. He still hadn't told her the complete truth, and he'd been raised better than that. Even if he couldn't be the baseball player his father had wanted, he could still be the man.

"You all right?" he murmured after a moment.

"Better."

Her hips were still resting against his groin. She didn't seem to mind, so neither did he. It was one of the advantages of being an adult, David thought. You really could just hold someone.

He looped one long strand of her hair around his hand. She had beautiful hair. It smelled good too. He would like to bury both his hands in it and rub until she sighed.

His erection got a bit more uncomfortable, and he had to shift.

"You wear Old Spice," Melanie murmured. "I didn't think anyone wore Old Spice anymore."

"My dad," he said absently, and moved on to examining the shell-like curve of her tiny ear.

"You're close to him, aren't you?"

"Used to be." Melanie Stokes even had pretty ears. Probably had cute toes as well, he thought.

"Used to be?" She looked up at him.

"Things change. They just do."

"The arthritis?" Her gaze narrowed shrewdly. "Is your father the same great communicator as you?"

"I learned it all from him."

"Ah. And your mother isn't alive anymore to run interference. What a shame."

"I suppose." He'd never thought about it that way, but Melanie probably had a point.

"Tell me about your mother," she murmured intently. "Tell me what it was like to grow up with people you knew were your parents and would always love you."

David couldn't answer right away. The pain beneath her words tightened his throat too much.

She said, "Please?"

"I don't know. I don't remember much. You know kids. You inherit the world and you take it for granted."

"Did your mom bake cookies? When I was in the hospital, I always imagined a mom in a white ruffled apron baking chocolate chip cookies. I don't know why that image was so strong for me."

"Yeah, my mom baked cookies. Chocolate chip. Oatmeal. Sugar cookies with green frosting for St. Patrick's Day. God, I haven't thought of that in a while." He rubbed his forehead. "Uh, she read us stories too. And made us clean our rooms. She even laughed at my father's stories from work. And she was very pretty," he said. "I remember thinking as a little kid that I'd gotten the prettiest mom on the block."

"She sounds wonderful."

"Yeah," he whispered softly. "She was. I remember . . . I remember her and Dad coming home from the hospital, sitting us down. I remember they were holding hands and my dad was crying. I'd never seen him cry before. Then they said 'Cancer.' Just 'cancer,' as if that explained everything."

"I can't imagine explaining that to a child."

"Neither could they, I guess. Dad told us Mom

would need more help around the place, so Steven and I cleaned it up pronto that first afternoon. We actually tried to clean the bathrooms for the first time as a surprise. For the record, hand soap doesn't clean stainless steel very well. Then you should've seen us with the vacuum cleaner. Oh, boy."

"Made a mess?"

"Sucked up half the drapes. Who would've thought?"

Melanie smiled. "It was sweet, though, both of you trying."

"Yeah. Mom went to chemo, we stripped the kitchen floors. Radiation treatment started, we did the windows. She relapsed, we shampooed the rugs. People in the neighborhood were always dropping by with casseroles, pot roasts, you know, because surely with the little wife feeling 'blue,' the husband and sons would starve. They'd comment on how great the house looked, how great Steven and I looked. What brave little troopers we must be.

"My mom went back to the hospital. We stripped beds and soaped down furniture and beat out drapes and polished silver and she came home. She came home and lay down in our perfectly spotless living room and died. Because that's what cancer does. It kills you even when you have perfect little boys and a perfect loving husband doing everything they know how to do to keep you alive."

"I'm sorry," she whispered.

He shrugged awkwardly. His voice had broken more bitterly than he'd intended. He couldn't find a good flippant retort to break the mood. He never thought about this stuff. He just didn't. Now he felt overexposed.

He untangled Melanie from his lap, climbed off the chair, and put some space between them. He could tell she was a little hurt, but he couldn't find it in himself to go back.

"It's . . . uh . . . it's not easy to talk about it," he said.

"I know."

"I just, um, need some space."

"David, I know."

"Jesus Christ, how much bad luck can one fucking family have!"

Melanie didn't say anything this time, and he exhaled in one angry rush. Time to get a grip, Riggs. Time to pull it together. He settled his hands on his hips and looked around.

"It's getting late, Melanie. What do you say?"

"Yeah, I guess it is time for bed." She suddenly flushed. "I mean to sleep. In our own rooms. In our own beds."

"You take the loft. I should be close to the door."

"You really will be gone all day?"

"I have to go to this meeting. My boss is a little excited about me firing my gun. In contrast to what you might think, it doesn't happen every day, particularly when you work fraud."

"You did well," she said, looking impressed. "Got me out. Wounded the guy."

David grimaced. "After all the times I've fired at paper, I should've put it where it counted."

"He was a human being, David. Not paper."

"Well, we'll see if we both still think that when he comes around again. I'll try not to be in the office too long. Why don't you sleep in, order up a big breakfast. Take a day to relax and catch your breath again."

"Maybe," she said at last. Then, "I should call my mother."

"No—"

"Yes. I can't just stay out all night without even a phone call. You have no idea how much she worries."

David gave her a look. "Don't tell her what's really going on. Until we know who is involved and why, it's too dangerous. Got it?"

"I'll say I'm spending the night at a friend's."

"Don't go into details. Details will only get you into trouble."

"So says the master," Melanie muttered. She turned toward the stairs. The minute she saw shadows gathering upstairs, her shoulders sagged.

"Why don't I leave the lights on?" he said.

"It's okay. I'm a grown woman. I know better than to be afraid of the dark."

"Yeah, but I'm an FBI agent, and frankly, we're all a bunch of wusses. There isn't an agent alive who doesn't sleep with the light on. I swear."

She smiled. It was filled with just enough gratitude to tighten his chest.

"Thank you," she whispered.

Melanie climbed upstairs. David watched her, feeling the cold water trickle down his back as the cauliflower melted in his jeans.

He turned on his computer. Fetched the fax sent by Chenney earlier in the evening. Started poring over a twenty-five-year-old case file, courtesy of the Houston police.

His back throbbed, his eyes blurred with exhaustion. He made some instant coffee and kept going.

"I'm gonna get you," he muttered. "Whoever you are, after what you did to little Meagan, I'm gonna get you good."

SEVENTEEN

PATRICIA WAS ASLEEP when the phone rang. In her dreams she was Miss Texas again, walking the runway with her Vaseline smile and beaded gown. Look at me, look at me, look at me.

And they did. The men roared their approval. The women cried to see such beauty. She had captured the hearts of her home state. She had made her father proud, and as they placed the diamond tiara on her head, she wished it would last forever.

Fairy tales should never end.

She walked backstage and Jamie O'Donnell wrapped his arms around her.

"Beautiful lass, beautiful lass."

She giggled and kissed him passionately.

She looked beyond his shoulders and saw her daughter's headless body.

"Bad Mommy, bad Mommy, BAD MOMMY!"

Patricia jolted awake with a scream.

Blackness, thick blackness. The phone rang for the second time, and she fumbled for it. She could read the clock now. Just after midnight. Harper was still not home.

She put the phone to her ear.

"Mom?"

Patricia was so disoriented, she almost screamed again.

"It's Melanie," the voice continued, and Patricia, rattled beyond words, just nodded. Then she gripped the phone tighter and commanded herself to pull it together for her second daughter. "Yes, Melanie love? Where are you calling from? It's after midnight—are you all right?"

There was a pause, too long a pause. Patricia felt the first whisper of unease. "Honey, is everything all right?"

Did you find a note too? Did someone slip into your locked car? Threaten you, snatch you, kill you? Oh, God, please, baby, please, baby, tell me you're all right. I swear I never meant—

"I've just had a long day," Melanie said. "I met up with a friend. We went to a few bars. I'm going to stay here for the night."

Patricia frowned. Her daughter never did things like meet an anonymous friend for drinks and then spend the night.

"Are you sure you're all right? I can come get you. It's no bother. Really."

"I'm fine."

"Are you having another migraine? Your father and I have been worried about you."

"You have?" She sounded genuinely surprised.

"Of course. Melanie, I don't know what's going on. You're calling me in the middle of the night, and you don't sound like yourself. Please, sweetheart, if you need to talk, if you've done something and now you need a shoulder to cry on . . ."

Her voice ending pleadingly, maybe desperately. Suddenly she had that same tightness in her chest she'd gotten the day she'd come home to police cars surrounding her house and a man she'd never met before calmly telling her they were doing everything they could to find her daughter.

"Melanie?" she whispered.

"Do you remember the first day you came to the hospice?" her daughter asked suddenly. "Do you remember the first time you saw me?"

"Of course I do. Why—"

"When I looked at you, Mom, I remember thinking you were so beautiful, so lovely. I desperately wanted to be your little girl. I don't even know why. I just did. What did you think when you looked at me?"

"I . . . I remember being very impressed, Melanie. You were such a small child, abandoned, no name, no memories. You should've been terrified, but you weren't. You smiled bravely. You told little jokes and made other people laugh. You looked . . . you looked strong, Melanie. You looked like everything I had always wanted to be."

"But why adopt me? Had you and Dad spoken about adopting a child before?"

"Well, no . . ."

"Then why change?" Melanie's voice had gained urgency. "Why suddenly adopt a nine-year-old girl?"

"I don't know! It was like you said, I suppose. The minute I saw you, I wanted you too."

"Why, Mom? *Why?*"

"I don't know!"

"Yes, you do, dammit! I want to hear it! Why me?"

"It doesn't matter—"

"Yes, it does! You know it does. Tell me. Tell me right now. *Why did you adopt me?*"

"*Because you looked like Meagan!* All right? Are you happy? Because when I saw you I thought of Meagan, and then I had to have you. I just had to have you—" Patricia broke off. She realized what she had said. The silence on the other end confirmed it. Oh God, what had she done?

"Meagan," her daughter said quietly. "You looked at me and you saw Meagan."

"No, I didn't mean that! Melanie, please, you confused me, you badgered me."

She didn't seem to have heard her. "I got a family

because I looked like a murdered little girl. The house, your love . . . All along you just wanted Meagan back."

"No!" Patricia cried. "No, that's not what I meant—"

"Yes, it is, Mom. Finally we are getting to the truth. Why is it so hard in our family to get to the truth?"

"Melanie love, listen to me. I am human. In the beginning . . . in the beginning maybe I was confused. Maybe I did see what I wanted to see. I *know* you are not Meagan. Remember when I dressed you up in those lacy dresses and did your hair? Remember what that did to you? And I saw it, Melanie. I realized how much I was hurting you. And I let it go. I realized I wasn't looking for Meagan after all. She was gone, but through God's good graces, I had gotten another little girl, a different little girl, Melanie Stokes, who likes used clothes and garage sale furniture. And I discovered I genuinely *loved* Melanie Stokes. You healed me, honey. You are the best thing that ever happened to me, and I swear to you, Melanie, your life has not been a lie. I love you. I do."

There was no answer. Just more chilling silence that signaled her daughter's doubt, her daughter's hurt.

Patricia closed her eyes. A tear trickled down her cheek. She didn't wipe it away.

"Melanie?" she whispered.

"Did you really love Meagan?"

"Oh, heavens, child. More than my own life."

More silence. "I . . . I have to go now."

"Melanie, I love you too."

"Good night, Mom."

"Melanie—"

"Good night."

The phone clicked. Patricia was alone in the darkness.

She thought of those warm, sunny days in Texas with the first daughter she had loved so much. She thought of the note in her car. She thought of her son, no longer speaking to his father. She thought of Jamie O'Donnell and all the sins that never could be undone.

She whispered, "No more, Lord. This family has paid enough."

DR. WILLIAM SHEFFIELD slept on the empty hospital bed the way he'd learned when he was an intern. Then the hand on his watch hit three A.M., and the tiny bell began to chime.

He sat up smoothly, going from deep slumber to instant wakefulness the way only a doctor can. He felt a faint hammering in the back of his skull. The whiskey, of course.

He'd brought a pint into the hospital with him earlier, finding a back room and spending hours bolstering his courage, fingering the gun he now wore beneath his white lab coat. He wasn't thinking of what he'd found in his house last night—piles of healthy pink organs and a shiny red apple on his bed, and on his bathroom mirror the words *you get what you deserve* scrawled in blood. The whiskey warmth had carried him to his special place, where he was the golden boy, the perfect anesthesiologist, the man who always won at the roulette table with his lucky number eight.

"Just a few more," Harper had repeated earlier in the day.

It's too risky, William had insisted.

Nonsense, Harper had said briskly, but William could tell he was scared too. The last few days, calm, controlled Harper Stokes hadn't seemed so calm or controlled. William had even caught him glancing over his shoulder from time to time, as if he expected to find something bad behind him.

"Three more, tops," Harper had finally said. *"You can handle it, William. Your credit card debts will be clear and you can start over, clean slate. Still making*

*over half a million as an anesthesiologist. As long as
you don't resume gambling, you should be able to live
a very good life, without anyone being hurt or anyone
being the wiser. That's what you've always wanted,
isn't it?"*

That was what William had always wanted. The
fancy house, the fancy car, the fancy clothes. Every
symbol of success dripping from his wrist, his feet, his
body. So William had agreed. He'd had his whiskey,
and an hour earlier he'd walked into the ICU, and in
plain sight of God and everyone, he'd injected a vial
of propranolol into the candidate.

Now he dug into the pocket of his lab jacket and
fingered the second needle.

He stepped out into the hall.

At three in the morning the hospital had adopted a
quiet, somber state. Lights were dimmed for patients.
The nurses talked softer. Machines pulsed rhythmi-
cally. There was no one in the halls as William slipped
into the ICU.

The candidate had been admitted that morning.
That's how William categorized them in his mind:
Candidates.

Tonight's candidate was a sixty-five-year-old male.
Healthy. Active. History of heart disease in the family—he'd watched his father drop dead of a heart attack at fifty—so at the first signs of chest pains, the
man had dialed 911 and hopped a ride to the ER.

He'd gone through the whole medical process, including a fluoroscopy, which had revealed he didn't
have any blocked arteries. Now he was drugged in the
ICU to keep himself from pulling out the catheter. His
heart monitor looked good. They still weren't de-
tecting any dangerous cardiac enzymes, and most
likely he'd be released in the morning, none the worse
for the wear.

Except an hour ago Dr. William Sheffield had injected him with the beta blocker propranolol, causing
temporary heart failure that had been reversed only

by the nurse administering .5 milligrams of atropine. That had been round one. Now it was time for round two, and the overworked nurse was once again out of the room, checking on someone else.

It was the fault of budget cuts, William thought dully. The fault of stupid nurses who didn't protect their charges from people like him. The fault of paranoid candidates who thought they could still eat pepperoni pizzas and garlic bread without repercussions.

The fault of everyone else but him. He was just a lonely, abandoned kid trying to make his way in the world. The rest of them should know better.

William grabbed the T-injection port on the IV and stuck in the second needle.

The candidate's heart rate plunged to below thirty beats per minute and the heart monitor screeched red alert.

William hightailed it for the door. He was just about to pass through, when he spotted the nurse racing down the hall, a second just coming around the corner behind her.

Shit, they would see him. How to explain leaving the room? What to do?

Hide. William dropped to the floor and rolled beneath a pile of soiled sheets just as one of the nurses rushed into the room.

"Come on, Harry, come on," the nurse was saying. "Don't you do this to me again."

The second nurse arrived on the scene. "I got a pulse."

"He's still breathing, what's the blood pressure?"

The rasping sound of the blood pressure cuff. The nurse cursed at the reading while the blood monitor alarm still screeched because Harry's heart refused to speed up.

"We need atropine," the first nurse declared. "Second time tonight. Come on, Harry, what are you trying to do to us? We like you here, I swear it."

She rushed out, then returned moments later. William heard her tap the needle to remove air pockets.

The atropine, he guessed. Please, please, don't let her drop the needle and bend down to pick it up.

"Come on, come on, come on," the first nurse muttered. Abruptly the beeping stopped. The atropine had successfully stimulated the heart rate back to normal.

"Well, he's stable for now," the first nurse said with a sigh.

"Have you called Dr. Carson-Miller?"

"Not yet, but I'll give her a buzz now. This is Harry's second attack in just three hours. That's not good."

"Anything you need me to do?"

"No, I'm all set. Thanks, Sally."

"Anytime. M&M's at four, right?"

"Wouldn't miss it for the world."

Sally exited. The first nurse picked up the phone and called the on-duty cardiologist.

Once again everything proceeded as planned.

Harper had explained it to him two years ago. *What is the weakness of a hospital? The fact that it's all routine. Each crisis has a process. Everything we do is planned and predictable. In the end, medicine is much more cookie-cutter than doctors care to admit, and we can exploit that.*

"He's gone bradycardic twice now," the nurse was explaining to Dr. Carson-Miller, no doubt having woken her up from her sleep in another empty hospital room. "I've administered atropine both times to restore rhythm."

William knew the cardiologist's response. "Twice, huh? Keep Harry NPO. We'll have his doctor check him out again in the morning, and bring in Dr. Stokes for a consult. Glance at his day, all right? Good night."

The phone clicked. William managed to breathe again. Everything was done. He still felt hysterical but wasn't sure why. After all, it went just like all of them went, smooth as glass. Inject twice, giving the candidate two bradycardic episodes. Cardiologist does the sensible thing and recommends the installation of a pacemaker to regulate the heart, Dr. Harper Stokes agrees, and it's done.

Why wouldn't the nurse leave now? William needed her to leave now.

He heard footsteps, loud, ringing footsteps coming down the hall. Men's shoes appeared in view. Brown suede Italian loafers.

"I'm sorry, sir," the nurse said immediately. "But you can't just walk into the ICU."

"Um," the man said. "I know . . . this is for family only—"

"During visiting hours," the nurse said firmly. "These aren't visiting hours."

"Ah, yes, um, I know. But I'm with the FBI . . ."

William bit his lower lip.

"I'm a friend of this guy. I mean, he's an old friend of the family. I understand he had some chest pains today and was rushed to the ER. We'd heard it was nothing, but then I found out he was in the ICU. I promised my pop I'd check in on him. Of course, my job doesn't let me come during normal hours. I was just gonna glance in, but the lady at the desk said he'd been having problems. Can't you at least tell me what's happening."

The man was lying, of course. Even a four-year-old could tell the man was full of shit. FBI agent appearing in the hospital at three A.M. to look in on a "friend"?

And then William understood. That's what the note had said—*You get what you deserve*. And the organs, of course, the organs were a symbol of what he and Harper were doing. Someone knew. Someone had sent the agent for him. At any minute the agent would make a pretense of dropping his gun, bend down, and shoot William.

You've been a bad boy, a very bad boy. Bad Billy.

"Oh, dear," the nurse said. "You really can't be in here. I'll have to ask you to step outside."

"But is he all right?"

"Mr. Boer has had a rough night, I'm afraid. Most likely he'll have surgery in the morning, but his doctor can tell you more about that."

"He needs open heart surgery!" The man sounded both stricken and triumphant.

"Well, he might."

"Please, nurse, tell me exactly what happened."

The feet started moving. The nurse was ushering the man to the door. But she was also beginning to explain.

William lay transfixed.

You get what you deserve.

Slowly he reached beneath his arm and pulled out his gun. He took off the safety.

He was ready, he promised himself. He wasn't some scared, spineless kid anymore. He'd learned a lot growing up as an undersized boy in a Texas orphanage.

Time to start thinking, William. Time to take control.

You get what you deserve.

William made his decision. If that's the way this thing was going to be played, he'd play it. Dr. Harper Stokes might think of William as harmless, maybe even a fall guy, but Dr. Stokes hadn't seen nothing yet.

EIGHTEEN

I N A DARK suite of the Four Seasons, just across from the Public Garden, just across from the Stokeses' Beacon Street town house, Jamie O'Donnell sat on a blue velvet sofa, brandy snifter in one hand, TV remote in another.

An old goat like him shouldn't be surfing the channels with the lights out. He should turn off the TV, go to bed. Snuggle up with Annie and savor the soft sound of her breathing. Beautiful woman, Annie. The best thing that had ever happened to him.

He remained in front of the TV, flipping the channels.

In many ways Jamie considered himself a simple man. He'd worked hard all his life, fighting his way up from poverty tooth and nail. He'd killed men and he'd seen them die. He'd done things he was proud of, and he'd done things he knew better than to think about late at night. You did what you had to.

He'd arrived in Texas at the ripe old age of thirteen. He started working the oil fields when he was just fourteen. By the time he was twenty he'd developed the broad shoulders and thick neck of a day laborer. His face was generally stained black, his nails too. Definitely not a pretty boy, but he'd never let it get in his way.

Come sunset, Jamie was always the first person off
the fields, into the showers, and then into town. College campuses, that's where he liked to go. College
campuses were where he could dream. And that's
where he'd met Harper Stokes.

Introduced by mutual friends, they'd sized each
other up immediately. Shrewd Harper had recognized
that Jamie didn't fit in—no way was this thick, dark
man a student. In turn, Jamie had known that Harper
didn't fit in—no way was this thin, overdressed
Poindexter really an aristocrat. They were the outsid-
ers, and they both knew it. So they spent the next few
months competing against each other to see who
would break into the golden clique of old money.
They schemed against each other and ridiculed each
other and somehow, along the way, they ended up
friends.

Harper liked to talk of money even back then. He
was obsessed with what other boys wore, what other
boys drove. Jamie understood. He'd spent enough
time in the oil fields to know he wanted to be someone someday too.

Harper lectured him nonstop about the power of
education, the proper way to talk and dress. Jamie
figured he might have a point. He cleaned up a little.
Then he taught Harper how to throw a proper right
hook. Now, that was something every man ought to
know.

And then on Friday nights, the mutual education
delved into deeper grounds. Bookish Harper, desperate for the perfect upper-class wife, couldn't even get a
date. Jamie, on the other hand, went through women
by the dozen. He adored them, and they sure as hell
adored him. So every now and then he'd try to send
one Harper's way. It seemed the least he could do.

Then Patricia walked into both their lives.

Ironic that the things men would do for love could
be so much worse than the things they'd do out of
hate.

Life worked itself out. Jamie knew that now. In many ways he and his old friend had gotten exactly what they wanted. Harper lived in a Boston town house. He had his showcase wife, his golden children, his glowing reputation. No third-generation blueblood would question the great Dr. Stokes these days.

And Jamie couldn't complain either. He jetted around the globe, he built a business empire. He stayed in all the right places, met with all the right people. Sure, not all his friends belonged in polite society. But he had power now. No one was getting rich off his sweat but him.

Two old men. So many years the wiser.

Perhaps when all was said and done, the biggest lesson of all was that familiarity did breed contempt.

One hour earlier Harper had called him on the phone, rousing him from his slumber. Harper's voice had been too calm. His anger too quiet.

"What are you doing, O'Donnell? It's been twenty-five years, I've kept my end of the bargain, and we are much too old for this shit."

Jamie had yawned. "Harper, it's two in the morning. I don't know what you're talking about, and I don't feel like playing guessing games—"

"The note in my car, dammit. This little vendetta against William. Breaking into his house to plant a pile of pig organs? Classy, O'Donnell. Just plain classy."

"Someone left a pile of pig organs in William's house?" Jamie laughed. "Did the poor boy get sick? I bet he did. I would've paid to see that, you know. I've always hated that spineless bugger."

"Oh, cut the crap. I want to know why you're doing this. Dammit, we all have too much to lose."

"You got it all wrong, sport. I don't know what the hell is going on or who the hell is doing it, but as of tonight, I also joined the club."

"*What?*"

"I got a present too. Hand-delivered to the concierge downstairs. Wrapped nicely, I have to say. The ribbons even made those pretty little curlicues. You'd like it, Hap, you would."

"What was it?" Harper sounded perplexed. He'd never liked the unexpected, and it was stealing his headwind of righteous rage.

"I got a canning jar. And floating in it, in some kind of shit I just don't want to know, is a cock and balls. A penis. A pickled penis."

There was a moment of horrified silence, then Harper laughed. Then his voice grew cold. "A castrated penis, how charming. Tell me, Jamie, do you still dream about her? Do you still lust after my wife?"

"For God's sake, Hap, I'm telling you again, I'm not the one responsible for what's going on. It's been decades, man. I've moved *on*."

"Ah, decades, of course. I suppose even beauty queens don't look quite the same after thirty years—"

"You're an idiot, Harper."

"That's what you'd like to think. But I'm the one who won the girl in the end, aren't I? And *I know* that still galls you, O'Donnell. You just can't handle that you've never understood Pat any more than you've understood me."

"Hap, you're missing the point."

"What point?"

"Somebody knows, Harper. After all these years, somebody knows about Meagan."

Harper shut up. He turned his attention to business, and together they ran through the facts. It wasn't encouraging. Harper had received a note. William had gotten a pile of organs and a note, and Jamie now had a pickled penis. Plus there were the hangups Annie had been receiving. Finally, Larry Digger was in town after all these years.

"It could be him," Jamie said after a moment.

"He doesn't have the imagination. Never did."

"What about Patricia? Has she received anything?"

"Hasn't said a word to me."

"She wouldn't say anything, Harper, at least not to you."

Harper didn't argue the point. No matter what he liked to say, his marriage had fallen a long way from being a love match over the years, and they both knew it. "She'd tell Brian though," he said at last. "And Brian would be angry enough to tell me."

"Even now?"

"I think you know as well as I do, O'Donnell, that my own son hates me more than ever. I would think that would make you happy."

"No," Jamie said honestly. "It doesn't."

Harper cleared his throat. He was shaken up about his son. Handling it badly, in Jamie's opinion, but genuinely shaken up. That made Jamie feel something he wasn't prepared to feel after all these years—pity.

Sometimes he hated Harper Stokes. He saw all the things Harper did that his family knew nothing about, and at those times he thought Harper Stokes could very well be the devil. Then there were moments when he confused even Jamie. Harper did seem to love his son. He had been honestly betrayed by Brian's little announcement.

"Melanie's migraine," Harper suddenly said.

"What about it?"

"I assumed it was due to stress, but what if it's not? Melanie hasn't had a migraine in ten years, not even when she split with William. So why now? Unless it's more than just stress. Unless it's her memories."

"It could be. It could be."

Jamie couldn't say anything more. He could tell Harper was equally spooked. Her memory was the wild card, the one thing that could undo it all. In the beginning they'd obsessed about it constantly. But after twenty-five years, all of them, he supposed, had grown comfortable.

"The truth has a life of its own," Jamie said at last.

"Maybe the only real surprise is that it took it this long to find us again."

"Who the hell could be doing this?" Harper exploded.

"I don't know."

"What about you? Or maybe Brian?"

"What would we possibly have to gain, old man? How could we come out ahead? Melanie would hate our guts, and maybe you don't care, but I know I do. And I'm sure as holy hell that Brian does."

"It's too late, O'Donnell. All of us have gained too much to lose it all now. I'm taking the family to Europe, that's it."

"Europe?"

"Oh, I didn't tell you?" Harper's voice grew innocent, and Jamie knew his old friend was moving in for the kill. "I asked Pat this morning. We're taking the whole family, including Brian, on vacation. Just gonna pack up our bags and go, to hell with everything. Very romantic, Pat said. She seems quite excited about it. I know I am."

Jamie didn't say a word. He simply gripped the phone tighter and listened.

"Don't you get it yet, *sport?* Patricia loves me. She's always loved me. I do know how to make her happy, O'Donnell. I am *just her kind*. So take care of this *person,* okay? We both know that getting dirty is your line of work, not mine."

Harper hung up. But Jamie whispered into the phone anyway. "Yes, she's always loved you. But you've never *cared,* old sport. You got the goddamn perfect family and you've never, ever *cared!*"

He slammed down the phone. And then he simply felt tired.

Four A.M. A one-minute roundup of local news came on. Jamie watched the report of a shooting in a downtown hotel. Reporter Larry Digger was dead.

Jamie froze. Harper had not mentioned it. Jamie certainly hadn't arranged it. What was going on?

He turned up the volume. The gunman had escaped and was being considered armed and dangerous. A sketch flashed on the screen and Jamie recognized the face.

He hurled the remote across the room and watched it smash into pieces. It wasn't enough. He tipped over the glass coffee table and listened to it shatter.

"You fucker. You panicked, shitless, spineless fucker. How dare you betray me like that? *How dare you betray me!*"

The bedroom door opened. Ann Margaret stood there, wearing a white bedsheet and looking at him in confusion.

"Jamie?"

"Go to bed!"

Ann Margaret didn't move. "Jamie, what's wrong?"

"Get away. Just get away."

Ann Margaret moved closer. Then she said calmly, "Nonsense, Jamie. There is nothing you can do that I can't handle. I love you, sweetheart. I do."

Jamie hung his head and groaned.

He knew he shouldn't. He did it anyway, crossing to her in three strides, his chest thundering, his body covered in sweat. He took her in his arms and he was at once awed and humbled.

This woman had her own kind of beauty and her own kind of strength. This woman had an indomitable spirit and a tough, sensible shell. No pedigrees, no fancy words, no phony pretenses. She was right; whatever he did, she could handle. Neither of them was better than the other, and neither of them was worse.

And he loved her for that. He loved her deeply, and it was one of the few things in life that scared him.

Jamie pulled out of her arms. There were things he had to do and they were errands best done in the dark.

The TV was still on, casting its ghostly light on the

room. He'd left the canning jar out in the open without thinking. Ann Margaret suddenly spotted it.

"Jamie?" she whispered.

He closed his eyes. "It came today," he said gruffly. "Someone's sick idea of a joke, I guess."

"It's about her, isn't it?"

"Annie, it was a long time ago—"

"But not long enough, Jamie. Not so long ago that someone still isn't remembering, that someone still doesn't want to see you pay."

Jamie couldn't reply to that.

"Do you still love her?"

"No, Annie, I don't."

"Did she get an adulterer's penis? Maybe a chastity belt?"

Jamie took her arm, forcing her to look at him. "Annie," he said softly, "it's not just about Patricia."

"How do you know? *What is going on?*"

"Harper got a note," he said steadfastly.

"What kind of note?"

"The kind that says you get what you deserve. Plus, Larry Digger is in town and Melanie is having migraines and, Annie, William got . . . he got a note too. 'You get what you deserve.' "

"Oh, God." Her tough, sensible shell shattered. "Why doesn't it ever end?"

"I don't know. Must just be the way of things, I suppose. Some people get a good life, and some people don't."

Jamie strapped on his gun. "Don't let anyone in, Annie, and don't answer the phone."

"Where are you going? What are you going to do?"

"I don't know yet."

"Jamie . . ."

He walked to the door. Opened it. Took a step. Turned again. He came as close as he could to saying what was in his heart.

"I'll look after you, Annie. You and Melanie. I swear it."

• • •

BRIAN STOKES JERKED awake. It was the fifth time in five hours, and his lover finally said, "Do you want to talk about it or should I just get you a package of razor blades?"

"Leave me alone."

"You were dreaming, you know. I heard you call a name."

Brian rolled away. "Shut up."

Nate sat up instead. Besides Melanie he was the only person Brian had ever trusted. He always pressed and he always saw too much. Now he tossed back the covers and adjusted his pajamas over his middle-aged frame, a sure sign he was gearing up for a serious discussion.

"You called out for Meagan," he said gently. "Brian, even when you're awake you never say that name."

Brian thought he was going to cry. "Fuck you." He got up, walked to the window, and stared out at the still-sleeping city. But the images in his head were all he saw.

The funeral on the gray, dreary day. His mother keeling over halfway through the service from grief and gin. His father, stony-faced, looking at her as if he hated her.

The silence in the days afterward. The huge house empty of little-girl squeals.

Harper screaming one night, "Where the hell were you all day? If you'd just come home . . ."

His mother replying, "I didn't mean . . . I didn't know . . . I thought Brian needed some time alone with me. You know how he can be, especially around her."

"Well, he's got you all to himself now, doesn't he? He's got that, all fucking right."

I'm sorry. I can't even tell you why I was so cruel.

Nate came up behind him. "You're worried about your sister, aren't you?" he asked, rubbing Brian's arms. "You've been like this ever since you went to see her."

"I don't want to talk about it."

"Of course not," Nate agreed amiably. "So how long are you going to hate yourself, Brian? And how long are you going to hate Melanie for daring to care?"

"I don't—"

"She came to you for help. You haven't even called her since."

"You don't understand."

Nate gave him a look. He'd seen Brian at his worst, when he was so filled with self-loathing he could barely crawl out of bed. Nate understood plenty. He said, "Then explain it to me. Give me one logical reason for blowing off your poor sister."

Brian shifted uneasily. "She's better off without me. She is."

"Hah," Nate said. "Your sister adores you. First sign of trouble, who does she call? Big-brother Brian. That's because she knows you care. Because you've always looked out for her. She *trusts* you. She loves you. Why are you being so difficult now?"

Brian gritted his teeth. "It's different."

"Your sister needs help. Not that different."

"It's complicated, all right? She doesn't know about Meagan. No one knows about Meagan. Dammit, *I* don't want to know about Meagan!"

Nate said quietly, "You know, you're the only person I know who came out of the closet to hide a bigger secret."

"I did not—"

"I've been around the block a few times, I know the signs. I've watched other men come out of the closet, and it isn't easy. But generally there is a moment of relief afterward. You haven't gotten that sense of relief, have you, Brian? Six months later you are just as tense and troubled as before. Why is that? If you are finally at peace with who you are, why are you some-how *angrier*?"

Brian couldn't answer. Nate didn't need him to. "Because that wasn't *the* secret, was it, Brian?"

Brian didn't answer.

FIVE A.M. DAWN was just breaking over the horizon, washing Boston's streets in shades of gold. The man finally turned away from the window. He was tired from a long, hard night, but also exhilarated.

The game was in full motion now, the players not just assembled, but moving around the board. He found it interesting that for a group of people who half hated one another, for twenty-five years they had stayed close together. It made it easy to monitor them.

Harper was looking over his shoulder. William was carrying a gun. Brian Stokes was suffering from long, sleepless nights. The rest of them were working franti-cally to keep their secrets.

A shooter had been unleashed and the first death recorded.

And Melanie? He wasn't even sure where she was, but assumed she was safe. Otherwise he would've heard.

Melanie was the king. She was the prize in the game, the one reason it all unfolded and the only thing he had to gain.

Come on, Melanie. It's all up to you now.

Time to remember, sweetheart. Time to put the pieces together.

Time to come home to daddy.

Time to come home to me.

NINETEEN

"ALL RIGHT," LAIRMORE said crisply. "What the hell is going on?"

At seven A.M. sharp, there was no messing with the supervisory agent. His double-breasted gray suit was impeccably tailored, his white dress shirt sharply pressed, and his military-cropped hair perfectly even. He sat behind his oversized walnut desk, while behind him, the blue FBI seal provided a halo of thirteen stars and a white banner declaring Fidelity, Bravery, and Integrity. Even during internal meetings there was always the feeling that Lairmore was conducting a press conference.

Still, David liked him.

At nearly fifty years of age, the head of the Boston healthcare fraud squad could tell you what *every* color and object in the FBI shield symbolized. He'd also go to his grave swearing that Hoover never so much as touched a pair of women's underwear; it was all a horrible misunderstanding. He was conservative, he was bureaucratic, but he also believed that healthcare fraud was the worst crime epidemic sweeping the United States since organized crime—ten cents of every dollar wasted, not to mention shoddy treatment, unnecessary procedures, and the risk of human life—and he worked his ass off to do something about it. A man who believed in his job. In David's mind, a rarity these days.

Now, Lairmore stared down two agents who hadn't slept a wink.

"Oh, for heaven's sake," he finally exclaimed, "couldn't you two at least have showered and shaved? This isn't a bachelor party."

David and Chenney looked at each other. They shook their heads.

"Watching Sheffield," Chenney mumbled. His eyes lit up. "Got a *big* break."

"Researched Meagan Stokes," David said. "Dodged bullets. Talked to Supervisory Special Agent Quincy. No breaks."

"You talked to Quincy? At Quantico?"

"Yeah, late last night. He's always at the office too. What the hell is it with this job?"

Chenney gazed at David with awe. "Cool."

"Ah, Jesus, Mary, and Joseph." Lairmore stood up from his chair. "In the hallway now."

He stormed out. They followed. He plugged the coffee machine with quarters, then handed them the steaming cups that came shooting out. They accepted. Then chugged. Then dutifully followed their disgruntled leader back to his office, where David received a personal lecture on overextending his case team and fracturing a "very important if not critical" investigation. David nursed the rest of his coffee and pulled his thoughts together so he could sound intelligent when he had the chance. It came sooner than he desired.

"Let's start with the Meagan Stokes case." Lairmore slapped the Harper Stokes/William Sheffield healthcare fraud case file on the desk. "How the hell did you end up working on a twenty-five-year-old *solved* homicide?"

David started at the beginning and ended by stating his growing certainty that the whole Stokes family had bigger secrets than fraud.

Lairmore half agreed. "Most perpetrators do have a

pattern of small-time fraud in their backgrounds. Maybe they cheated on auto insurance, then graduated to doctoring pharmaceutical billings. But in all my days, Agent, I have never heard of a person *starting* with conspiring to murder his own child for the insurance money and then trading *down* for white collar fraud."

David smiled wearily. "And we don't even know if Harper Stokes is committing healthcare fraud, let alone if he had anything to do with Meagan. Personally, Quincy favors the mother—"

"Harper's doing it!" Chenney burst in. "I got it. I *got* Sheffield!"

Chenney explained his previous night's adventure in one long adrenaline rush: Harry Boer suffered chest pains and was rushed to the ER. By evening he was in ICU, under sedation but appearing to be fine. Then, bam, he had two bradycardic episodes within five hours and was now undergoing an operation for a pacemaker performed by none other than Dr. Harper Stokes. And William Sheffield just happened to be spotted in the ICU ward several times, hours after his shift ended, with no patients in that ward. He was just "around." Conveniently around, if you asked Chenney.

"I called a pharmacist friend first thing this morning," Chenney announced. "She said that if you wanted to make it appear that someone needed a pacemaker, there are two drugs that would effectively interfere with the electrical conduction of the heart. They are propranolol and digoxin. Propranolol's a beta blocker, it's used to slow a racing heartbeat. Digoxin can also slow down the ventricles, but it might also accelerate the heart to lethal rates. Kinda risky, she said. Most likely, Sheffield's using propranolol.

"So," Chenney concluded with a flourish, "Sheffield sneaks into the ICU wards at night, that's why he's at the hospital so much. Injecting propranolol just once would cause concern but probably not lead to a cardiologist immediately recommending surgery. However, if a couple episodes happened right in a row . . ."

"Then the patients appear to have a circulatory disorder and need surgery," David said.

"Brilliantly simple," Lairmore said. "Must take Sheffield two minutes for each injection. Then they're all set for an hour-long procedure that garners Harper two thousand dollars for the surgery and another four thousand in royalty dollars as he uses his own custom-designed pacemakers. If they do a couple a week . . ."

"Sheffield has no problem paying off his gambling debts and Harper can spend all he wants." David sighed. "One thing we are learning about Harper Stokes, he likes a nice lifestyle."

Lairmore was nodding thoughtfully. Chenney had resumed looking troubled.

"But even if we can now prove Harper Stokes is making money from illegal surgeries, how does that tie in with what happened to Meagan Stokes twenty-five years ago?"

"That's what I want to know." David leaned forward, planted his elbows on his knees, and though he was dog tired from a night spent poring over documents and weathering aching muscles, he got into it. "I went through the entire Houston PD case file last night and a few key findings about the Meagan Stokes case emerged. One, in 1972, the Stokeses were in dire financial straits. They lived in a big house, but it was a gift from Patricia's father, not anything Harper could afford. He was just a resident, barely making ten thousand a year and scrounging to maintain the lifestyle to which his wife was accustomed. He'd taken out a second mortgage on the home and was already behind three payments when Meagan disappeared. Bottom line is that from a financial point of view,

Meagan's murder was the best thing that ever happened to Harper and Patricia Stokes."

"So we have motive," Lairmore said.

Chenney was not convinced. "If it was only about money, couldn't Harper have dreamed up his little operations back then?"

"No, residents are salaried, not paid by the procedure. One pacemaker surgery a week or a dozen, it would have been the same to him."

Now Lairmore was the one with an objection. "Still, Dr. Stokes could have done other things—sold drugs from the hospital, sought kickbacks from pharmaceutical representatives. We all know there are many ways for healthcare providers at any level to abuse their positions for money. So I believe Chenney's point still stands. We have established that Harper and Patricia Stokes needed the money, but you haven't convinced me yet that they are the type of people to cold-bloodedly murder their little girl to get it."

"All right, fair enough. That brings me to my second key finding. Not only did Harper have motive, but just about everyone in the family was having problems back then. To hell with having one suspect, in 1972 the police had four: Harper Stokes, Patricia Stokes, Jamie O'Donnell, and, believe it or not, Brian Stokes." David nodded at their startled expressions. "Exactly. This family doesn't just have skeletons, it has graveyards. So if you don't like Harper for the murder, let's look at everyone else.

"Patricia Stokes. Long before she met Harper, she was rich. Born into oil wealth, raised by a fairly domineering father, and the apple of his eye. Doesn't sound like her father liked Harper much, thought he wasn't good enough for his daughter—but that didn't stop him from giving his little girl a dream wedding and a mansion up on the hill. Unfortunately, when Patricia settled down to a future as a doctor's wife, she discovered she didn't like the scenery. Even before Brian was out of diapers, she was acting restless and bored. She took to spending lots of money. Went out partying. *And* she started spending more time with Jamie O'Donnell than with her husband, though her husband seemed to be spending more time with twenty-something nurses than his own wife.

"According to friends of the family, they did make an attempt at reconciliation. Harper started coming home more often, and they made a decision to have a second child, Meagan. This time it seemed to work. With two kids at home, Patricia gave up the party scene and finally settled into motherhood. She took up charity work, joined a few organizations, but mostly appeared content to dote on her children. According to the housekeeper, she and Harper shared a bedroom again, but the housekeeper never had to change the sheets, if you get my drift."

"A lot of marriages turn into that," Lairmore said mildly. "If that's a sign of criminal activity, we'd have to arrest all husbands and wives married more than five years."

David smiled. "Sure, but we're not done with the Stokeses yet. So now we have Meagan Stokes in the picture. We got Harper and Patricia and the two children and happily ever after. But then, six months before Meagan's murder, Patricia and Harper start fighting every night. One maid apparently said something to friends of the family, and Patricia fired her the next day. And wonder of all wonders, Jamie O'Donnell starts hanging around again."

"He and Patricia have a thing," Chenney said.

"Seems that way. Police couldn't prove it, but you can't believe he's hanging around the house for the cooking. And Patricia is already starting to hit the gin. Everyone says it was the murder of Meagan that sent her over the brink, but the police can trace it back to *before* Meagan's death. Right before, which means whatever was going on, it had put Patricia in a questionable state of mind. Who knows what women do in a questionable state of mind?"

Lairmore nodded slowly, pursing his lips. "Interesting. So we have a materialistic workaholic doctor, an unhappy alcoholic wife, and a love triangle with the family friend. Exactly what is Jamie O'Donnell's connection with the Stokeses?"

"Old friend of Harper's from college days, not that O'Donnell went to school. He's strictly self-educated and self-made. Started out working in the oil fields and took it from there. On the surface he and Harper make an unlikely pair, but they're both driven. Of course, they took entirely different routes to the top. Harper is now Mr. Community and Mr. Family, whereas Jamie O'Donnell *knows* people. Interpol has a file on the man."

"What?" Now he had Lairmore's attention. David waved it away.

"Interpol has been desperate to prove that he runs guns but has never found a thing other than he keeps interesting company. Otherwise he runs a legitimate import business, pays his taxes every April 15, and puts his pants on one leg at a time just like the rest of us."

"The rest of us aren't sleeping with Patricia Stokes," Chenney said dryly.

David shrugged. "Sure. So now we have the money motive and the love triangle. Maybe Harper was so angry at his wife, he decided killing Meagan would be a great way to spite her and solve his financial woes. Or maybe Jamie O'Donnell thought Patricia would never leave Harper as long as they had children together, so he tried to do something about it. Or maybe when Patricia was strung too tightly, had a little too much to drink, Meagan chose that moment to act out, and boom, bye-bye Meagan. Now we come to possibility number three—Brian Stokes."

"This family just gets better and better," muttered Chenney.

"Not exactly the Waltons," David agreed. "Brian in particular has a very troubled history. According to the Houston police report, he frequently broke items in the house and was known to reduce his mother to tears on almost a nightly basis. The interviewing officer wrote that the nanny had standing orders *not* to leave Brian alone in a room with Meagan. Apparently, he'd gone out of his way to destroy some of her toys. Then just to make it a slam dunk, Brian was seeing a therapist in 1972. It seems that Brian already had a history of playing with matches."

"You're kidding me." Lairmore sat up straighter. "Don't tell me he's also a bed wetter and an animal torturer."

Lairmore was referring to the violent triad developed by the profilers. For whatever reason, serial killers always had at least two legs of that triangle in their past. But not Brian Stokes.

"Just petty arson," David said. "Now, to make matters even more interesting, he and Patricia have no alibi for the day Meagan disappeared. Patricia told the cops that she took Brian to his therapist. The cops confirmed that, but the appointment was over at ten A.M. The cops got the call from the nanny at two P.M. that Meagan had disappeared from her car. At five Patricia and Brian drove up to the house, where they were both supposedly surprised by the news."

"What about Harper Stokes or Jamie O'Donnell?" Lairmore asked. "Do they have alibis?"

David shook his head. "Harper claimed to be at work, but no one could ever vouch for it. O'Donnell said he was out of town but never produced any proof. Better yet, the police aren't even convinced the nanny was telling the truth about when Meagan was taken. She barely spoke English, refused to meet their gaze when answering questions, and spent most of the time sidling closer to Harper. They thought she might be a little involved with him, or at least wanted to make sure he liked what she was saying. In all probability, Meagan could've been taken at any time from any place that day. One day Meagan Stokes is simply gone. The next day the ransom note appears at the hospital where Harper works, and nothing is seen or heard from the kidnapper again. Then eight weeks later Meagan's body is found by a man and his dog out taking a walk.

"Quincy is right. Everything about the Meagan Stokes case reeks to high heaven, and every single member of the family carries the stench. If Russell Lee Holmes had not confessed, the police would've investigated the Stokeses and O'Donnell until the cows came home. And as long as the investigation was active, the insurance company would not pay out the policy. Basically, Russell Lee's last-minute confession to Larry Digger earned the family the end of a very embarrassing investigation and one million dollars."

"How convenient, then," Lairmore murmured, "that Russell Lee Holmes confessed."

"Exactly," David said. *"Exactly!"*

"Quincy is going to reopen this case?" Lairmore asked.

"That's what he said. But I don't think he needs to officially reopen it. We're looking into it as part of our case."

"No," Lairmore said.

"No?"

Lairmore rewarded his incredulous tone with a stern look. "With all due respect, Agent, you are in healthcare fraud. Agent Chenney here has discovered we have a viable allegation against Dr. Harper Stokes and Dr. William Sheffield if we can prove their activities. That case is your job. That case needs your focus."

"But the shooter, Larry Digger—"

"Will be investigated by the Boston PD since it falls in their jurisdiction. Just as the Meagan Stokes case is in very capable hands with Quincy."

"Goddammit!" David bolted out of his chair, star-

ing at his supervisor incredulously. "This is my case! I've worked my ass off connecting these dots, I got a terrified woman in a hotel room who doesn't even know if it's safe to go home to her family, and I got a direct link with the case I'm already working."

"You do not have a link," Lairmore fired back. He gave David a warning look. David didn't take it.

"The hell I don't! Twenty-five years ago, the Stokeses needed money and their daughter died, providing them with a million dollars. Now Harper is once more living beyond his means, and he's come up with another way of getting money, cutting open innocent people for profit. It's a pattern of behavior."

Now even Chenney was looking at him as if he'd lost his mind. "There's no pattern. Murdering your kid is not remotely close to installing illegal pacemakers."

"One is insurance fraud, one is healthcare fraud."

"One is homicide! The other is criminal, sure, but an unnecessary pacemaker isn't even dangerous. The pacemaker would be activated only if the person had a heart attack."

"Someone could seize up and die on the table. Reckless endangerment of human life."

"Which is still a far cry from murdering your own kid."

"The rookie is right," Lairmore said. "You have established motive, Agent Riggs, but you haven't established character. We know Harper Stokes likes his lifestyle, maybe enough to commit fraud, but what evidence do we have that he would commit murder? Does he have a history of violence?"

"No."

"Child abuse, spousal abuse? Neglect?"

"No."

"By all accounts, he's raised two healthy children. No trips to emergency rooms, no arguments reported by neighbors. And in your first report on Harper Stokes didn't you write that he has a reputation for being a doting father and being exceedingly generous with his wife?"

David gritted his teeth. "Yes."

"And Patricia Stokes. I know Quincy has questions about the carefully wrapped body, but again, any history of abuse or neglect?"

"She has a problem with alcohol."

"Which resurfaced six months ago. Any reports of violence then?"

David was forced to shake his head.

"Which brings us to Jamie O'Donnell. Maybe we have a criminal past there. According to Larry Digger, he visited the midwife in Texas, but again, by all reports he dotes on his godchildren and is close to the family.

"That just leaves us with Brian Stokes," Lairmore continued. "But by your own admission, he adores his second sister and has always been extremely protective of her. Face it, Agent, this case is over your head. The motives are there and opportunity is there, but none of the players make sense, at least not to our eyes. So leave it to the experts. Leave it to Quincy."

"They are connected," David said stiffly, "and I'll tell you one last reason why."

Lairmore and Chenney looked impatient for his little display to end.

"The caller," David stated. "The anonymous tipster who alerted us to the healthcare fraud at the same time he was alerting Larry Digger to Melanie. His agenda seems to be revenge for Meagan Stokes, for making sure everyone gets what they deserve. So if he's bringing us in on it, they're related, they're all related."

Lairmore remained skeptical, but finally he sighed.

"All right, Agent. I'll give you one last shot. Establish character. Bring me any proof that Harper, Patricia, or Brian Stokes is cruel enough or cold enough or clinically unstable enough to engineer the death of four-year-old Meagan Stokes, and I'll let you work on it—in your own time. Right now I believe that health-care fraud is the only viable case my agents have."

"Fine," David said curtly.

Since Lairmore didn't want to hear anything more about twenty-five-year-old homicides, they focused on the fraud angle that Chenney had uncovered. They had no hard physical evidence, so their options were limited. They could prove motive—money—and opportunity. But they needed physical evidence or a good eyewitness account. Eyewitnesses, unfortunately, were notoriously hard to get in a hospital setting. There were too many nurses and doctors around for most patients to keep straight, and nurses and doctors had a code of silence. They did not rat each other out even when they saw evidence of a crime.

The consensus was to put Chenney in the hospital undercover as a janitor. He'd prowl the ICU, ask the nurses questions, maybe even catch Sheffield in the act.

David was given the fun-filled act of building the paper trail. Going over the financial statements to prove need. Looking for evidence of payoffs between Harper and Sheffield.

Then he turned his attention to Melanie Stokes, where he began his work in earnest. But by the end of the day he had merely proven Lairmore's point. Except for the migraines, Melanie was in perfect health, not a single broken bone, not a single unexplained bruise. She was reported as happy and well-adjusted, the recipient of the best birthday parties on the block.

By all accounts, her entire family simply loved her to death.

TWENTY

ELANIE WOKE UP Tuesday morning thinking of Meagan, of the family she loved so much and had assumed loved her.

She got up to stand in front of the dresser and stared at her reflection. Dammit, she *did not* look like Meagan. She was not nearly as beautiful.

She slapped the top of the dresser, then stormed downstairs.

David wasn't around but he'd left a note on the kitchen table.

Went to meeting. Will be back after five. Remember, *no going outdoors*. D.

She set down the note and roamed the room. She found frozen vegetables in the freezer and a jar of instant coffee on the counter. She boiled water to give herself something to do. While it heated up, she unburied her Day-Timer from her purse and looked up her schedule. The books were way overdue to the rare book dealer. She'd planned lunch with an old friend from Wellesley, followed by an afternoon meeting with the committee for the children's hospital winter ball. It was already nearly June and they had yet to line up entertainment. The whole thing was a disaster waiting to happen.

Melanie got on the phone and canceled everything. She had the flu, she said. Everyone was sympathetic. They encouraged her to rest. Of course they could manage without her.

She hung up feeling disappointed. She'd wanted dismay, she realized finally, cries of We need you, Melanie, we'll never make it without you.

You're special, Melanie. Indispensable. You are not *a substitute daughter.*

Dammit, how could her mother say she'd wanted Meagan again? How could she have looked at Melanie and seen *Meagan?*

Was it always just about Meagan?

Did they all feel that way? Her mother, her father, her brother, her godfather. The people who had taken her in and given her a home. The people she trusted and considered her own family.

Melanie thought, To hell with questions. She was going to figure out the answers.

On a pad of paper she drew a circle and labeled it Meagan. Then around it she drew circles for her mother, her father, her brother, and Jamie. Then she drew in Russell Lee Holmes, Larry Digger, and herself. Finally she added Ann Margaret. David seemed to feel she was involved, and at this point Melanie shouldn't exclude any possibilities. Considering that, she also drew in William Sheffield.

Nine different people, all surrounding one little girl.

She drew lines connecting Meagan to her mother, father, brother, and godfather. It actually bothered her, like acknowledging another woman in a lover's life. But it was true. Meagan had come first. Melanie added Larry Digger's relationship as journalist. She could not come up with any direct lines for William Sheffield or Ann Margaret.

Russell Lee Holmes was even more troubling. She wanted to write killer, but Quincy had raised too much doubt. Russell Lee was connected not directly to Meagan then, but to the other people encircling Meagan.

And after a moment's hesitation she drew a line between Russell Lee Holmes and herself. Father and daughter. There in black and white.

After that she found that the rest flowed easier.

A LITTLE AFTER five-thirty David rapped on the door three times, then entered. He was holding a paper bag. From the couch Melanie arched a brow inquiringly.

"Brought Chinese," David said at last. He held out the bag, trying to gauge her mood.

"Fine," she agreed.

He edged into the kitchen. "Spicy orange beef and General Tsao's chicken."

"Nice." Despite David's fear, she was not angry with him. She'd spent the day with her diagram and it had given her what she needed most—conclusive proof that her family could *not* have killed Meagan Stokes. It made Melanie happy.

She climbed off the sofa and followed David into the kitchen.

David's jacket was off, his green paisley tie loosened, and his white shirtsleeves rolled up to his elbows. He was getting to the point of needing a haircut. His hair held track marks from his fingers running through it one too many times, and those lines were back at the corners of his eyes.

He looked like he'd had a very bad day, and for a moment Melanie was tempted to cup his cheek with her hand. She wondered if he would turn his face into her touch. She wondered if he would move closer . . .

She had liked the way he'd held her last night.

He said, "The bowls are in the cupboard."

She got them down and they dished up their dinner.

They ate in silence for nearly half the meal before David spoke up.

"How was your day?"

"I watched Jerry Springer. Enough said. And yours?"

He dug deeper into his fried rice. "I would've preferred Jerry Springer. Did you sleep at all last night?"

"A little."

"Any more dreams of Meagan?"

"A blend. Meagan Stokes in that cabin. But you were there too."

He glanced at her in surprise. A grain of rice decorated his bottom lip, and without thinking she brushed it away with her thumb. The motion caught them both off guard, and she quickly pulled her hand back.

"Um . . . I was in the cabin with you and Meagan Stokes," she said a trifle breathlessly.

"Me?" He sounded frazzled himself and was studying his bowl intently. "What was I doing there?"

"Housecleaning."

"What?"

Melanie took another bite of food. "Meagan Stokes was in the corner of the cabin, clutching her horse and very, very afraid. Then you walked into the cabin and started cleaning. Swept the floor, removed the cobwebs, cleaned the windows. Oh, and you hung drapes."

"I hung drapes?" David looked stricken. "So much for to serve and protect."

"They were very nice drapes," Melanie said. "Meagan was happy."

"Housekeeper extraordinare," he muttered, pushing his empty bowl away. "Give me a cape and I'll call it a day."

He sighed, and it hurt her to see the weariness on his face. "Well," he said seriously, "do you want to know what I learned today?"

She pushed back her bowl and squared her shoulders. "Sure. Give it to me straight. What did you learn?"

"Nothing," David said bluntly. "The great FBI agent learned nothing. This whole case simply makes no sense." He stood and began to clear the table.

"The shooter?"

"Jax said they checked with area hospitals and locals. So far no sign."

"Any more evidence from Larry Digger's room? The notes?"

"Nope, not a thing." David walked into the kitchen, slammed the bowls in the sink.

"What about Meagan's case? Did you talk more about it?"

"Sure, I reviewed it with my supervisor and Chenney. We all agree that Quincy raised excellent questions. I sure as hell don't believe Russell Lee did it. That leaves us with your family, as you know. They do have motive."

"The money," she said flatly, and stood herself. The subject was too aggravating to handle sitting. "The million-dollar life insurance policy."

"Better than that. We think your mother and Jamie O'Donnell might have been having an affair back then."

"*What?*"

"Police notes. O'Donnell was spending a lot of time around the house and your parents were having a lot of marital difficulties. Screaming matches, that kind of thing."

Melanie shook her head. "My parents don't scream at each other. They have 'discussions' behind closed doors."

"Yeah, well, back then they were fighting enough to attract the notice of the hired help and friends. Seems that your father wasn't very faithful—"

"He *flirts* a lot." She held up a hand and conceded: "Maybe he does more than flirt, but as strange as this sounds, I don't think my mom minds. I've always had the impression she accepts my father's job and lifestyle as male prerogative. Boys will be boys."

"What's good for the goose . . ."

Melanie pursed her lips, not liking this newest allegation. But these days there seemed to be more she *didn't* know about her family than she did.

She moved to the coffee table and picked up the hotel pad that revealed her work for the day.

"Then we come to your brother," David said.

"Brian was nine years old!"

"And troubled enough to be seeing a shrink. Plus, your mom herself had given the nanny orders not to leave him alone with Meagan. He seemed to be very jealous of her and very destructive of her toys. Remember, he said that he'd thrown her toy pony against the fireplace.

"So now we have money, love, and mental instability all running in your family. But here's a twist. I did full background checks on your family, and there is simply nothing to suggest they're capable of murdering a four-year-old girl."

Melanie nodded vigorously and waved her notepad in the air. "Exactly! Look here. I wrote down what Quincy said about the person who did the crime, and I've done a little analysis of my own. I've been arguing that my family couldn't do it because I loved them so much. Since that doesn't carry weight in criminal investigations, I decided to look at it your way."

She sat down on the sofa and placed the notepad on the coffee table. David took a seat next to her. She could feel the warmth of his body against her leg. She spoke faster and kept her eyes on the diagram.

"Here is Meagan and my family. Here is what we know about everyone's relationship, and here is what we know about each individual. I was thinking of what Quincy said about profiling, that you look at the psychology under the behavior. I'm not sure I can objectively say that my parents are good or bad people, but I believe I can objectively say if they are smart or precise or sloppy."

"Okay," David said, studying her picture. "I can grant you that much."

"Here is what Quincy said about the person who killed Meagan Stokes. The person is precise and knowledgeable about police procedure. Then the person has to be clever enough and credible enough to approach Meagan. Also, I guess the person has to be tough enough to deal with the likes of Russell Lee Holmes. At the same time, however, the person is maternal, at least caring and remorseful enough to wrap Meagan in a blanket and bury the body. He'd also have to feel guilty for what he did, guilty enough to, well, decapitate her."

Even on paper that aspect of the crime still horrified her. She swallowed, and not wanting to lose momentum, for she clearly had David's full attention, she rapped the pencil tip against her diagram.

"Now, that's a unique combination of traits. Distinct, wouldn't you say? So let's look at our players. We have my father, who is very precise and smart. But frankly, as much as I love him, I can tell you he's not maternal. Hugs and kisses are definitely my mother's department. As for knowledge of police procedure, I don't think my father has even gotten a speeding ticket in his life. He doesn't watch cop dramas or read true crime, so I think he's a total washout there. Plus, tough enough to approach and/or intimidate Russell Lee Holmes? Please, this man can't bear to go a week without a manicure. Russell Lee would eat him alive.

"So, what about my mother? Now, she fits for being maternal, remorseful, and guilty. But do you really think my mother is precise? Haven't you ever seen how hard her hands shake? And while I think she's an intelligent woman, she's not this kind of clever, let alone knowledgeable about police procedure. And there really is no way she would ever approach a man like Russell Lee. Can you imagine that? So she doesn't fit either.

"Now, my godfather . . . I'll be honest. I've always had the impression that Jamie knows things. He has a way of moving, you know. If you're a female he loves, it's very reassuring, like spending time around the tough kid in school. He grew up hard and I imagine he could intimidate a man like Russell Lee Holmes. And he probably knows something about law enforcement. But Jamie isn't precise. He's blunt, physical, and rough around the edges. Also, I can't see Jamie harming a little girl. In his world that would be . . . dishonorable, I guess. He could be cruel to someone who threatened someone he loved, but he'd cut off his own hand before he'd harm a child. Actually, he's even a little maternal toward kids. Certainly he's affectionate and loving toward Brian and me. He's just not that combination of cold, precise, callousness.

"Then we have my brother."

"He's a doctor," David interjected. "So he must be precise."

"At the age of nine? And what would he know about police procedure, David? And how in the world would a nine-year-old convince Russell Lee to confess to a crime he didn't commit? Don't you see?" She turned, looking at him earnestly. "There is no one on this page who fits what Quincy is looking for. I'm not an expert, true, but put at this level, it doesn't work. The killer simply isn't my family. End of story."

Melanie finally relaxed. But then David took her chart from her. He took her pencil. He drew a few lines. And that easily, he burst her bubble.

"You're right, Melanie," he said simply. "You're absolutely right. Alone, no one individual meets all the requirements. And that's what the message has been all along. I was a fool not to see it earlier. It's not one person who's getting notes. It's all of them. And if you put them all together . . ."

He looked her in the eye. "Your mother, father, brother, or godfather could not have committed this crime. But this *family,* on the other hand . . ."

"No," Melanie said.

"Yes," he replied. "I'm sorry, Melanie. But yes."

She had to get off the sofa. She paced around the room a few times, her thoughts in turmoil.

"It's the combination," David murmured, making quick notes and seeming to speak almost to himself. "As individuals they fail. But as a group they cover all the traits and areas of knowledge needed to carry out the crime. Harper devising the ransom demand, coming up with the idea to make it a copycat crime. Your guilt-stricken mother wrapping up Meagan's body. Your godfather disposing of it, I think, and handling the deal with Russell Lee Holmes when the police started asking too many questions. Getting Russell Lee to confess to Meagan's murder in return for your family providing a home for his own child. Think of how much Russell Lee would've liked that. A lifetime of hating poverty, and one day he gets an offer to transport his child to the upper class. What a deal."

"But . . . but the murder," Melanie protested. "No one is cruel enough to commit the murder. You said yourself, *no one* is cruel enough to commit the murder!"

David looked up, his expression distracted. She realized with a start that this had become an academic exercise for him, a riddle for the great agent to figure out. She was shocked.

"What if it wasn't murder, Melanie? What if it was an accident? What if little Brian Stokes simply went too far with his jealous rampage one day?"

"Oh, God," she whispered in horror.

"Think about it, Melanie. Nine-year-old Brian. He harms Meagan out of jealousy or rage and what do your parents do? They've already lost one child."

"No."

"Your godfather also seems loyal to him. Plus, he'd

probably do anything to keep Patricia from suffering more. Finally we have a situation worthy of the three adults getting over their differences and working together."

"But the decapitation, the mutilation."

"Maybe they had to. Quincy said decapitation can also be about covering up a crime. They're trying to imitate a killer who strangles his victims. But what if it was an accident that killed Meagan? Maybe she fell down the stairs, maybe she was hit in the head. They must decapitate her or the real cause of death will be determined. If she was hit with a blunt instrument, there might even be paint or fiber or metallic particles buried in the wound that could be used to trace the murder weapon. So in for a dime, in for a dollar. They decapitate the body, remove the hands to hide other wounds or physical evidence, and devise a plot to imitate some serial killer they've been reading about in the paper."

Melanie was shaking her head.

"But the police aren't convinced," David continued. "Harper doesn't know enough details, so his copycat attempt fails. Then Russell Lee is arrested, so they decide to go straight to the source. Jamie. Jamie pays him a visit. And they strike a deal."

David looked at her somberly. "I'm sorry, Melanie, but that scenario works. You are Russell Lee Holmes's child and they took you in the night he died to cover up what happened to Meagan five years before."

"You're wrong, you're wrong," Melanie kept repeating.

She had wrapped her arms tightly around her waist and her voice came out sounding more desperate than she'd intended.

David rose off the sofa. There was a look in his eyes Melanie had never seen before. Maybe tenderness. Maybe compassion. He took her hands, and then, in a move she didn't expect, he drew her against his body and pressed her cheek against his chest. She realized for the first time that she was trembling uncontrollably.

And then he whispered roughly against her temple, "Maybe. But there's no arguing that Larry Digger was killed. Or that shots were aimed at you."

She collapsed. Her knees buckled and she would've fallen if David hadn't already been holding her. Her hands grabbed his shirt for support. Her body sagged into him and he gripped her tighter.

"It's going to be all right," David whispered against her hair. "I won't let them hurt you. I won't let anyone hurt you."

"My family, my family . . . I *love* them."

She buried her head against his shoulder and held on tight.

The storm lasted a bit. Gradually she was aware of David leading her over to the couch. He lay down with her, wrapping his lean body around her. He stroked her hair, her back. Then his lips brushed her cheek, the curve of her ear. Tender. Soft.

She turned to him savagely, caught his lips full-force with her own and kissed him hard. Lips bruising lips, teeth smashing, breath labored. She arched against him, tried to bury herself in the feel and taste and sensation. He ravaged her totally, his tongue plunging into her mouth, filling her, making her whole . . .

Then, when her breasts were swollen and her nipples tingling and her whole body restless and writhing, he pulled away. She could hear his ragged breathing and the racing beat of his heart. She could see that his hands trembled.

"No more," he said roughly.

"Why not?"

"Because it wouldn't be right. I want it to be right."

He got off the couch in a hurry, obviously realizing that she was in no mood to be denied and he was in no shape to win. The front of his slacks bulged with his erection, and he had to fist his hands in his back pockets to keep from reaching for her again.

Melanie contemplated forcing the issue. He wanted her, and she needed to be wanted. By anyone.

But he was right. She was too desperate and she'd hate them both later.

She rose from the sofa and walked to the window. "They've never harmed me, David. They've been so good to me."

He didn't answer. Minute ticked into minute.

"The police should find the shooter soon," David said at last. "Once we get our hands on him, he'll be able to tell us a thing or two."

"Such as who hired him."

"Exactly."

"And then we'll know."

"Exactly."

"Okay," she said. "Okay."

David raised his arms above his head and stretched out his back. "I gotta get some sleep."

"I know."

"You gonna stay up? Will you be okay?"

"I'll be fine."

"We're going to get to the bottom of it," he said again. "We will."

Melanie simply smiled. She wasn't so sure herself anymore. And she was wondering if there were some truths that should never be known.

David moved toward the bedroom. Then he stopped and turned, his gaze unreadable.

"You know," he said quietly. "You don't need them as much as you think you do. You're stronger than you know."

"What does that have to do with the fact that I love them?"

David didn't have a reply.

Melanie stayed up long into the night. She sat on the sofa with her knees pulled up against her chest and her arms wrapped around her legs. She thought of her parents and her brother and her godfather. The way they had held her and made her laugh and doted on her. The way they had lavished their time and attention on her as if she were a long-awaited present that was finally theirs at last.

Right before she fell asleep, she thought, If I really am Russell Lee Holmes's daughter, why did Quincy say my memories of the shack weren't right? And if all this was done to protect Brian, wouldn't it matter that he's now been disinherited from the family?

The shooter, she thought groggily. The shooter will tell.

But there was no such luck. The next morning she and David awoke to the hotel phone ringing. It was Detective Jax. He'd found the shooter all right.

Unfortunately, the man was dead.

TWENTY-ONE

"IT WON'T BE pleasant," David warned.

Melanie merely nodded, keeping her gaze out the passenger-side window, where semis barreled down Highway 93 and distant factories emitted plumes of smoke. They were approaching the harbor district of Boston. She caught the first whiff of salt.

"Jax said he was in the water," David said. "That always makes it look worse. Really, Melanie, you should wait until the body has been processed. You can ID it by video at the morgue."

"But it won't be ready until tomorrow morning, correct?"

"Boston homicide is a little overworked."

"Then I'll do it now," she reasserted firmly, as she'd been saying since they first got the call. "If it's him, and he's dead, then I can go home. No sense in delaying that any longer than necessary."

"Why don't we hold off on any quick decisions," David said vaguely, which was enough to let her know he was going to make an issue out of it. She shot him a quick glance, but he refused to meet her gaze. Obviously he didn't want to engage in the discussion then. Fine, it could wait until she saw the body. It wouldn't change her mind. She had spent a lot of time thinking since last night and formed some opinions of her own.

She turned back to the car window. The exit appeared on their right, and David careened across three lanes of traffic to take it. One tourist honked. No one else seemed to notice. The wharf came into view. As crime scenes went, this one was hard to miss.

Black and white police cruisers peppered the scene. Yellow crime tape draped across the road. One beefy officer had adopted an aggressive stance outside the perimeter and was waving them away until David flashed his creds. Like membership in an elite club, the FBI shield entitled them to a first-class viewing of a dead man.

They pulled in next to two dark sedans and one old clunker. David opened her door for her. She realized he always did that, even held out chairs. His mother's doing, she thought, and accepted his hand to pull herself out of the car. When he held out his arm for her, however, she shook her head. She preferred to walk this path alone.

They crossed to a group of plainclothes detectives and one medical examiner. The air was tangy with the scent of salt and underlined with the heavy sweetness of rot. This area of Boston's harbor was far from scenic, and Melanie had never spent much time down here. There was an old fish packaging plant that had seen better days. The dark, oily water was stagnant with dead fish, fallen sea gulls, and today, a man's corpse. In spite of all of David's warnings, Melanie recoiled at the smell.

Detective Jax turned to greet them. He once again worked a toothpick between his teeth, giving David a firm handshake and Melanie a sympathetic smile.

"How y' doin', Ms. Stokes?"

"No one's shot me yet. I must be doing better than Monday."

Detective Jax flashed a grin, then grew serious. "Just so you're prepared, it's not pretty."

"David warned me."

"Sure you don't want to wait for the morgue tape?"

"As I've said—"

"Okay, okay, I got it. You're tired of Club Fed and want to go home. Fine. Then here's the drill. You don't have to memorize him or nothing. Just take a glance. Tell us if you think it's him. One look, you're done."

"Go home and forget all about it?" she murmured, then followed Detective Jax to the body. David rested his hand on the small of her back.

There was no mistaking the dead man. He was faceup on the cracked asphalt. Puffed face gray and rubbery. Bloated hands over his head, picked ragged by feeding fish. Dark suit waterlogged and algae coated. Black holes on his white dress shirt where two bullets had fired home.

No blood this time. The water had washed it away.

"What do you think?" Detective Jax asked.

"That's him." She kept staring. She couldn't help herself. Dead never looked the way she thought it should. With Digger it had been too bloody. With this man it was too alien. The water had turned him into something resembling a wax doll.

"Looks like he'd been shot twice, close range," Detective Jax said conversationally. "Probably the day before. It's gonna take a bit to ID him—no papers and not much for fingertips. Guess the fish had a real banquet. We'll send him to the state crime lab for analysis. The water will make it tougher—he's a floater and a bloater—but I've requested Jeffrey Ames for the job. Jeff's the best."

"I know Jeff," David spoke up. "He's good."

"You know Jeff?" Detective Jax switched the toothpick to the left side of his mouth and peered at David curiously.

"I'm a member of the Mass Rifle Association," David explained. "Jeff shoots there too."

"You're a member of the MRA? Wait a sec, David Riggs. Are you Bobby Riggs's son?"

David nodded. Detective Jax lit up.

"Holy hell, good to meet you. I love Bobby. Man does beautiful work. Give your father my regards, 'kay? Oh, and tell him I wanna bring in my gun. Damn sight is driving me nuts."

"I'll tell him. When do you think you'll have the initial report?"

"Forty-eight hours maybe? I'm gonna put a rush on it, but we're a little backed up these days. Spring's rough around here."

"Do you know who killed him?" Melanie asked quietly. Her stomach was beginning to roll.

"Don't have any witnesses, if that's what you mean. We're still detailing the area, but so far no brass and no traces of blood, so he was probably shot somewhere else. Lab guys may find something on his shoes or clothing that can help us locate the murder site. It's amazing what a couple of good chemists can do these days."

"What about the notes he took? The papers from Larry Digger's room?"

Detective Jax shook his head. "Nope. My guess is he showed up for contact, delivering the goods and expecting to get paid. But maybe his employer wasn't so happy about the mess he made of things, or the job being only half done. So he closed out the deal with a couple of deliveries of lead. There just ain't no honor among thieves."

"So we don't really know anything yet," Melanie murmured. "Sure, this person is dead, but his employer could just hire another, and another, and . . ." Her voice was rising. She was losing it after all.

David and Detective Jax were watching her closely. She took a deep breath, focused on the warm, familiar feel of David's hand against the small of her back. She nodded and everyone relaxed.

"You guys care to start explaining things yet?" Detective Jax asked. "Or should I just wait until the next dead body?"

"I don't know," David replied. "When are you planning on finding the next dead body?"

"Oh, holy Lord, working with G-men sucks." Jax spat out his toothpick. "Look, I'm going after this with all I can, Agent Riggs. I don't have the resources of the Bureau or the experts of the Bureau, but what the hell, I like to think us poor local slobs run a pretty good show. Now, do you want to give me any hints, or should I just keep gnawing away at this like a Chihuahua?"

"Larry Digger said he had proof of who my birth parents are," Melanie offered. "It seems someone doesn't want me to know."

"Why? Everyone's finding their birth parents these days. It's about as popular as no-fat double lattes with whip."

"Because maybe my birth father was a serial killer. And maybe it would be embarrassing for my family if it was discovered that they had knowingly adopted the child of such a man."

Now she had Detective Jax's undivided attention. "Well, shoot me, that would make a difference. So this Larry Digger, he claimed to have proof of where you came from?"

"That's what he said. We never got to see it, but we heard quite a bit of his story."

"And he alleged your parents *knowingly* adopted you anyway? They got big hearts, or what? I didn't think the Beacon Street type liked to go outside established bloodlines." Jax gave her a look. "Ms. Stokes, I can dance as well as the next guy, but this tango is ridiculous. If you want me to help, you give it to me clean. I'll see what I can do. Welcome to the Jax School of Justice. 'Kay?"

"Needless to say," David said smoothly, "it's an ongoing investigation. Listen, Detective, if you want to help, here's what we need the most: Our shooter is dead, but we still don't know who hired him, and since the job wasn't completed the first time, there's a good chance that there'll be a second contract on Melanie's life. If you hear anything—"

"I think I'll let you know." Jax returned to Melanie, shaking his head. "I'll work on this as hard as I can and you got Mr. Personality here, too, but these things take time. It'll be days before I get the first lab report, and that's assuming the initial chem run yields findings. With bodies that have been in the water, it can take longer than that. I can already tell the bullets are soft lead, so they won't have any striations, which means the lab will have to determine gun type by class, not characteristic. That takes longer as well. Seriously, ma'am, we're looking at weeks before we start getting the first clue, and considering that you're already in danger . . ."

"He's right," David said, having found an ally for his case. "I'll take you back to the hotel, Melanie. We'll buy you clothes, come up with a good excuse for your parents. Hell, you can tell them you're off to find yourself. That's true enough. And it would certainly be a lot safer—"

"No."

"Yes—"

"No! I *know* who I am, David. I'm twenty-nine years old, I have lived the last twenty years in the Stokes household, and *that is where I belong.*"

"Like hell it is. They are going to get you killed—"

"You don't know that! We don't have a shred of evidence, just a bunch of far-fetched theories. I'm not going to walk away because of that. For crying out loud, we are never going to move beyond theory with me shut up in a hotel room anyway. At the very least, you can consider my going home as the most efficient means of moving the investigation forward."

"I will not risk you for the stupid case—"

"This isn't your choice, David. It's mine, and I'm going home!"

She pivoted, took a step toward the car, but David grabbed her arm.

"Don't you put yourself in the line of fire."

"They won't hurt me," she insisted stubbornly. "They won't."

"You are blind and stubborn and completely ignorant when it comes to your parents. You're so caught up in your romantic notion of what families mean that you're going to get yourself killed!"

"Why, thank you, David. I trust your judgment and intelligence just as much."

She jerked her arm free and stormed back to the car.

Detective Jax let out a low whistle. "I guess we pissed her off."

"She doesn't understand."

"The woman is standing in front of a corpse. I think she understands just fine."

"No, she doesn't." David turned on Jax. "You don't get her yet, Detective. She was abandoned and that has skewed her judgment. Her family is perfect. Her family must need her. It's a great dream, an understandable dream. And it's gonna get her killed."

Detective Jax shrugged. "And if it were your family, Riggs? If it was your father we were talking about? Who would be the naïve romantic then?"

"Oh, shut up," David said darkly, and stalked after Melanie to the car.

They drove downtown in taut silence, David tapping his fingers crossly on the wheel while Melanie stared resolutely out the window.

"You are a pigheaded fool," he said finally.

She smiled tightly. "I believe it runs in the family."

They made it another half-mile, then he exploded again. "Dammit, you can't ignore the fact that someone wants you dead."

"I'm not ignoring it."

"You're walking into the proverbial lion's den!"

"No, I'm not! I'm going home, which is my right. I'm going to kiss my mother on the cheek, I'm going to hug my father. I'm going to hunt down my brother for a serious heart-to-heart, and then I'm going to corner my godfather for a nice long chat."

"Because you believe they'll magically tell you everything?" His voice lowered with scorn. "Whatever happened to Meagan, they've kept it secret for twenty-five years. Now someone has even gone so far as to hire a paid gun. So really, I don't think they're going to simply confess. Not even to their favorite daughter."

Melanie drew in her breath with a sharp hiss. "They are not evil."

"Close enough. Dammit, Melanie." David suddenly slapped the steering wheel. "Are you going to make me say it?"

"Maybe."

"I'm an agent. It's out of line."

"Then I'll take it off the record, Mr. Riggs."

He growled, but she didn't relent. She had not realized how much this mattered to her until right that moment. She was leaning toward him. She was staring at him intently. She'd come to need him even more than she'd realized. She really wanted to know that he cared, as well. That the last few days had not been another illusion.

He spoke in a rush. "I care, dammit! You matter to me, Melanie, more than you're supposed to, and I don't want to see you hurt."

"I know."

"I sympathize, all right? They are your family, and while I certainly won't win son of the year award anytime soon, my family is important to me too. If it was my father or brother in question, I don't know that I would handle it any better."

"I have to trust them, David. They've loved me so well."

"Of course they've loved you, Mel. You're as close to Meagan Stokes as they're ever going to get."

Melanie recoiled. She knew he was trying to shock her, and it worked. Her eyes were stinging. She was on the verge of tears.

There wasn't anyone in the world who didn't long to be loved for simply being herself. It wasn't fair of him to state that no matter what she did, she would always be the substitute daughter.

She turned away and looked out the window.

David got off 93, whipped through the financial district, and emerged on Beacon Street. Three blocks from home. He slowed down the car. She groped for her composure. When he finally stopped the car, she still didn't feel ready.

"Be careful," he said quietly. The scowl had dropped. He looked genuinely worried and that touched her.

"Thank you." She brushed his hand.

He pulled it back, shaking his head. "I don't want your gratitude. I'm too far over the line to even pretend this is professional courtesy."

"Yeah, it's part of your charm."

"I *don't* have any charm. I'm old, arthritic, and cranky. Half the time I have the personality of a porcupine. Don't tell me I have charm."

"You do, because underneath it all I know there beats a good heart."

"Female fantasy," he muttered.

"Truth."

He looked like he might argue some more, but then he sighed and now he did take her hand with his own. "Melanie, for lots of reasons I think you know, I can't just stop by your house."

"I expected that."

"You really will be on your own."

"I understand that too."

"And you're scaring the shit out of me."

"Given."

"Okay, fine. This is my beeper number." He scrawled it on a piece of paper. "If you're in trouble, I'll come. Have a bad dream, I'll come. Have a bad memory, I'll come. Just dial the beeper, okay? I'll be there, Melanie. I will."

She took the piece of paper. "Thank you," she said, and saw him wince once more at her gratitude. "I need to go now."

"Mel, wait."

But Melanie didn't wait. She slipped out of the car. She started walking and didn't look back, not even when the car started up and drove away.

Then she was alone.

The cherry blossoms waved merrily. The scent of hyacinths was spicy and fragrant in the air. A beautiful day in a beautiful city.

Melanie looked up at the three-story brick house that was her home. She saw the solid walnut doors, the heavy iron gate. She saw the bay windows of her bedroom.

And for just a moment she shivered with fear.

Then she opened the door and stepped inside.

TWENTY-TWO

MARÍA, THE MAID, greeted her with a friendly nod. She looked at Melanie's wrinkled clothes and disheveled hair but took them in stride. Her parents and Señor O'Donnell were on the back patio eating lunch. Would she like anything?

Melanie shook her head and headed for the patio. Jamie came walking through the back door. He halted at the sight of her, his face registering surprise.

"Melanie?" her godfather said hesitantly, holding out his arms as he always did but clearly uncertain.

She went into the hug, realizing she needed the contact more than she'd thought. Before she was ready, he pulled back and held her firmly at arm's length.

"What's up, lass? I hear you've been gone for two days without so much as a by-your-leave. Why are you worrying your mother like this? It's not like you."

Melanie didn't answer immediately. Confronted by her first family member, she discovered she wasn't sure what she wanted to say. Or maybe she wasn't sure what she wanted to hear. David was right. This was more difficult than she'd thought. Her first question caught even her by surprise.

"Do you love me?"

"Of course, lass! You are my favorite woman in the whole world."

"Why?"

"Why?" Her godfather arched a brow and regarded her more seriously. "You are in a mood. Well, I don't know. Why do you love anything, Melanie? I suppose because you do."

"Is it? You've always been there for me, Jamie. For my coming-home party, my first day of school, my birthdays, my charity balls, everything. That's a lot of interest in a goddaughter's life."

"Well, you are a special goddaughter."

"But why? Why do you love me so much, Jamie? What is it you want from me?"

Her voice was rising a notch. Her godfather immediately waved away her distress. He said simply and calmly, "I love you for being you. And all I've ever wanted was for you to be happy."

Melanie thought it was one of the loveliest things she'd ever heard, and a heartbeat later she knew she didn't believe a word of it. For the first time in her life she doubted her godfather.

Moments passed, the silence growing strained. Jamie's expression changed from tender to wary.

"If something was going on with you," he finally asked, "you would let me know, wouldn't you?"

"I don't know. If something was going on with *you,* you would let me know, wouldn't you?"

"No, I wouldn't."

"Why? I'm twenty-nine, I'm ready to hear—"

"And I'm fifty-nine, which is still older than you and wiser."

"Wiser about what, Jamie? Wiser about a reporter named Larry Digger, or a midwife to Russell Lee Holmes? Wiser about Brian and Meagan Stokes?"

Her godfather studied her. His eyes, she realized, were much more sharp, much more knowing than she'd ever given him credit for.

"Not Brian," he said. "But you, lass. You."

"Jamie—"

He moved away, making a show of dusting off his trench coat, flicking at lint. "I'm going to be in town a bit, Melanie. Business is booming, what can I say? So if you need anything, of course"—he looked at her meaningfully—"call me at the Four Seasons. Day or night, I'll come."

"Jamie—"

"I've met a woman, Mel, have I told you that? I'm thinking of settling down, maybe becoming a local. What do you think? Can you see me as a married man? Bah. You're right, you're right. What am I doing looking at myself as a family man? That's Harper's gig, you know. Pipe dreams again. I'm getting maudlin and foolish in my old age."

"Jamie—"

"At the Four Seasons. Just call the number and your old godfather will be here. Now try to get some sleep."

Then he was gone.

After a minute Melanie opened the French doors and walked onto the patio.

Her parents were dining alone. Harper was wearing hospital scrubs and reading the paper; he must have had a surgery this morning. Patricia sat across from him, sectioning out bites of grapefruit, which she followed with nibbles of dry toast. For as long as Melanie could remember, her mother had dined on only grapefruit and plain wheat toast.

Patricia turned at the sound of Melanie's approach and her eyes grew wide. They looked at each other uncomfortably, memories of a phone call stretching between the two of them. Melanie had never felt awkward around her mother, but now she did.

Finally, Patricia smiled tremulously and held out her arms for her daughter's embrace.

Melanie's knees almost gave way. This was what she wanted, she realized. After the last forty-eight hours, she wanted to come home to her mother. She wanted to inhale the scents of Chanel No. 5 and Lancôme face cream she'd known most of her life. She wanted to hear her mother say, as she had so many times over the years, "It'll be all right, child. You're a Stokes now, and we'll always take care of you."

And then Melanie thought, Oh, God, what did you people do to Meagan?

"How was your evening?" Patricia asked lightly.

"Fine," Melanie said. She stared at the patio floor, then fingered the petals of a pink climbing rose. Her mother's arms finally came down. She turned back to her grapefruit, shaken, and Melanie felt worse.

Her father lowered his newspaper. He looked at her, then at Patricia, then her again. He frowned. "Melanie? Are you all right? We haven't seen you in days, which is not like you."

"I just needed some space."

"That may be, but we're still family. Next time, make sure you call. That's common courtesy."

"Of course," she murmured. "How . . . how is life around here?"

"Busy," her father said with a sigh. He looked pale and overworked, his face showing his age. "Got called in this morning for another pacemaker installation. I swear, that hospital never lets me get any rest."

"Your father and I have been talking," her mother interjected suddenly. "We think it's time the whole family went on vacation. Even Brian."

"Europe," Harper said.

"What?" Melanie couldn't have been more surprised.

"I've always said we should take a family vacation," her father continued reasonably. "Finally I said to your mother that maybe we should just pack our bags and go. We'll spend six months traveling around France and England and the Mediterranean. It will be the time of our life."

She was bewildered. "I don't want to go to Europe. Not now."

"Nonsense," her mother said. Melanie thought her voice was too bright, as if she were placating a child. "You need a vacation, Melanie. You deserve one. It will be wonderful. We'll relax and bask in the sun."

Melanie shook her head. She looked at her parents, but they wouldn't return her gaze. Patricia was wringing her hands on her lap, then twisting her wedding band. Harper was tapping his foot, shifting a bit to the left, shifting to the right, in a way she'd never seen her father do before.

This wasn't a vacation, Melanie realized. This was escape. Had they gotten a shrine? Or maybe a phone call telling them they got what they deserved. Were they panicking and resorting to fleeing once more, as they'd fled from Texas to Boston?

"I won't go," Melanie announced.

Harper frowned. "We're offering you a vacation to Europe, Melanie. Of course you'll go."

She shook her head. Her hands were knotted at her sides, and she realized as she spoke that her voice was climbing. "This has nothing to do with a vacation. You *never* go on vacation, Dad. One would think if you spent more than ten minutes away from your precious hospital, you'd turn to stone."

Her father's gaze narrowed. "I don't know what you are talking about, young lady, nor do I appreciate your tone."

"I'm talking about the truth," Melanie cried. "I'm talking about what happened to a little girl named Meagan Stokes."

A silence descended upon the patio. Melanie saw her mother pale. Then the silence was broken by the sound of metal screeching on flagstone as her father pushed back his chair and leaped to his feet, his face an unhealthy shade of red. "Don't you dare, young lady. Don't you dare bring this up in front of your mother!"

"Why not? It's been twenty-five years. Why don't we ever speak of Meagan? It's not like you guys don't think about her. Or that I don't find Mom staring at her portrait, or you yourself gazing at it over a glass of Scotch. Brian still calls out her name at times, Jamie used to stutter every time he had to say Melanie. Meagan's here. She's in this house and she's part of all of our lives. So why don't we ever speak of her? *What are you so afraid of?*"

"Young lady, that is enough. You will not speak to your parents like that—"

"My parents. Yes, my parents. One more thing we never mention. Why didn't we ever look for my birth parents, Dad? Why didn't you ever suggest hypnosis or regression therapy or anything that might help me reclaim my own identity? Why were you at the hospital that night and not watching the execution of Russell Lee Holmes?"

"Melanie!" her mother gasped. "What . . . what is this?"

Melanie didn't get a chance to answer. Harper thrust up a hand, immediately silencing his wife. He stared at his daughter, and there was a cold expression on his face Melanie had never seen turned on her before.

"How dare you." His gaze burned the way it had when he'd looked at her brother the night Brian had announced he was gay. "How dare you stand in my own house and speak to me this way. After everything I've done for you. Goddammit, I took you in, I put a roof over your head. I've done everything a father is supposed to do, looked after your health, paid for your education, guided you through life. I've never short-changed you, young lady. I have never treated you as less than my own child, you spoiled, ungrateful—"

"What?" Melanie goaded softly. "Killer's brat? Is that what you're trying to say? Is that how you *really* feel, Harper?"

"You little bitch." He raised his arm and smacked her hard. Melanie fell onto the patio without even a murmur. As if from a distance, she heard her mother's soft cry of distress.

Slowly Melanie raised her head.

"It's not going to go away, Dad," she whispered. "The truth is out now, and not even Boston's best cardiac surgeon can control this mess. Not even you can make it go away."

"You don't know what you're talking about—"

"Stop it," Patricia yelled. "Just stop it."

They both turned to her. Patricia was getting shakily to her feet. Her body swayed tremulously, her eyes filled with unshed tears.

"Please," she whispered. "No more. This is our daughter, Harper. Brian is our son. They are all we have. What are you doing?"

"I'm trying to teach them some gratitude. You see what happens when you give them everything, Pat? How they are both turning out—"

Patricia placed a hand on his shoulder. "Harper, please."

He yanked his arm away, his expression too angry, too hurt.

"You too, Pat?" he growled. "Goddammit, I have had enough. Who bought this house and the cars you're driving and the clothes you're wearing and the food you're eating anyway? Certainly wasn't you or your father. He left all his money to charity, remember? Told us we could earn ours. So I did. I go to that hospital every day, I work my ass off in a stressful position you couldn't even imagine, and what kind of respect do I get for that? What kind of appreciation from my own wife?"

He whirled on Melanie. "And you. Your charity work is great, but how the hell does it pay the rent? What kind of responsibility do you show around here? You just went off for two days as if you hadn't a fucking care in the world.

"Now, what would happen if I did that? Huh? *What would happen?* Don't you people get it yet? My own children dance and play and join freak shows while *I* pay the fucking bills. My wife shops and nurses her self-pity while *I* get up and go to work every single day regardless of rain, weather, or mood. Jesus Christ, Pat, all I ever asked of you was to be a good mother. Then Meagan dies and you weren't even that. You became a mourner, a full-time professional mourner. Is it any wonder that Brian became a freak? Of course he had to turn to men. It wasn't like he was getting any affection from the women in his life!"

Patricia inhaled sharply, but her husband was far from done.

"So don't you turn on me!" He stared directly at Melanie. "Don't you speak to me in that tone of voice! This is *my house*. Paid for by me, maintained by me, because that's what my life is all about—taking care of the rest of you whether I feel like it or not. You guys get to play. I have *never* had that luxury. Not even when my little girl was murdered, you selfish, self-centered—"

Harper's voice broke off abruptly. He was near tears, Melanie realized. Oh, God, she'd driven her father to *tears*.

He wiped his face with the back of a hand, quickly composing himself, but still angry.

"I'm going to the hospital. While I'm gone, I expect you two to give this some thought. And you, Melanie. I want an apology to both me and your mother by morning. And then you can start packing your bags. Because whether you like it or not, this whole family is going on vacation and we're all going to be happy, if it kills us!"

Harper banged through the French doors. Moments later they could hear him storming down the hall and then slamming the front door. Then the house was silent.

Patricia was staring at Melanie, who tried to think of something to say, something to do. She found herself fingering her cheek; it still stung. Her mind couldn't grasp it. She'd never seen her father violent before.

"He just needs some time to cool off," Patricia murmured. "He's been under a lot of pressure lately. . . ."

Melanie didn't say anything.

"It's going to be all right," her mother said more anxiously. "This is how families are. We have spells, bad spells, but we get through them, Melanie. We all get through them, and that's what makes us strong."

"Maybe we shouldn't keep getting through them," Melanie said tiredly. "Maybe what this family really needs is to fall apart."

She staggered to her feet. Her legs felt rubbery. Pain gathered behind her left eyeball. Another migraine was coming.

"You're only twenty-nine," her mother was saying. "Only a twenty-nine-year-old would say something like that. The bottom line is that families must forgive, Melanie, and families must *forget*."

"Why? We have never forgotten Meagan. And you and Dad have obviously never forgiven each other, or how could he have said even half of what he did? What did you guys do back then? What did you do?"

Patricia paled again. Then her shoulders sagged and Melanie supposed she'd finally gotten what she wanted. Her mother broke, looking hurt and frightened beyond belief.

Melanie decided there was no satisfaction in it after all.

IN HER OWN room, the colors greeted her sharply. Red, green, and blue. Yellow and orange, and Lord, what a mess.

She shed her dress and climbed into the shower. And there beneath the protective spray, she sobbed simply because she needed to.

When she climbed back out, all the emotion had drained away. She was no longer scared or angry or overwhelmed. She was exhausted.

She took her Fiorinal, cocooned herself in bed, and within seconds fell asleep.

Once she woke up and saw her father standing in the doorway, his hands on his hips, his face filled with menace.

Then she was sucked back into the darkness, where she ran through a dense underbrush, thorns snatching at her hair and the scent of gardenias cloying in the air.

I want to go home. I want to go home.

Run, Meagan, run.

The sound of laboring breath coming closer . . . coming closer . . .

RUN, MEAGAN, RUN!

The gardenias, the branches, twigs, the heavy foot-steps falling so close—

Nooo.

When she woke up again, Patricia sat at her bed-side, stroking her hair.

"It's all right," her mother whispered. "I won't lose another child. I won't."

_____

TWENTY-THREE

DAVID WORKED LATE. Hunched over his desk, he raked a hand through his hair and sifted through stacks of paper. His eyes were blurred by fatigue, his neck muscles ached, and his lower back had locked up. He pushed himself harder, consumed by the notion that there wasn't much time left.

Chenney had investigated William Sheffield's trash early that afternoon. He'd discovered an entire bag filled with pig organs, stained bedding, and one shiny apple. Unless Sheffield had taken up a macabre hobby, David was willing to believe the items had been left as some kind of shocking display.

After twenty-five years, had one of the co-conspirators finally had enough? Or was there a person they had yet to identify? And what other kinds of messages might have been delivered that the Bureau simply didn't know about yet?

David hated that question most of all. He was left with an overall feeling of being herded, that the messenger wasn't moving just with speed, but with competency. Hitting everyone's buttons and moving on. Advancing them all through some highly complex game where he already had an ending in sight.

That ending worried David quite a bit.

"What you got?" he demanded from Detective Jax at four in the afternoon.

"Forty-two cases and two unidentified stiffs. And how are you?"

"Overworked and underloved. Have you ID'd the shooter?"

"Nah, the tarot card reading came back inconclusive. Now I'm thinking of contacting a medium. Maybe get the guy's name and a song by Elvis Presley. You know, 'cause us local boys have nothing better to do with our time."

"What about the pay phone records? Know who Difford spoke to?"

"Yo, Agent, keep your pants on. It takes a little time to subpoena public phone records and wade through the mess, unless, of course, you want to do the paperwork for me."

"It's your case," David said stiffly.

"As a matter of fact, it is. So why the hell am I talking to you?" Detective Jax hung up. Apparently forty-two cases took their toll on a man.

David was left with gnawing frustration and a really bad mood. Subpoenaing records did take time. Sorting through the records of a downtown Boston pay phone with its extraordinary high volume of calls took even longer.

He just wanted answers now.

Seven P.M. arrived.

Lairmore stopped by on his way out the door. "Where are we?"

"Same as yesterday, plus one additional corpse."

Lairmore scowled. David raised an inquiring brow. "Bad day, Lairmore?"

"Bad week," the supervisory agent said. David didn't push. Lairmore's business was his own, just as David's business was his own. The red message light on his phone was already blinking with the third message left by his father.

After a moment Lairmore walked away.

David returned to the open file on his desk. He was surrounded by stacks of materials, as if they were pieces of a giant jigsaw puzzle just waiting to fall into place. He had a file on the Stokes financials, which he was dutifully compiling for his next seven A.M. meeting with Lairmore. Nothing revolutionary there. Money came in, money went out. Someone had better tell Harper there was more to life than Armani suits.

David sighed. He'd left two messages with Brian Stokes, but neither had been returned. At eight P.M. he paid a visit to the exiled son's house. No lights on, nobody home. Next David tried the private practice where Brian worked, only to be told that the doctor had called in sick.

Forty-eight hours without a single sighting of Brian Stokes. David still wasn't sure what that meant.

Nine P.M. He followed up with the lab. They didn't have conclusive news yet. No prints. Candles were a local-made brand available from a factory in Maine and sold in several hundred locations in the state. The toy did seem old. Most interesting was the scrap of dress that had yielded two blood types. They were hoping to have DNA test results by end of week, and that was considered a rush job. Of course, for DNA results to be useful, you generally needed someone to match them against.

Back to the normal investigative world of hurry-up-and-wait.

Nothing you can do anymore, Riggs. You are trying to help her, you are.

I lied to her, he thought bluntly, finally left alone with his guilt. I never told her I was investigating her father, or that we probably do have a case against Harper for healthcare fraud.

That's your job. You have to do your job. That is how you help her.

What if it makes a difference? What if knowing that much about her father would give her perspective, help keep her safe?

You don't know that, Riggs. As Chenney likes to say, there's still a world of difference between reckless endangerment of human life and hiring a hit man to kill your adopted daughter.

He finally headed back to his place.

He slipped on boxers, crawled into bed.

He fell asleep with his pager cradled against his cheek, and he dreamed he was in a wooden shack but with Melanie, not Meagan Stokes. He was cleaning, scrubbing the floor furiously, as if that would save them all.

But he could still see Melanie laid out in the middle of the floor, and no matter how hard he scrubbed, she didn't move.

In the doorway Russell Lee Holmes stood laughing.

CHENNEY WAS TIRED. Really tired. He'd managed to snag an afternoon nap, but between trying to track down William Sheffield's garbage and his history at some boys' home in Texas, he'd still had a long day. At least he'd learned interesting information. According to one of the nuns, Sheffield had been a bit of a monster at that boys' home. She even thought William might have poisoned one of the older boys, not enough to die, but enough to put some fear of God in the child and keep him away from William. Clearly, there was more to the thin, overeducated anesthesiologist than met the eye.

Now Chenney trudged through the dim halls of City General, pushing a cart loaded down with cleaning supplies, a giant trash can, and rolls upon rolls of toilet paper. Halls were empty, dimly lit. His cart echoed against the linoleum floor and gave him the willies. He didn't like big institutional places.

When the ICU nurse had moved on to other patients in the ward, he'd managed to sneak a glance at the charts. He couldn't understand any of the shit— that was Riggs's department.

He'd finally focused on two older patients who were hooked to heart monitors and IVs. One looked in pretty rough shape. Toothless jaw open beneath the oxygen mask. Skin settling into folds around her neck. Flesh tone nearly gray. Chenney figured whatever condition she had, it was real.

The other man was younger, probably in his fifties. Fairly fit, actually. Good haircut. Nice spring tan, a bit of a roll around the middle and upper arms. The next time the nurse was around, he'd inquire politely about the man's condition.

Chenney turned the corner, slogging ahead, and thinking he really had to get up to speed on healthcare fraud.

"Oh, excuse me." Chenney had been so lost in thought, he'd run into a doctor.

The man turned around, equally startled, and Chenney found himself face-to-face with Dr. William Sheffield.

Chenney gripped the cart to hold himself steady. He was just a janitor, he reminded himself belatedly.

"Are you going to move?" Sheffield inquired tersely. Chenney caught a faint whiff of whiskey.

"Sorry." Chenney eased back his cart. He had to stare at the floor now, or he was sure his face would give him away. Luckily Sheffield wasn't in the mood to chat. The anesthesiologist brushed by in a snit and kept walking down the hall.

Okay. Now what?

Chenney should swing back around to the ICU. Would Sheffield really strike two nights in a row? Anything was possible.

Chenney picked up his footsteps, never seeing Sheffield turn around with a last annoyed glance, his gaze falling to the janitor's shoes. William took one look at the retreating Italian loafers, and his stomach plunged, and his mouth went dry.

He bolted into the nearest bathroom. He vomited into the sink. He grabbed the two vials of propranolol from his pocket, wiped them clean with paper towels, and shoved them deep into the trash can.

Harper was setting him up, that son of a bitch. Looking for a fall guy so he could once again sail away into the sunset.

Well, Harper Stokes had another think coming. William was not going down without a fight. Particularly not when he knew a thing or two.

"WE HAVE PROBLEMS," Harper stated at the other end of the line.

"Would it kill you to let me sleep?" Jamie O'Donnell yawned, annoyed at being woken up for a second night by Harper. Jamie glanced at the clock glowing next to his bed. Two A.M. Bloody hell.

"Hang on." Jamie pushed back the covers and crawled out of bed, conscious of Annie sleeping beside him. Jamie touched her cheek once, then picked up the phone and carried it with him to the adjoining room of the suite, shutting the door behind him so he wouldn't disturb her.

"What's up, sport? Did you just get your tickets to Europe?" Jamie yawned again. The European vacation still rankled him. Harper riding off like the good cowboy with the tall white hat.

"Fuck Europe," Harper said. "This is about William. He's cracked. Called me in total panic, told me he was being pursued by a pair of Italian loafers, and that he wasn't going to let me get away with this. Then he slammed down the phone. I tried calling back twice, no answer. I went by his place. Looks as if a tornado has blown through, and both William and his car have vanished."

"You're right. The kid's gone Humpty Dumpty."

"Jesus Christ," Harper exploded. "He's ranting that I set him up. I've done no such thing. Just who the hell is behind all this? I thought you were going to figure it out."

"I'm trying. As a matter of fact, I'd thought I'd talk to Larry Digger about it, but I couldn't. Seems that Larry boy is now dead."

"*What!*"

"Oh, don't play dumb with me, Harper. I know you did it."

"I did not!" Harper sounded shrill. "What the hell is going on? Somebody is setting me up, Jamie. You have to believe me. Somebody is just plain fucking with everything. My God, even Melanie came home accusing me of doing something to Meagan."

For a moment Jamie didn't reply. He'd never heard his old friend sound so out of control before, so genuinely afraid. He kept waiting for some feeling of satisfaction to come to him, but it didn't. He still carried the suspicion that this too was an act. It was always so difficult to tell with Harper.

"You really didn't arrange to harm Larry Digger?"

"No!"

"Well, I didn't do it."

"But, but . . ." Harper was definitely losing it now. "*Who?*"

"I don't know."

"You have to fix this, Jamie. Everything is falling apart. It can't just happen like this. Not . . . not after all this time. It makes no sense. This was over and done with, end of story."

"You started it again with the surgeries, Hap. I warned you to keep your hands clean—"

"Fine, fine, I'm stopping them. Just find Sheffield for me. Work this out with him."

"What makes you think he'll listen to me? He hates me as much as anyone."

"Because, Jamie, he's your kind. Remember?"

Jamie was silent. Then he had to shake his head. Leave it to Harper to lash out even when he was down. There was more than a bit of the street fighter in prim, proper Dr. Stokes.

"All right," Jamie said finally, reluctantly. "One

last time, I'll take care of things. Just give me a day or two." He added as almost an afterthought, "Oh, Harper."

"What?"

"Have you spoken to your son lately?"

"No. I've been meaning to call. Tomorrow I'll do it."

"Well, I wish you the best of luck, then, old man, because I've been trying to reach him for twenty-four hours now, but Brian seems to have also disappeared. I wonder what that means, Hap. I wonder."

TWENTY-FOUR

M ELANIE WOKE UP with her cheek still stinging. She fingered the bruise gingerly. Painful, but nothing that wouldn't heal. She supposed that assessment characterized much of her life these days.

When she came downstairs, the house was quiet. No Harper or Patricia. No María.

She called her brother. Brian wasn't at home. She tried him at work. He was still out sick, the receptionist informed her. Something about a forty-eight-hour flu bug. Melanie didn't believe that for a minute. If Brian was sick, he'd be at home. Now what?

The phone call, the anonymous tip that supposedly had come from her own house. In the chaos of the past few days, she'd never followed up on it. Now she dialed the local phone company and arranged for a listing of calls to be sent. That would be a start. And until then?

Melanie roamed the downstairs, feeling strange and outside her own skin. Her home looked like a setting from a play to her now, a carefully crafted backdrop. Living room hung in rose-colored silk, perfect for social gatherings. Front parlor with golden Italian marble, perfect for impressing hospital administrators. Dining room with the huge walnut table set for twelve, perfect for family dinners and long, intimate conversations as the Stokeses unwound from their day.

Back patio with its clay urns of climbing roses and wrought iron table, perfect for a father to strike a daughter.

Enough. Melanie went down to the basement, where there rested a pile of boxes that shared one common label: MEAGAN STOKES 1968–1972.

When Melanie had turned twelve, Patricia lobbied to finish the basement as a rec room for the kids. Harper denied the motion. Families needed places to hide their junk, he'd insisted. Basements served useful purposes.

It may have made sense, except the Stokeses had no junk. No boxes of old clothes, old books, jigsaw puzzles, or games. No stained carpet or too-old furniture. Harper was scrupulous—all outgrown items were catalogued, evaluated, and sent to the Salvation Army for the tax deduction. Everything had its worth. Except these boxes, whose content was priceless.

She'd searched these boxes before, as a nine-year-old child desperate to learn more about her new parents' life. She'd run her child's hands reverently over the lace baptismal dress, the red velvet Christmas dress, the hand-knit pink "blankie." She'd examined the small bronzed shoes, the tiny handprint made in clay, the first works of Crayola art. She'd looked through the boxes feeling both guilty and enthralled, knowing she should stay away but consumed with the desire to know more.

This was all that remained of Meagan Stokes, and Melanie wanted to know about the real love in her family's life.

Melanie began with the box of photos.

They started with the Texas days. Jamie, Harper, and Patricia in an old white convertible; Jamie and Harper in pin-striped suits, looking like fifties gangsters; Jamie with his arms wrapped around a young, beautiful Patricia, beaming at the camera; Jamie shaking his head while a dashing young Harper kissed his future wife.

Wedding photos. Patricia and Harper inside a yawning cathedral, holding hands. Patricia wearing the perfect princess dress, flounces and flounces of white tulle cascading down her slender frame.

Outside with Jamie again, posing in a white tuxedo jacket with black trim as Harper's best man. Her godfather was still smiling, but now he stood far away from Patricia, often half cut out of the camera's lens. Despite what the three friends must have said, the wedding had changed things.

Suddenly, baby pictures. Brian Harper Stokes, February 25, 1963, 8 lbs. 10 oz. Brian being cradled in Harper's triumphant embrace. Patricia smiling tiredly. Brian crawling, Brian walking. Three-year-old Brian reaching for a figurine poised just out of his reach in a hallway. Three-year-old Brian looking stunned at the now-broken statue. Patricia's notation: "Brian's first encounter with art. When will he learn?"

Brian dressed up for Halloween as Satan. "Brian still in his 'devil phase.' At least it suits him."

Then Patricia was pregnant. Brian faded to the background. The lens focused in on tall, slender Patricia now radiantly in bloom. Patricia cradling her stomach. Patricia in profile, looking far away at something Melanie couldn't see. Patricia at a picnic, Brian running beside the blanket. Patricia very, very pregnant, holding up a stuffed bear for the camera. Brian's face barely visible behind her. Jamie's notation, "Pat 1968. Looking beautiful as always, lass."

Melanie turned the page. Meagan. Patricia cradling the newborn against her breast, the ruddy face pudgy and sleepy, the tiny little hand forming a tiny little fist. Brian sitting beside his mother and newborn sister. Jamie, standing beside the hospital bed laughing, his thick finger securely caught in baby Meagan's tight little fist.

Suddenly both Brian and Meagan were growing up very fast. Picture of Brian feeding Meagan. Brian reading to Meagan. Brian pulling Meagan in a little red wagon, beaming happily.

Three Halloweens later, Brian still dressed up as the devil, but Meagan now at his side as Raggedy Ann. They were both smiling. Next photo, Patricia, Brian, and four-year-old Meagan Stokes, beaming into the camera, a beautiful young mother and her two incredibly happy, incredibly beautiful blond children.

Melanie put the album down. Her hands were shaking.

She knew what happened next. A hot, summer day in Texas. Patricia and Brian had left Meagan with the nanny one morning to go to the doctor. And something had occurred that afternoon so that Meagan Stokes ceased to exist on this earth.

They really had been such a perfect family.

There was no mention of Russell Lee Holmes in the box. No newspaper clippings of the case, not even condolence cards from the funeral. One page Meagan Stokes beamed for the camera, the next she was gone, the end of the story never given.

Melanie flipped through the book again. Jamie, Harper, and Patricia. Harper and Patricia. Baby Brian. Brian growing up. Pregnant Patricia, baby Meagan. Meagan and Brian.

Something niggled at the back of her mind.

Pregnant Patricia, baby Meagan. Meagan and Brian.

She couldn't get it. What she wanted haunted her, a word on the tip of her tongue, but she couldn't get it.

Pregnant Patricia, baby Meagan. Meagan and Brian—

Oh, Jesus! Where was Harper? Why wasn't there a single picture of her father with his new baby girl?

Abruptly a sound came from upstairs. The front door opening, then slamming shut. Footsteps on the floor above her head.

Someone was home. Melanie scrambled to replace the photo album. The Meagan boxes were sacred, and at the rate things were going these days, she didn't want to be caught rifling through them.

More footsteps. Crossing the hall into the living room, moving down the back hallway toward the office . . . Harper then. He'd returned from the hospital and was now going to catch up on his paperwork.

Melanie crept up the old wooden stairs, cracked the door, and seeing that the coast was clear, sneaked into the foyer. Seconds later she stood in front of the hallway mirror, dusting off her hands, her denim shorts, and blue and yellow top.

She could hear Harper banging around in his study; from the sound of it, he was not in a good mood.

She surveyed her reflection one last time and decided, what the hell.

Her father was never generous when backed into a corner, but sometimes, on his own, he'd been known to reach the independent conclusion that he was wrong. She could start with her own apology, see what he would do. It was worth a shot.

Melanie walked into her father's office. She expected to find Harper in green surgical scrubs hunched over his desk.

She found William Sheffield, surrounded by flying papers and holding a gun.

WILLIAM WAS HAVING a bad day, a bad week, a bad life. But he was coming out on top of this mess at whatever the price. He just needed proof. Surely Harper had some financial records somewhere.

"William?" A female voice called from the doorway. "What are you doing here?"

William stilled, turned slowly. He saw Melanie standing in the doorway, with her hands stuck in her back pockets. Her gaze rested on his gun warily.

"William?" she asked again.

"You shouldn't be here, Mel," he said. He'd thought the house was empty. He'd thought it would be a simple in and out. But now she'd seen him, and sweet Melanie always told Daddy everything. He couldn't have that.

"What are you doing, William?"

"Enjoying your house." He gestured at the expensively paneled and decorated room. "Quite the place. I've always wondered what it would be like to come home to this day after day. Who would've thunk my mama would've been kinder if she'd drugged me up and dropped me off at an emergency room?"

"You need to leave," Melanie said coolly. "Harper's not here right now, so you shouldn't be in his office."

"Well, you know what?" William strode toward her, catching her off guard and making her gaze flicker once more to his gun. "I don't give a flying fuck what you think. You're just Harper's adopted daughter and you don't know jack shit!"

"William . . ."

She tried to retreat. He knew she'd never seen him as a threat before—but now he charged, and had the satisfaction of seeing her gaze widen with fear. Too late. William pinned her against the wall.

"Move away," she said.

"Why, Mel? I've already seen all of you. Already had all of you."

"Dammit, William—"

He grabbed her hair and yanked. She yelped and immediately blinked back tears. She'd always liked to play tough, play cool. William decided it was time for a little change. Time to finally have some fun at Harper's expense.

"Getting it yet, Mel?"

"I don't . . . no."

"Of course you don't. You know, for a supposedly smart woman, you don't know shit about your family. Yeah, that's right. Stare at me defiantly, try to think you're better than me. You're not better, Mel, you're just more naïve. After all, I figured out your father in less than five minutes, and you still haven't a clue after twenty fucking years. Who's so smart now?"

He yanked her hair again cruelly. This time she couldn't suppress the hiss of pain. He liked that.

"Your fine daddy thinks he has me beat," William drawled. "He thinks he can set me up to take the fall for all his little illegal operations and I'd be too stupid to figure it out. Yeah, you don't know about that either, do you, Mel?" William swept the barrel of the gun casually around the study. "See all this, sweetheart? *Tainted.* Your daddy may be the best cardiac surgeon in Boston, but he knows nothing about money. Man digs himself in deeper and deeper all the time. But do you think that means he cuts back, keeps his family in any less style? Oh, no, not the great Harper Stokes.

"He simply concocts a plan to slice open innocent old folks and slap pacemakers in their chest. 'Nobody gets hurt,' he likes to say. 'Insurance companies can afford it.' Now, how is that for class, Melanie? How is that for your dear old dad?"

Her lips trembled. But then Melanie looked him in the eye and stated in that cool tone he hated so much, "I don't know what you're talking about."

He rewarded her brave words by slapping her hard. She didn't wince, which disappointed him, but her bottom lip cracked. Flecks of blood appeared. The lip began to swell.

William said, "Well, say good-bye to Daddy, darling, because I have no intention of coming home to another surprise gift. You get what you deserve, my ass. I spotted that FBI agent at the hospital. I know what the hell he's up to, and I sure as *hell* am not going to take the fall."

"Oh, my God. You got a note."

"A note?" He frowned at her angrily. "I didn't get a

note. I got a goddamn message scrawled across my mirror in blood. Who would've thought your father had it in him?"

Melanie was shaking her head. "But how are you connected with Russell Lee Holmes? Did you know Meagan?"

"What?" William didn't know what she was talking about and didn't care. He shut her up by pressing his body against hers, watching her gaze flicker more frantically.

"You want to know the truth, Mel? I'll give it to you straight, you dumb little fool. Your father is a con man who would rather slice open healthy people than admit that he's broke. Your mother is an unstable lush who can't keep her own husband satisfied, and your brother is a fucking fruitcake who can only get it up for men. And to top it all off, your godfather is little more than a dressed-up thug. Now, how is that for a sweet family portrait? Two criminals, a lush, and a fag. And what does that make you, Melanie? It makes you a patsy. The world's biggest *patsy,* conned for over twenty years. How do you like that?"

William smiled. Melanie's chin came up like she wanted a fight. But he could also read doubt in her eyes, a bit of pleading, as if she wanted him to take the words back. Like hell.

He leaned back and casually smacked her across the face. "How dare you dump me like that, you stupid bitch."

"How dare you treat me like shit!" she cried, and tried to knee him. He blocked her easily. Then he reached down, caught her wrist, and began to squeeze.

"I need the combination for the safe, Melanie. I need *all* of Harper's papers."

"I don't know it—"

He let go of her wrist and pistol-whipped her. Her head hit the wall, then she slid down to the floor, her eyes blinking groggily.

"Larry Digger."

"What are you talking about? I want the combination for the safe!"

"Did my father . . . did my father shoot Larry Digger?"

William shook his head. "I don't even know what you're talking about. Harper's into money, not murder. Now, I want that combination."

"What happened to Meagan?" she murmured. "What did they do to Meagan?"

"Forget fucking Meagan. Give me the combination, or I'm going to kill you."

He wrapped her long hair around his left hand and in one quick tug jerked her back up to her feet

And the rest simply happened.

Sweet Melanie Stokes drove her shoulder into his gut. Air whooshed out of his lungs. She slammed the broad part of her hand into his sternum and stomped on his foot.

"Fuck!"

He hopped back, cursing, and finally getting the gun between them.

"Fuck you!" he heard himself screaming. "I'm going to kill you, bitch. I'm going to fucking blow your brains—"

"Stop it," she gasped, gripping his hand, wrestling for control.

The gun went off with a blast. They froze in the middle of the torn-up study. William's eyes were wide, startled. Melanie gazed at him with equal shock as he slowly slipped to the floor.

Now she could see the hole in his gut. Blood was pouring everywhere. It was on her hands, on the papers, on the floor. Just like Larry Digger, she thought.

"*Mi Dios!*" a voice breathed in the silence.

Melanie turned to find María standing in the doorway, holding bags of groceries.

"I didn't mean to," Melanie began weakly.

María whirled and ran. Belatedly Melanie realized

she was still holding the gun in her hands and her arms were splattered in blood.

All she'd ever wanted was a family. People who would love her. People who would be there for her. A place that would finally be home.

Lies and blood. Lies and blood.

Her body moved on its own.

She grabbed her purse. She burst out of the front door of her house. She started running, and she didn't stop.

TWENTY-FIVE

LAIRMORE WAS RIPPING new assholes for his investigating agents when David's beeper went off.

"Got to take this," David said calmly, and left the conference room. Lairmore grumbled something unkind, but David ignored him.

The number on his beeper was not one David recognized, but his call was picked up immediately. The sound of background traffic and voices filled the line.

"This is Riggs," he said.

There was a moment of silence, then he knew it was her. "Melanie?"

"You lied to me."

"Melanie, where are you?"

"You told me you weren't investigating my family. You told me it was William you were looking into. I bet you slept well that night. The super agent did his job."

"Melanie, listen to me. I'm trying to help you—"

"Fuck you, David Riggs. How dare you lie to me. How dare you not tell me the truth after everything we went through."

"Melanie—"

"The shooting was accidental, just so you know. William was going to kill me. You can tell that to my

family, but I don't know if they'll care. I don't know
what they care about at this point. I guess you were
right, and I didn't know them at all."

"Melanie, tell me exactly where you are. I'll be
there in minutes."

"No. No more games. No more manipulations.
From the very beginning I've let everyone mess with
me. Well, now I'm doing this my way. Good-bye."

The phone clicked. David swore furiously, earning
a round of stares. Lairmore came out of the conference room, trailed by Chenney.

"Riggs!" the supervisory agent warned.

David grabbed his coat. "Get Detective Jax on the
line. That was Melanie Stokes. According to her, she
just shot William Sheffield."

THE STOKES HOUSE had suddenly become a very popular place. Two ambulances and three police cars barri-
caded the front, blue lights flashing and uniformed
officers milling. Two TV stations had arrived in cam-
era-mounted vans; the local ABC affiliate was probably not far behind.

Between the reporters, the neighbors peering from
doorways and windows, and the tourists who were
snapping photos, traffic on the whole four-lane street
had ground to a halt.

David Riggs yanked over his car one block away
and ran the rest, Chenney huffing and puffing at his
heels. He'd tried calling Melanie back without success. Then he'd gotten Detective Jax long enough to
be told there had been a shooting all right, and Boston
homicide had a few questions for their good friends at
the Bureau.

David flashed his creds to the patrolmen. Chenney
simply muscled his way through. They followed the
stream of crime photographers, homicide detectives,
and beat officers to the study at the rear of the house.
Patricia Stokes stood in a corner, her thin arms

crossed in front of her and a jeweled hand fluttering at the hollow of her throat. She looked confused and frightened, as if the slightest sound would shatter her.

Her husband was in the opposite corner, scowling and rumpled. He must have just been called from surgery. He had a green mask down around his neck and his arms akimbo on his hips, the stance belligerent.

Jamie O'Donnell occupied the doorway. He had already adopted a careful expression of both concern and distrust.

"Of course María tried to clean things up," Harper was saying tersely. "She's a maid, it's her job."

"She tampered with a crime scene," Jax pointed out, standing in front of Harper.

Harper shrugged. "How's she supposed to know that? She thought she was just doing her job."

David saw Jax's point immediately. The blood was not in a clear puddle or splatter pattern but instead had been smeared all over the floor, making it hard to interpret the scene. On the perimeter of the streaky mess, the blood formed razor-crisp lines at random intervals, as if it had spread along the edge of pieces of paper. The paper was gone. One could interpret that scene as William being shot, incriminating documents at his feet.

Detective Jax seemed to have arrived at that conclusion himself. "If I find out you had anything to do with this, Dr. Stokes, I'll bust your rich hide for interfering with an investigation, tampering with a crime scene, and aiding and abetting. Just so you know."

Harper smiled tightly. "You do that, Detective, and my lawyer will eat your badge for lunch."

"Please," Patricia interjected in a tremulous voice. "Can you tell me what happened to Melanie? Where is my daughter? Is she all right?"

"We're still looking for her, ma'am."

"I'm sure she didn't do this on purpose," she continued desperately. "There was no reason for her to hurt William."

"We don't know that." Harper glanced at his wife wearily. "After that scene yesterday? Face it, Pat, our daughter is obviously very troubled these days. Maybe she took the end of her engagement with William much harder than either of us thought. I don't know."

"Harper!" Patricia exclaimed.

"She's been having migraines and not sleeping well! She didn't even come home the night before. I'm not going to lie to these people. You and I don't know a thing about our children anymore."

David wasn't thinking. One moment he was standing beside Chenney, listening to Harper incriminate his own daughter, the next moment he was across the room, grabbing a fistful of Harper's scrubs and shoving the startled surgeon against the wall.

"Don't you set her up for this," David growled. "You don't give a rat's ass about this investigation. William's death is the best thing to happen for you and your little operations. God, this is just a game to you, isn't it? You could've gotten her killed. Do you hear me? You almost killed your daughter. *Again!*"

"D-d-dammit," Harper spluttered. "Let me go!"

"Easy there," O'Donnell said softly from behind David. "Easy there, sport."

Slowly David became aware that the only person in the room surprised by what was going on was Patricia Stokes. Harper, who was being strangled by a man he'd met only as a waiter, was not surprised. Jamie O'Donnell, faced by two men he'd never seen before, was not surprised.

They knew. They knew who David was and who Chenney was, and probably more about the investigation than the federal agents did.

David released Harper. He stepped back briskly and split his gaze between Harper and Jamie.

"How?" David asked.

Both men gave him blank looks.

"No," David said, shaking his head. "I don't buy it.

I don't think even you two realized what Sheffield would do when pushed too hard. I bet you figured he was a spineless shit, just like we did. But he came up with his own agenda, didn't he? Did the stupid thing and put everything in jeopardy. In fact, the only person today who's shown an ounce of common sense is Melanie, isn't it? She's outplaying you. Outplaying us all."

A muscle spasmed in O'Donnell's jaw. "Don't know what you're talking about, sport."

"Sure you do. Congratulations on putting your goddaughter in danger. It's not every day a man almost gets a beautiful young woman killed. But then, you must be getting used to that feeling, huh, O'Donnell? By my calculations, this makes two. First your hired gun, and now your hired lackey. I think you're getting old."

O'Donnell's gaze went black, confirming David's stab in the dark. "Be careful, sport. Be very, very careful."

David just smiled. "I'd say ditto, *sport,* because I'm getting smarter every day and a whole lot closer. You know there's no statute of limitations on homicide, don't you? Especially of a little girl. Especially of a *poor, helpless* little girl who had no idea what you were capable of. I bet she loved her family too. Just like Melanie."

He strode for the door. Behind him, he heard Patricia say, "What's that man talking about? What has happened to Melanie? Has anyone thought to call Brian?"

"By Brian, do you mean Brian Stokes?" Jax inquired.

"Of course," Patricia said, sounding even more bewildered.

"His 'friend' filed a missing persons report two hours ago. Seems Brian Stokes went out for a walk two days ago and hasn't been seen since."

The news apparently was too much. With a small

cry Patricia fainted. Her husband didn't catch her. Jamie O'Donnell did.

"WOULD YOU MIND telling me what is going on?" Chenney panted, barely keeping up with David outside the house. David strode down the sidewalk, his back killing him and the rest of him beyond caring.

"We got a leak. We've never met them before, and yet they knew who we were."

"Shit," Chenney said. "Think Melanie told them?"

"Melanie didn't know I was investigating her father." David reached the car. He yanked open the driver-side door with more force than necessary and climbed in. Chenney rushed to catch up. "Don't answer to anyone but Lairmore at this point. Things are just beginning. They weren't surprised by my comments about Meagan either. They knew exactly what I was talking about."

"They were in on it."

"Up to their eyeballs." David shoved the car into drive, then frowned. "Except for Patricia. She had no idea what was going on."

"Yo, where are we going?"

"Brian Stokes's condo, of course. Where else could Melanie have gone?"

David pulled away with a roar.

Chenney said after a while: "You lost it back there. I mean, you *lost* it. Lairmore hears about you going after Harper Stokes like that, you'll be suspended for a month."

David didn't reply.

B RIAN STOKES'S CONDO reminded David of a sterile museum. He and Chenney got the building maintenance man to let them in; apparently his services came with the condo fees. Once inside the third story residence, they found themselves confronted by four rooms filled only with crystal-clear glass, chrome frames, and one black leather sofa.

"There's not even a family portrait on the wall," Chenney said.

"He isn't so pleased with his family."

"The adopted daughter is grateful for her parents," Chenney murmured, "the older son is dying to give them away. Can you imagine these guys on *Family Feud?*"

"Only if they were playing opposite the Donner party."

They drifted from room to room. Not a speck of dust, a streak of lint, or a stray item of clothing. The man could've given David and his own brother lessons all those years ago.

"Just beer and yogurt in the fridge," Chenney reported.

"No messages on the machine," David said, then frowned. "Can you really believe after two days there're no messages on the machine?"

"Maybe he calls in and checks them. Those machines let you do that these days."

"Yeah, maybe."

They gave the condo a second pass. Brian seemed very neat and no-frills. A troubled young man, David thought, because no sane person kept anything that sanitized.

The maintenance man claimed not to have seen any blondes entering the building that day, but he also confessed a weakness for daytime soaps. He hadn't seen Brian around. Not that he noticed the male residents much, he said with a shrug, hitching up his slacks and rubbing his beer gut. Some of them were definitely swinging on the wrong side of the field, if you know what he meant, and he didn't want them to get no ideas about him.

Chenney and David headed back downstairs. They'd just reached their automobile when a voice stopped them.

"Special Agent Riggs, Chenney."

Both agents turned as one, Chenney going for his gun. Brian Stokes stepped out of a shadowed doorway. He looked as if he hadn't slept a minute in days.

"You can let go of the gun, Chenney," David said dryly. "I don't think Brian Stokes is here for a showdown."

"I just want to talk," Brian seconded.

"Do you know where your sister is?"

Brian shook his head. "I just got a message. That's my role in the family."

"And was that your role twenty-five years ago when Meagan disappeared?"

Brian looked at him curiously. "You think Meagan was my fault," he said, and then smiled. "Of course. It's nothing I haven't thought myself."

"Brian—"

"Come with me, Agent. There's something I need to show you and something I should have told you. Something I should've told everyone a long time ago."

• • •

THEY FOLLOWED BRIAN Stokes on foot, passing block after block of neat brick town houses lined up like toy soldiers. A few streets over, Brian led them into a narrow street lined with older but still stately—and expensive—homes. He let himself into the last one with a key. A flower box filled with yellow daffodils waved to them as they passed through the heavy wood door, but none of them noticed.

"My . . . friend lives here," Brian said at last, leading them up the stairs.

"You mean your lover."

"You could say that. In theory, no one knew the name of the man I'm seeing or the fact that I often spend the night at his house."

"In theory?"

"Tuesday morning I received a package. Hand-delivered to my name, here, at his place."

David and Chenney exchanged looks. "And you've been hiding out ever since?" David asked.

"I needed some time to think."

"And the missing persons report?"

"I asked Nate to do that. To throw him off the trail."

"Him?"

"I don't know, Agent. I was hoping you could tell me."

They reached the third floor. Brian unlocked the front door and led them both inside, disappearing almost immediately into the kitchen. This condo celebrated hardwood floors, a redbrick wall, and piles and piles of suede pillows and soft wool rugs—it was everything Brian Stokes's condo wasn't.

"Is Nate home?" David asked. One question was solved. This was definitely Brian's "home," and the other residence mere window dressing.

"At work. He's a doctor as well."

"And Melanie. When did you see her?"

Brian reemerged from the kitchen, carrying a cardboard box and giving David an impatient look. "I already told you, I haven't seen her."

"But you know William Sheffield has been shot."

"I checked my machine thirty minutes ago. Two messages. The first was from Melanie. She sounded so calm, I almost thought it was a joke. She said William had tried to shoot her, but she'd shot him instead. She wanted me to know that she was all right. Then she mentioned your name and that you were investigating our father, probably with good cause. Then she said—"

Brian's voice faltered. "She said she knew Russell Lee Holmes hadn't killed Meagan. And then she said—" His voice broke again. He cleared his throat forcefully. "She said that she loved me. And she thanked me for the last twenty years."

Brian's gaze was fixed on the box in front of him. His jaw was tense, and David could see a muscle spasm. Then he got it. Brian didn't just have a small self-confidence issue. He loathed himself. He genuinely loathed himself and held himself responsible for all the bad things that happened in his family—including the fates of his sisters.

"You said you had a second message?"

"From my godfather. He's been leaving three a day. He also told me about William's shooting. He said he knew something was up and that we really needed to talk about it. Seems that he got a gift too. I think they all have."

"They all have?"

"My mom, Dad, Jamie, Melanie, and me. Everyone who was involved back then, though some of us remember it more than others. Let me show you."

He lifted the lid of the cardboard box. There, resting on white tissue paper was a blackened, shriveled cow's tongue.

Brian looked at them both. "It came with a note, 'You get what you deserve,' but I know what it's talking about. I'd already lost my sister, you see. I didn't want to lose my father too."

David sat down. He got out his spiral notebook and picked up a pen. "Let's start at the beginning here, because I'm dying for answers and we got a lot for you to explain. Where were you the day Meagan Stokes was kidnapped? What did you and your mother do?"

Brian took a deep breath and then, staring at the dried cow's tongue, he began.

"I wasn't a good kid, all right? In this day and age they'd probably diagnose me with attention deficit disorder. Back then I was simply hyper and high-strung and no one, least of all my mother, knew what to do with me. Frankly, our family wasn't sweetness and light back then either. I don't know how my parents started their marriage, but by the time I came along, my father seemed to be a withdrawn workaholic who gave his best at the office and had nothing left for home. Mom was hurt and sullen half the time, spending money as a hobby, doing anything to get attention. I think I was eight when I figured out it was worse than that—that Dad wasn't always working late, that my mom knew about the other women and seemed hell-bent on becoming a bit of a party animal on her own. I don't know, it was like being raised by a robot and a sixteen-year-old. Nobody ever said anything bad about the other, but, the undercurrents when they were both in a room . . . Kids just *know* these things, okay?"

"Yeah," Chenney said heavily, which earned him a surprised look by both David and Brian. He shrugged. Apparently he did know.

"Then Meagan came along," Brian continued after a moment. "She was so sweet, always smiling. No matter what happened, she'd beam and hold out her hands to you. Everyone loved her. Women in super-markets, for God's sake, the neighbors, stray dogs. If you had a pulse, you automatically loved Meagan

Stokes and she automatically loved you. Sure as hell no one ever thought that about me. And, yeah, I was jealous. I'd get angry. But . . . but I wasn't immune to her either, Agent. Even when I was jealous I loved her. Sometimes I even crept into her room at night just to watch her sleep. She was so peaceful, so happy. I never understood how my family could create a little girl who was so *happy*.

"And then I would grow afraid. I would think that my parents would ruin her too. She would love them like I did, and they would make her pay. Harper would abandon her and Patricia would grow bored, and she'd realize one day that her parents were two completely self-centered, overindulged people. I started breaking her toys, stealing her stuff. I kept thinking if I was mean enough, she'd get strong, learn to protect herself. I hurt her and I still believed I was doing her a favor." He smiled lopsidedly. "Welcome to the Stokes version of family."

"And that last day? What did you do then?"

"I had fun, Agent. I honestly enjoyed life for a moment, and that was probably my biggest sin. That day . . . that day was my fourth therapy appointment. Afterward the shrink asked to speak to my mother alone. I don't know what he said. But she took me for ice cream, though it was only eleven in the morning. She even had some, and this is a woman who's dined on grapefruit and dry wheat toast for the last fifty years. We hung out, Agent, I don't know how else to describe it.

"After a while Mom told me that things would be different. The family was having a rough spell and she understood that they'd been pretending I didn't know what was really going on. She would spend more time with me. She and my father would work things out. She realized now that her family meant more to her than anything, and she was prepared to do whatever was necessary to hold it together. She told me she loved me, she really loved me, and everything would be all right.

"We played in the park after that. She pushed me on the swing even though I was too old to be pushed, and I liked it. I remember thinking that I was almost happy, and it was sort of curious and strange. I wasn't sure I'd ever been happy before.

"Then we went home and the police officer told us Meagan was gone. Just like that. Are you a fatalist, Agent?" Brian smiled. "I sure as hell am."

"You were with your mother all day?"

"All day."

"Did you see Meagan get into the nanny's car?"

"No. We left before they did."

"Brian, do you know absolutely that Russell Lee Holmes kidnapped Meagan Stokes?"

"I honestly thought he had," Brian said. "I insist, if the devil had a human face, Agent Riggs, it would look like Russell Lee Holmes."

David frowned. He believed Brian Stokes. So if Brian and Patricia were together all day and had nothing to do with Meagan Stokes's death . . .

"Then what about the tongue?" he asked in frustration. "If you had nothing to do with your sister's kidnapping, why the 'gift'?"

Brian thinned his lips. "I'm not sure. The shrine in Melanie's room caught me off guard. That she might be Russell Lee Holmes's daughter . . . God, I don't know. All I can say is that there were some things the police didn't catch back then, and someone seems intent on getting out that info now. For example, three nights ago my godfather got a penis in a jar. Three guesses as to why."

"Him and Patricia?"

"Yep. In spite of what people might think, not all of my parents' problems were caused by Dad's work habits." Brian shrugged, took a deep breath. "As for the tongue . . . My father didn't have a hundred thousand dollars for ransom money back then. He was just an overworked resident still trying to pay off his student loans, let alone keep up with my mother. So Jamie supplied the money. I was there when he arrived with the briefcase filled with one hundred thousand dollars in cold, hard cash. And—"

Brian looked up, met their gazes. "And I was there to see that my father did not take that briefcase to the drop site. He took his briefcase instead. Empty. I know, because when I spotted Jamie's briefcase under my parents' bed, I pulled it out and opened it. All that cash, sitting right there. Do you get it? My father didn't pay the ransom. He was so damn greedy, he kept the money for himself. And Russell Lee Holmes . . . Russell Lee Holmes *killed* my baby sister."

Brian's breath came out in angry gasps. "And I never said a word. I never went to the cops or Jamie or my mom or anyone. I just stared at Harper night after night, watching him eat dinner and assure my mom it would be all right. Night after night. He lied through his teeth, sold out my sister for a hundred thousand dollars, and I never had the courage to call him on it. Never. Goddammit, I wanted to say it so badly and I *couldn't*. I just fucking *couldn't!*"

Brian swept the cardboard box off the oak coffee table. It didn't do him any good. The tongue tumbled out, then lay on the rug in plain sight.

"Shit," he said after a moment. Then again, "Shit."

David shared that thought. So Brian and Patricia Stokes hadn't harmed Meagan. The family had not rushed into cover-up mode to protect their son. If Meagan had been harmed, it had to have been by Jamie or Harper, and it had to have been cold-blooded murder.

Of a four-year-old little girl with big blue eyes and curly blond hair.

He said, "If it's any help, I'm ninety percent positive that Russell Lee Holmes *did not* kidnap or murder Meagan Stokes, which may explain why your father didn't take the money to the drop site. He already knew he didn't have to."

"Come again?"

David regarded Brian Stokes seriously. "I don't think your father was after a hundred thousand dollars. I believe he was after a million."

"*What?*"

"The life insurance, Brian, or didn't you know? Both you and Meagan were insured for one million bucks."

Brian Stokes hadn't known. In front of them, he went pale as a sheet, then his face twisted with rage. *"That goddamn son of a bitch!* I will kill him. I can't believe . . ."

"The ransom note that was delivered was too sophisticated for Russell Lee Holmes. Meagan did not fit his victim profile. They *never* found any physical evidence tying him with the crime. In fact, all they had was his confession—"

"Why would he confess?"

"In order to have his child raised in style. Melanie is Russell Lee Holmes's daughter, Brian. Your parents raised her to cover their own tracks. Now you tell me, for your sister's sake, does that make a difference?"

Brian was silent for a moment. "No. Of course not. Melanie is Melanie. She is the best thing that ever happened to this family. Maybe it just figures that it takes the devil's own daughter to love the Stokeses."

David decided to let that comment pass. "Okay, now you have to help me. Originally we had reason to believe you or your mother might be involved. You understand that in seventy-five percent of cases, it is the family, so we have to think that way. Now we know you and your mother had alibis. What about Harper?"

"He worked. At least I thought he was at work. I don't know. My father can be a cold SOB, but I can't imagine him kidnapping . . . killing . . ." Brian shook his head. "He's not the type to get his hands dirty."

"Yeah? Well, what about Jamie O'Donnell?"

Brian hung his head, which was answer enough. "He loved us, I'd swear to it. He played with us, brought us presents, spoiled us, indulged us. But—"

"But?"

He whispered, "But there's more to him than that. He's done some things. Known some things. I get the impression— If Harper hates getting his hands dirty, then Jamie is most at home in the muck."

"He's that kind of man," David said.

"Yeah, maybe. But Meagan was just a little girl. I can imagine Jamie taking on a grown man, or maybe somebody who'd wronged us, but I can't see him hurting a child. Especially Meagan. Did you know that his name was the first word she learned to say? Dad was furious."

"Let's approach this from a different angle," David tried after a moment. "We have two different things going on here. We have the person or persons who harmed Meagan Stokes. Most likely Harper or Jamie. Then we have someone who knows the truth, who seems intimately aware of what everyone did or didn't do twenty-five years ago. This person is trying to get out the truth, in a sick and twisted way. Maybe, if we can identify this person, we can cut to the chase and ask directly. Who knew that you saw the ransom money but didn't tell?"

Brian shook his head. "I didn't think anyone knew. If I'd thought I'd had an ally anywhere, I would've confessed."

David gave him a look. "That's not possible. Someone had to have seen to know to send you this cow's tongue."

"No kidding. And I'm telling you, Agent, no one knew!"

"Russell Lee Holmes," Chenney said excitedly. "He must know all the details. That Harper never delivered the money, that the family had a love triangle. Before he confessed, he probably demanded all the details. He's sick and twisted enough to enjoy a little game like that."

"Russell Lee Holmes is dead," Brian said flatly and with a trace of vehemence. "I watched it."

"Things can be switched, faked. Maybe it was part of the deal." Chenney shrugged again. "Why should we assume he did it solely for his child's future? Maybe he got away for *life*, huh?"

David gave the rookie a look. "We have no proof that Russell Lee Holmes is alive."

"We have proof we're missing some piece of the puzzle," Chenney argued. "You can't deny that."

"Let's get back to the facts," David said flatly. "One, someone knows what happened twenty-five years ago and is intent on shaking things up. Maybe he guessed about Brian and the ransom money. He also had to know where Meagan's toy horse and clothes were all these years, so he has to be connected to the family. Hell, maybe it was William Sheffield. Maybe Harper got drunk one night and said too much and William thought this would be a great way to twist everyone for extra money. We'll have to search his place.

"That brings us to the person who actually did the crime twenty-five years ago and is desperate to keep it covered up. He hired the shooter to take out Larry Digger when he got too close and Melanie when she began to remember."

"What?" Brian said sharply.

David filled him in. "Whoever is doing this," David concluded, "is playing for keeps. I think, Dr. Stokes, that having Nate declare you missing might not have been such a bad idea.

"And I'm asking you again: Understanding now that Melanie is in danger, that we are dealing with someone who murdered a four-year-old girl, do you know where she is?"

"No, Agent. I just got her message."

"Okay, she knows she isn't safe at home, she knows she couldn't find you. She's not experienced enough or prepared enough to drop off the face of the earth, so where would she turn next?"

Brian's face lit up. "Ann Margaret. Her boss at the Dedham Donor Center."

IT WAS A thirty-five-minute drive to the Dedham Red Cross Donor Center. Chenney handled the wheel, David worked the cell phone. He offered Detective Jax the tidbit that Melanie had left a message on her brother's machine saying she had to shoot William in self-defense. In return, Jax told him that they had witnesses testifying that Melanie had used a pay phone in Government Center. They had one forensics team already searching the area for the murder weapon. They'd also found the taxi driver who had driven Melanie to Brian's condo. He'd described Melanie as being pale, quiet, and "a little spooky."

Now the police were canvassing the neighborhood, talking to taxi dispatch stations, monitoring the airport, and getting financial records from her bank. They figured they'd turn up something shortly. How long could one debutante hide?

David said uh-huh a lot. He didn't bother to mention his current destination. FBI agents were supposed to cooperate with local law enforcement, but that didn't preclude staying one step ahead of them.

They pulled into the parking lot of the Red Cross Center a little after three. Melanie had now been on the run for over two hours, plenty of time to get down to Dedham by taxi or train.

They found Ann Margaret inside the vast white blood-donation center, sitting in a tiny office doing paperwork. The desk looked makeshift, the plastic chairs utilitarian. Industrial metal bookcases and gray metal filing cabinets.

The woman fit the office. Short, sensible, gray hair capped closely in tight curls. Lined face carrying the permanent stamp of a southern sun. Trim, neat figure clad in nurses' whites. Though not large or imposing, Ann Margaret looked like the kind of woman you could trust to get the job done.

At their approach, she glanced up, frowned, then paled as they showed their credentials.

"What is it?" she asked sharply, as if part of her had been expecting bad news for quite some time. "What happened?"

"We'd like to ask you some questions about Melanie Stokes," David said.

The lines of her face turned to confusion. Apparently the presence of FBI agents didn't surprise her, but FBI agents asking about Melanie did.

David motioned to two yellow plastic chairs. "May we?"

Ann Margaret was too well mannered to refuse, so he and Chenney took a seat.

"I don't understand what you need to know about Melanie," Ann Margaret said, setting down her pen. "She's not even scheduled to work today."

"She's volunteered here for a while?" David asked.

"Five years." Ann Margaret frowned. "Is she all right? What's going on?"

"Do you know William Sheffield?"

"Yes, Melanie's ex-fiancé. Now, see here"—she leaned forward, her lips thinning into a firm line—"I want to know what is going on."

"William Sheffield was found shot two hours ago. We have reason to believe that Melanie pulled the trigger."

Ann Margaret was shaken. "No," she whispered.

"Yes, ma'am."

"But . . . but . . ." She couldn't seem to find her bearings. Her hands fluttered on her desk as if seeking anchor. "Is he dead?"

"Yes, ma'am. But we'll need you to keep that under your hat until we notify his family."

"He doesn't have a family. He was an orphan too. It was one of the things he and Melanie had in common."

"What do you know about their relationship?"

Ann Margaret still looked shell-shocked. "I don't . . . I mean. Melanie is more than just a volunteer, I'm her friend. I remember how happy she was when he first proposed."

David waited patiently.

"Her father introduced the two of them, I believe. They dated six months, seemed happy. I know Melanie said once that William was a bit jealous that she'd been adopted by such a rich family and he hadn't. She didn't understand that. He'd become a doctor after all, lived a very good life. I guess it caused a rift between them. She hasn't really talked much about him since they broke up. I assumed the parting was mutual."

"Did she ever allude that she wanted him back or felt injured?"

"Not at all. And even if—listen to me, young man." Ann Margaret pulled herself up. "William and Melanie weren't a good match, but you don't kill someone over something like that. William was really a nice boy, very smart, a good anesthesiologist. And Melanie simply wouldn't hurt a fly. Plus, their breakup is ancient history. There must be some other explanation."

"Did she talk to you about anything else going on in her life?"

"Well, I haven't really spoken to her for four or five days. She hasn't been feeling well. Problems with migraines . . ." Her voice trailed off. She seemed to realize that could be significant.

David waited, but Ann Margaret had obviously decided it would be best if she didn't say anything more.

"We really need to speak to Melanie," David said evenly.

"I'm sure you do."

"If you know where she is—"

"I don't know any such thing."

"You're sure she hasn't contacted you?"

"I am her boss, Agent, not her mother."

David said in a low, steely voice, "If we find out you're hiding a fugitive . . ."

But Ann Margaret remained unmoved. If she did know more, she simply wasn't saying.

David placed a business card on her desk. The blue FBI shield emblazoned on the card stared up at her as he and Chenney walked away.

As he was passing through the doorway, David suddenly turned.

"Ever hear the name Angela Johnson?"

He thought she flinched.

"No."

"What about Annie?"

A muscle flickered in her cheek. "My name is Ann Margaret Dawson. That's all I go by, Agent—at least on a good day."

"Of course."

She smiled thinly. "Of course."

David and Chenney walked out. "What do you think?" Chenney asked as they got into their car.

"I don't know yet."

"She seemed to take the news rather hard."

David tapped the steering wheel a few times, then started the engine. "I think she may be worth watching."

"I don't know. Melanie Stokes is spooked and frightened. If you were spooked and frightened, would you really run to Dedham?"

"No, but if my name was really Ann Margaret Dawson, I wouldn't flinch at the mention of Angela Johnson."

"Who's Angela Johnson?"

"Russell Lee Holmes's wife?"

Chenney's eyes got round. "You think . . ."

"Ann Margaret, Annie, Angela. Lots of Annes to be a coincidence."

"And she's from Texas."

"And she's about the right age."

"Oh, my God," Chenney said.

David just nodded and drove. He had a thousand things on his mind, but first and foremost he remained worried about Melanie.

Chenney didn't speak again until they were almost in Boston. "Shit," he declared. "Riggs, we're male chauvinist pigs."

"Probably."

"Think for a moment. The Stokes family doesn't have motive to stir things up. We don't think O'Donnell has motive to stir things up. Melanie certainly doesn't, and you're determined to believe that Russell Lee Holmes is dead."

"Yes, I definitely believe that."

"So what about Russell Lee Holmes's *wife?* What about this Angela Johnson and everything she must know from back then?"

"Oh, God," David said as the pieces started to fit. "We *are* male chauvinist pigs."

"She'd probably know all about the details of the crime and life in the Stokes family."

"That would explain the shrine in Melanie's room. If you were a woman and you gave up your daughter twenty years ago to protect her, to give her a better life, you'd have to wish—"

"That she'd remember. Or someday come looking for you."

"Christ. First thing tomorrow morning—"

"Everything I can find on Angela Johnson—"

"Ann Margaret Dawson."

"Got it."

TWENTY-SEVEN

D AVID DIDN'T RETURN home until ten P.M. He felt a moment of apprehension standing in front of his apartment door. Melanie knew where he lived. Would she come here on her own, give him a second chance?

He unlocked his door and pushed it wide open. Moonlight cascaded over the dingy mess that passed for his private refuge, illuminating his old green couch and the dusty collection of trophies he never could bring himself to throw away.

No Melanie. Damn.

By eight P.M. the police had traced two ATM withdrawals to her checking account. Her bank reported her coming in late in the afternoon and withdrawing an even larger sum of cash. At this point she had a few thousand dollars on her. She could get pretty far on a few thousand dollars. David wished he knew where.

He limped into the kitchen and grabbed a bag of frozen peas. His back was a mess.

His career wasn't doing so great these days either.

The press was all over the shooting of William Sheffield. Reporters were already calling the Bureau's press relations agent, stating they knew two FBI agents had been present at the scene and they wanted to know the Bureau's involvement in the case. So far

Lairmore had issued the generic "We are merely assisting local law enforcement in any way they see fit," a party line nobody was buying.

It would be only a matter of time before someone found out about the investigation into Drs. William Sheffield and Harper Stokes. Then someone would place Larry Digger at the Stokes residence, connect the dots with his recent murder, and the story would gain real momentum. While the Bureau remained looking bad. Agents leaving a trail of unsolved homicides. The Feebies—always a day late and dollar short. The potential for Bureau bashing was unlimited.

The Bureau had already had enough bad press in the nineties, Lairmore had informed Riggs and Chenney curtly after five o'clock. They'd better perform some damage control quick, or they would become the first agents in the history of the Bureau reduced to serving as meter maids.

David paced his living room. He jerked off his tie, shed his jacket. To hell with Lairmore, David couldn't stand not being able to put this case to bed.

Twenty-five years earlier Harper cut a deal with Russell Lee Holmes. Something happened to Meagan Stokes, and Harper wanted Russell Lee to take the fall. Harper gets a million dollars. Russell Lee's daughter gets a good home. Everyone lives happily ever after until one day Harper needs money again.

This time he comes up with scheme number two, slicing open healthy patients for profit. No harm, no foul, he must have thought. Piece of cake after disguising a murder.

But he didn't cover up all his tracks this time, and someone was after him now. Maybe he/she wanted vengeance for Meagan or maybe he/she wanted Melanie back or maybe he/she was simply sick to death of Harper Stokes. David sure as hell was. Killing one daughter. Adopting another and leading her on for twenty years, only to hand her over to the police on a silver platter. The man had to have ice water instead of blood in his veins.

The phone rang. David quickly snatched it up.

"Melanie?"

There was a pause. "David?"

Not Melanie, but his father. David was disappointed, and he sounded it. "Dad? Is everything all right? It's late."

"Sorry. Didn't mean . . . Just couldn't get hold of you during the conventional times, you know. Did you get my messages? I've been wondering."

His father sounded humbled and hurt. David grimaced.

"I'm fine," he said. "Just   busy."

"Work going well?" Bobby's voice picked up. "I got some new ideas for your gun."

"My gun's fine, Dad. Uh, I'm doing some work with Detective Jax. He told me to give you his regards."

"Oh, Jax. I like him. Good man. Pretty good shot, but you're better. Coming out to the range anytime soon?" Bobby asked eagerly. "I could meet you there."

"I don't know. I got a pretty rough case now."

"More of that doctor stuff?"

"Yeah."

The call drifted to silence. David shifted restlessly, cold water trickling down his back. He should say something more. *Hey, Dad, how are the Red Sox doing? No, don't tell me. It'll just break both of our hearts.*

"So," Bobby said presently. "Your brother is doing better. Sent his lead pitcher to the bench like I recommended. Brought up the rookie. Good kid, lots of potential. Got ten strikeouts his second game."

"That's good."

"I painted the house. Gray, dark blue trim. Not that different."

"You should've told me, I would've helped."

"No need, I have plenty of time. Business is kind of slow right now."

Another edgy silence.

"How's your back?" Bobby blurted out.

"Fine," David lied.

"Taking those pills the doctor talked about?"

"Nope, no need." Lied even more.

"David," Bobby said. "I'm your father. Can't you at least tell me what's going on?"

David hung his head, then stared at the big trophy in the back, the state championship, won on the day his father had hugged him so hard, he'd thought his ribs would break. He hurt. He hurt too much and it had nothing to do with solidifying vertebrae and spasming muscles. He'd failed his dad. That was the bottom line. He could get over many things, but he couldn't get over that.

He said weakly, "I'm uh . . . I'm just busy, Dad. A lot of work right now. I really should be going."

"I see. Fraud?"

"Fraud. Homicide. I'm not doing so good at staying ahead of these guys."

"You'll catch up." His father sounded confident.

David squeezed his eyes shut and said tightly, "You don't know that. Christ, Dad, it's not like I traded in a brilliant pitching career for a brilliant law enforcement career. I'm in *healthcare fraud*. I read reports, not change the world. As a matter of fact, because of me some young woman had to shoot a man to save her life today. Now she's on the run, frightened and scared and God knows what, and *it's all my fault!*"

"You'll help her," his father said.

"*Dammit!* Listen to me, Dad, just listen. I don't save lives, okay, or the world. I save dollars and cents. That's it. I spend most of the year reading hundreds of pounds of subpoenaed documents. I don't need a souped-up Beretta with radioactive sights. *I need Wite-Out!* Wite-Out!"

The phone line fell silent. David realized what he'd just said, how much he'd said. Oh, Christ. He tried to backpedal furiously, though he knew it was too late.

"I'm sorry. I'm just working too hard. I'm not getting enough sleep—"

"I don't understand your job," his father said somberly. "I try, David, I do. But I'm not book-smart like you. I didn't go to college. I'm good with my hands and I'm good with guns and I'm good with a baseball. When you were doing that too, I could understand. Then you got a degree, I mean a real degree instead of going to college for ball, like we thought you would. You got into the academy. God almighty, I can't imagine ever being chosen for something like that. Now you analyze things, you take on doctors and hospitals and insurance companies, and those people aren't stupid.

"No, David, I don't get your job. I'm just good with my hands and I'm good at fixing up your gun. Because you won't play ball with me anymore, David. Customizing your Beretta is pretty much all I have left. So that's what I do. I can't advise you, I can't coach you. Half the time I can't even speak to you. So I fix your gun. Maybe that seems silly to you, but I'd rather be silly than completely shut out."

"Dad . . ." David didn't know what to say. He should reassure his father. Play nice. Get off the phone before he made anything worse. And then, strangely, he found himself whispering, "Dad, I failed a woman today. I mean more than professionally. She trusted me. She needed me. And I shut her out. I lied to her and told myself it was all right because of my job. I did something I know you'd never do. I don't know what I was thinking."

His father was silent for a moment. He said quietly, "You're a good man, David. You know you made a mistake and now you'll fix it."

"I'm not even sure where she is."

"Then figure it out. You're the smartest man I know, David, and I mean that. When the doc told me your condition was hereditary, caused by genetics, I had a bad thought. Made me feel guilty for days, but I think it's still the truth."

"What?"

"I thought that if one of us was meant to get it, marked for it, then I was glad it was you. You may have had the better arm, but, son, you also just had *more*. Where would Steven be without baseball? What would I do? You, on the other hand, you took after your mother. You got her brains. And now you're an FBI agent. An honest-to-God federal agent. Haven't you ever figured out how envious your brother and I are of you?"

David couldn't swallow. He said, "I guess not."

"You did well, son. You did well."

David couldn't reply. His throat had closed up on him.

"Ummm," his dad said. "It's getting kind of late. I know you have a lot of work to do."

"Yeah, yeah. I'll, uh, talk to you soon. Maybe bring in my Beretta. You can play with the sights."

"Okay. I'll even bring some Wite-Out."

David laughed a little hoarsely. "Thanks."

"Good night, David."

"Good night."

He hung up. He sat for a while longer in the dining room, feeling a little wrung out. A little . . . reassured.

It had been a long time since he'd really *connected* with his dad. He was thirty-six years old. He kept telling himself his father's approval shouldn't mean much anymore, but that was a load of bunk. A parent's approval always mattered, regardless of age—

He stopped the thought cold. Comprehension washed over him.

Melanie Stokes on the run. Melanie Stokes feeling

betrayed, as if her whole life had been a lie. Melanie Stokes wanting to know once and for all who she was.

He knew exactly where she'd gone.

He picked up the phone and roused Chenney out of bed.

TWENTY-EIGHT

NN MARGARET DIDN'T go to sleep. She sat in the shadowed darkness of her little bungalow, still wearing her nurses' whites. She knew he wouldn't arrive right away, but later, when he thought no one was paying attention.

The back door finally opened. He walked quietly into the living room, hardly making a sound.

"I guess you heard," he said at last.

She stared at Jamie from across the room. She realized there was nothing he could say that would make it right. She'd been foolish to wait up for him, but they had been through so much, first as friends, recently as lovers. She'd thought of him as her second chance at happiness. She'd thought she'd finally gotten it right. This time love would be kind.

She'd forgotten that she always fell for the wrong kind of man.

"I'm sorry, my love," Jamie finally said softly. "I am . . . so sorry." He took a step forward.

"Don't."

"Annie, please, listen to me."

"The agents told me Melanie shot him. Why would that happen, Jamie? What could've gone wrong?"

"I don't know, Annie. You can't believe for a minute I wanted this to happen. It's a real shame. I'll do whatever it takes to make it right."

"The omnipotent Jamie O'Donnell." Her lips twisted. She finally rose, surprised to find that her legs would support her. "If I said anything now, after all these years, you would kill me, wouldn't you, Jamie?"

"Don't say that, love. Don't talk like that."

"It's true though, isn't it? You like to think you're better than Harper, but you're not, Jamie. You both piss on the people you love. Men should spend less time with guns and more time in childbirth."

She brushed by him, her steps forceful. He tried to catch her shoulder, and she slapped him so hard the room rang with the blow. The muscle on his jaw twitched. They both knew it was in his nature to always fight back, even when in the wrong. But he checked himself now. He fisted his hands at his sides and weathered the blow for her. She supposed that meant he really did love her . . . and Patricia Stokes.

"I'm sorry, Annie," he said again.

"Go to hell."

"Even if you hate me, sweetheart, you struck a deal and I'll expect you to keep up your end."

"Sold my soul to the devil."

"Twenty-five years, Annie," he said softly. "Very fine life. Better than you could've done on your own, and you know it. I kept my word. I told you that very first day that Jamie O'Donnell always keeps his word, and I meant it."

Her eyes suddenly filled with tears. The sight struck him more forcefully than her slap. He'd never seen Ann Margaret cry. Not once. He'd first respected her steel core, then grown to love that about her.

"Don't," he said hoarsely. "Annie . . ."

"I loved you," she whispered. "I thought it would make things better, but it only makes them worse."

"It doesn't have to change."

"But it does. You've always known, haven't you, that it would come to this?"

For his answer, he tried once more to take her hands. She pulled away.

"I don't want to see you or any of the Stokeses ever again," she declared. "I made a mistake back then. I paid for it, but I won't keep paying for it."

"You can't mean that—"

"And if anything happens to Melanie," she continued, "I will hunt you down, Jamie O'Donnell. I will kill you with my bare hands. Don't think I didn't learn anything from the company I've been keeping, and don't underestimate me. When men are cruel, it's capricious. When women are cruel, it's serious."

She twisted away from him and stalked down the hall.

Jamie watched her go, feeling that tightness again in his chest. In the back of his mind a little voice whispered he was having a heart attack. The rest of him knew better. His heart was breaking. He'd felt exactly this way the night Patricia walked out of his arms and told him she was going with Harper forever, going to give the bastard one last try. Jamie might be her passion, but Harper, sniveling Harper, was her kind.

It didn't change Jamie. It didn't and for that he was sorry.

Now Jamie O'Donnell whispered, "Don't do anything stupid, Annie my love. Please don't make me kill you."

PATRICIA STOOD IN front of the liquor cabinet. She opened the door and took out the nearly full bottle of gin. Her hands moved slowly, as if weighed down by fifty-pound barbells.

She was alone. Her husband was off doing whatever it was he did at odd hours of the night, and she didn't care. She didn't care about anything anymore, and if she had been able to summon any emotion for her husband, it would have been a cold-hearted rage that would have forced her to hurt him once and for all.

She stared at the bottle of gin.

Don't do it. You don't have to make the same mistakes again. You don't have to fail again.

But maybe I do. Did we ever fix any of the problems in this family, or did we all just run away? Both my husband and my son still carry so much rage . . . and my daughter, my precious adopted daughter forced to shoot a man while still carrying the imprint of her father's hand upon her face.

The phone rang. She picked it up, uncapping the gin and saying, "What?"

"Mom," her son replied evenly.

"Brian?"

"Are you drinking yet? I figured that's what you would do."

"Oh, Brian." She started crying. "I want my baby back. What have they done to Melanie, how could I have lost Melanie?"

"I want to hate you," Brian said hoarsely. "Why can't I hate you?"

"I'm sorry, I'm sorry, I'm sorry for everything." She set down the bottle and cried harder.

"I'm standing here tonight, figuring this ought to push you over the top," Brian announced. "And I keep thinking, I shouldn't care. It's not my problem. I can't take care of you. I can't fix things for you and Dad, and I surely never figured out how to make either of you happy. But then I think of Melanie and how disappointed she'd be in me if I did nothing. Dammit . . . do you love her?" he asked abruptly. "Tell me, do you at least honestly love her?"

"Completely."

"So do I," Brian whispered, then blurted out, "What did we do wrong this time, Mom? How could we fail twice?"

And then he started to cry too. They cried together, in the dark, because they had been the ones who had wanted Melanie. More than Harper, they had been the ones determined to make a fresh start. And in loving Melanie and failing her, mother and son finally found common ground.

After a moment Brian pulled himself together. He told her about Larry Digger's arrival and accusations. About the altar in Melanie's room. Then Larry Digger's subsequent murder and Melanie's growing belief that she really was Russell Lee Holmes's child and that the Stokeses had somehow made a deal.

"That's ridiculous," Patricia stammered. She reached once more for the gin.

"Is it?" her son asked. "Come on, Mom, I know you and Dad were fighting all the time back then and both of you hate to fight. For God's sake, what could make Dad angry enough to yell?"

Her heart thundered too hard. It was unfair, she thought, that a mother would have to expose herself like this to her son.

"It was Meagan, wasn't it?" he filled in calmly. "You were fighting about Meagan."

"Yes."

"And Jamie."

Patricia closed her eyes. She couldn't say the rest.

Her son expelled a breath sharply. "Jesus Christ, she was Jamie's daughter, wasn't she? That's why she was so happy, so pretty. I knew this family couldn't produce anyone so happy! I knew it!"

"Brian—"

"He killed her, dammit! Don't you get it yet, Mom? Not Russell Lee Holmes. The police have *proof* he could not have killed Meagan. It was Dad! He murdered her for the million-dollar life insurance. And because he knew she wasn't even his own kid. Oh, God, he destroyed our family because he needed money. And we let him, Mom. We never suspected a thing."

"You don't know," she said desperately. "We don't know—"

"*I saw the fucking ransom money, Mom!* That day Jamie brought it over, but Dad didn't take that brief-case—"

"No!"

"*Yes!* I found the real briefcase under your bed. I saw Jamie's money. Dad pocketed it as well, because he knew he didn't really have to pay the ransom. *Because he knew Meagan was already dead.*"

"No, no, no! Don't say these things. You are his son, how can you say these things? He's always loved you—"

"He kicked me out of the family—"

"And he's been trying to reach you for days to let you back in. We're going to Europe. We're going to Europe as one big happy family!" Her voice had risen to fever pitch. She heard herself speak like a raving lunatic, and her bravado collapsed.

They were not one big happy family. Her own husband had kicked her son out of the family and had tried to turn her daughter over to the police. He had not paid Meagan's ransom. He had known Meagan was really Jamie O'Donnell's daughter. Oh, God, she had been living with the man who killed her own daughter and, worse, *she had loved him.* She had been grateful he brought her flowers, grateful for each crumb of attention, grateful that someday he would retire and truly be all hers.

Even now she was thinking, poor Harper, you're so desperately afraid of being commonplace, of never rising above your parents. You don't even realize how talented or loved you are.

Especially by Melanie.

Oh, Lord, she was going to be ill.

"I won't protect him anymore, Mom," her son said quietly. "I can't believe what he's done to us."

"He's your father—"

"Mom, you're an alcoholic, and your own husband keeps bringing home booze. Doesn't that tell you something? I'm going after Mclanie. I already failed one sister, and I won't fail another."

Brian hung up.

Patricia was left alone in the dark. She twisted off the cap of the gin, her hands shaking. She carried the pint into the kitchen, held it upside down in the huge stainless-steel sink and listened to the gin pour down the drain.

You get what you deserve. You get what you deserve.

No! That is not true! I did not get what I deserved. I deserved two healthy, happy children. I deserved to watch my four-year-old daughter grow to adulthood. My only crime was being too human, and even that I was trying to fix. I had sent Jamie away, I had vowed to put my family first.

I told Harper that. I told him I loved him.

She found the whiskey and poured it down the sink. Astringent odors burned her nose.

The peach schnapps, the Cointreau, the pear brandy, the blackberry brandy, the Courvoisier, Kahlua, Baileys, Glenfiddich, Chivas Regal. Now the vodka, six bottles, all down the drain. She followed with vanilla extract, almond extract, and cough syrup, working her way through the kitchen, the downstairs lavette, the upstairs bathrooms. She cleansed the house of alcohol, ferreted out each and every conceivable source, dumped it out and kept purging.

He murdered her for the million-dollar life insurance. And because he knew she wasn't even his own kid.

Melanie, you were right. I should've let it all fall apart. We would have been better as a family if we'd fallen apart.

She returned to the kitchen with another bottle of cough syrup, dumped it out. It wasn't enough. She needed to do more, purge more. What else?

Her gaze fell on the refrigerator. Seconds later she

ripped open the huge doors and plumbed the chilled depths. She tossed salads into the garbage disposal and ground them up. She followed with whole apples. She opened bottles of mayonnaise and ketchup and mustard and dumped it all in. Bread, beer, wine, cheese, eggs, yogurt, grapefruit.

Now she was in a frenzy, her hair whipping around her, her movements desperate.

Melanie, sweet Melanie, who deserved so much more. I will save this daughter! I will fight! For once in my life I will stand up for my children!

I am not just a drunk!

Harper walked through the kitchen door just as she stuffed half a turkey down the drain. He drew up short, staring at her with shocked, bewildered eyes.

"Are you fucking nuts?" he cried.

She snapped on the disposal and listened to it whir as it ground the bird to smithereens.

"Pat, what the hell are you doing?"

She finally turned toward her husband, her eyes falling on his bandaged right hand. He didn't seem to notice it, though, as he stared, flabbergasted.

And then he lifted his left hand toward her slightly, his expression softening into concern. Lord, he was handsome when he looked at her like that. She thought of all the years between them, the mistakes he made, the mistakes she made, her overwhelming certainty that it could all be forgiven, that they could move beyond and be happy. They both deserved at least that much.

Oh, Harper, where did we go wrong? How could we have hurt each other so much? How could you have harmed Meagan? She called you Daddy. She learned Jamie's name, but she called you *Daddy.*

She said, "I'm leaving you."

"Pat, sweetheart, what is going on? You've obviously worked yourself into a state." He glanced at the floor, the empty bottles of booze. "Please tell me you didn't . . . You've been doing so well. . . ."

"I am doing well. But then, what do you care? You're the one who brings home the booze."

"Pat! What's gotten into you? We're going to Europe."

"Running away, that's what it was, except I was too stupid to see it. You got a note too, didn't you, Hap? That you get what you deserve."

He stiffened, his handsome features shuttering in answer. She finally found her strength, bringing up her chin.

"No, we don't get what we deserve in the end, Harper. Because I deserved a helluva lot more than to lose my little girl. And you . . . if you really did harm her, you deserve to rot in hell!"

She charged forward, piloted by anger and desperation. She had to get out of the room. She had to get away from him before he turned those eyes on her once more and she broke.

Just as she shoved by him in the doorway, he grabbed her arm.

"Pat, let me explain . . ."

"You can't explain hurting our little girl. She thought of you as her daddy. I don't care what genetics said. You were her dad!"

"I didn't harm Meagan!"

"Bullshit. Brian said—"

Harper grabbed her other shoulder, wincing because of his bandaged hand, then shook her. "Dammit, look at me," he demanded. "Look at me! I have been your husband for thirty-five years, and I swear to you, I did not hurt Meagan!"

"The million dollars—"

"She was four years old, Pat. Jesus Christ, what kind of man do you think I am?" He sounded so hurt.

She shook her head. "I don't know anymore! You kicked out our son. You told the police our daughter may have shot William because he dumped her—"

"I can explain it all. Oh Pat . . ." His voice gentled, he moved closer, pinning her with those eyes, those deep blue eyes. He whispered, "You just have to give me some time. Oh God, everything is falling apart. More than you know. Don't leave me now, Pat. I need you. Don't you understand? I *need* you."

Patricia hesitated and looked at Harper. She saw turmoil and pain in his eyes, fear and shame. She thought, this is why they had ended up together, because she knew the same emotions filled her own gaze. They were both so self-centered. Whatever had made them believe they were capable of being good parents?

"Good-bye, Harper," she said simply, and yanked out of his grasp to head upstairs.

"Everything is in my name," he cried out behind her. "Walk out that door and I'll cancel your gold cards, your bank cards, everything. Within ten minutes I'll have reduced you to nothing!"

She said, "I don't care," and five minutes later, armed with only one suitcase, she sailed out the front door.

The night wind greeted her warmly, filled with the scent of tulips. Across the street the gas lamps glowed softly in the Public Garden as taxis whizzed by.

"That is it," Harper yelled from their bedroom window. "Don't even try to crawl back, Pat. We are through! Do you hear me? We are through!"

On the empty sidewalk Patricia opened her arms and embraced the balmy breeze.

"I am free," she whispered to the city. "Melanie love, I am free!"

IN THE UPSTAIRS bedroom Harper slammed the window shut. He tried to take a step, and the room spun so dizzily he fell down hard on the edge of the bed. For a minute he just sat, shell-shocked, listening to the ringing filling his ears.

She'd left him. Patty had left him. Jesus, Patty had left him.

The pieces he'd been juggling for so long were falling down around him, he thought wildly. The notes in his car. The pile of organs in William's house. Jamie O'Donnell's present, the change in both his wife and daughter. William's wild accusations, Jamie's reports that the FBI was closing in on the fraud rapidly.

He'd gone too far; he'd never get out of this one. And then he thought, he had to get out of this one. He must protect his family.

He'd never meant for it all to come to this. In the beginning he'd viewed Pat as simply the perfect companion. Gorgeous, graceful, confident. A great hostess for a rising doctor, a suitable mother for his children. He'd pursued her almost clinically, armed with books on the subject and, of course, Jamie O'Donnell's advice.

And then the slow-budding wonder that such a creature truly could love him. That she believed in him more than he did. That she could look beyond his humble roots and view the man he desperately wanted to be.

Somewhere along the way he'd fallen hopelessly in love with his own wife, and it had all disintegrated from there. The mutual hurt, the mutual betrayals. The confusion on his part because he could see that he was failing her without understanding what it was he needed to do.

Then, finally, anger, when he discovered her affair with Jamie O'Donnell, anger that had turned his love to dust and made him want to smack her beautiful, lying face. He'd thought it would be better after that. He would never be vulnerable to her again. Business partners, that was the way to run a marriage.

Then they'd come to Boston. Struggled with their son's growing mood swings. Worked diligently on their adopted daughter. And he'd spotted sometimes the way his wife watched him, the quiet yearning in her face, the acceptance.

Somehow over the years the anger had also turned

to dust and he'd rediscovered the love. Softer this
time. Gentler.

He had wanted to give his wife the world. His son
too; Brian would grow up with everything he hadn't!
And maybe Melanie would as well. Because even if
she wasn't his, even if he knew exactly where she
came from, she had looked up to him, and he wasn't
immune to that. There were weeks on end when even
he was convinced they were the perfect family.

But the money ran out so quickly. Retirement
looming around the corner with nothing saved, and
what was he supposed to tell his former-beauty-queen
wife? That at the age of sixty she might want to start
thinking about getting a job?

He'd come up with a plan. No one would get hurt.
A little extra money, and it helped out William too.
Everything was fine. No harm, no foul. Just a little bit
longer . . .

You get what you deserve!

Christ, he didn't know what to do. And the house
of cards was caving in fast. . . .

Earlier tonight the pretty redhead at the Armani
bar, sitting in the same chair she'd occupied for the
last week. Himself, going there for comfort, losing
himself in the living, pulsing rush of money.

Buying the redhead a drink. Then another, then another.

They'd gone to the Four Seasons. Beneath that
shimmering black top she wore something frothy and
made of pure lace. He remembered struggling with the
clasp. The room growing blurry, faraway . . . And
then . . .

Waking up in his car in a seedy section of Boston.
Doors locked, keys in the ignition, a song playing on
his tape deck. The Rolling Stones, "Sympathy for the
Devil."

The blood dewing the white bandage on his right
hand. The tingling in his fingertips. Lifting the ban-

dage slowly, gazing at what lay beneath in gauze, the pounding of his own heart.

"I didn't hurt Meagan!" Harper groaned in the room. "Why doesn't anyone believe me? I never hurt *anyone!*"

THE MAN IN the darkened room moved quickly now, throwing everything into bags. He hadn't gotten to deliver everything he'd wanted, but the big gift had gone down today and that was good enough.

Time to move on.

William Sheffield was dead. Melanie Stokes had pulled the trigger. That was unexpected but filled him with pride. That's my girl!

No time to dwell now, though, little time to contemplate.

Things were happening fast.

He zipped up the last bag and walked out of the room. He already had his ticket for Houston. He knew for a fact that so did Brian Stokes and he guessed that very soon Patricia and Harper Stokes would have tickets as well.

The trap was set and baited. Everything would end where it began.

For you, Meagan. For you.

TWENTY-NINE

ELANIE DISCOVERED THAT for a rich girl, she was pretty good at running away. First, after withdrawing as much cash as possible from her accounts, she dumped out all her plastic but one in an alley. In a city like Boston, some thief ought to be kind enough to recover the cards, use them, and lead the police on a merry goose chase. At least one could dream.

Next, she purchased a baseball cap—thought of David, his arthritis, his baseball pictures, forced herself to dispel such thoughts—and stuffed her hair beneath it. Sunglasses, oversized T-shirt, and cheap canvas backpack transformed her into a young college student prone to furtive glances.

She proceeded to the downtown Boston Amtrak station, which brimmed and bustled with hundreds of people. Boston's South Station led her to New York's Penn Station. A taxi took her to Kennedy Airport, and there she ran into her first obstacle. Getting into an airplane required a valid ID, and she was hardly running around with a fake one. She had to use her real name after all and hope no one would think to check the New York airlines. From Kennedy she flew to Houston.

At Hobby Airport, she followed the signs to the information desk.

The man stationed there was very helpful. He got a map for her and drew out her route to Huntsville, approximately ninety minutes away. Real hard to miss, ma'am, he assured her. Stay on I-45 all the way to I-10, and follow the signs. Finding a place to stay shouldn't be a problem, ma'am. This is Houston. Everything is done to a Texas scale, with strip malls and motels and family restaurants every fifty feet. Why, it's not uncommon to witness three to four funeral processions a day, ma'am. There's that many people living here, and that many people dying. You take care of yourself, y'hear?

Melanie proceeded to the car rental booth. Renting a car required a valid driver's license and a credit card. She was on borrowed time, she thought grimly as she signed the forms.

She got out onto the interstate and drove as night began to fade to black and the world took on a vast, alien scale.

Strip malls loomed, car dealerships, and Motel 6's for as far as the eye could see. Houston sprang up on her right, tall, imposing buildings bursting out of flat land like moon craters in the falling light. The traffic halted for one funeral procession, then, twenty miles later, she stopped for a second.

It was like driving on a giant treadmill, she thought, feeling the first bubbles of hysteria. Pass a hotel, see it again five miles later. Pass a car dealership. Oh, here it is again. Everything so gray, so concrete. By the time she came to I-10 and spotted yet another Motel 6, she figured she was due to get off the road.

She paid for her room with cash. Another friendly man was behind the counter. He told her where a pharmacy was and a grocery store and a hardware store, and was doing so well she went ahead and asked him about a gun shop. He didn't blink an eye but nodded approvingly. A young lady traveling alone needed protection. Particularly this close to Huntsville. Did she know that this town, the headquarters for the Texas Department of Corrections, housed over seventy-two hundred inmates?

She hadn't known. She jotted down everything he said, and rather than going straight to her room, she headed out for the stores.

She bought fruit. It made her feel almost normal. Then she bought scissors and makeup and hair dye, and in another frenzy of activity she went into a local discount store and bought bags and bags of clothes, cheap, trashy.

She dragged them back to her room. The hour was much too late for purchasing a handgun. She locked each of the three locks on her door and finally looked at herself in the mirror.

Pale, pale face. Fine white-blond hair. Deep purple smudges framing cornflower-blue eyes.

She suddenly hated everything about herself. She looked like Melanie but she was not Melanie. She was Daddy's Girl. Abandoned, nameless. No identity, no past, no parentage.

You looked like Meagan, all right? her mother cried. *I looked at you and saw Meagan!* Killer's brat, killer's brat, Larry Digger hissed. Tell me, do you look at children and feel *hungry?*

She picked up the scissors and started whacking. Her hair rained down around her, and she kept ravaging. If she shed enough hair, maybe she wouldn't be Melanie Stokes anymore. If she massacred enough strands, maybe she wouldn't see William's blood on her hands or Larry Digger's body on dark blue carpet. If she cut off enough hair, maybe Daddy's Girl would show her true face and she'd finally feel some recognition.

All I ever wanted was for my family to love me as much as I loved them.

Not since she was nine years old and waking up in a white emergency room had she felt so alone.

•   •   •

AT SIX A.M. Melanie got up. She ate half a cantaloupe for breakfast and a cheap cheese-filled Danish that came out of a plastic wrap. She washed it down with bitter motel coffee, black. Then she showered again and donned a new outfit. After she plastered on some makeup she was ready.

Huntsville didn't just house Texas's extensive prison system, it also housed the Huntsville Prison Museum. The museum opened at nine and Melanie planned on being the first person through the doors. If any place could tell her about Russell Lee Holmes, surely the museum would be it.

She stopped by the visitors' bureau, picked up slick, brightly colored maps, and continued straight into town. Huntsville looked surprisingly pleasant for the city that had hosted more executions than any other in the United States. Old West storefronts, clean sidewalks, wide streets. An impressive stone courthouse set atop an emerald sea of grass and the all important old-fashioned ice cream parlor.

In a town so square and quaint, it took her all of three minutes to locate the prison museum. She pulled her car into a space that still had the bar for hitching a horse. She walked up a gently sloping sidewalk on a bright warm day that promised heavy humidity and booming thunderstorms. A small family of tourists was in front of her, merrily snapping photos.

The small museum was sandwiched between a jewelry store and a western shop. It wasn't much to look at. Dark walls, drop ceiling, faded brown carpet. The room mostly boasted a large model of the Huntsville prison system and many freestanding exhibits of the individual units that comprised the Texas Department of Corrections.

Melanie followed walls covered with portraits of the corrections officials who'd built the prisons. She learned of the famous prison rodeo. She got to stare at Old Sparky, appropriately on display in a fake execution chamber, the wood still rich and gleaming, the broad leather straps and metal electrodes fully functional. Next to the chair, the museum had posted the last meal requests of many men. Three hundred and sixty-two men served.

Melanie found what she was looking for in the small room marked PRISONERS' HALL OF FAME. It featured pictures of such notorious felons as Bonnie and Clyde and, of course, Russell Lee Holmes. Unfortunately the neatly typed placard next to Russell Lee's picture said very little: Convicted of murdering six children. The first prisoner to be executed by Old Sparky when the moratorium on the death penalty finally ended, and, due to his hands and foot blowing off, the last.

"Do you have any more information on specific prisoners?" Melanie asked.

"We get books and tapes donated all the time. Some of them are more specific."

"Where would I find them?"

"Stacked against the wall, honey. Help yourself and take as long as you need. Huntsville prison has some of the most exciting history in the United States, and we're here to share it."

Melanie sorted through the pile of old, faded novels.

Hour dissolved into hour. The curator left and a young man took over, reading *Gray's Anatomy* at the front desk until midafternoon. Then, when it became obvious Melanie wasn't going to budge, he offered to lock her into the museum while he ran across the street to grab a sandwich. Vaguely Melanie was aware of the ding as the door opened again, then the tall, ropy medical student was asking her if she wanted pastrami. She didn't.

She was reading about the deaths of men, the many, many deaths, and the intricate process that culminated in capital punishment. The book was written by the journalist who'd had the death beat in Huntsville, Larry Digger.

Melanie kept reading. Another person entered. She heard the bell and then she simply knew. In fact, she realized now, she'd been waiting for this. She'd known that of all people, he would deduce where she'd gone. After all, he was the person she'd told the most to. He was the person she'd trusted.

Melanie didn't look up. She waited until she felt the warm, hard body of David Riggs standing behind her.

"Melanie," he began softly.

She pointed to the black and white photo in the middle of Larry Digger's book. She said, "Meet Daddy."

THIRTY

"OKAY, MELANIE, START talking." David planted his feet in the middle of Melanie's motel room, looking harsh. He'd been up most of the night and traveling since six that morning. He wasn't in the mood for excuses and he was pissed—no, he felt guilty, scared and sick to his stomach with the worry that something might have happened to Melanie. He wasn't used to worry. He resented it. Then he looked at her face, bruised from William's fists, and he returned to feeling pissed.

Melanie wasn't helping matters. Apparently she'd decided to try out a new look—a black denim skirt that used less material than a headband, a white cotton T-shirt that was at least two sizes too small, and blue eye shadow that appeared to have been applied with a trowel.

He was afraid he knew what she was trying to prove, and it made him feel worse.

Now she arched a brow at his growling tone and shrugged. "Sorry, Agent, but I'm pleading the Fifth."

"Melanie—"

"What do you think? Does this outfit work for me? Very Texan, you know. Younger too. I think Russell Lee would be proud."

"Enough, Mel. You're taking this too far."

"On the contrary, I don't think I'm taking this far enough."

"You are not some piece of trash! You are not this . . . this *chick*."

"Oh, then, who am I, David? Just who am I?" She stormed away. He grabbed her arm.

"You've been dreaming again," he stated bluntly. "The nightmares, right?"

"Maybe I have, maybe I haven't. Maybe it's simply that I've never been to Texas before and yet everything in this damn state looks familiar."

"Melanie, you're falling apart."

"Yeah, well, what do you care?" She jerked her arm free and skewered him with a withering glance. "Why are you here, David? Suffering a change of heart? Well, let me do you a favor—too late."

"Dammit, you're wanted for questioning regarding the death of William Sheffield."

"Are you arresting me?"

"I'm questioning you!"

"Then let me get out the thumbscrews."

"What will it take to set things right? You want sorry? I'm sorry. You want remorse. Hey, I can do remorse. But figure it out, because I am trying to help you, and you need help! Your father has already gone on record as saying that William dumped you, that you haven't been yourself lately, and that you pulled the trigger out of spite. You shot a man and your own father has hung you out to dry. This is *serious*."

She flinched. Her overly made up face finally stilled, but not before David caught the bleakness in her eyes. She turned away and sat down on the edge of the bed, the black miniskirt hitching up to the tops of her thighs.

"Well," she said finally with forced nonchalance. "Easy come, easy go."

"Bullshit. I don't believe Harper. Neither does your mom or your brother. You have allies, Melanie. You do."

"So you found Brian?"

"Yeah. He's sorry he missed your call."

"Is he?" She spoke wistfully, then caught herself and fisted her hands on her lap. "What about my mother? How is she doing?"

"She's shaken but managing. And your brother did clear her. We don't believe she or Brian harmed Meagan."

"Which just leaves dear old Dad. You know the men in my life. . . ."

"He doesn't have an alibi," David said. "He may have engineered Meagan's death so he could collect the million-dollar life insurance. He definitely needed the money."

"If he did it, he didn't do it alone. He would never approach a man like Russell Lee Holmes. Jamie had to have helped him."

"I'm getting the impression that Harper and Jamie come as a package."

Melanie smiled thinly. Then her shoulders slumped and he could practically hear her unspoken thoughts. Two of the men who meant the most in her life plotting the kidnapping and death of a little girl. Who did the planning? Who did the murder? How much could a four-year-old child plead? How much had she screamed—or had she never seen it coming?

"William said my family was an illusion," Melanie murmured after a minute. "My straitlaced father has been operating on healthy people for profit, my mother is a lush, and my brother is gay. And I'm their patsy, he said. Their audience of one because I always believe whatever they show me. I'm not loved, I'm just stupid."

"William's an ass."

Melanie remained unconvinced. "You knew about the surgeries, didn't you, David? You were in my house not because you were investigating William, but because you were investigating my father. White collar crime. The 'case' you would never discuss with

Detective Jax or Agent Quincy. And I never put it together. I was stupid for you too."

"It wasn't that cold—"

"Of course it was! For God's sake, don't continue to treat me like an idiot. For once in my goddamn miserable life, I want to hear the *whole truth*. Why is it so hard for anyone to tell me the truth?"

David fisted his hands. His own temper was sparking, and now he found himself saying more crisply than he intended, "Fine. You want the truth? Here you go. We have reason to believe William and Harper were selecting healthy patients and injecting them with beta blockers to make them appear to need pacemakers. It garnered your father up to forty grand a month, and your father loves money. Hell, he probably murdered his own kid for a million, so what's a simple surgical procedure for six thousand a pop? Can we prove it? No. We have no proof. We'd hoped to catch William red-handed in the hospital and squeeze it from him. But then you shot him, so . . ." He shrugged.

Melanie bolted off the bed, stalking toward him, her eyes narrowed dangerously.

"You mean I made your life messy, Agent? Added some complications, screwed your plan? Welcome to the club, David. Welcome to the goddamn club!"

She jabbed a finger in his chest. He winced. But then he saw the tears gathering in her eyes. He stared at her bruised cheek, her swollen lip, her shaking hands, and everything in him gave way.

"I'm sorry," he found himself saying hoarsely. "I'm sorry, Mel, I'm sorry."

He took her in his arms despite her protests. She kicked at him.

"I hate you, I hate you, I hate you!"

He held her closer. "I know. Shh, I know."

She started to sob, the grief and anger racking her frame. David pressed her against his chest. She smeared blue eye shadow and black mascara all over

his white shirt. He held her tighter, but it wasn't
enough. He had hurt her. He had not been the man
his father had raised him to be, and this time around
he couldn't blame it on his medical condition. He'd
played it safe when Melanie had deserved more.

When he had wanted to give her more.

Suddenly her head angled up. Her hands dug into
the back of his head as she dragged him down. There
was nothing passive about the kiss. Melanie was upset
and angry. She turned on him violently, seeking an
outlet for her rage. He went along with it. Hell, he
found himself responding to it, and then they were
tearing at each other's clothes like savages.

He ripped her T-shirt off and pushed her onto the
bed. Her hands grabbed his belt, cracking leather as
she ripped it from the pant loops. He just managed to
get the back of her skirt unzipped before she'd hooked
her thumb inside the waistband of his briefs and
pushed them down around his ankles.

Then she was slithering out of her skirt and sprawling on the bed in her simple cotton underwear. The
sight of it grounded him, brought him back to reason.

"Easy," he whispered. "Easy."

He feathered back her hair, stroked her cheek, trying to get her writhing body to relax.

"I'm sorry," he whispered again. "I'm sorry." He
ran his fingers down the delicate curve of her jaw to
the vulnerable hollow at the base of her throat. Her
pulse pounded against his thumb. He kissed her collarbone, felt her shiver a little. His lips came lower, his
cheek brushing the high, firm swell of her breast. He
waited a heartbeat. She moaned softly, almost a sigh.
He drew in her nipple deeply and sucked hard.

She shivered. Then she tightened her legs around his
waist and he went tumbling off the cliff of reason.

He kissed her breast, her waist, her navel. His hand
slipped between her thighs, stroking her folds, feeling
her dampen for him. She was so passionate, so re-
sponsive, and it had been a long time for him. He was

torn between taking her right that instant and making the moment last.

He managed to pull away long enough to root around the floor for his wallet. He always traveled with a condom, the eternal optimist.

When he rose back up, foil package triumphantly in hand, he had a clear view of her, her slender body sprawled on the dark blue comforter, breasts high and pink-tipped, skin all cream and rose. Makeup was smeared across her face, but he could see her beneath it, her lips parted, her eyes heavy-lidded with passion.

"Look at me," he demanded hoarsely. "This isn't just some fling, Mel. Once this is over, I'm not ever going away."

He smoothed on the condom, his gaze still on her face, and entered her in one fierce thrust.

She cried out.

"Melanie. Sweet Melanie."

Her gaze darkened. "No," she muttered, then gasped as he began to rock. "Not Melanie. Not anyone."

"You're wrong. You're Melanie, sweet, loving Melanie. *My Melanie.*"

He thrust harder. Her teeth sank into her lower lip. He could feel her body tense. Then he got to see the small moment of wonder as her climax broke and brought fresh sheen to her face. She was lovely.

"David . . ."

The traffic roared and rushed beyond the curtains. He closed his ears to the sound and followed her over the brink.

MINUTES LATER HE rolled off her. Not wanting to completely break contact, he spooned her body against his. Her head rested on his arm, her gaze focused on the far wall. He was struck once more by her tiny size, the delicate shape of her arm, the long, graceful line of her back. She hardly made a dent against his own darker, larger form. He thought of her having had to take on William Sheffield, and he wished the man were still alive just so he could kill him.

Now Melanie was retreating, mentally withdrawing. He wondered if she was remembering William too. Maybe the way he'd cheated on her, or maybe the look on his face right before he struck her. Or maybe she was thinking of Harper, of the man she'd grown up calling Dad whom she knew now as, at the very least, a cold-blooded felon, if not a child murderer. Then there was Russell Lee Holmes, the genetic dad, who'd also killed little girls as a hobby.

"I'm not going back to Boston," she said abruptly. "I can't yet. There are answers here. I have to know what they are."

His fingers stilled just above her elbow, his hand settling on her arm, cupping it lightly. "If you agree to stay in my custody," he said after a minute, "I may be able to buy us both some time. We can work on this together, see what we find."

"We made love."

"Yes."

"You're an agent. I thought they had rules about such things."

"There are rules. I've crossed the line."

"What will they do?"

"I don't know. I might get written up. I might lose my job. It's possible."

She rolled over, looking at him with a fierceness that hit him hard. "Regrets, then? Tell me, I want to know."

He said honestly, "No regrets, Mel. For you, not ever."

She whispered: "I'm ripped up, David. There aren't enough pieces left to make a whole. I'm so frightened of what I'm going to find. I'm angry and I'm scared and I . . . I can't believe what William did. I can't believe Harper hates me this much. I can't believe I loved them all and I didn't know them at all. I feel so completely, utterly *empty,* and I don't even care."

"It's going to get better, Melanie. It will."

"I don't even know myself anymore. Why I do the things I do or say the things I say? I want to buy a gun. I used to hate guns. What is happening to me?"

"It's going to work out, Mel," he tried again. "I'm going to help you."

"David, I don't believe you."

He had to nod. The words hurt, but she had the right. He drew her back into his arms. At least she didn't protest.

After a moment he said against the top of her head, "Why don't you rest now, Melanie. You've been the strong one through this. Now it's my turn."

She seemed to nod against his chest and they drifted off to silence together, then sleep. When David awoke, Melanie was untangling herself from his arms and crawling out of bed.

"I need to shower," she said. "I have an appointment."

"With whom?"

She gave him a small smile and strode toward the bathroom. "Russell Lee Holmes."

THIRTY-ONE

WHEN THEY PILED into David's car, a thunderstorm was rolling across the sky. Clouds teemed and broiled, blacking out the sun and settling an eerie heaviness over the city. They drove in silence for fifteen minutes, watching the horizon crackle with lightning while the air conditioner blasted their cheeks.

David pulled over at the Captain Joe Byrd Cemetery. "The sky looks like it's going to go."

"It's only water." She got out of the car and headed straight into the graveyard.

The cemetery didn't have a fence. Some flowers had been planted at the perimeter, now leaning over and panting from the heat. The rest of the cemetery was filled with rows of white crosses marching steadily backward. They rolled back as far as she could see, the last dozen rows so wind-scarred, the dates and prisoner numbers had completely eroded. Those were surrounded by hard-packed ground and thick, old grass. Then there were the front rows, the fresh new graves with the black earth still mounded from recent filling.

The sky cracked, the first fat raindrop splashing on Melanie's nose as an owl hooted and lightning danced across the sky.

"We'd better hurry," David called above the growing wind, his dark suit glued to his lanky frame. "The storm's almost overhead."

"We have to look for the prisoner number," she called back to him, and rattled off the information.

Lightning cracked again, so close they felt its charge zip through the air. The wind was whipping up now. The owl hooted again, agitated and uncomfortable. Then thunder boomed. More lightning. Melanie could feel the static electricity raising the hair on her arms, rippling up her spine, accelerating her heart. She began to feel panic. The rain hit her face. She was breathing too hard. She could feel the thunder still echoing in her belly, and suddenly she felt like a little girl lost in a sea of white death, trying to find her father.

David was suddenly at her side. He took one look at her face and ordered her head down between her knees. He grabbed her hands and gripped them tight. "You're having an anxiety attack. Calm down."

The sky abruptly gave up. It burst like a giant water balloon and deluged them in a sheet of rain.

David led her over to the grave he'd found. She stood beside him in front of the white cross. Prisoner number and date. That was it.

Melanie thought she should feel something. She *wanted* to feel something. This was her father's grave, her real father. Please let it mean something to her, give her some sense of closure.

She felt hollow. The marker meant nothing to her. Neither did the dead man who'd once been her father. These were abstract concepts that couldn't begin to compete with the real, vibrant, warm memories of Harper, Patricia, and Brian Stokes. David had been right, she did have a family and she missed them and she loved them. No going forward, it seemed, and no going back.

David put his arm around her shoulders. He led her back to the car through the stinging sheets of rain and held open the door for her. Then he removed his jacket, and tucked it around Melanie's shivering shoulders. Then he fastened her seat belt.

When he pulled back to close the door, his gaze was liquid gold. Understanding, she thought. Simple understanding.

"He is not what you're about, Melanie," he said. "You can spend your time in prison museums and graveyards if you want, but you are not the legacy of Russell Lee Holmes."

He shut the door, and she watched him cross rapidly in front of the car to the driver's side.

He knew her, she realized, even when she had stopped knowing herself. He did have enough faith for both of them.

And then she thought, I want to go home.

She turned away so David wouldn't see her tears.

LATER DAVID HELPED her shower and crawl into bed, tucking the covers around her shoulders. She was too exhausted to fight him, falling almost immediately to sleep with her head buried against the feather pillow.

David got out the phone and prepared to do more work.

Their clothes were strewn all over the room, damp puddles reminding him of the choices he'd made. His suit mingled with her T-shirt, his loafers rolling over her sandals.

His FBI shield next to her makeup on the blue Formica counter.

Chenney picked up the other end of the phone line just as Melanie began to mutter in her sleep. David turned his back to her for more privacy and searched for a neutral tone of voice.

"Hey, rookie. What's the status?"

Silence over the line. Then a long, hard sigh. That told David enough.

"Lairmore didn't buy it, did he?" he said.

"I think he's gonna write you up," Chenney confirmed. "It's going in your files. Jesus, Riggs, you're not exactly the most popular guy around here at the moment."

"I went after a suspect in a murder case. I wouldn't think that would be such a breach in protocol."

"Oh, yeah, Riggs. You flew across the country without backup, discussion with your supervisor, or any solid leads. And the Bureau has such a reputation for loving cowboys. Did you sleep through the academy, or what?"

David managed a ghost of a smile. For so long he'd been convinced he hated his job. Now that he was tossing it away, however . . .

"Things blow over," he said at last. "Just give me an update."

"You need to come back, Riggs, I'm serious."

"I have a lead. I've traced Melanie Stokes to the William P. Hobby airport and a rental car agency. It's not a goose chase, Chenney. I'll leave Lairmore a report."

"Then let me come out there and help you."

"You don't want to come here."

Another small silence as comprehension dawned. "Shit. Riggs—"

"Just give me the update, Chenney."

Chenney exhaled in fury. David waited.

"Fine. Here's where we're at, but if Lairmore drills you too hard—"

"You had nothing to do with it. Trust me, Chenney, I know."

Chenney didn't sound mollified. Maybe he liked Riggs after all, maybe they had formed some version of partnership. Stranger things had happened.

"Well, we got some answers and some questions. Which do you want first?"

"Go in order. Where are we with the Sheffield homicide?"

"Well, I'd think you'd know more than me—"

"Chenney."

"Yeah, fine. Okay. Jax is heading up the case, and let me tell you, he's riding Harper with a vengeance. Jax ordered fingerprinting powder over every damn square inch of the study, and every time Harper makes a condescending remark, Jax simply has more floorboards ripped up and sent to the lab. Yesterday he even tore down the curtains. Soon Harper's gonna be living in a crime lab."

"And this is teaching us . . ."

"How to have a good time. No, we don't have many leads other than Melanie Stokes. Lairmore has us attacking it from the healthcare side. I was over at the hospital yesterday conducting the interviews on Sheffield. Interestingly enough, another anesthesiologist, Dr. Whaler Jones seems to know an awful lot about Sheffield. I get the impression she was a little jealous of all the surgeries Sheffield got to pick up. She can put Sheffield at the hospital at all sorts of times he had no good reason to be there, that's for sure."

"Still circumstantial."

"Yeah, that's the problem we have. Too many circumstances. Lairmore is toying around with having all pacemaker patients receive a second evaluation, but from what we've heard, that won't fly. The attorney general tells us we could be sued by Harper for ruining his reputation. To be on the safe side, we got all the serial numbers of the pacemakers Harper has installed in the past five years. Quite a list, let me tell you. The FDA ran a cross-check. They've received only *one* complaint on the batch, which is actually well under the industry average. So we can't even go after the pacemakers that way. Everything appears perfectly legit.

"At this point, we'd have to bring in patients, remove the pacemakers, and then hook the patients to a heart monitor to see if they're truly bradycardic. Let's just say both the legal and medical experts agree that's not a great idea. On the other hand, the pacemakers naturally expire in five years and will have to be removed, so if we're willing to be patient . . ." Chenney shrugged, declaring bluntly, "We got nothing, Riggs. At this point Harper's coming away clean."

"What about the outline of the papers next to William's body?"

"That's the thing. There's gotta be documentation somewhere. We've ripped apart Sheffield's apartment, but no such luck. Bank shows Sheffield deposited some rather large checks from Harper, but Harper claims the money was a gift to his one-time future son-in-law, and who are we to argue? We couldn't find any propranolol in William's place, no notes, and no friends who have an inkling what he was into."

"Jamie O'Donnell might know something."

"Well, that brings us to the second point. Jamie O'Donnell seems to have skipped town. Checked out of the Four Seasons yesterday afternoon and nothing's been heard from him since."

"Hmmm." David tucked that information away. Of all the people to come after Melanie, Jamie O'Donnell would be it.

"Patricia Stokes has also bolted," Chenney said.

"Huh?"

"Yep. I was over at the Stokes house earlier this afternoon. Harper's playing cool about it, but the maid told us Patricia packed a bag last night and walked out the front door. Boston homicide talked to the people at the Four Seasons, but they claim they haven't seen her around. Most likely she finally got sick of Harper's shit. I mean, trying to turn in your own daughter . . ."

"Not endearing," David agreed.

"Oh, I almost forgot. Harper has on a bandage today. His whole hand is wrapped up. Seems he injured it somehow, but he won't talk about it. Jax even asked him point-blank what he'd done and Harper told him point-blank to go fuck himself. You know, I don't think Harper has that fresh feeling anymore."

"Think if Jax pushes him hard enough, he might crack?"

"I don't think it's Jax," Chenney said. "I think our mystery manipulator is pulling out the stops. It's what she wants, right? All those little gifts reopening old wounds. Melanie's on the run, Brian's removed from the family, Patricia finally left her husband, and O'Donnell has gotten the hell out of Dodge. Harper's alone and feeling the strain. Ten to one, the man is frightened. I don't put anything past him at this point. I'm trying to run down information on Ann Margaret, by the way. Nothing immediate comes up on the computer though, and I haven't had time to do anything more in-depth. Kind of need more hands at this point."

"Don't we all. What about the Texas angle? I'm here, so let's use me."

"Actually, you may be helpful, Riggs. I think I may have a break in Texas."

"That's my boy."

"Okay, Jax and I went through the public pay phone records yesterday. *Nada*. I mean zip. But Jax—give him some credit here, Riggs—didn't subpoena just the Boston records, he got Larry Digger's Houston phone records as well."

"Son of a bitch. He never told me that."

"Of course not, we're the feds, remember?"

"Oh, yeah."

"Well, you were the one who said Digger reported the anonymous call three weeks ago. Sure enough. Twenty-five days ago, Digger's phone records suddenly exploded with calls. I got them from Jax. Then to entertain myself this morning, I cross-referenced the names of the people Digger called with the midwives association's list of Texan members. And guess what I found . . ."

Chenney rattled off the name, David quickly wrote it down. "I'll look her up first thing in the morning. If she remembers Russell Lee Holmes, she must remember his wife, so maybe I can tie in Ann Margaret from this side."

"Yeah," Chenney said, but he sounded troubled now. "Riggs . . . I got more news."

"That's what they pay you for."

"I . . . uh . . . I kinda started exhumation proceedings for Russell Lee Holmes."

"Jesus, Chenney."

"My off-the-wall theories aren't so off the wall anymore, Riggs. I even got Lairmore scared. Remember the shrine in Melanie's room? The blue scrap of fabric with the two types of blood?"

"Of course. Come on, Chenney, spit it out."

"Okay. They've positively ID'd one blood sample as belonging to Melanie Stokes. It's an absolute match. A lot of blood work was done when she was first found twenty years ago, so they had plenty to go on. Which brings us to the second blood sample . . . They did a DNA test, Riggs. There is a fifty percent match between the second DNA and Melanie's DNA, what you'd see between parent and child."

"Oh, shit." David closed his eyes. He already knew what Chenney was going to say next.

"I think we finally found the missing player in our game, Riggs. We've just sent away for Russell Lee Holmes's medical files and blood samples to confirm, but we can already tell you that the second bloodstain is an XY chromosome. We're talking Melanie Stokes's genetic dad. And, Riggs, the lab swears that bloodstain is less than one week old."

THIRTY-TWO

HARPER STOKES STOOD alone in the middle of his study. He had turned on the lights earlier, but the illumination had only frustrated him, revealing the glowing powder, the torn curtains, the ripped-up floorboards. For the past twenty-four hours Boston homicide had swarmed his home, investigating every carefully decorated nook, manhandling every lovingly acquired antique.

It seemed there was no place he could go anymore without being watched by a uniformed officer. No refuge left in the respectable life he'd spent his whole life building.

Jamie was gone. Patricia was gone. He wondered if she was finally happy with Jamie O'Donnell, and that thought left him gutted.

No Brian. He'd called his son's practice. They said Brian had been out for days. He didn't believe it. He'd swallowed his pride, begged for his own son's emergency number, knowing it would probably belong to some man. It had.

Nate had been polite. Brian was gone. He didn't know where. He did consider him missing.

Harper had hung up the phone feeling suddenly old and, for the first time, lonely.

Empty house. Crime-scene tape. A bandage on his

hand. Once again smug Jamie O'Donnell was right. It had all come full circle.

He couldn't just stay here and mourn forever. He was a man of action. It was time to get something done. For his family. For himself.

He went up to the bedroom. From a locked safe in the walk-in closet he pulled out a gun. The bandage on his right hand made it too hard to grip, so he unwound the gauze. The fresh tattoo blazed up at him: 666.

He muttered, "But I am not the devil. I didn't harm Meagan, dammit, and I'm not even close to Russell Lee Holmes."

At least, not yet.

THIRTY-SIX HOURS AFTER abandoning her husband, the euphoria had left Patricia Stokes.

She'd tried to use her credit card; it had been canceled. She had tried to use her ATM card; it had been declined. She was fifty-eight years old, carrying a suitcase of designer clothes, and she was penniless. A wave of fear had hit her, and she simply wanted to run to the safest place she knew—the arms of her husband.

She'd spent the previous night with friends. It had gotten her through the first few hours. With daybreak, however, had come the realization that she needed a purpose. For once in her life she needed to take control.

She'd tried the Four Seasons. Jamie O'Donnell was gone. She'd tried her son's apartment. She found her son's lover packing up her son's things and telling her that Brian had left town. He had no idea where her son had gone.

Patricia knew only one other person to try.

Now she stood with her suitcase in front of the home of Ann Margaret Dawson. She knew Ann Margaret only as her daughter's boss. Now Patricia swallowed her pride and knocked.

After a moment the door cracked open. Ann Margaret peered out cautiously, as if she were expecting something unpleasant. Then her eyes widened in surprise.

"Patricia," she said, and opened the door all the way.

"I left Harper," Patricia blurted out.

"Are you looking for Jamie?"

"No," Patricia said in bewilderment. "I'm looking for you!"

Ann Margaret closed her eyes. There was something sad about her expression. "Do you love him?"

"Who?"

"Jamie."

"Of course not. That was years ago. I just want my daughter back!"

Ann Margaret said quietly, almost gently, "Patricia, I believe it's time we talked."

BRIAN STOKES HUNKERED down lower in his seat at the airport waiting lounge. The first flight to Houston wasn't until morning, so he might as well catch some sleep. He was anxious though, already worried that he was too late.

He'd done wrong by Meagan. There was no escaping the hard, cold facts, he thought. His troubled mother had had an affair with his godfather. She'd given birth to Jamie's child and Harper had found out. Harper had engineered the death of Meagan, probably out of rage but also out of greed. His dad had killed his sister for a million bucks.

And Brian had never said a word.

Well, he'd been a child back then. Now he was an adult, and he vowed to do more for Melanie.

He fidgeted in his seat, trying to stretch out his spine, then stiffened.

He could have sworn he caught a glimpse of someone familiar, but when he looked again, no one was
there.

MELANIE WAS NOT sleeping well. She was in the cabin.
In the cabin in the middle of the woods, watching the
spider ease across the window. And Meagan was behind her. Meagan was rocking back and forth, clutching her pony.

"Please let me go, let me go, let me go."

You have no idea what he can do.

Then a shadow fell across the wood floor. A man
filled the doorway and he took a step into the room.
Cold wind swept through the cabin. Meagan shrank
back and Melanie already knew that all was lost. He
was back and it would only get worse.

"No," Meagan whimpered.

"*No!*" Melanie cried out.

"It's okay," David Riggs murmured in her ear, and
cradled her close. "I've got you now, Melanie. I've got
you."

She whispered, "Too late."

THIRTY-THREE

WHEN MELANIE WOKE up next, she was alone in the bed. The room was shadowed, the thick curtains tightly drawn against a blazing Texas sun. In the background came the rhythmic hum of cars racing over a concrete interstate. Closer was the rattle of a metal cart wheeling across the balcony as a cleaning woman performed her rounds.

Melanie blinked a few times. Her head was fuzzy, the impression of lingering dreams still hovering around her like a shadow she couldn't dispel. A dull throbbing had burrowed in behind her left eye. Not a full-blown migraine yet, but she should probably take some aspirin.

She finally turned her head and searched for signs of David.

Clothes were strewn across the floor. She spotted his slacks and his suit jacket, carelessly tossed by the chair.

Then Melanie heard a new sound, low, half muffled. A moan of pain.

Melanie rushed to the bathroom. She wasn't prepared for what she found.

David Riggs was writhing on his stomach on the cold tile floor.

"Oh, my God, it's your back."

She went down on her hands and knees beside him, but David didn't reply. His face was bone white and contorted into a horrible expression as he beat the floor with the heel of his hand.

"Do you need ice? What about medication? Surely you're on something for this."

For answer, his legs kicked out and another guttural moan escaped his lips. She leaned closer, and when she looked into his eyes she saw something worse than pain—she saw impotent rage.

"Go . . . away," he gasped.

Melanie compromised. She threw on clothes and went running for ice. When she returned, he was still on his stomach, but he was crawling now. In many ways it was an even more horrible sight.

So this was arthritis. This was strong, capable David Riggs's world.

Melanie discovered tears on her cheeks. She put the ice in his dress shirt with shaking fingers and fashioned a clumsy ice pack.

"I'm going to put this on your back," she told David.

David muttered something that might or might not have been a curse. Melanie plopped the makeshift ice pack on his naked lower back. Immediately his body arched, the muscles in his neck cording, and his lips curled back to bare his teeth.

"I'm sorry," Melanie whispered. "I don't know what else . . ."

"Leave . . . it," David snarled. "Time." His head sagged between his shoulder blades, his body still convulsing.

Melanie sat beside him and waited. Eventually his limbs stopped twitching. His face relaxed more, still red and flushed. He finally got to curl his legs up, assuming the fetal position.

"How is it?" she ventured.

"Fucking . . . awful."

"Does this happen a lot?"

"Has . . . phases."

"Surely there's something you're supposed to do. Exercises, medication . . ."

David didn't say anything, but his gaze darted toward his travel bag. Puzzled, Melanie got up and opened it. Inside she found a bottle of orange pills. Naproxen, she read. The date on the bottle was almost a year ago, but it looked completely full.

"David, I don't understand."

"It's arthritis," he muttered, looking cornered. "My spine is fusing. Sometimes I wake up at night with the muscles locked around my ribs so tightly, I can't breathe. On my really good days, maybe I can skip to work. But then I get days like this to bring me back to earth. What's a fucking pill gonna do about all that!"

Melanie touched his cheek. "You're afraid, aren't you? You're afraid that if you take this first pill that you'll finally be giving in. You'll finally be admitting that you have a chronic disease and you will have it for the rest of your life."

"No, goddammit! I'm afraid I'll take that damn pill and *it won't get any better.* That *nothing will change* and what will I look forward to then, Melanie? What will I have to hope for then?"

"Oh, David," she whispered. "Oh, sweetheart, you have arthritis, not cancer."

The haunted look on his lined face undid her. He broke and she took him into her arms, cradling his head on her lap, rocking him against her.

"They put her through chemo so many times," he muttered hoarsely. "So many times and they never did any good, and we cleaned and it never did any good. Nothing ever did any good."

"I understand, I understand."

"I wanted to make my father so proud. I wanted to make him so damn proud."

"He is, David, he is."

"Goddammit, Melanie, I loved baseball. And

there's nothing I can do. I'll never be everything I wanted to be. Never."

"Oh, David," she said quietly, "none of us ever are."

Eventually the worst passed. She remained curled up on the floor with him, still stroking his hair, neck, shoulders. And then she became aware of the smooth feeling of his skin, the distinct delineation of lean muscle and sinew right beneath her touch. His head came up. She saw his fierce blue eyes, and then she was on her back and they made love again, fiercely and with unexplained need.

Afterward they lay without speaking, intertwining their fingers over and over again, and listening to each other's heartbeats. It told them enough.

"I have a name and an address for the midwife," David said finally, hours later.

"All right," Melanie said.

They both got up and dressed.

THE ADDRESS LED them to a nice neighborhood, much nicer than what Melanie expected of a woman who had once assisted Russell Lee Holmes. The modest ranch house was nestled in one of the new suburbs bursting up all around Houston, where every fourth house looked exactly the same, just painted slightly different. The yards were lush, well manicured. A few young saplings thrust toward the sun, their meager year's worth of growth marking the age of the houses around them.

A few kids on dirt bikes looked at them curiously as David pulled over. He returned their stares with a level gaze of his own and they quickly sped up. There was just something about FBI agents, Melanie thought. You could spot one twenty feet away.

David opened the car door for her. Melanie had to take a deep breath, then she walked ahead of him to the doorway.

The woman who answered on the second knock was not what Melanie expected. In comfortable beige slacks and worn white shirt, she had dirt stains on her knees and a gardening trowel in her hand. Her silver-white hair was all but hidden beneath her straw hat, making her an easy match for someone's favorite grandmother, down to the warm blue eyes and scent of fresh baking hanging in the air.

"May I help you folks?" the woman asked politely, going so far as to smile at the strangers. She had an easy smile. Melanie found herself returning it.

"Mrs. Applebee?" David inquired somberly.

"Yes, sir," Mrs. Applebee agreed amiably. "Though I should tell you now, I'm a happy retired woman right down to the fixed income. No encyclopedia sets or nouveau religions for me. At my age, all I need is a pack of sunflower seeds and a few more grandkids— but don't tell my daughter I said that."

David grinned, then caught himself and struggled for professionalism. Melanie could tell Mrs. Applebee had also taken him by surprise.

"I understand that, ma'am," he assured her. "Trust me. Actually, I'm Special Agent David Riggs with the FBI, and I'm here about a man you spoke to three weeks ago—Larry Digger."

Rhonda Applebee stilled, the friendly smile replaced by wariness. She looked at Melanie curiously, then she looked back at David, who was now holding up his credentials. She said finally, "I see. Well, then, I suppose you should come on in. I'll get us some iced tea."

Mrs. Applebee led them both through a modest, tastefully decorated house to a back patio that was surprisingly lush. Huge palm trees and brightly flowering bushes enclosed a kidney-shaped yard. The dirt was turned over in one shady corner, where Mrs. Applebee had obviously been at work planting before they had arrived. She gestured to a glass patio table, where they took seats, and she adjusted the yellow and blue umbrella for better shade.

They murmured polite comments about the yard. She thanked them graciously and returned to the house for a pitcher of iced tea and a large plate of cookies.

"Oatmeal cookies?" she inquired. "Made them fresh this morning."

David looked at Melanie. She wordlessly agreed. This woman was so perfectly lovely, and now they were going to pick her brain about Russell Lee Holmes.

"You were a midwife?" David began finally.

Mrs. Applebee gave him a brisk nod. "Yes, I was a midwife. Retired ten years. And, yes, thirty years ago part of my practice was serving poor neighborhoods, where folks couldn't afford a doctor, medication, or hospital. Those were the days when we still put people first regardless of income. You know—the days before the HMOs."

"Larry Digger tracked you down?" David pressed.

"Yes, but I'll tell you honestly, I didn't care much for him or his questions. The sins of the fathers, my fanny. Each child has its own right to live and let live. I really didn't want to be a part of tracking down some poor soul just because of what its father did."

"What exactly did you tell Larry Digger?"

"Well, he had a picture, of course, of Russell Lee Holmes. And, yes, I recognized the man. Back then it didn't mean much. I made the rounds, and as much as I hate to say it, one poor, mean skedaddling father was pretty much the same as another. None of them stuck around for the birth of their child, I can tell you that much. They'd show up, give you a once-over, and then go off drinking with their buddies while their wives or girlfriends squeeze out their next progeny on dirty sheets. Childbirth is women's work, and they sure as hell don't want to be involved."

"Where was this?" David had out his notepad now

and was preparing to write but Mrs. Applebee shook her head.

"That neighborhood doesn't exist anymore. It wasn't much more than a shantytown when it did, and the city bulldozed it years ago in favor of middle-income housing. Progress, you know."

David set down his pad. "Mrs. Applebee, I understand your concern about not wanting to inflict the sins of the fathers upon a child. Frankly I think I know who Russell Lee Holmes's child is, and it doesn't bother me a bit. We need confirmation, however, and we need to know exactly what Larry Digger told you. Last week, you see, he was shot dead."

Mrs. Applebee's frank blue gaze ran David up and down. Then she gave Melanie the same appraisal. Finally she seemed to make up her mind.

"All right, Agent. What is it you need to know?"

"Let's start with Russell Lee Holmes. Did you spend much time with him?"

"No, not really. I said hi, how is she? He shrugged, told me I'd know better than him, and to call him when it was over. Then he was out the front door and I worked with his wife—at least he called her his wife, though I didn't see any wedding bands."

"What was she like?" Melanie spoke up urgently. Rhonda Applebee looked at her curiously, and Melanie fumbled. "His wife, I mean. The mother."

"Oh, she made more of an impression on me than he did. A real tough one, that girl. She was already nearly fully dilated and effaced when I showed up, but she didn't so much as shed a tear. Just twisted those sheets tighter in her hands and held on for dear life. She struck me as smart—she asked good questions. She also looked me in the eye, which requires some self-respect. She mentioned that she'd been using a diaphragm and that people like her had no business having children." Mrs. Applebee murmured wryly, "Smart *and* a realist. But I guess her husband found out about the birth control and put an end to it. She wasn't happy, but I suppose she figured the damage was already done."

"Did . . . did she seem to want the child? Did she seem to care about her baby at all?" Melanie asked.

Mrs. Applebee's face softened. "When that baby finally came bursting out, you could tell she was tired and you could tell she was already worried about its future and hers, but, boy, the smile that lit her face, the glow that filled her eyes . . ."

"What happened next?" David said.

"When I was just cleaning up, Russell Lee finally came home. He was a bit wobbly on his feet—probably had a few congratulatory beers from his friends. Of course the first thing he did was wake up his wife and child.

"She showed him the child. He looked it over, nodded a bit, seemed satisfied. He even stroked his woman's cheek, which was about as nice a gesture I got to see in those parts. He seemed honestly proud of his kid, poofing out his chest, strutting around the house like he'd gotten a new car and done it all himself.

"Finally he asked me what he owed. I told him what he could afford. He gave me ten bucks, inspected the piles of diapers and formulas, and grunted. I told him to call me if they needed anything more, and that's the last I saw of the couple.

"Years later I pick up the paper and lo and behold, there's the same man, now identified as a baby killer. I really didn't know what to think."

"Did you contact the police?"

"What for? I helped deliver his child, that was all. Besides, I may not be a doctor, but even a midwife values confidentiality."

"But that wasn't the end of it, was it?" David asked shrewdly.

Mrs. Applebee finally hesitated. "No, it wasn't. Just weeks after the first article appears in the paper, some man shows up on my doorstep with a thick mane of red hair and an Irish brogue. Tells me to forget everything I ever knew about Russell Lee Holmes, his wife and child, and tries to offer me money. Well, I never. I do my job and I do it well and I'll tell you the same thing I told him—I keep my own to my own for my own and he and his dollars could take a flying leap."

"And what did he say?" David asked.

"Why, he laughed. Very charming really, but still, you could tell . . ." For the first time, Mrs. Applebee looked troubled. "There was just something about him," she said finally. "In my line of work I've been about everywhere, seen about every kind of folk, some good, some bad, some kind, some cruel. You realize after a bit it's not in the clothes or the way they walk or in the way they live. You can tell a man by the look around his eyes, and that Irishman, he had that look. He was a man who knew things, who'd done things, who was capable of doing many more things. . . ."

She shook her head, shivering a bit even after all the years. "Let's just say I got the message. Whether I took the money or not, it was best that I forget everything I ever knew about Russell Lee Holmes." Her gaze lowered, and she added more softly, "And for a time I suppose I did."

David was looking at Melanie. She nodded miserably, understanding his silent message. Larry Digger had been telling them the truth. Jamie O'Donnell had indeed visited the midwife. Her godfather had paid this woman a visit and had threatened to harm her if she ever told anyone about Russell Lee Holmes.

"Larry Digger implied you wanted money," Melanie murmured finally. "Do you?"

Mrs. Applebee appeared affronted. "Look around you, child. Why would I need money. My Howard provided for me just fine!"

"Why are you telling the story now?" David pressed more diplomatically. "Last you knew, your life had been threatened."

"Ah, well." She shrugged. "I was scared, Agent, I can admit that. But I was forty years old then and maybe a bit more aware of my own mortality and my children. I'm seventy now, and my children are grown. What do I care about some Irishman? And what do I care about Russell Lee Holmes? That's all water under the bridge these days. Even you must realize that the world does not rise and fall based on the actions of one man, not even the actions of one bad man."

"Other than that visit twenty-five years ago, and Larry Digger's visit, has anyone else asked you about Russell Lee Holmes?"

"No."

"Have you ever seen the mother again?"

"No."

"Do you have a name for her?"

"Angela Johnson, the name she used thirty years ago. Mr. Digger told me it was an alias."

"Can you describe her?"

"Oh, I don't know, I saw the poor thing when she was giving birth. Not a great time for a woman. She was . . . a little over five feet, I suppose. A short, tough build, like a pistol. Blue eyes. Dark hair, naturally curly. She was in her late twenties, so I suppose she's nearly sixty now."

David was looking at Melanie. "Does that sound like anyone you know?"

"No—"

"Ann Margaret," he whispered.

Her eyes went wide. "No!" But in fact, he had a point, and while Melanie was still trying to absorb that shock, David turned to Mrs. Applebee and asked an even more absurd question.

"By any chance have you seen Russell Lee Holmes lately?"

"What?" asked Mrs. Applebee.

"He's dead!" exclaimed Melanie.

David said, "I'm sorry, Mel, I couldn't think of a

way of saying this, but we received new information on the scrap of fabric found in your room. It contained two types of blood. The first is yours, and according to the DNA test the second sample most likely belongs to your father."

Melanie felt the pounding pick up behind her eyeball. Wooden shack. Little girl. Shadow looming in the doorway.

"Wait a minute," Mrs. Applebee was saying. "You believe *she* is the child of Russell Lee Holmes?"

"Yes, ma'am."

"What in the world made you believe that?"

"Larry Digger," David said with equal bewilderment. "Why?"

"Because she *can't* be his child, Agent. Russell Lee didn't have a daughter. Russell Lee had a *son*."

THIRTY-FOUR

IT WAS JUST after noon when Brian Stokes pulled into the Motel 6 in Huntsville, Texas. He'd been traveling since five in the morning, and after a rough night of fitful sleep in the airport, he felt tired, grimy, and anxious. At least he'd also been lucky. For twenty bucks a pop, he'd found a person at each car rental company willing to look into their records. Once he knew Melanie had a car, he'd thought to stop by the information desk, where her big blue eyes had made quite an impression on the older man who worked there. That had brought him to Huntsville, where the first hotel he encountered was a Motel 6.

He stepped out of his car. The heat and humidity slapped him fiercely, plastering his shirt to his skin. Welcome home, Texas, he thought. Christ, he didn't miss this state.

In the motel lobby he got the blushing receptionist to confess that while she didn't have a guest with Melanie's name, she just happened to have a guest matching her description.

Brian rewarded her with a wink. The twenty-year-old blushed harder and stammered she could take a message. Brian decided against leaving one. He wasn't sure what state of mind his sister was in these days and didn't want to spook her into running more. He'd wait, approach her in person.

He walked back into the parking lot feeling much better about life. He had found Melanie. He would take care of her. Everything would be all right.

Then he turned toward his car and found himself face-to-face with his father.

"What the hell are you doing here?" Harper Stokes demanded first. His white dress shirt was soaked through, his dark tie skewed. If Brian had passed a restless night, his father had suffered a completely sleepless one.

"Looking for Melanie," Brian said, then frowned. "What the hell are you doing here?"

"What I should've done twenty-five years ago."

"What, tell the truth? I know what you did, Dad. I know you didn't pay the ransom. I know you sold out your own daughter for the fucking life insurance. How dare you—"

"I held this family together—"

"You ripped us apart!"

"I did what had to be done!"

"By sacrificing your own child?" Brian screamed. "By selling out my sister?"

"You hated her! You ruined her toys."

"*I loved her*. She was *Meagan*. She smiled at all of us, she believed in all of us. Hell, she even believed in you. How could you do that to a four-year-old girl? *How could you do that to me?*"

Harper's face darkened. He said, in a tone Brian had never heard before, "You ungrateful little shit. You don't know anything, and I refuse to stand here and explain myself to my own son. I raised you. I did everything for you, and this is how you repay me? For the last time, I did not hurt Meagan! I didn't! And now, I've had enough."

Harper brought up his hand. Brian noticed the white bandage. It looked like such a big wound, and on his father's hand, the place any surgeon felt most vulnerable. Then, much more slowly, the rest of the picture registered. His father was holding a gun. His own father was actually pointing a gun at him.

Brian stared at Harper and felt unbelievably calm.

He realized for the first time that all he'd wanted was his father's love and that's where he'd gone wrong. Harper hadn't been worth it. It was his mother and sister who should have counted. They were the ones who loved him, and now it was too late.

"I won't let you hurt Melanie," Brian said matter-of-factly. "I won't lose another sister to you."

"I know. So trust me, Brian, I'm doing this for your own good."

Harper Stokes ripped off his bandage. Brian saw the raw, bloody wound. A fresh tattoo: 666.

The final present, Brian thought. Then his father's hand whipped toward him with shocking force.

Brian tried to block the blow. He moved too slowly, and the handle of the gun caught him squarely on the nose. He heard a cracking sound. His own bone breaking.

He thought, Melanie, I'm sorry.

Then the world went black.

"I DON'T UNDERSTAND," Melanie was murmuring in the car. "I don't understand."

"We just took a wrong turn somewhere. That happens in investigations. We need to backtrack," David answered.

The fight had left her. She sagged in her seat, turning morosely toward the window.

"Why do I know the shack, David? I keep picturing that damn shack and Meagan Stokes," she whispered after a moment. "Why can I smell gardenias, plain as day? Little girl sitting in the corner. Little girl suddenly getting a chance and bolting for the door. Running away through thick, brambly underbrush. But she won't run fast enough. I know. I know."

David was quiet for a moment. "Maybe Larry Digger steered us wrong. He was the one who made the big leap that you were Russell Lee Holmes's daughter. The rest of us merrily followed him into the sea like a pack of lemmings."

"But I can see—"

"Can you, Melanie? Remember what Quincy said. He had a picture of Russell Lee's shack in front of him and he told you that you were wrong, that you *were not* picturing Russell Lee's hut. At the time we both just ignored that. Maybe we shouldn't have."

"But then, how come I can picture Meagan and Russell Lee Holmes?"

"There's always the power of suggestion. You never knew where you came from, a whole part of you is blank and probably hungry. Then suddenly a man appears and gives you a morsel of fact. You know what Meagan looks like, Mel, her picture has hung in your house for twenty years. Maybe once you even looked up Russell Lee Holmes. His name wasn't completely new to you."

"No," she admitted. "I remembered having heard it before."

"So the seeds were sown deep in your subconscious. And when Larry Digger appeared, your impressionable mind took over. Turned his snack into a five-course meal, adding all sorts of details to round it out. But of course you couldn't get it all right."

Slowly Melanie nodded. Larry Digger had appeared so out of the blue and had made such a big impression . . .

She was rubbing her temple. "If that's true, David, why did the scent of gardenias work? You were the one who told me that scent would trigger memory. If it was all a fantasy, why would it be triggered by a scent?"

"Let's back up," he announced curtly. "What do

we know? Someone murdered Meagan Stokes, and it was not Russell Lee Holmes."

Melanie nodded.

"Your mother and brother didn't do it because they seem to have an alibi and they have been as destroyed by it as anyone."

"Okay."

"But your father may have been involved. We know he needed the money. And your godfather probably helped him."

"To approach Russell Lee."

"Exactly. So we know Meagan was killed for money, but they botched the 'copycat' crime, so to speak. Thus they went to a backup plan, approaching Russell Lee to confess and get them off the hook. Now, Russell Lee did confess to the murder, so he must have been promised something."

Melanie hesitated. "The blood on the fabric. Maybe Russell Lee is alive. Maybe that's what he was promised. He could be the one pulling all the strings, messing with everyone."

"No," David said forcefully. "I don't buy it. The man was executed in front of witnesses. Even if the state coroner had been bribed to pronounce him dead when he was really still alive, his hands and feet blew off. You can't fake that."

"Unless it wasn't him in the death chamber."

"And who could they have gotten instead? What kind of moron agrees to be fried in someone else's place? It's just too far-fetched. Besides"—David's voice picked up suddenly—"the blood on the fabric is *not* Russell Lee's. The DNA test said it was *your* genetic father's. So if you're not Russell Lee Holmes's daughter, then someone else is your father. Who the hell is your father?"

David became very excited. Melanie shook her head. Her head hurt. Dim pictures of a time and place that had been . . . Dizzy. White lights. She closed her eyes futilely and rested her forehead against the car window.

But David was obviously feeling better about things. "You were right, Mel!" he said excitedly. "Dammit, you were the one who was right all along."

"I—I was?"

"Your family honestly loves you. Your family isn't violent. Your family is exactly who you thought they would be. That's why the pieces never fit. We've been trying to solve a murder that never happened. Shit!"

"What?"

David was no longer talking. He glanced over his shoulder, shot the car in reverse, and while she was still jerking forward, he put the pedal to the floor and squealed them onto the freeway.

"It's going to be okay," he declared.

"My head hurts."

"I know. Hang in there for me. I have one last place for you to see. And then, if my theory is correct, you'll know exactly who you are, and we'll finally get to the bottom of all this."

"I *want* to get to the bottom of all this."

"Of course you do, Melanie. Or should I say *Meagan*."

THIRTY-FIVE

"I CAN NEVER THINK of Texas without feeling like a failure," Patricia Stokes was murmuring. "As a wife, a mother, a lover. When Harper told me we could move, I swore I would never come back. I never wanted to see Texas again. I blamed the whole state for breaking my heart."

"I made a similar vow myself," Ann Margaret said, "but more out of necessity, I'm afraid. I always figured Larry Digger would keep pecking away at things, or, if not him, then someone else. When I was a child, I used to think a mistake was simply a mistake. You make it, you pay for it, you move on. Now I think some mistakes are more like a pebble hitting a pond. They start as a small ripple, then get bigger and bigger, an exploding circle of mistakes, until they become a tidal wave and you simply drown."

Patricia glanced at her. They'd been traveling since dawn, and up talking for most of the hours before then. There were things that had finally been said and many more things each was still struggling to grasp.

"How could you love a man like that?" Patricia had to ask.

Ann Margaret smiled. "Don't you think that's my line?"

Patricia winced. The more she learned about Harper, the less she had a right to judge others.

"When you're young," Ann Margaret added gently, "you love who you were raised to love."

"Our fathers."

"Exactly."

"And when we're old enough to know better—"

"It's too late to do anything about it."

"I can't believe I didn't know," Patricia sighed. They finally reached their destination, and Ann Margaret pulled into the grand old Georgian that had been Patricia and Harper's first home. The white pillars still stood tall, but the paint was peeling and looked mildewed on the top. This house had been so beautiful to Patricia as a young bride flushed with the heady rush of newly pledged love. It was dated now, one of those tired homes real estate agents labored to sell.

The house had been on the market for a year, she and Ann Margaret had learned that morning. The rooms were empty, the owners already off to Florida and retirement. The grass could use mowing, the flower bed needed weeding.

The house wasn't the way Patricia remembered it; its obvious age reminded her too much of her own.

"Oh, God, Annie, I failed my little girl."

"We all did."

"But I was her mother!"

"I know, that's why you adopted her again. Haven't you ever realized why you loved Melanie from the moment you saw her? Because a part of you knew, Patricia. Even though your mind had accepted that Meagan was dead, the mother in you knew."

"What must she have been thinking these last few days? And then that scene with William. My poor baby, having to shoot a man she'd once cared for. How do you get over such a thing, even when you know you're right? It's too much. She shouldn't have

had to go through any of that! We should've taken
better care of her!"

"She's tougher than you think, Pat. Maybe she has
more of her mother in her than you realize."

"I don't want her to have to be strong. I want her to
be safe. I want her *back!*" Patricia fisted her hands.
She wanted to strike something, lash out again in hurt
and rage. She could do nothing but calm herself and
remain focused for her daughter's sake.

"So tell me," she said after a minute, when she'd
gotten her hands to relax. "We're here. I know what
happened twenty-five years ago. Now what do we
do?"

Ann Margaret shrugged. "If she's seeking her past,
sooner or later she'll come here. And if Harper and
Jamie are looking for her, sooner or later they'll try
here as well. So now we wait."

DAVID WAS FINALLY slowing the car. Melanie opened
her eyes. She had fallen asleep almost the minute they
reached the interstate, her mind hitting a wall and
shutting down. Now, her limbs felt sluggish, her body
heavy, as if a great weight were pressed against her.
She could feel moisture on her face, sweat dampening
her upper lip and brow. Her throat was parched.

She fumbled for a can of Coke on the floor by her
feet, then took a long sip. The liquid didn't lighten the
thick cloak of impending doom that had settled
around her.

David quietly asked, "Does any of this look familiar? Take your time, Melanie. We'll go slow."

They'd arrived at a crumbling group of houses built
into a curving hillside. It might have been well kept
once, but it looked neglected now. Tall weeds waved
along the cracked asphalt roads. Small groves of trees
that might have once been pleasant, shady retreats,
were now tangled and overgrown with brambles.

When Melanie rolled down her window, she caught the unmistakable scent of gardenias.

Her mind lurched. She clutched her soda as if for balance.

"I've been here," she murmured. "I've been here."

"This is where your family used to live. Patricia, Harper, Brian, and Meagan Stokes."

A minute later a tall white house emerged into view. Big white columns. Grand Georgian style. A huge gnarled cherry tree on the front lawn, perfect for climbing. *Help me up, Daddy. Help me up.* A tall, overgrown hedge, once perfect for hide-and-seek. *You're never gonna find me, Brian. I'm smart!* A graceful curving drive once marked up for hopscotch. *Look at me, Mommy, look at me!*

Two women standing next to a red rental sedan in the driveway. Crisp gray hair. Golden, gleaming blond.

Mommy, Mommy, I'm going to grow up someday to look just like you.

Melanie turned toward David slowly. His eyes were concerned. And as she watched, he suddenly seemed to spin far away.

She was falling back in time, a tumbling down into a gaping black abyss . . . until she was in a dusty wooden shack and she was four years old.

"I want to go home," she heard herself murmur. "Dada Jamie, why can't I go home?"

"It's okay, Melanie. You're here with me, David, and you're safe. You are Meagan Stokes. Your family never hurt you, they never even abandoned you. Your father just faked it for the million dollars. Insurance fraud. Very clever insurance fraud. It's Harper's MO."

"You don't understand," she said. "You don't know . . ."

In the distance, a car engine suddenly gunned and roared. Another car, coming up behind them fast. The two women turned and stared. David glanced in the rearview mirror. Melanie watched them all fatalistically. They didn't know. They couldn't understand. She had tried to run once too. She had learned . . .

"Shit," David said. He stepped on the gas. Melanie looked at him sadly.

"You shouldn't run," she declared softly. "It's only worse if you run."

"Hang on, Melanie. Dammit, hang on."

He roared down the hill toward a grove of trees. Melanie heard shouts. The women were running. Everyone was running, even she was running in her mind. She remembered it clearly now. The fourth day, the desperate bid for freedom. Just wanting to see her family again . . .

Not fast enough though. Never fast enough. *Ah, lass, can't you see that when you run away, you only hurt yourself?*

Melanie was snapped back by a savage curse. She glanced at David and saw sweat pop out on his face as he frantically cranked the wheel. A sharp turn had suddenly appeared in the road. And they were going so fast. Much too fast. When you run, you hurt only yourself.

David swearing again. Back tires squealing, trying to break loose. David fighting them, yanking at the steering wheel so hard, the muscles in his arms bulged. David praying, maybe, then at the last moment, glancing at her apologetically. David whispering her name.

She thought, I love him. And a heartbeat later, I'm so sorry.

The back tires won. The whole car snapped around. So much screaming. Oh, God, that was her voice, screaming.

You hurt only yourself when you run.

The other car hit them hard. Melanie had a brief impression of Harper's shocked face. Then the front of their car snapped over the top of the other and they sailed through the air.

David's hand found hers. She felt the warm, rough texture of his fingers entangling with her own.

Then the ground rushed up fast. The car landing. A new screech of metal. A scream cut short. Black.

THIRTY-SIX

J AMIE O'DONNELL'S BREATH was coming out hard as he frantically focused the binoculars on the street overlooking the Stokeses' old home. He felt like he'd been running a marathon since six that morning, but more likely he was too old for this, and now that the moment was at hand, it was too real. His hands were shaking, and he had not felt this afraid in a long, long time.

First he followed Brian to the airport because he was worried about the kid. Then, when he figured he must let Brian forge his own way like a real man, he bought a one-way ticket to Houston for himself.

He'd landed at Houston Intercontinental, a place that always brought back too many memories for him and few of them good. It had occurred to him for the first time that none of them ever came to Texas. They avoided the entire state as if it carried the plague.

That was a shame in some ways. For as many of the memories were bitter, a lot were sweet. Patricia. Texas nights. Watching baby Brian grow. The miraculous birth of Meagan. Christ, the first time she'd gripped his index finger, such a tiny, tight fist. His baby. Jamie O'Donnell's girl!

Finding Melanie in Huntsville had been easy. She was smart and resourceful, he was proud to say, but it was a simple matter to trace her to the motel and set up watch. The arrival of the FBI bloke had made him nervous, but they seemed to have a thing between the two of them. Not bad really. He'd run a check on Special Agent David Riggs in the very beginning, as he'd done with all of his daughter's acquaintances. It was a father's prerogative, he liked to think, to want to know his daughter's associates.

The Riggs man had checked out well. Middle-class roots. Good rep with the Bureau, and Jamie had heard this from an inside source who hated to give praise. Shame about the arthritis, but the boy seemed to move well enough and was certainly above average in the brains department, as he'd figured out Harper Stokes quickly enough. That alone made him A-OK in Jamie's book.

The man's presence, however, had made shadowing Melanie a lot trickier. He doubted Melanie would ever think to check her rearview mirror, but Riggs was a trained professional. Jamie had had to follow them the hard way, staying three car-lengths back, occasionally turning off. Once they'd reached the neighborhood where Mrs. Appleebee lived, it had been easier. He merely pulled over at a gas station on the main road and waited.

When their rental car had finally reemerged forty-five minutes later, Jamie had had a clear view of Melanie's face. She'd looked pale, shaken, and anguished.

Mother of God, his heart had lurched in his chest.

It seemed that all the times he tried to protect his daughter, he only brought her pain. And that left him with the horrible, bitter thought that maybe Harper was the better one of them after all. She'd run into his arms naturally enough when he'd adopted her. Called him Dad, went out of her way to make him smile. Seemed happy.

When Jamie had crouched down to see his daughter, his own daughter whom he'd protected at great

personal risk for five long years, she recoiled from his
embrace.

He still remembered the moment clearly. The way
his heart had simply stopped beating in his chest. The
taste of dust in his mouth. The way his reaching fingers had curled into a fist.

Harper's smug smile from across the room, enjoying Jamie's pain.

And the sudden realization of just how much he
hated the son of a bitch.

From that day forward, Jamie had wanted nothing
more than for Melanie to remember. She should know
the true nature of self-centered, money-hungry Harper
Stokes. She should know the true nature of Jamie and
how honestly he had loved her over the years.

But it never happened. Melanie was happy as Melanie. Harper was surprisingly good to her, maybe because he knew it rankled Jamie so much. Or maybe he
had cared for Meagan too, more than he would ever
admit. Patricia and Brian adored her, falling back into
their roles as mother and brother so gratefully, it had
made Jamie's chest ache. And Melanie . . . Melanie
grew into such a lovely, content young lady, Jamie's
rage lost all momentum.

He could want only what was best for her, he discovered. And though his pride demanded action and
his shame and hurt feelings rankled, he never made a
move to interfere. Loving a child, he learned, was
humbling. How the mighty had fallen, and how easily
he'd accepted the tumble from grace.

Then, six months ago, Harper foisted William Sheffield onto Melanie. Harper kicking Brian out of the
house over such a thing as being gay. And then cold,
petty Harper letting Patricia dissolve into drinking
again, until Melanie's whole family was once more
ripped apart. Pretending to be better than his whole
damn family while all the while he was slicing open
healthy patients for a buck.

Jamie had had enough. He'd given Harper the

world twenty-five years ago. A fresh start with a million bucks, and as soon as the time was right, his own daughter to make Harper's family complete. There was nothing more one man could give another. There was nothing more one man could do to ensure Patricia Stokes's happiness. How dare Harper piss it all away for a buck.

Even in a rage Jamie could be remarkably cold. He'd plotted his strategy, made his plan, set the wheels in motion.

Harper would finally get his due, and Jamie would finally get his triumph.

Except so much had happened along the way. Harper hiring a hit man to take out Larry Digger and his adopted daughter. Jamie had figured it out the minute he saw the police sketch on TV—that was one of his acquaintances, whom he had introduced to Harper in the past, and Jamie sure as hell hadn't hired him to attack Larry Digger, so that meant Harper must have. Jamie had to hunt the fellow down and plug three bullets into his heart simply for principle's sake. You did not mess with his daughter.

As for Harper's due . . . all in good time.

Except Harper surprised him again. Pushing William so hard the boy cracked. Then trying to finger Melanie in the boy's shooting. As if Russell Lee Holmes's son had deserved any better.

Then today, just forty-five minutes earlier, Jamie caught sight of Harper Stokes here in Houston, obviously trying to track down his daughter.

The players were assembled, but the pieces were moving faster than Jamie had expected. And for the first time since he'd started this a month before, he was genuinely afraid.

Nor for himself, but for Melanie.

Now he was parked on the road above the Stokeses' old house with a clear view of the street. He saw Patricia and Ann Margaret arrive. And then he spotted Harper, parked along a side street, waiting.

David and Melanie approaching. Harper pulling out. Harper gunning the gas. And then the cars were racing. Up over one hill, thundering down another.

The squeal of tires. The crash of metal. Jamie watched all his worst fears pass before his eyes and was too far away to do a thing about it. The car spinning, hitting the other, sailing into the air. The sickening crunch as it landed, the hood popping up.

He could hear Patricia and Ann Margaret still shouting from the house, beginning to run. Screaming.

He waited himself, breath held, for sign of his daughter.

A car door opened. Melanie staggered into view. Blood on her forehead. She seemed dazed and confused. Suddenly she plunged into the woods.

Jamie tried to call out for her, but he was too far away. Harper had spotted her from his own car. He was out. He was wielding a gun. He was plunging into the woods.

No sign of life from Riggs yet, and no time to check. His first thought, his only thought, was always Melanie.

And this is how it all comes down, Jamie thought fatalistically.

He started moving. He had a weapon, he had experience, he had training on his side. And yet as he plunged into the woods, he was thinking of his daughter, and he had never been so afraid.

You don't know enough yet, lass. You don't know . . .

Ah, Jesus God, you may take my silly life, just keep my little girl safe. Just protect my little girl from Harper.

FOUR-YEAR-OLD MEAGAN *was running. Running, running, running. Branches caught at her hair, cut her cheek.*

Low, scraggly bushes tore at her favorite blue dress, trying to hold her back.

She kept slogging forward, little legs pumping. Had to run. Had to run fast. Had to run fast, fast, fast.

She wanted to go home to her mommy. Time to go home.

Meagan pushed faster, but behind her, she could still hear the footsteps pounding closer.

Dada Jamie was going to get her. Dada Jamie was going to force her back to the shack. No, no, she wanted her mommy. She wanted Brian!

You can't go home, Meagan. They don't want you anymore. *Want to go home!* It's going to be okay, lass, I'll take care of you, we'll get you out of here and to someplace much much nicer. Why, you'll get to live like a princess in a faraway kingdom called London. *Want to go home!* I know, love, but you can't. Harper . . . your da, he's not safe for you right now. He's not even your real da, love, and I'm afraid all he really wants these days is money. *WANT TO GO HOME!* Love, no!

Footsteps, closer. Crashing underbrush, crackling branches.

Run, Meagan, run. Faster, faster.

Footsteps closer . . .

Run, run.

Breathing closer . . .

RUN, MEAGAN, RUN!

The hand whipped out and caught her hard around the middle. Melanie tried to scream. A second hand slapped over her mouth while she was yanked against a big, burly body.

"Shh, lass," Jamie O'Donnell whispered in her ear, dragging her deeper into the thick underbrush. "Don't make a noise."

And for the first time, Melanie became aware of more sounds of crackling in the underbrush. Harper suddenly appeared twenty feet in front of them, making his way through the trees and holding a very large gun.

DAVID WOKE UP to ringing in his ears. He blinked his eyes, wondering what he was doing in the shooting range. Then he wondered why it was so bright inside the shooting range. Then he wondered why his face was so wet.

He raised a hand. Brought it back down. He had blood all over his face.

He reached for Melanie, then saw that she wasn't there. The car door was wide open, seat belt dragged out into the dirt. A second car sandwiched behind them, the driver's door also flung open into the breeze.

David shoved against his door. Nothing. Shit. His hands were shaking, a first-class lump burgeoning on his temple. For once in his life he felt pain somewhere other than his back. Jesus Christ, he had to get to Melanie.

He finally got his seat belt off. Scrambled across the passenger seat, tried to get his feet beneath him, and fell down into the dirt. The world was turning, then spinning.

He forced himself to stand up, using the car for balance. He had his gun, so he was not helpless. Melanie was still out there, no doubt dazed and confused and vulnerable.

Time to focus, David. Time to get control.

He ripped the tie from his neck and wrapped it around his forehead. That cleared the blood from his gaze. He dug his fingernails into the palms of his hands. The sharp sensation made the world stop spinning.

David took the safety off his souped-up Beretta, thanked his father for the first time in years, and plunged into the forest.

• • • •

MELANIE WAS STANDING stock-still, her heart thundering in her chest. The world had gone so quiet around them, every move, every sound exaggerated. Her godfather pinned her against his body until she could barely breathe. Her father, so close, stalked through the underbrush as if he were hunting small prey. The gun held in Harper's hands. The gun carried beneath Jamie's jacket, the bulge pressing against her ribs.

A single scene floated up in her mind.

She tripped over a tree root, sprawling to the ground. The air whooshing from her lungs. No more running. She was caught. Blood on her knees, twigs in her hair. Not even enough air left to cry.

Dada Jamie kneeling beside her, looking tired too. Funny that Dada Jamie should be the one with tears in his eyes. Brushing back her hair slowly, checking her for broken bones, examining her bloody knee.

Dada Jamie gently, so gently, picking all those nasty little rocks from her knees. Dada Jamie murmuring over and over again that it would be all right. She just needed time to adjust, then she'd realize he would never do anything to hurt her. Dada Jamie calling her his little girl.

Hating him anyway because he was keeping her from her family and she wanted to go home!

Something crashed in the underbrush right behind him. Jamie swiveled, Harper's head came up. Melanie saw both of them staring off at the sound, and then she moved.

She drove her elbow into her godfather's gut. He grimaced, tried to recover, and she stomped the inside of his foot. He was shocked enough to loosen his grip, and she pushed back with all her might. He tried to grab her arm. She ducked and burst free, making a beeline for the right, away from both men.

"Dammit!" Jamie swore.

"Melanie!" Harper cried.

Melanie lowered her head and ran harder.

And then it all happened at once. Sounds of crashing twigs and crackling branches. She thought she was moving quickly, but her godfather was already there, reaching for her shoulder. And then Harper was there, to her left, bringing up his gun.

She burst into the clearing just as gunfire erupted from the side.

She watched the bullet come right at her. And then she saw her godfather leap up. Jamie flying through the air, stretching out his whole body, staring right into her eyes, so earnest, so determined, so sad.

The bullet ripped into his back, bowing his body and sending him crashing to the ground.

Harper came into view, standing right in front of her with smoke still pouring from his gun.

"Goddammit," he said, "that man was always in the way."

And then he leveled his gun at his adopted daughter.

DAVID WAS CAREENING through the underbrush. Leaves tangled in his hair. Roots clawed at his feet. His vision was starting to clear, but now he found he was lost and disoriented in the woods, not sure where he'd come from or where he was going.

He found himself back at the roadside, right where he'd started, except now he was aware of banging coming from the trunk of the other car.

"Hey," a male voice was calling. "Somebody let me out!"

David found the keys still dangling from the ignition and popped the trunk. Brian Stokes sat up.

"Are you okay?" David asked, lending him an arm to help him climb out.

Brian was fingering the bridge of his nose, which looked as if it had been attacked with a hammer. "Harper," he mumbled. "Got a gun. Hit me."

"He hit you? Why?"

"Didn't want me to . . . help Melanie. Gotta help Melanie."

He tried to lurch forward, but he collapsed on the asphalt. "You don't understand," he said. "Harper has to cover his tracks. Harper . . . has to . . . kill her."

"Why? She's his daughter."

"No, not his daughter. Jamie's daughter. Don't you see? She's Jamie's . . ."

The last few pieces clicked into place in David's mind, and then right on the heels of that came the thought that Harper really could be driven to kill Melanie. Shit!

As if reading his mind, a gun blast suddenly ripped through the air.

"Help Melanie," Brian cried. *"Run!"*

David ran.

MELANIE WENT DOWN on her knees in the grass, ignoring Harper and his gun. Jamie's blue eyes were locked onto hers, his hand fluttering at his side, his lips searching for air. She heard a sucking sound and realized that he'd been shot in the lung. The air was literally leaking out of him.

Oh, God. Though she didn't know why, she looked at her father for help. Harper didn't move. He seemed to be in a state of shock. Maybe he hadn't meant to pull the trigger. Maybe he hadn't meant to harm any of them.

"Please," she whispered. "You're a doctor. Dad . . ."

He didn't reply.

Melanie gave up on him and turned her attention back to her godfather.

"I'm . . . s-s-sorry," Jamie gasped.

"Shh . . . it's all right. You just rest, you can explain everything later.

"You . . . w-w-w-wouldn't remember. I w-w-wanted you . . . to . . . r-r-r-emember . . ."

Blood was foaming on his lips. His eyes started to roll back, and Melanie gripped his hand more tightly.

"No, dammit. You won't die on me, Jamie. I won't let you. . . ."

He looked at her sadly, and she knew it was too late. He whispered, "Selfish . . . like Harper. Annie right. I am no better. Meagan . . ."

"Jamie."

"I love you, lass . . . my little girl."

"No, Jamie, no—"

His body convulsed. She tried to hold him still, tried to plug the bullet hole with her shaking fingers. Blood, so much blood, leaking from his ribs, from his lips. She could feel him shudder again and again.

"God damn you," she cried. "Don't you dare die on me. Don't you do this to me now!"

You will always be my little girl, he had said. *And no place you go will you ever be alone.*

I forgot, I forgot. I never remembered a thing. Oh, Jamie, I am so sorry.

"M-M-Meagan," he whispered.

"What, Jamie? What is it?"

"Say it . . . once . . ."

"Say what?"

"Call me . . . Dad."

"Dad," she wept. "Dad."

The last breath escaped him as a soft sigh and finally the struggle was over. Jamie O'Donnell lay perfectly still. He was gone.

Crashing emitted from the underbrush. Patricia Stokes and Ann Margaret suddenly burst forward, their hair filled with brambles. Another sound of scattering birds from the right. David Riggs burst onto the scene, his gun out.

Everyone stared. Jamie O'Donnell's bloody body on the ground. Melanie leaning over him with tears staining her cheeks. Harper Stokes standing there—

David pointed his gun at the same moment Harper recovered and leveled his 9mm at Melanie.

"Back away," David said. "FBI."

"Harper, for God's sake," Patricia cried.

"Shut up!" Harper snapped. "Anybody move, and I'm going to open fire!"

How strange, Melanie thought. She felt as if she were seeing her adoptive father for the first time. The features she'd always found golden were faded and lined by strain. The square chin was really weak, the bright blue eyes uncertain.

This was the man she'd loved as a father for most of her life. A spineless, self-centered, insecure man who'd traded her away for a million bucks, and had single-handedly destroyed his own family.

She said savagely, "Say it, goddammit. Stand right there and tell everyone once and for all what you did."

"You don't know anything!" Harper spat out. "I did what had to be done. I did what was in the best interest of my family."

"You took away our daughter!" Patricia shouted. "How was that in our best interest?"

"She wasn't *our* daughter. She was your brat. Yours and O'Donnell's, and you foisted her on me as if I'd never know. Did you think I was stupid? God, Pat, you of all people. I *loved* you."

"Did you, Harper? It was so hard to tell, when you were always at work."

"I was trying to build something for both of us. Or didn't you ever think about where the money was coming from when you went out shopping?"

"I went out shopping because there was nothing else to do! For heaven's sake, if you'd only said something. You stupid man, I would've lived like a pauper for you. I even gave up Jamie for you. I really did love you, and I owed it to you to make it work. I really did want—oh, God, I was planning on how to save our marriage and you were kidnapping our daughter! Did you tie her up? Did you drag her screaming from the nanny's car?"

"It wasn't anything like that! I didn't even do it. Jamie did."

"Because he had to," Ann Margaret interrupted. "Because you went so far as to imply that if he didn't help you fake Meagan's murder for the insurance money, you might commit the crime for real."

"I was hurt, I was angry—"

"You were greedy," David stated flatly. Melanie could see him appraising the scene, moving slightly to the side so he'd have a better line of fire. He nodded toward her slightly. She realized he was trying to tell her that he was more in control than anyone thought, and it would be all right.

She didn't care. Her real father was dead at her feet. Her adoptive father had a gun pointed at her. She was feeling betrayed and angry. And then she remembered that Jamie's gun was still tucked beneath his jacket.

"How did you do it?" David was asking Harper, sidling a bit more to the left, where he could take his best aim. "You were angry, you were broke. You decided you would have to make the situation work to your advantage. Get rid of Meagan and gain a million dollars. Very clever."

"Brains have always been my strong suit," Harper said. "Don't bother, Agent. I'm not going to confess it all to you."

"You don't have to," Ann Margaret responded contemptuously. "I know it all. I was there too. As Russell Lee Holmes's wife."

She gave David a brittle smile. "Let me start at the beginning for you. Harper hatches his horrible plan. He knew Meagan wasn't his daughter—no matter that she'd adored him for four years—and he wanted her out of the house. Jamie would do anything for the girl, so he agreed. He'd fake a kidnapping of Meagan, take her someplace safe—"

"A goddamn shack!" Harper exclaimed. *"That's* how he treated his child."

"Well, what was he supposed to do, Harper? As a friend of the family he'd be expected to help out with the search and recovery. Plus, he couldn't very well magically have a new little girl traveling with him. If he left her with a friend, that person could blackmail you later. If he put her in a hotel, someone would surely notice a weeping girl all alone every day. You were the one insisting it be so perfect. So, yes, he locked her in a shack in the middle of the woods, where no one could find her. It was hardly ideal, and it tore him up. But it also worked.

"She was tucked away, you could fake the ransom demand, and Jamie could cough up another hundred thousand dollars to help you out."

"The ransom money that Brian knew Harper had never delivered," David stated. "God, Harper, even when you're greedy, you're greedy."

Harper wasn't looking so steady with the gun. Every time someone spoke up, he'd jerk a little in that direction. David had noticed it. Melanie too. She was sinking toward the ground, edging closer to the front of Jamie's jacket.

"The police," Ann Margaret continued, "started investigating immediately, just as Harper and Jamie figured. Harper was smart, however, and no one could trace the ransom note back to him. On the other hand, you immediately realized you had overlooked a few details, right, Harper? You'd gotten yourself a quick hundred thousand, but you couldn't exactly start spending it—the police would notice. No, you needed money you could account for. The life insurance. Of course, for that you needed a body, and none was appearing the way you hoped. So once again you went to Jamie. To pull this off, he had to find a body for you. A body of a four-year-old girl who roughly matched the description of Meagan."

Her hand already on Jamie's jacket, Melanie froze. "He didn't . . . he didn't kill anyone, did he?"

"Of course not. Identifying bodies was his job, remember? He waited until he saw one that was close enough. It took four months, four nail-biting months while the police turned on your whole family. Then he stole the body from the Mississippi morgue. He mutilated the fingertips. He cut off the head so the body couldn't be ID'd from dental records. And then he wrapped the body in a blanket. He told me about it years later. Alone in the woods with that little body. Digging the shallow grave, making sure he covered his tracks. Feeling lower than low, as if he really were a child murderer. He felt so bad, he almost couldn't do it. She was so small, some beautiful little girl who would never go home. He wept. Then he placed her in the grave for the cadaver dogs to find. She was so close in height and size to Meagan, so the police simply accepted it when Harper confirmed her ID as Meagan. God, that was a sad day."

Patricia nodded gloomily. Even Harper looked pained. Then he swore.

"But the damn police wouldn't go away," he said. "We had done everything as planned and then they went and caught Russell Lee Holmes and realized he had nothing in his little shack that belonged to Meagan. Jesus Christ, how were we supposed to know they'd actually catch the bastard the next week?" He looked at Ann Margaret mutinously. "Your husband was certainly nowhere near as smart as me."

She replied dryly, "Thank heavens."

"And then what?" David said conversationally. He had gotten three feet closer to Harper. With so many people around, it was best to shorten the distance to the target. Then David realized that Melanie had moved as well. She was almost sitting on top of Jamie's body now, her hand beneath the jacket. What the hell was she doing?

"Harper sold his soul to the devil, that's what,"

Ann Margaret stated. "Sent Jamie into prison to deal with Russell Lee himself. And what a deal it was. All Russell Lee had to do was confess to yet another kid's death, and in return Harper Stokes and Jamie O'Donnell would personally guarantee that our child was raised in style. Everything we could never give him, he would magically have. And while Russell Lee was surely the devil himself, he was damn proud of that boy. What is it about men and their sons?"

Melanie looked at Ann Margaret quizzically. "They really did agree to take care of Russell Lee's child? Then, who is that?"

"William, sweetheart. William Sheffield was my son. I turned him over to the boys' home the day they arrested Russell Lee, terrified some reporter like Larry Digger would find us both and make his life hell. I honestly thought it was for the best.

"Then, when Russell Lee and Harper agreed on the deal, I drew up papers. Harper and Jamie both had to sign a confession to all they'd done, and then I put it in a safety deposit box with instructions that it was to be opened and turned over to the police if anything happened to me. Finally I moved to Boston, where I could start over too, make something of myself, and, of course, keep an eye on Harper. As for William . . ."

She hesitated, and then she flushed. She said quietly, "I was so sure he was better off in that boys' home. I sent money every year so he would have the best of everything. The brothers promised to take very good care of him. . . . He could get a clean start, never have to worry about some reporter connecting him with his father. And with all that money . . . I grew up so poor myself, I was so sure money was the one thing that would make a difference. I guess I'm not so much better than Harper after all."

"No," Melanie said. Something had come over her, and it showed in her face. Something cool. Something fearless. "We are all better than Harper. Because it didn't stop there, did it, *Dad?* Five years later Russell Lee is finally due to be executed, then no one will ever be the wiser. But how is your family? Your family you thought would be so thrilled with a million bucks? Mom's drinking, Brian's still in therapy. You work all the time just so you don't have to face your own handiwork. And even then you didn't do the right thing.

"Jamie called you. I can remember being in the study of the hotel room in London, hearing it all but not understanding. Jamie telling you that your plan had worked, you'd done well, and now couldn't you give something back. I was so miserable without my mom. And Mom and Brian were so miserable without me. He could set it all up. Erase my memories so not even I would ever know. Drop me off at the hospital for Harper to 'find.' Then you could literally adopt me back. You wouldn't even have to pretend to be my real father this time. This time you could be the generous adoptive dad taking in an abandoned little girl. You liked that, didn't you, Harper? It made you look good."

Harper glared at her stubbornly.

"And even then," she said, "you *fucked it up!* Kept spending, didn't you? Became a brilliant surgeon, making more and more money, but it was never enough. You learned *nothing* from ripping your family apart. Suddenly it's twenty years later and you're not the great provider you pretend to be. You're slicing up healthy patients for profit. You're violating your own doctors' oath. Why not? You've already committed a heinous act and gotten away with it—"

"I never hurt anyone!"

"*You hurt everyone!* You hurt my mom, you hurt my brother. You hurt me! And you risked your patients who trusted you with their health. And then you got mean.

"The man who shot Larry Digger, who tried to shoot me, that was your doing. Someone had found out, someone was sending you little notes, and you were afraid that finally, after all these years, the truth would come out. So you hired someone to kill me. And did you kill him too? Because you were too cheap to part with the payment money?"

"No, no," Harper protested. "Jamie did that. Jamie shot the man. He's the killer!"

"Jamie is the protector! He did what he had to do to keep me safe. Just like he dove in front of me when you opened fire. For God's sake, he was your friend, and you killed him!"

"He cheated with my wife!"

"You cheated with half the nursing staff. How dare you!"

"Goddammit, you don't know anything!" Harper's voice had gone too high. He lost whatever control he'd had on himself, and in a fraction of an instant David realized it was all going to hell.

He aimed at Harper's forehead just as Patricia Stokes jumped into the way.

"You will not hurt my daughter!" she cried.

"Patricia, no," David shouted.

And now Ann Margaret was moving and Harper was leveling his gun at his wife, screaming at her to get out of the way or he'd kill her too. And how could she have hurt him when he'd loved her so much and why hadn't she just let things go, why hadn't she been able to get over the loss of Jamie O'Donnell's daughter. Because she still loved O'Donnell, that's why. She'd always loved O'Donnell more.

And while David tried desperately to get a bead, Patricia was yelling that it wasn't true, she had loved Harper more, it was his own pride that had never let him see it and she had been so certain they could have been happy together. What had happened to their dreams? How could he have brought them to this? How could he have threatened their daughter and murdered his own friend?

And then he heard Melanie. Melanie crying for her

mother. Melanie realizing that Harper was beyond
reason, that he really was going to shoot his own wife
and David couldn't stop it, and then she was pulling
something out of Jamie O'Donnell's jacket. The gun.
Melanie had Jamie's gun.

"Ann Margaret, down!" David roared at the same
time Harper spotted the new threat and jerked toward
Melanie. Shit, Patricia Stokes was still in the way. He
couldn't fire!

Harper screamed. His face twisted, something horrible and bleak passing over his eyes. Melanie rose to
face him, looking calm, looking fierce.

"Melanie, no! Patricia, goddammit, get down. Get
down!"

And Brian Stokes stepped up behind his father with
a tree limb and slammed it across the back of his
skull.

Harper crumpled. David rushed forward, already
pulling out the handcuffs, and snapped them on. Ann
Margaret and Patricia were still standing in the way,
pale and dazed.

Brian stared at them all, the tree limb gripped
tightly between his hands. With his bruised and battered face he looked like hell. Then his eyes found his
sister.

"Meagan?" he whispered. "Oh, Meagan . . ."

"Brian," she cried, and then she dove into his arms.
Patricia ran there too, throwing her arms around her
children, cradling them feverishly against her. Together at last, the three remaining Stokeses began to
cry.

David and Ann Margaret stood on the outside
while the woods once again settled down, and after a
minute the birds resumed chirping as if all were as it
should be.

When the police arrived twenty minutes later, Patricia Stokes was still crying with Brian. But Melanie
had moved into David's arms, and now he held her
against him tightly and gently stroked her hair.

EPILOGUE

I T WAS RAINING the day they laid Jamie O'Donnell to rest. It had taken weeks to get his body from the Texas medical examiner. Patricia had found a Catholic priest for the service. Ann Margaret had known he wanted to be cremated. Brian and Melanie had chosen the Newport Cliff Walk to scatter his remains; he had taken them there often when they were children, claiming he loved to listen to the sound of the waves battering the rocks. It reminded him of Ireland.

Now Melanie, Ann Margaret, Patricia, Brian, and Nate stood silently in front of the priest. Melanie found she could not concentrate on the words. Promises of hope and glory and charity meant little to her these days. She was tired of words. They were too easy to say and too tempting to believe.

She watched the dark, angry water frothing below. She thought as strange as it sounded, Harper should be here. This funeral was about him too, and whether he'd ever admit or not, she suspected he missed Jamie O'Donnell and grieved over him too.

Dr. Harper Stokes was now in jail. The states of Texas and Massachusetts and the FBI were currently fighting over him, each arguing they had the best case and should get first dibs. So far the feds were winning.

David's healthcare fraud squad had descended upon
their Beacon Street home in a frenzy. Bank accounts
were frozen, assets seized, files plundered. Melanie,
her mother, and her brother had been called in for
questioning so many times, the desk man at the Bureau knew them by sight.

Melanie had gotten to spend equal time with Detective Jax, going over that last afternoon with William.
So far no charges had been filed against her. Her attorney assured her that the abrasions on her face,
combined with the fact that the gun had been William's, made her self-defense argument plausible.
Most likely the D.A. would not want to waste the
state's time prosecuting the case. She supposed she
should be grateful for small favors.

She would not go through life as a murderer, then.
And yet she had killed a man. She wasn't sure what
that made her, but then, she was unsure of so many
things these days.

One day, exactly two weeks after Jamie's death,
she'd awakened in a cold sweat. She'd been dreaming
again about the shack and then the days in London.
Except this time Jamie said he couldn't stand to be her
father anymore. She was a dreadful little girl, he hated
her, and he was giving her back.

In a frenzy, she'd driven straight to the jail where
they'd been holding Harper and had demanded to see
him. She had to know, she had to ask him. Could he
tell her if Jamie really loved her? Would she fill in the
missing pieces for her? Her memory was still so hazy,
and she wanted to hear that both men had cared, that
Harper never really would have hurt her, even the hit
man had been a mistake. He loved her, Jamie loved
her, everything had simply gone awry. Two men and
their jealousy, one man and his greed. It was everyone's fault but hers.

Harper, however, wouldn't see her. Since his arrest,
he had refused to see anyone, even his wife.

She'd gotten back in her car, driving mindlessly.

The next thing she'd known she was at David's apartment. She hadn't had a moment alone with him since the police had arrived in Texas. He was back to being Special Agent Riggs, lead investigator of the growing healthcare fraud case against Harper. Agents, of course, were not allowed to consort with witnesses in a case. She had understood. Agents had rules, and for the most part David respected those rules. That's what made him so different from her two dads.

That night, however, she'd said to hell with it. She'd banged on his door, and the moment he'd opened it, she'd thrown herself into his arms. He hadn't argued. His expression had said everything she felt, the hunger, the yearning, the need for connection, for a reminder that Texas had been real, they were real. They'd made love right there on the entryway floor. Then again in the kitchen, then finally they made it to the bedroom, where they'd started all over again.

Hours later she'd gotten up, gotten dressed, and as wordlessly as she'd arrived, she'd left. He had never called her. She expected that until the investigation was concluded, that would be the case.

She'd waited five days before showing up again. Then three days after that. They never spoke, as if both realized that would cross the line and breach the agent-witness protocol. Instead, they let their hands and mouths and bodies speak for them, urgent and hungry and fierce. Melanie trusted those silent, feverish interludes more than she trusted anything else that had happened in the last twenty years of her life.

Her mother and Ann Margaret were trying to help. Most afternoons now the three women sat out back on the patio, Ann Margaret and Patricia relating the early days in Texas to Melanie, trying to give her some perspective.

Melanie learned a lot about Jamie in those sessions. The way he had loved her mother but had never completely won her away from Harper. The way he'd loved Ann Margaret but still chose the destructive course. The way he seemed to love his daughter, though even that love was strange and tragic.

He had made Melanie his primary heir. Swiss bank accounts holding millions of dollars were hers, ensuring that she and her mother would never want for anything. Ann Margaret was to receive a generous annual stipend for the rest of her life.

The police uncovered the electronic voice distorter he'd used for his anonymous calls. They also found ostrich feathers and a strange picture of a woman and two horrible beasts no one could explain. Last gifts, Brian said. The ostrich feathers for Patricia, for burying her head in the sand when it came to her husband's activities, and the picture for Ann Margaret, for having cavorted with not one, but two monsters in her lifetime.

According to Ann Margaret, Jamie had knowledge of everyone's crimes. The apple on William's bed symbolized that the apple never fell far from the tree. He'd even seen Brian pulling out the briefcase with the ransom money, then had waited breathlessly for Brian to blow the whistle. Of course, Brian never had.

Also, Jamie had the knack for bypassing various security systems, for ferreting out the little details of everyone's life so he could deliver the intimate gifts most intimately.

Finally, Jamie O'Donnell had had motive. According to the Texas medical examiner, Melanie's father had possessed one last secret—he'd been dying of stomach cancer, most likely with less than six months to live.

It appeared that he'd decided to use the brief time he had left to reveal the truth. That's what the FBI said.

Ann Margaret had a slightly different theory.

When you were first adopted, Melanie, you got to meet everyone again for the first time. Just as Jamie predicted, you seemed to "know" your mother in-

stantly. The same with Brian. You even accepted Harper quite naturally and were very protective of him.

Then your parents introduced you to Jamie. Do you remember what you did, Melanie? This was your birth father. The man who'd purposely removed you from the country to help appease Harper and protect you. The man who'd rearranged his life to care for you and then out of love for Patricia and you had given you up again. And you took one look at him and recoiled. You were afraid.

I don't think he ever forgot that moment, sweetheart. I don't think he ever stopped knowing that Harper was the one you ended up loving, while he was the one who had inspired fear.

Some things are even more powerful to a man than cancer. One of those has got to be love.

" 'When I was a child, I spake as a child,' " the priest at the service intoned. " 'I understood as a child, I thought as a child: But when I became a man, I put away childish things. For now we see through a glass, darkly; but then face to face: now I know in part; but then shall I know even as also I am known.' "

That was Melanie's cue. She rose. She picked up the urn. It was amazingly heavy, substantial, and yet nothing at all compared to what Jamie had been on earth. At the priest's nod, she took off the top.

Did we ever see face-to-face, Jamie? There is so much I want to ask you. So much I wish I understood . . . So much about you to love and admire, and so much to hate.

I believe you loved me, that you did what you thought was for the best. You sacrificed for me, you sacrificed for my mother, and because of that, I love you, Jamie O'Donnell, and I forgive you everything. Go in peace and God bless.

Melanie tipped over the urn. The ashes floated

down in the damp, misty air, into the ocean, where they swirled and then were swept away.

Patricia and Ann Margaret walked back to the road together in the lead. Behind them came Brian and Nate, their heads huddled together and speaking quietly. That left Melanie alone in the rear. She tried not to feel lonely, but it didn't entirely work.

They arrived at the end of the Cliff Walk, where their three vehicles were parked. Melanie saw that a fourth had joined them. And as if reading her mind, a dark-suited man leaned against the passenger door and his head came up at the sight of her.

Melanie started running, and she didn't care who saw her.

"David!"

She drew up short at the last moment, suddenly self-conscious and unsure. He wore a navy blue suit, which made him look official. But then his face softened, his eyes began to glow, and she felt the knot loosen in her chest.

"Hi," he said.

"Hi yourself."

"Nice ceremony."

"You heard?"

"I walked out for it but didn't want to interrupt."

"You could have interrupted," she said immediately. "I wouldn't have minded."

He smiled slightly and brushed a finger down her cheek. She closed her eyes so she could concentrate on the feel of his touch, and when she opened them again, she saw that the tip of his finger was damp. He'd brushed away her tears.

"Are you still investigating my father?" she demanded. "Tell me, are you here as part of your special duties, because you are just killing me—"

"I'm done."

"Done?"

"Done. Wrapped up this morning, handed over to

the attorney general. I'm a free man, Melanie Stokes. So I thought I oughta find you."

"Oh, David," she said, and then she couldn't speak. "Oh, David," she tried again. She gave up words and threw herself against him. He folded her into his embrace.

"I missed you," he said.

"Me too."

"I wanted to know how you were doing."

"I know, I know."

He was suddenly angling back her head, his eyes fierce. "I'm taking meds," he declared in a rush. "I can walk better, move better. Got promoted too. I have job security. But, Mel, I haven't done as right by you as I could."

"David, I love you."

He stopped talking and held her close. After a moment he muttered, "Thank God. My father told me I was probably messing this whole thing up and I should've introduced you to him weeks ago. Somehow or other that would've made a difference. I don't claim to understand him. Actually, after everything I blabbered, I think he was hoping for a chance to court you himself."

"Really? My mom asked if you were ever going to come around again. Ann Margaret told her to be quiet and mind her own business—they were in no position to give advice on men."

He laughed. "Interesting point."

She grabbed his lapels. "Say it, dammit! It's been a bitch of a month and I want to hear it. All of it!"

"I love you, Melanie. I want to settle down with you, raise two point two children, and grow old together. I want to be with you every single day of my life."

She melted against him. The knot left her chest completely. The haze of the last month cleared from her eyes. Now she could see it all clearly. Herself, him, probably two point two children. Maybe a golden retriever.

Family. At last, a family of her own.

Funny, but in her mind she saw Jamie O'Donnell beaming and four-year-old Meagan Stokes finally happy.

Melanie Stokes whispered, "Yes."

And in hardcover

THE KILLING HOUR

by Lisa Gardner

Look for it at your favorite bookstore